From Grandeville - A Tale

Tale 13

SEEMNA and CHYNDRA

Two Daughters.

One Warrior, One Witch.

George R. Mead

E-Cat Worlds Press

This is a work of fiction. All the characters and events portrayed are creations of the imagination, nothing more, nothing less.
Comments and questions? –> gmead01@gmail.com

Seemna and Chyndra

Copyright 2014 by George R. Mead

LCCN 2014919056

Mead, George R.
Seemna and Chyndra. /
George R. Mead.
p. cm. – Seemna and Chyndra. Two Daughters. One Warrior, One Witch. (From Grandeville - A Tale; Tale 13)
ISBN-13 978-0-9890927-6-0
1. Fantasy. I. Title. II. Series.

E-Cat Worlds established its publishing program as a reaction to the large commercial publishing houses currently dominating the book industry and the smaller intellectual clones. It is interested in publishing works of fiction and non-fiction that are often deemed insufficiently profitable or commercial or that are not necessarily reflective of current literary trends and fads.

E-Cat Worlds, 57744 Foothill Road, La Grande OR 97850
www.ecatworldspress.com
SAN 255-6383

In the middle of nowhere - Creativity.

First Edition:
Printed in the United States of America

Fiction

From Grandeville.
Portal
Lair
Not Again
And Again.
Magiwitch
Rebirth
Offspring
Holiday
Treasure
E'Nilt
Braidna
Seemna and Chyndra

A Tale of The Feyra
Jonathon and Dee
Dee Of The Fontala
Dee and The People
Dee and The Golden Cartouche

The Seven Lands
Seventeen Siblings (assisted by Zakke L. Zacog)

Nonfiction

A History of Union County
The Ethnobotany of the California Indians, 2nd Edition
A History of The Chinese in The West: 1848-1880
Yachats. The Town Called "Dark Water at the Foot of the Mountains."

Cden Odo. Many Long Ago.

Five over and one down, Ab Ster, also known as The Unhinged, shoved his greatest creation out the door and on its way hastily telling it what to do. Slamming the entrance shut, Ab Ster, hurried back to investigate the properties of a certain rare substance that came from a dragon.

He knew that most folk thought that dragons were merely figments of fanciful imaginations trying to explain what they didn't understand. Some time later, deep inside his investigation, having totally forgotten what he had released and the orders that he had issued, garbled as they were, he hurried to explore his most recent enthusiasm. He was in a rush as per usual.

In the act of prodding that certain substance with a powerful investigatory rod, everything some distance from his dwelling shattered, including Ab Ster.

Just Another Day

Grandeville. Tinker's Place.

In the moonless black of night.
She coasted over the house.
She coasted along.
Over the house.
Just inches above the upper ridge line.
A silent, dark shape.
Seeking her prey.
Coasting over the house.

Her prey, drifting moth silent, floating on the evening breeze, was listening intently. She was listening intently, not for the beat of wings, but for the faint sound of air flowing over wings, the slightest of flutters.

The clouds touched cotton wisp feather soft damp tickle across her back and wings.

In the faintest of faint light she searched for a dark shape crossing between her and the grey patches down below, the shadow grey patches that marked pasture and lawn, house and garden.

Then something new entered the night.
Headlights.

A car had turned off the county road and started up the long driveway that led to the house over which she was slowly circling. The car was traveling at a normal rate of speed so she assumed that it wasn't anything to worry about. It probably wasn't the bearer of bad news.

But this was a curious event.

Visitors at this late hour.

Visitors at this very late hour of the night.

The headlights flickered. Something had passed between them and where she floated. Smiling happily, she curved, a wide, lazy turn. Down there was the hunter, attracted by who ever it was that was driving up the slope headed for the parking area next to the house.

She made a long, slow spiral down and saw her, the hunter, perched on the garage roof, a neo-gargoyle, wings folded forward, around herself, peering down toward the approaching vehicle. The prey fell, hawk swift controlled plunge, wings folded in. And snatched the hunter from her perch.

"Gotcha!"

Early Dawn laughed. "I heard you coming."

The pair settled on the roof of the house, just over the kitchen to watch the automobile. Fair Morn folded and folded and folded her great butterfly wings.

Early Dawn nodded and popped her dark leather bat wings away and tucked her shirt back into her jeans. "Who is it?"

The pair were both magical jests created by Big Red, one of the pure magical forces in the universe of universes. He had been teasing John Tinker during two of his visits by sending a magical jest to bother him. Tinker and group had been visiting Paradise, the place created by Big Red. But Messenger, feeling sorry for the jests had snapped the magical bonds linking them to Big Red, turning them from magical jests into alive beings with unique characteristics. It was a unique skill. Smoke had merged Fair Morn into their poly-mind. For her folk it was a normal thing to do.

Early Dawn was a visitor.

The vehicle slid to a halt, engine and lights going off. Two people climbed out, from either side of the front seat.

"It's Doc and Bad News, friends," whispered Fair Morn. "We better get inside."

The pair ran lightly across the roof, jumped down to the front porch and hurried into the front room, snapping on lights as they headed for the back porch. To let their visitors in.

And met Smoke, Doc, and Bad News in the kitchen.

"I'll make more coffee." Early Dawn stepped over to the row of coffee makers and began to load the one not already set on a timer. And filled cups from the one already full and hot. The hunter and the prey had started that one some time before.

Doc watched, furrows creasing his forehead in curiosity. He hadn't met Early Dawn before. And smiled at Smoke and Fair Morn.

"Sorry for the early morning visit," he said. "Or the late evening visit. But I need your help. A rather sudden trip and I require J.C.'s presence." He shrugged. "But I do not know where he went camping or how to contact him."

"We can do that." Smoke handed Doc a cup of coffee and nodded at the refrigerator for Bad News, Doc's constant companion, who gave her an almost imperceptible nod, opened it and took out the orange juice and filled the glass handed to him by Smoke.

"Ummmm," umm'd Doc as he took a sip, enjoying the coffee. "But I am in a bit of a hurry. We need to leave soon. As soon as possible. This evening." He laughed. "That is after the sun comes up and sets again."

Smoke urged them into the living room and reached out with her minds speaking both to Tinker and Fair Morn. *Wake up, MindMate, we have visitors. Get Dat up. She will know where they are.*

Ummmmmmm? Tinker stared at the bedroom ceiling and wondered, not for the first time, why does this always seem to happen. Visitors turning up at inopportune times.

Doc and Bad News are here. In the living room. They want us to tell J. C. to come back to town from his camping trip.

He rolled from the bed, snatching up his pajamas from their usual rumpled heap next to the bed, tucked the covers around the still sleeping lump in the bed and headed for the living room.

Fair Morn snatched an ornate ring, an ornate ring with a jewel cut in such a manner as to appear like an eye, from one of the book shelves, and hurried into the three-story atrium of their bedroom complex, the area they all called The Chamber. She rapped the ring on a table top.

"Wake up, Dat! Wake up!"

A tiny figure seemed to leap from the ring, stretched and yawned, and glowered up at her. "It is not nice to disturb indjinns when they are taking a nap!"

"You have been asleep for two weeks!"

"A small nap for an indjinn" She yawned again just to make a point. "What do you want?" she grumbled.

"Doc wants J.C. to stop camping and come home. Since Je'leel is with them that means you can tell us where they are."

"Of course I can." The tiny figure nodded. "Indjinn mothers always know where their daughters are."

"Will you tell me how to find them?"

"I will go with you!"

"NO! J.C. doesn't need to know everything about us."

"He already knows about me."

"Not about your size changing."

Dat smiled, fangs just showing. "I will ride inside your shirt and give you directions as we go."

Fair Morn picked up the tiny figure and dropped her inside her shirt. "Watch those claws!"

"Almost as beautifully formed as me," observed Dat.

"Thanks." Fair Morn headed for the back door, patting Early Dawn on a rear pocket as she passed her in the kitchen. "Let's go, Sis. You'll enjoy the flight." *Smoke, we are on our way. You and he can explain something to Doc.*

Stepping away from Early Dawn, out in a large space on the far side of the parking area, she began to unfold and unfold and unfold her great butterfly wings. With a soft pop, Early Dawn's long bat wings snapped out and open. "Which way, Dat?" asked Fair Morn.

A tiny head popped out between two buttons of Fair Morn's shirt. "North."

The pair surged into the air and were soon soaring just below the cloud layer.

"Clouds are lifting," called Early Dawn. She pointed toward the east and at the faint glow of another day beginning. "Be light soon."

"Turn northwest now," urged Dat. "My daughter is still sleeping."

John Tinker sat slumped in one of the couches, coffee cup cradled on his stomach and peered at his long-time friend through heavy-lidded eyes. "Awfully early for this sorta stuff."

"Really quite sorry." Doc was wide awake and looking not at all that sorry. "But we do have to leave as soon as possible. And I really do require J.C.'s considerable skills. A very exciting find in south-central Europe with some interesting peculiarities." He beamed happily at the thought. "There is quite a load of literature to read before we get there. J.C. can easily do it on the way."

They drifted over the dense forest slightly above the tree tops, carefully watching the ground below. This was an area with few roads and a place where few of the folk, local or otherwise, visited. Those were the exact reasons why J.C. had picked the spot for camping and getting away.

"Straight ahead," directed Dat. "There is a meadow by a rock ridge."

The pair gently settled in the grass near the tents, folding and furling their wings. As they did, a slight figure slipped from one of the tents and drifted silently over to them. "I felt you arrive," sighed the morning breeze.

"Morning, Reep. This is Early Dawn, a friend. Is J. C. awake?"

Reep sat on a fallen tree, a grey and sun-bleached log, the bark long ago having sloughed away. She waved in breakfast. "Soon." And beckoned them over to join her. She nodded at Early Dawn as the pair did. "Another large appetite." Her dark eyes watched Early Dawn as she ate. "Another Big Red creation?"

Early Dawn stared at her. "I am real, no longer a magical jest. It was Messenger done."

"Yessssssssss."

One of the tents shuddered and a tall, surfer handsome man crawled out, stood and stretched. "Wowie, breakfast and visitors. Hi, guys." He sat next to Reep and slid one arm around her waist. "What are we having?"

"Whatever you would wish," whispered the morning sun.

"The usual."

She nodded and handed him a large plate filled with steaming food.

As he ate, he asked, "What brings you guys way out here?"

So Fair Morn explained. And J.C. nodded. "Sounds like Doc alright. We'll pack and head back to town."

A young woman slipped from her tent and joined them on the log. "Hello, Fair Morn. Hello, Early Dawn." Then Je'leel laughed, knowing where her mother was hidden. And knowing that this interesting fact was being kept from J.C. Reep nodded at Je'leel and handed her a plate.

"Thank you, Aunt." Je'leel began to eat.

"Vacation's over" announced J.C. "Duty calls. Doc is in another rush." Then he tickled Reep with his free hand. "We can drive. It can't be that big of a hurry."

And, as soon as breakfast was done, J.C. took over the dismantling of the camp, storing everything in his battered van. With the last tent set inside, he slammed the rear door shut, urged Reep and Je'leel inside, and drove rattling down the dirt road, waving jauntily from his window at Fair Morn and Early Dawn. He didn't see their truck anywhere but figured that they had to have parked down one of the side trails to give him room to drive out. It was a very narrow road.

"We are going to have to be very careful on the way back," stated Fair Morn. "It's daylight."

"If we fly high enough no one can tell." Early Dawn pointed upward. Great patches of blue were showing through the cloud cover. With a soft pop her wings deployed, her great black leather, bat wings. She watched Fair Morn unfold and unfold and unfold her great butterfly wings, the multi-colors glittering in the sunlight of this new day.

And then.

They were just two tiny specks.

Soaring above the clouds.

They were almost home when it happened.

"Airplane!" shouted Early Dawn, banking sharply to the right.

A small, private airplane suddenly rose up through the clouds, passing them, going in the other direction. Before the startled pilot could bank his plane around and take another look at what he thought he had just seen, the pair had fallen, plunging head first into the safety of the clouds, out the bottoms, and down toward their first pasture and into the edge of the forested slope. On their way down they had noticed that Doc's car was gone.

They stood in the shadows of the woods and waited until they were sure that the airplane was not coming down and around for a look. They headed for the house, folding and furling their wings as they walked. "Sounded like it was heading north," said Early Dawn.

"No one will believe him," replied Fair Morn. "Let's have a snack."

"Roast beef," suggested Early Dawn.

"On sour dough buns," added Fair Morn, throwing a comradely arm around the slightly shorter young woman. "Let's not tell him about the airplane. He'd only grumble."

Early Dawn nodded, and grinned. "Him" didn't need to know everything.

Inside the kitchen, Fair Morn unbuttoned her shirt. "Out!"

The tiny indjinn leaped onto the counter top. "Cocoa, please."

"Sure." Fair Morn began to make it. Early Dawn opened the refrigerator and began to assemble their snack. Dat sat on the counter edge and kicked her legs back and forth as she waited for the cocoa to be ready to drink.

It was some hours later when J.C.'s battered van drove up to the house and dropped off Je'leel and her camping gear. Smoke, Sha'gar, and Chicken met them and thanked him for taking their daughter camping and then returned to washing their large van as J.C. backed around and headed back to town and to Doc's place to see what his employer was up to this time.

Tinker wandered down from his work room and joined his daughter in the living room. He dropped into the couch next to her, coffee cup in hand. Je'leel had a cup of cocoa. Dat sat on the back of the couch, near Je'leel's head, looking very pleased.

"So, how was camping?"

"J.C. really likes to do that."

"I know."

"I took lots of books. Reep even read one. She said that reading books was not something that witches do very much unless they are spell books or scrolls."

He laughed. "So you read a bunch and Reep read one and J.C. camped."

She nodded. "They hiked around in the woods a lot."

"Which one did Reep read?"

"A Robert Jordan one. She said that he had gotten all the magic user stuff wrong."

He laughed. "Well, he is writing fiction and doesn't have her experience to draw upon."

"She camps because he likes to."

"Sure."

"And lets him do the cooking. Most of the time."

"Cause he likes to do that also."

"Sure." She looked at him. "Dad?"

"Oh, oh. What?"

"J.C. wondered what you were doing with Early Dawn."

"Nothing. Nothing at all. She just decided to visit. And Fair Morn enjoys having her company. So what else did you read?"

"All my text books."

"What? Text books?"

"So did J.C. He said that if I wanted any help he would be glad to tutor me."

He laughed. J.C. could probably do that in almost any subject she chose. Dat shook her head. "No need. My daughter is very smart, indjinn smart."

"College?"

Je'leel nodded. "The Princess said that I should go to college."

"Away to college?"

"No. Here. J.C. said that it wasn't really a bad place to go."

"You apply."

"Not exactly."

"Ummmm?" He looked puzzled at her. "How does one not exactly apply for college?"

"Sha'gar and Szart fixed their records, the school's records. All I have to do is enroll." She sat straighter and looked very proper at him. "I really do not have to go."

"Ummmmm?"

"But the mothers like the idea. Especially Chantal."

He nodded slowly and muttered, "So you are going, right?"

"Yep." She sipped her cocoa. "But I am still living at home. Chantal is buying me a car and going with me to get my driver's license. Just like my high school friends."

"A lovely daughter," gurgled Dat.

He reached out with his mind into the multiminds of their

being. *Sha'gar! Dat needs to be large.*

Of course.

Dat sat next to her daughter and smiled broadly at him. "I like being large. Do you wish to play with my body?"

"Mother!"

"Behave," he growled at Dat.

"Gimble, gimble, gimble," grumbled Dat. "Indjinns are always well behaved." And whispered in Je'leel's ear, "He likes to play with my body. It is how I got you."

Je'leel tried to not laugh. "I know, Mother."

He sighed.

Je'leel stood. "Going to unpack and then visit the rear deck." She strolled into the hall and outside to fetch her belongings.

Dat slipped sideways and leaned against his side. "Kiss me!"

"What?"

"You are my Great Master and have been neglecting me."

"Oh?"

"Yes."

"You have been sleeping for weeks."

"Just a little nap. Kiss me."

He looked at her and frowned. "I didn't think that Great Masters had to listen to their servants. Especially their indjinn servants, or whatever you are."

"You are different. An exception of a Great Master."

"You up to something?"

"Indjinns are not devious." She smiled, long canines showing. "Most of the time."

"Sure?"

"Of course. Wellllll?" She frowned back at him.

"Ooooooh kay." He slid his arms around her and did as exceptional Great Masters were supposed to do.

Szart nudged Sha'gar. They were sitting in the shallow end of the swimming pool. "Chantal will be very angry. She has The Ring."

Sha'gar shrugged.

"He has the indjinn on the couch."

Sha'gar shrugged again. "She is his."

It was the next day and they stood in the parking lot. Their van sparkled wet clean in the mid-morning sunlight. Large puddles of wash water were slowing sinking into the gravel. The van had been washed again for some unknown reason.

She snarled and growled and suggested in the strongest terms possible that all his ancestors were bent and vile perverted. And that he was the most vile and perverted of them all.

He laughed and smiled at her. "Good golly, Miss Molly, are you related to that green-skinned witch that Dorothy splashed?" He arched his back and curled his fingers into claws and cackled and then sobbed dramatically, "I'm melting . . . I'm melting . . . "

"Ptar par rak tak!" She stomped over and glared up at him as she was rather short. The ideas that the folk had about witches in this elseplace were warped and ugly.

"You don't appear to be melting," he observed.

"Piz gak!"

"Must had washed off the green makeup," he added.

Her glowered darkened.

Two others walked from the house just to see what was going on in the parking lot. Other than washing the van again.

"Great Agitating Prince, do cease thy irritation of this Our Own Sweet Szart." Princess Chicken frowned at him.

"Yah, bully!" added Messenger, standing next to her.

"She started it," stated Tinker. "Threw a bucket of water at me."

"Poz ga!" suggested Szart.

"So I squirted her," he added by way of explanation. And grinned at his victim. "Pretty nice shirt, all plastered to everything like that."

"PERVERT!" yelled Chantal from the top of the stairs by the back door.

"Yah!" agreed Messenger. "Goggle-eyed body ogling berbit!"

"Berbit?" He stared at her.

Szart nodded. "That is you! The abuser of witches."

He nodded. "I think that the van is clean."

"Most true," observed Chicken.

"Good." He turned the hose back on . . . and soaked them all, then hurtled for the house.

He had been lounging in their great hot tub for some time when he heard the crying and wailing begin. Lurching up and out, he grabbed one of the large white robes from the pile that was always there, and ready to be used. He shrugged on the robe and headed for the large living room as it seemed to him that all the racket was coming from there. "Now what's going on?" he mumbled to himself. "This time."

As he stepped into the room he could see that they were all gathered in a large, loose circle staring at a heap of black clothes on the floor. All eyes shifted to him as the crying and wailing increased in tempo. Ever face trying to look as upset as possible.

"What?" he asked through the noise.

Chantal pointed. "Nothing left but that puddle of clothes."

"Huh?"

"She just melted away," explained Early Dawn.

"Most over watered, Our Prince," added Chicken.

He looked over at Sgenn. "Now what's going on, Quiet?"

She shrugged and nudged her sister Sha'gar who said, "You dissolved Szart."

"Dorothy," added Smoke, smiling at him. "Must have had a gender change."

"I," he stated firmly, "am not Dorothy. This is not The Land of Oz." He pointed at the heap of clothes. "And she is not The Wicked Witch of The West." And frowned at them. "I think."

She stepped from behind one of the couches where she had been crouching and hiding and poked him in the back. "I am Faan, not Wicked. Never heard of that Oz clan!"

He whirled around, scooped her into his arms, and spun back to the assembled crowd. "Bug nutz," he announced. "You are all bug nutz."

"Not us abusing people," stated Messenger, picking up the pile of clothes and handing them to Szart, who was also wearing one of the thick white robes. "Here."

Tinker set Szart down. "Go get dressed, Witchy Poo!"

She snarled at him and stomped from the room.

Sighing heavily, he dropped into one of the couches. "Anyone gonna explain?"

Fair Morn dropped down next to him. "What?"

"My question, exactly."

Early Dawn settled next to his other side. "You have not been treating us nice."

"Since when?"

"For days and days and days and days," intoned Messenger. "You are turning into a troll!"

"Trolls are piz kak!" growled Sha'gar.

He waved at hand at the room. "There is neither a bridge nor a cave here that I can see."

Szart returned, stood behind his couch, and poked at one of his ears.

"STOP THAT!"

"Checking," she grumbled.

"OUCH!" She had just given one of his ears a sharp tug.

"For troll traces."

"Trolls," explained Sha'gar, "have long and pointed ears."

"And," added Messenger, nodding sagely at him. "They maltreat beautiful young maidens. Really really." She nodded violently.

"That's us." Smoke dropped into a nearby chair.

"So there!" snapped Messenger, shooting him between the eyes. With her water pistol.

"HEY!"

"Straw," suggested Chantal.

"Dead grass." Smoke grinned at him.

He sighed heavily, heavily he sighed. "Nobody's gonna tell me, are they?" He looked from face to face.

"What, pray tell, Great Prince of Our Heart?" Chicken took a seat next to Messenger and looked royal quizzical at him.

"Why," he grumbled, "are you all going on the way that you all are going on?"

"What's your problem now, Grumble Butt." Chantal took a sip from her cup. Loudly.

"THAT'S MY QUESTION!"

"DON'T YOU YELL AT ME!" Chantal looked at Smoke. "I really don't understand why you and Chicken started this bunch with him."

"Bad taste," suggested Smoke, grinning widely.

"Merde," he growled and turned toward Early Dawn. "O.K., fleidermaus, what's the problem? This time? Now? Huh?"

"Kiss me," she demanded.

He did. "That's the problem?"

"Nope."

"What?"

"You have been ignoring us."

"For days and days and days and days and days," intoned Messenger.

"No one can ignore you guys," he mumbled.

"It is true," insisted Early Dawn.

"Yah," agreed Messenger. "And then you melted Szart, our poor, beautiful, and innocent witch self."

"I am not innocent," grumbled Szart as she came into the room. "I am a witch." Witches were never innocent. Everyone knew that. Well, most everyone did. Being called "innocent" was almost as bad as being called a "lady."

"How?" he asked.

"Preoccupied," stated Chantal.

"With water," replied Messenger.

"Really?"

"It is bothering us," added Chantal. "Not the water."

"For days and days and days and days and days," intoned Messenger.

"Well, then why didn't someone say something?"

They mobbed him.

"Merde," mumbled someone from the bottom. "There has got to be a better way to communicate."

"Heh heh heh," cackled Sha'gar.

"So," he asked into the tangle on and around himself, "what sort of attention is required to stop all this nonsense?"

"Shopping is good," suggested Chantal.

"Oh boy oh boy," bubbled Messenger. "Clothes?"

"Groceries," stated Smoke. "Also."

"Cheap," he mumbled, "at twice the price. Or whatever."

So they unpiled, hauled him to his feet, and headed out to their large van after everyone dressed appropriately for going into town. Messenger sat behind the wheel and started the engine. She liked to drive.

And off they went.

Into town.

The whole mob.

Grandeville, Greater Downtown.

They wandered along the sidewalk in a rather loose

cluster, mostly window shopping. He was trying to keep an eye on them all, nervous and wondering if they would behave.

"Damn worry butt," grumbled Chantal, walking by his side.

Clusters of twos and threes were forming and breaking apart with lots of chatter and laughter as this or that item in this or that shop window attracted someone's attention.

Just as the group was nearing and then passing *Chen's Chinese Restaurant* they bumped into Sandy coming from the restaurant, carrying small white paper containers, headed back to her office.

"Wow!" She grinned at him. "You let them all come to town at the same time." She winked at Chantal. "Think that is safe, Shooter?"

"Sure." Chantal indicated Tinker. "If we can keep him from frightening children with that glower of his."

"Pish tosh," he grumbled, glowering at her.

"Like that," said Chantal.

Sandy smiled at him. "How about telling your hard working attorney why you decided to invade Grandeville?"

"Cabin fever," he explained. "Or something like that."

"We had to get him out of the house," explained Chantal.

Looking past Sandy's shoulder he saw the rest pouring into *Rachel's Thing Shop*. It was a place that specialized in New Age crystals and other "magical" items as well as an extensive collection of books and magazines dealing with subjects of a similar nature.

"Better see what they are up to," he said.

"Cool it, Cowboy," grumbled Chantal. "The world is

safe."

Sandy laughed. "Gotta go. Lots of paperwork." She spun and headed into the door that opened onto the stairs that led up to her office.

"Later," called Chantal to her friend. "Come on, grump," she said to him.

As they stepped inside the shop, he took a quick look around, checking for chaos. Szart and Sha'gar were looking through various books of "magic" and nudging each other. Messenger was checking a collection of magic wands. She was standing beside Chicken who was pushing a finger around in a tray of rings and talking quietly with Sgenn. Fair Morn and Early Dawn were examining a number of kites of various sizes hanging from the ceiling. In a corner, Smoke was checking out a number of books dealing with food magic.

"Looks pretty quiet to me," murmured Chantal in his ear.

Messenger looked up and beckoned them over and then pointed at a particularly strange looking "magic wand" in the pile of magic wands. The wands came in all colors with various odds and ends attached to them: quartz crystals, feathers, beads, and cloth streamers. Some were more plain.

"Pretty ornate," observed Chantal.

"I like the one with the pink feather," said Tinker. He picked it up and tickled Chantal's ear with it. "Pretty handy."

"It's real," whispered Messenger.

He looked at the feather. "Yep. Just dyed pink."

"The wand," she said.

"Really?" He laughed and waggled it dramatically.

Rachel hurried over, looking worried. "May I help you?"

"Sure," he said. "I'll take this one. I like the feather."

Messenger pointed. "And that one. Put it in a big bag please? By itself."

Rachel nodded, picked up the strange wand, walked to her counter, and began to write out the bill. She did everything by hand.

Chicken walked up, dragging Sgenn along, and handed a jade ring to Rachel. She felt that Sgenn needed it. Fair Morn and Early Dawn joined them and pointed out which kites they wanted. Smoke dropped two books on the counter and winked at Tinker. Szart and Sha'gar were now thumbing through magazines, mumbling to each other about the advertisements.

Finally they all surged outside, allowing him to pay for their purchases. Messenger carefully carried her paper bag by the upper edge, neatly folded over and stapled. He shoved his wand into a shirt pocket.

"Come again," called Rachel from the door to her shop.

"Let's eat," said Smoke.

Fair Morn pointed. "Chen's."

They headed that way and inside.

And eventually headed for home.

Carrying a number of small white paper containers of left-over Chinese food.

Tinker's Place.

They sat on the couch. He reached over and tickled Chicken's ear with his "magic" wand.

"Desist!"

"Heh heh heh."

"Foul feather poking cur!"

"Now you are under my control," he intoned in a deep

rolling tone.

"Pish tosh!" She made a swipe as the feather and wand were yanked to safety.

"Humpf," he snorted. "Didn't work very well. Guess we should have asked for operating instructions."

She batted him with a pillow. "Pesky Lord!"

"Just giving you a little attention. As ordered."

"Thee do be most ferli."

"Ferli?"

"Indeed! Most!"

"That's bug nuts," explained Chantal, sitting next to him. "And you can keep that feather to yourself."

"Indeed!" agreed Chicken.

"Piffle," he suggested.

"Piffle Us not, Sirrah!" Chicken frowned most royally and darkly at him.

"Damn right," agreed Chantal. "If anything is, it is you and that ghastly pink feather."

"What I get," he grumbled. "Taking you guys to town."

"Har tak rak tak!" snapped Szart, as something popped.

"Ooooooooopsie!" said Messenger.

"Ptar zak nar," growled Sha'gar.

"Now what?" He looked over to where that trio sat on the floor. Green fumes were lazily drifting up toward the high ceiling.

Messenger looked up and then over at him. "Told you that it was real."

"What?"

"The wand."

He held it out and bobbled it up and down. "This?"

"The one that I bought." She held out the wand. It appeared to have been carved from a rather thick dowel, incised and painted in a number of colors, with a crudely shaped, pointed end.

"Really?"

"Yep!" She nodded vigorously. "Really really." Messenger was the only one who could actually see magic as it swirled around magical objects or beings that could control magic.

He stared at her. "You bought a real magic wand in Rachel's Thing Shop in Grandeville?"

"Yep. But it is being stubborn."

"Ptar tik," grumbled Sha'gar along with other magician unhappy comments under her breath.

Szart nodded.

"You're kidding."

"Nope," stated Messenger. "But we don't know why."

"Take it outside before it fogs up the house."

Messenger headed for the front door. "You better behave," she said to the wand. Szart and Sha'gar followed her, the air crackling softly around them.

"Most strange," observed Chicken.

He sighed. "I don't like this."

"Knock off the worrying," growled Chantal. "They will figure it out."

"Every time something like this happens, we get sucked into someone's problem or disaster."

She snatched the wand from his hand and tickled his ear with the feather. He batted her with a pillow.

"Yep," she said. "Doesn't work."

"Merde."

"Damn grump!"

Come out back! The call echoed through their minds.

"Let's go." Chantal yanked him to his feet, and hurried him toward the rear deck.

On the rear deck, he leaned on the railing and looked up.

Two very large kites soared back and forth. One bat. One butterfly.

"Figures," he said, watching as the pair tugged on the kite strings and laughed happy at their kite's antics.

"Think if we tied strings to them you could tell the kite from the real thing?" Chantal nudged him in the ribs.

"Don't even suggest it," he grumbled at her.

"I brought cups, pots, and coffee cups," said Smoke.

He filled his cup and looked back. Now only one kite flyer was flying a kite. The great bat kite swerved back and forth and smiled down at him.

"I didn't say anything," laughed Chantal.

He sighed. "Can always give her back to Big Red."

Then the kite landed and the kite flier and the kite raced up to the deck. Tears trickled down the kite's cheeks. Fair Morn glowered at him.

"It was a joke," he mumbled.

He hugged Early Dawn. "Sorry."

"I forgot about your acute hearing." He gently wiped her face with a handkerchief. "But you should know better."

Early Dawn nodded.

So did Fair Morn. "You're forgiven."

"For what?"

"For being such a damned grump," explained Chantal.

He released Early Dawn, turned, and leaned back against the deck railing, arms crossed over his chest. "I am never gonna speak to you guys again. I am taking a vow of silence."

"Bush walla," suggested Chicken, handing him his refilled coffee cup.

"Probably what is really on his mind," said Smoke.

"Huh?" he stared at her. And took a sip from his cup.

"Wants to drag one of us into the bush and walla around." She burst into laughter.

He sighed. Then he leered at her.

"See." Smoke grinned at him.

Messenger popped from the side door to the house. "Next!"

He looked at her. "For what?"

"After Smoke."

"Huh?"

"Walla." She nodded vigorously. The wand was poked through her belt over her left hip. "It's behaving now," she explained.

"Who? It?"

"The wand. And we know its name, also."

"Name?"

Szart and Sha'gar joined them.

"Yes," said Messenger. "Really really."

"The Wand of Cation Guisin Ombor," stated Szart in a witch firm tone of voice.

"Unknown," added Sha'gar.

"To live or indulge oneself fully," intoned Fair Morn, "with animal pleasure."

He stared at her. "What?"

"Wallow," she explained. "What happens when you drag one of us into the bush."

"Oh, boy!" gurgled Messenger. She stared at him, her eyes going all round. "Really really?"

He sighed. And gave up. Once again. And mumbled, more or less to himself, "Maybe I can talk with B.R. and see if he can do something."

"Oh no you don't," snapped Chantal, glowering at him. "I am not having Big Red, that piece of magic with a warped sense of humor, messing around with me!"

"Vitamins?" he suggested. "Minerals?"

"Knock it off," she snarled.

"Fruit punch?"

"Chocolate chip cookies?" offered Messenger. They were her favorite. For eating. For baking. She nodded violently at him.

"Most fine chocolate cake." Chicken smiled at him, and licked her lips slowly.

"Popcorn," suggested Fair Morn.

Smoke winked at her. "Roast beef."

"Black licorice." Szart nodded at Sha'gar who nodded back.

"I like roast beef also," stated Early Dawn. "With horseradish."

He glanced over. "Well?"

Sgenn shrugged.

"Fine. How about we put all this energy into doing the chores?" He headed for the tool shed. It really needed straightening out, again.

The rest scattered.

Fair Morn and Early Dawn took their kites inside to hang them on the walls of the atrium of The Chamber.

Then they all talked inside their mutually joined minds about how much fun they had today. And what to do about "him."

In the midst of all this conversation, Szart, Sha'gar, and Messenger discussed the strange wand.

Szart sent a message to her mother as did Sha'gar.

Messenger suggested that they ask Shem as he had specialized in the history of magic and magic users.

And, eventually, Smoke, Chantal, and Fair Morn headed into the kitchen to start dinner.

Late at night in the sleep still house, in the dim light of a moonbeam stroking over the collection of objects on the book shelf in the large living room, something crackled.

The red cube slide sideways as a small figure appeared next to the ornate ring with a jewel carved to look like a eye. She walked over and kicked the strange wand. "You there! Be quiet! I was sleeping!" Then she kicked it again. "And no arguing!" She disappeared back into the ring.

Far across the universe of universes something woke up.

Another Daughter

Bahn Duhr Tohr. The Quarters of the Royal Advisors.

She cackled.

He gasped.

"A strange . . .

time . . .

for . . .

that . . ."

"We will have a daughter," she stated.

"You sure?"

"Of course. Just now. You did it." The great dark eyes blinked at him.

"Just me?"

"I helped, Husband Forever." She shivered and tightened her arms and legs around him. "But do not stop. Yet."

"My pleasure, Ebony Delight."

Grandeville. Tinker's Place.

She slipped into the bedroom on silent bare feet and knelt next to the large water bed set flush with the floor. And reached over and gently nudged the hump under the blankets that was him. And did it again. And again. And, eventually, his head poked out. "Ermmmm? Huh?"

"Soon I will have a new sister," explained Szart.

He struggled back and leaned against the wall. "What?"

"Mother will birth soon. We have to go for the naming."

"Damn early in the morning for birth announcements." Chantal yanked the covers down and glared up at Szart in the early dawn light.

"We in a hurry?" he asked.

"No. We have two of your days."

"Then?"

"We must go."

He nodded. "O. K. We'll go."

She nodded and left the bedroom, gently closing the door.

Chantal gave him a poke with one forefinger. "Slide down here, Stud. We have lots of time." And glanced and glared at the nearby alarm clock. "I'll tell my partner to cover while we are visiting."

He slid down. "Lot's of time? For what?"

She grabbed him. "As Dat so elegantly stated it, yesterday, to play with my body. Com'mere, Cowboy."

Szart sat next to Sgenn at one of the large wooden tables on the rear deck. And waved in breakfast for both of them.

"It was necessary."

Sgenn looked over and took a bite out of her toast.

"Chantal wanted him and he was sleeping."

Sgenn fed a few crumbs to a very brave sparrow.

"Heh, heh, heh," cackled Szart.

"Not nice."

"She was about to wake him up anyway." She twitched. "We must leave tomorrow. My sister is early."

"Name?"

"Ripple daughter Faan websmith Seemna."

Sgenn twisted around and stared at Szart, soft grey eyes staring into midnight jet. "Websmith?"

Szart leaned close and murmured. "A very devious witch talent. Extremely rare. She will require special training. We have to find Fasbaq the Blue Udaz for her training."

Sgenn nodded and sent something all dark angles and strange shape to search for this person. The deep down always did what a Theurgist thought.

Adeby Lukme.

He wandered through the small market place and sampled various of the locally produced foods, offered and prepared for sale in the numerous booths.

It was a large building thronged by the folk from several of the nearby towns as well as by the locals. His loose fitting clothes were colored a soft powder blue artfully trimmed with a slightly darker blue.

Moments before a very strange messenger had appeared while he had been walking casually toward this very town following the wide path through the woodbent forest. Then it disappeared. And shortly thereafter he had received another message.

Now, as he ate a little of this and a little of that, he pondered whether he wanted to get involved with that witch clan. That clan, the Faan clan, was known far and wide as a very dangerous and a very volatile witch clan. They were probably the worst of the worst as far as the witch clans go. And that was truly something to worry about. He wondered what spell they had used to send bring such ugly into existence.

Then he tried something green and crunchy. He swallowed and thought that this witch clan would owe him witch debt, always something nice to have, and would pay him very well, also something very nice to have. After all, there were very few with his gifts.

He nodded to himself. And sent a message to the Clan Head.

And smiled to himself.

Bahn Duhr Tohr. The Quarters of the Royal Adviors.

They had been gathering in for the past three days. All the sisters and daughters had arrived. With one exception. The exception was the daughter that lived in that strangely primitive far distant rather isolated elseplace.

Ripple stroked the jet black hair of her new daughter and admired the large dark eyes, eyes that looked up at her with a knowing intelligence. There were a number of white specks in each iris.

Hanred peered down at his daughter. "I have never seen a child with eyes like that. Not even any of the others."

"Websmiths are different." Ripple smiled at him. "She will be beautiful."

He smiled back. "Of course. It runs in your clan."

"They are slow," she grumbled.

He shrugged, knowing who *they* were. "It is a long way to come."

"Reep and her's are already here."

He nodded. "True."

A small scroll fell from somewhere and landed in her lap.

She told it open and read it. "Hum, hum, hum. He wishes to meet in Doth Lamex."

"A very cautious person." Hanred gently touched his new strange daughter with a fingertip. She smiled at him. "He wishes to bargain and stay alive," he explained.

"What does he want?"

He shrugged. "Something we don't expect, I suspect. Something that your clan will not want to do, probably."

"Hum hum hum." She smiled. And some of the light was sucked from the room. "Then I shall let you come, most devious Mate, and, if need be, bargain with this cautious person. And I shall prepare something, hum, . . . special." She ran a finger down her daughter's forehead and nose. The light returned to the room. "Very special."

"Be careful."

"I am always careful."

He winced.

Dark began to twist into a tight rope in the middle of their room.

"Enter!" snapped Ripple.

They swirled in.

Szart and all the rest of herself.

Szart liked that effect.

"Hayou, Mother. Hayou, Father." Szart walked over and peered at her newest sister. "Lovely." She bent close and told her, "I am Szart, sister."

"Yessssss," gurgled Seemna.

"Oh my gosh!" gasped Messenger. "She pulls it very close." And looked at Ripple. "All her magical strands are coiled tightly around her. Really really different." She violently nodded. Messenger had that unique ability to see such things. She could, if she wished to, reach out and manipulate those strands.

And all the rest of them crowded around to admire this newest member of the Faan clan.

Two days later, after the naming ceremony, Ripple's sisters began to leave, each in their own fashion. But her daughters remained. It was an opportunity to visit and to find out what the others had been doing since the last time they had seen each other. And to discuss their newest sister, their newest and very strange sister.

A year had passed and now the newest sister had returned from witch raising, witch training. A year had passed for most. Twenty years had passed for the newest sister. It was normal. For the witch clan it was how things had always been done.

Shitar sprawled comfortably on the couch and against Mantara, her mate-for-life, who was relaxing because he could feel her relaxing, at least as much as a witch ever did relax. "What does anyone know about websmith?" she asked. The sisters and their's had gathered together again.

"Nothing." Szart shook her head.

Sook frowned. "They are told devious beyond devious." And wondered how her husband, The King, was doing. He had been gone most of the days visiting his parents, the King and the Queen of Bahn Duhr Tohr.

Santar held her hands out, fingers extended, her palms a

hand width apart and watched something form in the empty space inbetween. "They are very rare. None of the witch clans that I have met have had one."

"Hum hum." Shitar sat upright. "During her final training we must all be there." Her sisters gasped and stared at her. This just was not done. One or two helped, at times, but never all.

"My King will not come!" stated Sook. "I will not allow that!"

Shitar nodded, recognizing the Mate Protection hiss around Sook. "He is your's. We would not presume."

The air settled in the room.

Mantara lightly touched Shitar's ear with a fingertip. "I will help as well." He winked at the rest looking at him. "After all, I have already aided a few in training. Seemna can use a touch of green magic as well." He slid a cautious arm around a narrow waist. "Perhaps your Aunt, the urh-witch, could be convinced to add something as well. Or your cousin, Sedeem of the three colors?"

Sisters looked from one to the other and then at Shitar and stared hard at Mantara. He was suggesting strange behaviors, mostly non-witch.

Everyone jerked. Szart was staring into space and chewing on the tip of a glittering grey wand. No one moved, not even Mantara. They all knew that this sister had been given all of the spells that their late aunt, R-Bar, had known, including those in The Book of Banned Spells, just before that aunt had died. Gifting on that magnitude had made this sister's spell repertoire greater and more lethal that anyone in the room and most, if not all, of the Aunts as well.

The black eyes refocused. "I will ask him. And Messenger." She shrugged. "No promises."

"Witch true," agreed Santar.

Something flashed away.

"I sent a message to Sedeem," explained Shitar.

Someone knocked on the door which carefully opened itself. And he walked in. "Greetings, Dark Ones." Frinda bowed to each of them in turn. And then he pulled a chair over to sit next to Sook. "Such a sea of serious faces. Anything that I might do?" He laughed happily at the thought.

"It would be best if our newest sister could be trained in one of the far meadows of Our Kingdom, My King." Sook took one of his hands in her's.

"Anywhere that you might wish. Shall I ring it with troops?"

"No need!" snapped Sepanix.

"Perhaps some tents for our guests?" suggested Santar. "If they come." They could always wave in whatever anyone needed, but it would be witch proper to allow him to that in his lands.

"Whatever you wish." Frinda gently squeezed Sook's hand. "Tell me what and it shall be done." He leaned close to her. "Who is coming?"

"The Chosen One and his. Perhaps his daughter Sedeem and her's." Sook looked into his eyes. "Your sister, The Queen, his Queen, will probably visit as well, if he does."

Frinda laughed. "Without a doubt if she knows that he will be there."

Doth Lamex. The Place of Healing and Relaxation.

They waited in their assigned place. Some relaxed, some not so relaxed. Hanred and Mantara were relaxed. Shitar and Ripple were just being witch. Witches did not wait well. Or relax well either.

And then he finally strolled into their private area, a very self-assured stroll. He was a tall, pleasant looking man who didn't look as large as he was until he stood close and looked down at you. His clothes were colored a soft blue with nicely decorated darker blue accents.

"I am Blue Udaz Fazbaq. Who sent that ugly messenger? A year ago."

"Ah, ummm, associate of my sister," snapped Shitar, not liking his tone of voice at all.

"I merely sent a message," cooed Ripple, instantly causing Hanred to start to worry. A cooing witch was not a good sign.

"Nerpa," suggested Fazbaq. "Compliments to your sister's friend. She has a unique taste in ugly." He sat, a very relaxed slump. "What do you wish, Faan witch Clan Head Ripple? I have waited long."

"Even so, a daughter requires training."

"I only train the rare."

"She is websmith."

"Ahhh um, the very rare." Fazbaq's eyes slid from face to face. "And . . . ?"

"My sisters," stated Ripple, as firmly as only a witch could state when she was being firm, "and others will also help train."

Fazbaq stared at her. "That is unusual, most unusual."

"It is necessary."

Fazbaq shrugged. "My fee?"

"Witch debt," stated Ripple.

"Witch debt, "echoed Shitar.

He shrugged again.

"What else," hissed Ripple.

"Speak!" snarled Shitar.

"It is said," began Fazbaq carefully, "that the Faan witch clan are the blackest of the black."

"Hum." Ripple watched his face closely.

"I am," stated Fazbaq, "a most talented warlock for training the very rare."

Ripple blinked.

"And not hard to look upon, either." He smiled at her. "Much as the Faan are not hard to look upon."

Shitar growled deep in her throat.

"I would have one," stated Fazbaq.

"Ptar nar nar," hissed Ripple.

"Antak nil tik," suggested Shitar.

He nodded at them. "As coarse as is told." And straightened up, suddenly a sense of arcane power and deep strength. "It is my price. Witch debt and witch mate. Decide!"

Ripple looked at Shitar. "Strong daughter?"

Shitar stared at him. "The Faan pick their's. They are not chosen by anyone else. Nor are we given!"

"Kaa maap da!" Fazbaq stood. "That was not told."

"Wonderfully coarse." Ripple flowed to her feet. "Who?"

Fazbaq shrugged. "Other than you two, I have met none. Who can say?" His eyes narrowed. "How many daughters do you have, Clan Head. Name me names."

Ripple nodded at her daughter. "Shitar. Her's is Mantara, Grenzanr."

Fazbaq smiled at Mantara. "A green. How nice."

"Sook," said Ripple. "Her's is Frinda, a King." Fazbaq gasped. She continued. "Santar. Seemna, to be trained. Szart, her's is The Chosen One."

For a fleeting moment Fazbaq looked startled. But only for a fleeting moment. "This clan is many tangled."

"Witch true," agreed Ripple. "Sepanix, the wild," she added.

He looked at Shitar. "All are as lovely as you?"

Jet black eyes bored into his. "Like mother, like daughter."

"And all these sisters will help train?"

She nodded.

"And all will owe witch debt?"

"Yesssssss," hissed Shitar.

"But," interjected Ripple. "The Faan control how the debt is defined."

"Hap nap nap," growled Fazbaq.

"Where did a Blue Udaz learn such vile?" Shitar leaned back against a convenient tree and crossed her arms over her chest. Dark eyes watched him carefully.

He sat, once again in a very relaxed slump. "I did wander most widely. And trained subtle on Karfar Daz, a near hidden elseplace." He nodded at Ripple. "Which is now to your clan benefit and to your newest daughter's benefit."

"Hum," murmured Ripple. Shitar shot her a sharp glance, recognizing a certain tone of voice, a certain change of expression. Her mother was thinking devious.

Fazbaq stood. "Shall we go? Such training as we must do is long and hazardous."

Ripple nodded. "We have a special training place." She led them down the path and around to the entry area of Doth Lamex, a vast paved area with many tall columns spaced widely, all glaring white. And took them out in a burst of midnight.

Bahn Aahn Tohr. The Special Training Spot.

The selected spot, far in the interior of Frinda's lands, far away from any place that non-witch folk might wander, had several tents strewn along one edge of a large and quiet meadow. The meadow was a great open place of short grass. A number of people were seated around a table just finishing an early morn meal. They watched the small group approach, nodding and smiling greetings to the four that they knew and watched carefully the one they did not.

He stood, a proper distance away, and watched and bowed and said, "I am Blue Udaz Fazbaq. I am here to train Faan websmith Seemna." His eyes drifted from face to face, wondering which one she was.

Ripple waved one hand. "These are some of my sisters, the unmated ones. All witches. Riz, Reptar, Rumtah, and Rotak."

Four pair of dark eyes stared at him, frank appraising stares. Three young women appeared and strolled over and joined the group. "Santar," stated Ripple. "Sepanix, and Seemna. Seemna is the one wearing the green belt."

The taller of three stepped over to him, all feral grace. He could feel the beyond in her soft smile. She had the high cheek bones and slightly slanted, great jet filled eyes that marked all members of the Faan witch clan.

"Sooooooo," she said. "You are the Fazbaq." And pointed. "Out there, in that meadow."

He nodded, turned, and casually strolled, in a very controlled manner, out into the meadow. And turned to watch her approach. She was gone.

"Ha'a'kapt!" He slashed the air with a sputtering purple wand.

And she was there. Watching him.

"I am the teacher," he growled. "And you are the student." And cast.

She countered.

The meadow erupted.

And so the day passed.

Finally, some days later, as the sun touched a nearby ridge, Ripple called, "Enough!"

The environment settled down, more or less.

He had her by one arm and was wildly hacking away entangling web strands with the other as she snarled and cast.

Then she did the unexpected.

With her free hand she punched him in the solar plexus. He gasped and released her. She grabbed either side of his head and yanked it down, into a rapidly rising knee that smashed into his forehead.

As he stumbled backward, casting heal, she leaped backward and watched him.

Their clothes were tattered and torn, more rags than garments.

He stepped close to her, glaring, and demanded angrily.

"Where did you learn such hakpt?"

"From my Uncle."

"Who is?"

She indicated with her chin, the group sitting around two of the tables. "Him. The Chosen One."

"That was not-witch!"

She shrugged. "The Faan are not gazed upon except by their Mate-For-Life." She cast repair. The front of her blouse, mostly gone, quickly rewove itself.

"The Faan," he growled, "are worse than any told." He waved his robes into new.

"Of course!" She spun away and strolled over to where her mother stood.

Santar grabbed her by the hair as she passed by and yanked her backward as Sepanix came in low and upward, a gleaming golden wand clenched in her fist.

The world shifted.

"ENOUGH!"

And exploded.

And returned.

Seemna stared at her side where bright green was seeping in all directions from the golden wand sticking out.

Ripple stomped over, gestured the wand away and glared at trio, the air crackling angrily around her. "You all will do as you are told!"

And three daughters tried to look as contrite as a witch could, which was not very, and answered in unison. "Yes, Mother."

Sepanix waved away the green and kissed her sister. "We will train tomorrow. With Santar."

"Of course." Seemna hooked an arm around either waist and tugged them towards the tables. "I am hungry."

And every day, more day after more day, Aunts and Sisters, and Fazbaq, attacked and taught all manner of arcana to their student until all were exhausted, save one.

"Sister," announced the short witch, shorter than any present. "I am Szart."

"Hayou, Szart sister." Seemna stared at this sister. She had been told about every clan member and all the others associated with the clan. This sister was not as innocent as she appeared to be. She cast terrible.

Seemna crashed onto her back, far across the training spot. Leaping to her feet, she watched Szart stalk toward her, a midnight dark wand held in one hand.

Seemna slid sideways. Stared at her feet. She was anchored to the ground. Hissing angrily, she freed herself and leaped away. The bolt slashed past her side, plucking at the material of her blouse.

She spun and cast.

No one was there.

The wand plunged into her back and out the front of her chest, sputtering blue fire.

"Ptar ptar nar!" Yanking it out, she cast heal and turned, sagging to her knees, feeling her cast being deflected away.

Szart blew black dust from a cupped palm and watched it settle over her sister. And watched her begin to dissolve.

With the calm of knowing death, Seemna relaxed, and pulled it all together.

And was gone.

And returned.

Kneeling.

She bowed her head. "Forever witch debt, Sister."

Szart tapped her on top of the head with her wand. "Stand. Faan to Faan, no debt."

The much taller woman did and hugged her. "We are finished, are we not?"

"Yesssssss. Finished." Szart yanked Seemna's head down and kissed her on the forehead.

They walked back to the group standing and watching.

Szart tapped him on a shoulder. "Lap!"

He sat, drew up his knees so she could sit on him. "Kinna bossy, aren't you, Shorty?"

"Yesssssss." She kissed him. "That sister is finished training. Very nice."

"Uh huh." He frowned at her. He didn't like that last comment. It always led to things, or events, that were, in his opinion, unwanted.

"She is Faan lovely."

"Of course."

"Young, witch raised, now only twenty of your years old. And beautiful."

He sighed, heavily he sighed. "Stop stating the obvious, short and devious. Now what's going on?"

"Hum hum."

"You're gonna get dumped on your humming witchy butt in a minute," he growled.

Seemna gasped and stared at the pair and their strange conversation. And waited for her sister to attack him. No-one talked to witches that way. Then she wasn't sure what she was seeing. Szart had leaned against his chest and was now poking a finger inside his shirt and tickling him.

"Merde," he grumbled. And wondered what was wrong with Seemna. She was standing there, staring at them.

Ripple glanced at Shitar who shrugged.

One witch wandered past and stopped in front of Fazbaq and stared up into his face. He was a bit taller. "I am Reptar, Blue Udaz Fazbaq. I am going to visit Partnar and a small specialty shop located in that elseplace. Have you been there?"

He looked down, just a little, into great black eyes. "No, Faan witch Reptar, I have not. What do you do there?"

"Spell buy."

"Hada." He nodded, buying spells was always a nice thing to do. "Perhaps some company, some very talented company, would be in order and permissible?" he asked in a very warlock polite tone of voice.

"It would be allowed."

"I am always interested in new spells and new elseplaces, urma, new places to me."

In a soft rumble of black they were gone.

"Hum," observed Ripple.

Tinker stared at the rest of himself. "Is anyone going to tell me what this is all about?" He nudged Szart, she being the *what* that he was referring to.

Blank faces looked back at him.

He nodded. "O. K., if that is the way it is going to be then the answer is NO!"

Szart frowned up at him.

Seemna hastily cast protection. She didn't want to be injured by spell splash.

"My sister requires safe and calm for some time."

"Ah HA!"

"Yesssssssssssss."

"And if I refuse?"

Szart beckoned over Seemna. And said when she stood close. "She will be very well behaved."

Seemna frowned at her sister.

"Witches are never well behaved," he grumbled.

"Ptar tak," suggested Szart.

"Grumble butt," added Chantal, joining the group.

Messenger bounced over. "She is very pretty," she bubbled. "Really really."

Seemna jerked back. "This is not-Faan," she snapped. "Sister!" Black began to form around her.

"Behaving?" he asked.

Szart looked at her sister, all blank face. And blinked.

Seemna readied herself for the attack. "I will not be given!"

"Of course," agreed Szart.

"Sister?"

"You require rest. Where I, we, live is much calm and great comfort. Safe safe."

"Sorry sorry." The black faded away.

Tinker poked Szart with a finger. "She can sleep in your room."

"Of course."

"Why didn't you just say so instead of dancing all over the place, um, so to speak!"

Chantal stomped closer. "Cause you are such a grumble-butt, Cowboy! Let's go home!"

Szart stood, nodded at Sha'gar. They waited for him to stand.

In a swirl of twisting black the group was gone.

"Mother?" Shitar was frowning darkly.

"Her training was harder than any. She was near far." She chewed on one corner of her mouth. "You may visit."

"Yes, Mother."

Visitors and Visiting

Molus Halma.

Zaruna, Occiis witch, hurried through town gathering the energy that she required as she went. The situation was worse than they had been told. Something had to be done soon before it was too late. Zarna, the clan Head, had selected her to do this. It would be a long journey. Not necessarily a hazardous journey, just a long one. Her clothes were a pale yellow decorated here and there with touches of a bright red that glowed softly in the two suns of this elseplace.

It was a most strange mission that she had been set upon. What the clan understood seemed to be a mixture of folk tales and gossip intermingled with the fantastical stories told here and there. But from the few facts buried in all that, the clan felt there was enough to be worried about, and to take action. It was those few facts, the small knowledge, that now propelled her so swiftly down the street toward the edge of town.

As soon as she stepped over the town boundary, she was gone.

A soft flash of yellow in the air.

Then empty space.

Grandeville. Tinker's Place.

She faded in and onto the rear deck, settling softly down. Szart looked up and smiled at her sister. "Hayou sister.

Welcome to our elseplace."

The exploding water balloon splashed a number of the others as well as drenched its unintended target who snarled and snatched in a glowing bronze wand and cast.

"OOOOOOOPS!" said a voice from a high balcony. "Wrong person."

The bolt flashed upward, past Early Dawn's head. She yelped and leaped over the railing, landing with thump on the wooden deck in front of the startled witch holding the bronze wand. And punched her.

Fair Morn grabbed Early Dawn as Szart staggered sideways under the sudden weight of a limp body.

"HOLD IT!" He stomped over, glaring at everyone. It was an all-purpose glare. "Now what's going on?"

Early Dawn pointed at the now standing, held upright between Sha'gar and Smoke, Seemna. "That person just tried to kill me!" She grinned at Fair Morn who now stood by her side. "So I punched her lights out. Just like my sister showed me."

"Merde." He frowned at everyone and wondered once again why this was always happening. "Less than three seconds and it's already started. A new world's record for turmoil." He headed for the house. "Szart, you explain. It is your sister. And your idea!" He took two steps and jerked to a halt.

A small scroll had just fallen from somewhere and landed with a thump on one of the wooden tables.

"Sook sent," observed Szart, nodding at him. She wondered why her sister had done that.

"Now what?" He glowered again, frown wasn't working, at her, she shrugged, and walked over to look at the thing. And was joined at the table by Szart who looked at the label writtem in witch script, and said, "For you."

He picked it up and unrolled the scroll and read the message out loud so all the curious, that was everyone standing around, would know.

Great Lord King Husband.

Greetings from thy Queen, Lurin.

We do hear, We do, of a visit, not far distant, in Our Own Brother's lands, of many strange folk. And it was said that among this gathering was My Very Own King. Have We been abandoned that some small visit was denied? Our folk puzzle over this and mumble worry and concern for the affairs of this Our Kingdom.

And we do miss thee greatly.

Lurin, In Her Own Hand.

"Merde." He turned and looked at Seemna. "You may come or stay." And beckoned to Chicken. "Princess, any reason why we can't go for a short visit?"

"Naught, Sweet Prince. T'was most vast a'breach of protocol."

"Just over witched, I guess. Most vast is redundant."

Seemna, now fully recovered, looked at Szart, who shrugged.

Chicken stuck her tongue out at him.

Early Dawn nudged Fair Morn. "May I come? This time?"

"Sure. Hang on to my hand." She grabbed one of Early Dawn's. "It's a nice place."

He looked at Szart. "O. K." And ignored Chicken's tongue and frown.

Szart nodded at Sha'gar.

Black twisted them away.

Partnar.

The tall woman wearing a black vest over a black shirt with an ornate pattern woven in the side panels of the vest in grey walked down a narrow trail. Her long black skirt swirled close to her ankles as she stepped along. Her black sandals did not leave a mark in the soft dust of the way.

Her slightly taller companion was making dust puffs and leaving tracks.

"A special skill," she explained. "Light walking."

He cleared his throat.

"Yes?" She glanced at him from the corners of her eyes.

"It is said," he began, very cautiously. "That the Faan witch clan is many entangled."

"Most true."

"How?"

"My youngest witch sister, R-Bar, now gone far, did much. Ripple clan head agreed, saying that the clan was now headed in new directions. Some links were through chosen mates. Would you like to know who?"

He cleared his throat. "If you wish to tell, I would listen."

"Most polite, Blue Udaz."

"It is told that when speaking with Faan that it is healthy to be so."

"Hum." She nodded a slight nod. "Vanderlaine and Hacto."

He jerked. "Mage!" And quickly recovered.

She nodded again. Another slight nod. "Tanpak. Zwar. Grenzanr. Hinta."

"Many linked witch clans."

"Yesssssssss. Tell of the Blue Udaz."

"Of course." He cleared his throat. "Long before before, witch Evata of the clan Nadinat learned unique and founded a sub-order Udaz named after that unique. Many many later, during the Great Witch-Demon War, the Nadinat became no more. The Udaz chose blue on blue, a remembrance of the Nadinat. Ever since we have been a select few specializing in the training of the very rare of the very rare."

"True?"

"Witch true."

"How is it, tall Udaz, that you remain unmated?"

His eyes popped wide. And this time he didn't recover all that quickly. "Hap napna!" he muttered. "None told Faan were so randap!"

She stopped walking, twisted her head around, and snapped, eyes flashing midnight. "Randap!"

"Indeed! Most randap!" He glared back at her. "Most!"

"Hum." She jabbed his chest with one pointed fingernail. "And what do none tell of the Udaz that tear open young female's garments during training to stare at their beauty?"

He stepped away from that sharp forefinger, frowning darkly at her. "Vile agnar witch! She did that, not I! And tried to deform me!"

She stepped closer, the air crackling around her. "My

niece exposed herself to you? You speak ptar kar words!"

"NO!" He batted away her thrusting finger, unsure of her dialect word choice. "Her spell blast! Ripped the garb of us both. Cease!" The air thickened, soft blue haze.

"Most zata." Reptar admired the blue mist. And reached up and unfastened the top button on her shirt. "Would you admire me, staring Udaz?"

Yanking in a long blue wand, he rapped her on top of the head with it. "Hapna hisdta!" The wand bent.

Reptar folded her hands over her chest and just looked at him. "Hum hum. Why unmated?"

"Marbar marnar," he grumbled, mostly to himself. "Are all Faan so?"

"We are as we are." She watched him from a witch blank face. "Answer! The question asked!"

Waving the air clear, he stepped further back. "None seen were wanted."

"And," she demanded, "is this old witch as easy to view as my young niece?"

He snarled at her and stomped one foot. Dust eddied to all sides. "The face is beautiful." And waggled one hand. "The rest is unknown."

"Hum hum hum. Is that a clever ploy to divest me of my garments?"

Thunder crashed and the wind blew. Fazbaq stomped his foot again. The ground split open.

Reptar floated gently backward. "You may continue to travel with me, Blue Udaz Fazbaq." She turned away and strolled up the path leaving not a mark in the dust.

Hahn Dohr Kahn. Realm of The Dragon.

The servant slipped into the room and waited until she looked up from the document that she was reading. It was not good to interrupt her.

"Majesty, The King is here. He and his Company are all in the main dining hall."

She dropped the document on the table, wrote a short note in the right hand margin, and tossed the thing into a small container. And stood and followed the servant from the room.

As she strode, a determined warrior stride, into the main dining room, he smiled at her. "It was an oversight. I'll, umm, explain later."

She bowed her head. "Of course, Great King," she murmured.

Wincing at her tone, he waved one hand. "This is Seemna, Szart's sister, her newest sister, who is visiting us. This is Early Dawn, who is also visiting us. They wanted to come along." He stepped close to The Queen. "So, how are things in the kingdom? And our son and daughter-in-law?"

"All pear well. This great edifice is near complete. Our Son, The Prince, and His Princess, are exploring yet another piece of our unknown lands. And We did miss thee." Her eyes bored into his, it was a Royal Queen firmly in control look. "Come, stroll with me to The Great Quay. We would have thee see Our new vessel."

He smiled at her. "And your folk, The King."

She grinned. "That also."

"We shall Ourselves," stated Chicken, "also stroll about town and see what else do be new."

So, they headed out. Each group going their own way.

Smoke kept them all within her sensenet, a great sphere of awareness, guiding her group as she did so.

On the end of the quay, named The Great Quay, the pair stood, listening to the gentle creak of timbers moving in the gentle ocean swells headed toward the shore and the edge of town.

He looked up at it. "Certainly big. Certainly white."

"Indeed, Our King. This vessel is the largest yet constructed in all the Kingdoms, Old or New. This be Our very Own, fitted for exploration. We have two more a'building in the yard. They can haul all manner of supplies. Our Brother does likewise."

She slid an arm around his waist. "A small swift vessel of one of the sea folk did report most astonishing thing. South and west they were storm hurled and did barely manage to return to Us, more dead than alive. The Ship Master, a sturdy, honest fellow, did swear that he saw faint hint of land as they came about for home."

"What?"

She laughed. "Indeed! If this be true, t'will be yet more vacant land We suspect." She waggled a free hand at her ship. "This one, and the others, apply provisioned, might sail there and back, crew sound and healthy."

He turned and wrapped her in his arms. "You will be careful, right?"

"Most assuredly for We remain, to manage both kingdoms, while Our Brother King does venture forth. He does require and enjoy the challenge of such a journey. Much more than We do."

"Good." He kissed her. "We may not visit very often, but

we do worry a lot about things here."

"True?"

"You betcha."

"What?"

"Yes."

"Oh." She smiled at him. "Would thee care to board and see Our Quarters?"

"I suppose."

She tugged him toward the gangplank. "My room has a most comfortable and roomy bed."

"An offer that I can't refuse."

Several blocks from the base of the quay, Chicken nudged Smoke. "Most sly a'Queen and most eager a'King."

"Yep." Smoke eyed the food stuffs in the booth near where they stood. She strolled over and pointed. "I'll have some of that."

"Me too." Fair Morn stepped over to the booth accompanied by Early Dawn.

"Right," agreed Early Dawn.

The trio ordered the largest selection offered. It came with adequate napkins.

Seemna looked at Szart. "How did she know what he and that Queen were doing?"

So Szart explained that they were all mentally linked together.

Seemna blinked. "Sister! What have you become?"

"Nothing strange. We are merely a special creature unlike anything in any elseplace other than Smoke's. But I am still Ripple daughter Faan witch Szart, your older sister."

"Hum hum."

"Hum," agreed Szart.

Sourthe.

The trap was very clever.

But she escaped.

Rumtah had traveled widely and had trained and studied with the many and the varied.

Hissing wildly she slipped sideways in a twist of black, hauling away the one who had tried to trap her, dragging that one by the hair.

Cardsan.

It was a small clearing in the midst of dense forest, a small spot of green and warm sunlight. One of the giant trees ringing the meadow reached a long limb into the open space.

She hissed and growled, her long hair gathered into a rope, anchored to that long limb, just above her head. While she could stand, neither her arms nor her legs would obey her although her legs did function just enough to hold her up.

Her captor stood just beyond spitting range and idly chewed on the tip of a gleaming red wand. "Sooooooooo witch, name me a name. What clan?"

"Kispit!" spat the other.

"Hum." Rumtah stepped closer and poked her. With the tip of her wand. And watched the dark eyes fly wide and the tears as they wandered down the moonlight pale face. "Speak! Not-kispit!"

"Beris."

"Witch clan Beris. Hum hum. And your name?"

"Ninar."

"So Beris witch Ninar, why attempt to trap me? I know you not. I know clan Beris not."

"Kispit nat nar!" she growled.

Rumtah nodded. "Wonderfully vile." And slashed Niner's blouse open from her neck to her belt buckle. "Hum. Shall we see what we shall see?"

Splitting the seam of both sleeves from cuff to collar, she yanked the material down. "Not too bad." And trailed the tip of her wand over the bare torso and gently jabbed. "Which one shall we remove first? This one?" Another jab. "Or this one?" And jabbed again. And stared at her captive. "You may answer."

"Release me, napik witch!"

"When I am ready." She reached out. "This one? Shame to loose such beauty." And shrugged. "Once gone, never restored." The wand turned into a long, thin blade of ice blue.

"What?" Ninar stared at the blade as it rested on soft flesh.

"Trap?"

"Witch debt."

"To?"

"Clan Occiis."

Rumtah frowned. "Clan Occiis and clan Beris. I am Faan and never have Faan tangled with Occiis or Beris. Why trap me?"

"Know not." Ninar blinked. "Release me!"

Rumtah wrapped them in black and took them out.

Bahn Duhr Tohr. The Quarters of the Royal Advisors.

They crashed in.

"Sister," snarled Ripple, leaping to her feet, black surging overhead. "What is this?"

"Sorry sorry. Some hurry." Rumtah glared up at the black boiling across the ceiling and told it to go away. It growled at her until Ripple nodded. Then it went away.

"Sister," grumbled Ripple, "are you collecting toys? Now?"

Rumtah waggled one loose hand. "This is Beris witch Ninar. Not my toy!" She frowned at Ripple.

"Do Beris always garb themselves, hum hum, so revealing?"

"Very nice," observed Hanred, stepping to Ripple's side.

"She didn't want to speak tell," explained Rumtah.

"For Beris," grumbled Ripple. "Do you know of clan Beris, Huband?"

He shook his head.

"Or Occiis?" asked Rumtah.

Hanred stared somewhere for a moment. Then refocused his eyes on Rumtah. "A strange clan that dresses in pale yellow." He flicked one sleeve with a finger. "With red touches?"

Rumtah jabbed Ninar with her wand.

"Yes," gasped Ninar.

"Husband?"

Hanred walked to the table and sat in one of the chairs. "From what I was told, the Occiis are zealots who believe that they have the only true claim to witch and begrudgingly interact with a few selected other witch clans." He looked at Ninar. "Is

Beris one of them?"

"It is so," stated Ninar.

"This nar nar tak," hissed Rumtah, "tried to trap me?" She was still very agitated by the very thought that someone would attempt to do that. "Claims witch debt to Occiis."

"Hum." Ripple ran her eyes over Ninar. "We could give her to the demons. They might enjoy her?"

Ninar shuddered and wobbled.

"Spell bound?"

"Of course," snapped Rumtah.

"You could keep her," suggested Ripple.

Rumtah glared at her sister. "I have no need for such."

"Release me," whispered Ninar.

Ripple glanced at Hanred. "No! You may not have her."

He shrugged. "You are my only. Then?"

"Perhaps," wondered Ripple, "we could give her to Szart. Her's seems to collect all kinds of females."

"No," replied Hanred, shaking his head. "He could get very upset. Seemna is visiting with them. Not good if he became angry with us."

She nodded. "Then we shall just have to visit . . . talk." And spun to face Ninar. "You, tell me the name of your elseplace and the name of your clan head." She stomped over and grabbed Ninar by the throat. "NOW!"

Hahn Dohr Kahn. Realm of The Dragon.

She nudged him awake.

"Umpf?"

"Workers will soon swarm over Our Ship readying it for sea."

"Huh?"

The door was flung wide and Szart stomped inside. The air crackled around her.

He jolted upright, covers flying. "OOOOOOOP!"

Lurin laughed. "It is only Szart."

He stared at the very agitated witch. "What?"

"Ripple and Rumtah travel angry to visit some witch clan named Beris."

"And?"

"We should go."

"Why?"

Szart hissed at him.

"That bad, huh?" He looked around, searching for his clothes.

Lurin pointed at a chair. "Over there. Do fetch Us Our attire as well, My King?"

He stood, hurried over, and dressed. And handed Lurin her garments.

"Do return," ordered The Queen, as she quickly finished fastening her shirt. "This thy visit t'was most short."

"We will," stated Szart witch firm, banging back out the door and onto the deck where the rest of them waited.

"We do be most ready, Our Prince." Chicken waggled her sword and grinned at him.

He sighed and glared at Szart. "You have any idea of what's going on, this time?"

"Not told."

"Ummmmmm. O. K. Just like always." He pointed at Early Dawn and Fair Morn. "You two stay in the back and out of the way." And nodded at Szart. "Let's go, short and agitated."

Szart looked at Sha'gar.

In a swirl of black they were gone.

Piznar Hindo.

They shimmered in.

Startling the woman standing there.

"NINAR! Brazen, BRAZEN! Reclothe!"

"I am unable to do so. These will not allow."

The woman glared at the others, all strangers, black forming behind her. "Then they will die!"

Ripple stepped close and slapped her, rocking her head to one side. "Not at all." And pinned her in place and looked at Ninar. "Who is this one?"

"Clan head Nuart."

Ripple nodded and looked at the angry witch. "Beris witch Clan head Nuart, I am Faan witch Clan head Ripple and I would have some answers from you and your's."

"Pisna!" spat Nuart.

"Very witch," observed Ripple, reaching in a long, green wand. "Which part of you wishes to hurt first?"

They swirled into the room in a twist of black.

Szart cast protection over everyone.

"Oh my gosh!" Messenger stared at Ninar.

"Nice bod," observed Smoke.

"Mother!" gasped Seemna, staring at Ninar. "This is ptar kak pak zar!"

Ripple shrugged. "It was Rumtah done."

Szart frowned at Rumtah. "Aunt?"

Rumtah crossed her arms over her chest and glared back.

"She didn't want to speak tell."

"Hi, Hanred. What's going on? This time?" Tinker walked over and stood next to Hanred.

He shrugged. "I am not sure. But they are very agitated." He leaned closer and whispered. "It is not good to get in the way of agitated witches, especially very agitated witches."

Tinker nodded and walked over to Rumtah. "Let her put her clothes back on."

Rumtah frowned, but obeyed, allowing Ninar that amount of freedom. He was a Witch Master after all. It was a gift that he had been given some strange time before.

Ninar stared at him as she ordered her clothes back into place, fully repaired. "What are you?" She had never heard of anyone who could casually order a witch to do something. Then she looked at the rest of the group that had so suddenly appeared. Unasked for. She only recognized two witches and one magician. And a female warrior. The rest looked strange.

"No one in particular," he mumbled, stepping over to Ripple. "What's going on?"

"Witch business," she growled. "Why are you here?"

"I brought," stated Szart. "Mother."

"No need," snapped Ripple. She jabbed Nuart with her wand. "This ptar rak is of no concern."

Rumtah glowered at Szart and indicated Ninar. "This tried to trap me, Niece."

Szart walked over and kicked Ninar. "Then why does she still live, Aunt?" And whipped out a long bronze wand.

"HOLD IT! HOLD IT!" He glowered at everyone.

Witches hissed, glowered, frowned, and looked puzzled.

He stepped over and threw an arm around Szart's

shoulders. "Someone explain what is going on with your group this time or we are leaving."

Hanred cleared his throat and looked at Ripple. Her glower loosened. A little.

So, Hanred told Tinker.

"Ah, ha." He nodded, mostly to himself. "O. K., everybody calm down and we sit around that table, relax, and discuss it, without killing anyone." He looked at Ripple. "Release them."

Looking as unhappy as only a witch could, she did. And waved in a larger table, chairs, cups, and jugs. She dragged a chair over, dropped into it, and stared at Hanred. Who quickly did the same, sat next to her, grabbed a jug, and filled her cup. Then his own.

Sighing heavily, Tinker sat next to Hanred. "These guys are such a pain in the butt!" Every witch hissed or growled. Hanred filled another cup and handed it to him while Tinker watched them all seat themselves. Then he asked, "O. K., who are you?" He pointed.

"Beris witch Clan head Nuart."

"Beris witch Ninar."

He nodded. "And why are these Faan so, ummmm, agitated?"

Eyes jumping around the table, especially from witch face to witch face, Nuart explained.

Hahn Dohr Kahn. The Realm of The Dragon.

They swirled into the dining room, a large room paneled in light wood over the stone walls, startling the servant. The large table was square, glistening rose wood. It added a slight additional order to the faint wood smell from the walls. The Queen looked up and smiled at them. She was just finishing breakfast.

"Honey," he laughed, "I'm home."

The servant hurried away to bring more food and additional help. His Queen was very calm so it must be all right.

Lurin frowned at him. "Honey?"

So he explained.

She nodded slowly as he explained. "A strange thing to call someone, sweet, small flower sucker, spit."

He sat next to her and laughed again. "Ah well, some things just do not translate very well. But we did return."

"Indeed."

Chantal flopped into a chair. "Damn witches are settling some damn witch argument." And glowered at Szart. "And not one damn word from you." And then at Seemna. "And that goes for you too, toots!"

Szart indicated to Seemna to stay silent. Seemna nodded. One almost imperceptible nod. She recognized a bad case of witch bother when she saw it.

Then breakfast arrived. Smoke, Fair Morn, and Early Dawn had lots. They always had lots. The rest ate, for them, a more normal-sized breakfast.

Lurin smiled at him as he finished. "You were seen when last we did stroll."

He nodded. "So everyone is content again?"

"Most true. And a great excitement. Our Brother will sail next morn with our six new vessels."

He choked on the last piece of his bread. "WHAT?"

"It has been three months, I believe you call them, since

thy last visit. Our ships builders as do My Own Brother King's have labored long and hard."

"I'll never get used to it," he grumbled.

"Time, Me'Lord," stated Chicken, "do itself pass most differently in these elseplaces."

"It seems to twitch around too wildly for me." He looked at Lurin. "Tomorrow?"

"Most true." She smiled at him. "Attend Us at the Great Send Out? It is a Fest Day."

"Oh boy," gurgled Messenger. "Party time."

Most of them laughed.

Szart leaned sideways and explained what they were talking about to Seemna.

"These folk do not fret witches in their midst?" asked Seemna.

"Your sister Sook is Queen to her brother, the one who sails."

"Most not-witch." Seemna nodded. Then she remembered being told about her sister Sook's choice of mate.

"The Faan are becoming new-witch."

"Hum hum."

"Hum," agreed Szart.

Lurin looked around the table. "Would all wear Our Royal Garb on the morrow?"

"Most assuredly," stated Chicken. She felt that it was the proper thing to do and wanted to help Lurin in all matters, Queen to Queen.

"You also," whispered Szart.

"Sister!" hissed Seemna. There was little that could shock a witch. Dressing strange was something that could.

"Consider it as training."

"Yessssssss." Seemna pondered these very unusual not-witch behaviors and decided that her training had lacked much. And that her mother hadn't told her everything that there was to know about this sister.

The servants hurried away to see that the appropriate clothes would soon be delivered to all.

Lurin stood. "My King, do join Us on Our balcony. We would thee see Our fleet."

On the balcony, a small semicircular extension from the floor to ceiling window, which now stood wide open, he stood behind her, arms wrapped around and peered over her shoulder across the low roofs of the town at the Great Quay. Five vessels were anchored off shore, the sixth at the end of the quay. In all there were one white, one black, four grey.

"The white, as you know, is Sky Cloud, Our Royal vessel. The black is Storm Wind, Our Brother's. All be most ready to sail. In the morn a brief ceremony and then all do be out to sea to seek the new lands if these places do truly exist."

"Well prepared?"

"Indeed. The warrior Princess E'Nilt is aboard Sky Cloud and commands a full Band of handpicked Hephira warriors. Numerous artisans and craftsmen, both our folk and Hephira, fill each of the grey vessels as well as supplies, building materials, and on and on and on, including great quantities of suitable food and water."

"Planning on staying?"

"If this new land do be there, and empty of inhabitants, we mean to establish some small town and claim all, for the

New Kingdoms, and the Hephira Kingdom as well. Thus we bind ever closer our two peoples. Of course, if it do be inhabited, Our Royal Brother will have to make most appropriate agreements with them." She laughed. "And then we shall allow Our Parents to politic the New Kingdoms for sublands." And laughed deep in her throat.

"What?"

She looked down. "Thee does caress our middle."

"Cause it is there."

"It is always there. But thee are not."

"What?"

"There."

"Ahhhhhhhh?"

"Our King?"

"Have you lost weight?"

"Some. Roofing this great edifice do be most hard and hot work."

"Roofing?"

"Most hot and dusty. All do sweat great amounts." She undid the last of the buttons. "The sea folk will have eyes for naught but those great vessels."

Hapran gasped. And yanked the far-seer from his eyes. She was wrong.

"Aye?" asked Rarnat, his shipmate.

"Our Queen be as lusty as any wench that I know."

Rarnat grabbed the instrument and looked. "Bet a fair galoon," he gasped.

Hapran snatched back the far-seer, collapsed it, and headed back up the Great Quay. "Not a word to any." And laughed. "Maybe later."

They exited the foot of the quay and entered *The Wet Way*, the hangout of the sea folk.

She leaned back against him, arms thrown back. "Husband King, there be a most pleasant couch here, or my great bed in another room, or shall I stand like an alley wench?" She laughed.

Couch," he mumbled. "Couch!"

They were down in the immense open space, the paved square that separated the town from The Royal House, strolling about. Smoke nudged Chantal.

"What?"

"I think that it will be a girl."

Chantal stopped, turned, and stared at her.

"Lurin is very fertile right now."

"And he is . . . "

Smoke grinned.

Chantal shrugged. "Let's go see what kind of a gift that we can find here. The way time flies in the elseplaces by the time we make another visit here she'll be full grown. So you can't start shopping too early."

Szart grabbed Seemna's arm. "When we leave, you will remain here. Rest and heal and guard the new Princess."

"What new Princess?"

"The one soon to be born."

Seemna's eyes darted around the open space. "SISTER! Your's is up there raping The Queen? This is ptar nak vile vile!"

Szart spun and struck the side of her sister's head with a white wand. "He is her's. Also. Husband and wife. King and Queen."

Seemna rubbed the side of her head. "Explain. Everything!"

So Szart did.

She carefully explained how it all began when Big Red, one of the few pure forces in the universe of universes, took John Tinker from his world, called elseplaces by most of the folk in the universe of universes, and set him upon a task which Big Red could not do himself as the several laws of magic kept him from interfering directly.

Smoke of the Velvet Mist, a telepathic predator from a hidden elseplace that no-one can find, was one of the others taken from their elseplaces to aid Tinker. At that time she was a gigantic cat-like being.

Princess Chicken was created from an Easter egg fluffy toy, a thing of Tinker's elseplace celebration.

Toward the end of the quest designed by Big Red, Smoke, agreeing with Chicken, had linked Tinker's and Chicken's mind with her's, a skill unique to Smoke's folk. This was the start of their polymorphic being, a being that had separate and independent bodies but could, when wanted, merge themselves into a single mind or separate clusters of thought and conversation.

Later Smoke and Chicken added Messenger when she was dying from a kind of culture shock. Only later did they realize that her upbringing and special diet had made her into a magical adept, the only one ever who could actually see magic and, if she chose to do so, manipulate it.

Then Messenger liberated Fair Morn, a magical jest created by Big Red, and she became a real person.

And over time, for various reasons, the group added other members.

And so it went. Most were added deliberately although Chantal was an accident when witch Ripple tried to heal her, thinking that she was part of them.

When Szart finished, Seemna knew that her training had really left much to be learned.

Early the next morning they all stood on the ceremonial platform at the end of the quay, dressed in royal garb. Lurin hugged her brother and stepped back as he strode to the front edge to speak to the gathered crowd.

"We do sail into a hoped for new era for Our Two Lands. During Our absence Our Sister will be Queen of the New Kingdoms. When We return, all will have great cause for Fest, or so We do hope. Wish us well, for it do be time for to depart."

Frinda waved gaily into the roar of the crowd, turned and led Sook up the gangway onto the deck of their new vessel, glistening black in the early dawn light.

Hawsers were released, the gangway yanked to safety as sails dropped and popped, billowing in the gentle breeze. Echoing sounds came from all the other vessels as anchor chains rattled upward and the sea folk swarmed everywhere in the rigging.

The fleet headed out to sea and slowly turned south and west.

New Beginnings

Grandeville. Tinker's Place.

They were mostly on the rear deck relaxing in the later afternoon. Everyone, with one exception, was wearing as little as possible. The exception was trying to relax in the hammock, a large pillow tucked under his head, a tall glass held in one hand. He was watching them very carefully through hooded eyes. He had been watching them for some time. As far as he was concerned, from his careful obvervations, there were far too many whispered conversations going on. It was definitely something to worry about. So he watched them and worried, a little bit.

Messenger suddenly squeaked and hit Chicken with a large inflated alligator, knocking her into the swimming pool. Then as the spitting, swearing woman surfaced, banged her on top of the head with the green monstrosity. "Nasty, nasty! Really really!"

"Wench!" snarled Chicken, yanking the inflated weapon from her attacker's hands.

"Clothes snatcher!"

Chicken tried to look indignant. "We do naught but pluck some small bow a'loose. Thy garment do itself leap away for to lie pon fair deck."

Smoke walked over and rolled her eyes at Messenger. "It

looks to me like you haven't been wearing all that much for some time. I don't see any tan lines." She knelt, snatched the alligator free and wacked Chicken on top of the head with it. "Take that, skinny trouble maker!"

"Vile villain!" Chicken surged from the pool and made a grab for Smoke who dodged, leaped backward, and passed something to Messenger who dashed down the deck waving a strip of cloth in the air.

"Foul feline," snarled Chicken.

Smoke slipped behind one of the large wooden tables. "Not bad for sorta small," she observed, rolling her eyes at Chicken's bare chest.

"Body insulter!" snarled Chicken, circling around the table after her.

Smoke turned and leaped into the pool and swam for the far side towing the alligator.

Fair Morn and Early Dawn came around the far corner, sandwiches in hand, and hurried over to see what was going on.

"I didn't think that it was that warm out." Fair Morn took another bite from her thick sandwich. "Or are you just showing off again?" Chicken stuck her tongue out. Fair Morn looked over at him.

He took a sip from his glass. "I'd stay out of it, whatever it is, if I were you."

Fair Morn sat on the edge of the hammock and kicked it back and forth. "Costume du jour?"

"Just the Princess agitating." He frowned at Early Dawn. "Keep it on."

Fair Morn smiled at her. "Wouldn't want to drive him into a male lust frenzy."

Early Dawn smiled back. "Would he do that?"

Fair Morn took another bite from her sandwich and chewed thoughtfully, kicking the hammock into motion again. "Can't be helped. One glance at your bare torso and that male animal would go out of control. Surprised that he is still lying here, what with the Princess and Messenger trying to overstimulate him."

Early Dawn licked the mustard from her lips. "I didn't realize that he was such a beast."

Fair Morn jerked. She had just been pinched. "We better relocate before he snatches one of us and does vile things to our helpless selves." She stood.

Fair Morn smiled at him. "Shall I stay so you can?" Fair Morn yanked her away, over toward the edge of the pool.

He crooked at finger at Sgenn who walked over and looked down at him. "Why are the Princess and Messenger running around with their tops off?" he asked.

She shrugged and smiled a soft half-smile. "Shall I remove my garment?"

He sighed. "No. Keep it on." And really began to worry, a whole bunch.

She turned and sat on the edge of the hammock and watched the rest of them. Something dark gently rocked the hammock back and forth. It belonged to her.

Silca Dergart.

Zaruna huddled over the corner table and talked in very low tones to her dinner companion. The bar was crowded with loud folk so she felt confident that none would be able to overhear their conversation.

The woman dressed in grey and black hissed, "It is told that they have released a web wraith who now travels with a mythological band. Child scare tales."

Zaruna stared back at her. "Beris witch Ninar was taken and abused."

"E'nipta!" Fasna's eyes darted around the room, checking. "How?"

"Know not. But that clan has severed from us."

Fasna squinted at her. "What does this mean?"

"Strike sudden, strike hard!"

"They are told vicious beyond vicious."

Zaruna nodded. "It is told that way."

"You do not believe?"

"They are pretenders, tale spinners. Clever tale spinners who frighten small clans."

"Like the Beris?"

Zaruna nodded. "So it is."

"Pact?"

Zaruna nodded.

Hahn Dohr Kahn. The Realm of The Dragon.

The pair had been summoned.

"Great Queen?" asked the young woman dressed in black, her face a carefully held hard to read blank mask.

"Mother Queen?" asked the slender young woman standing next to the one in black, dressed in very grimy but recognizable Royal garb. Her left cheek, glowing a bright red, was beginning to puff up.

The Queen crossed her arms over her chest and looked at the pair. And nodded. "Chyndra, it is the custom of Our Royalty to do a long journey before they are allowed to take on adult duties. Faan witch Seemna wishes to accompany you on this quest journey."

"We have no need of a keeper!" She tossed the large sword she had been holding on the table and watched it slide a short distance. "Just better than this."

"I am keeper to no one," hissed Seemna.

Chyndra spun and wrapped her arms around the witch and hugged her. "Didn't mean it to sound so mean." And kissed her cheek.

"It is also the custom," continued Lurin, the Queen, "for the Faan witch clan to do wander as part of their education."

Chyndra turned back to her mother, her arm now around the shoulders of the witch. "We do know that."

"Shall We make it a Royal Command?"

Chyndra blanched. "NO! Mother." Her eyes bored into her mother's. "Are We ready?"

Lurin laughed and relaxed and unfolded her arms. "As ready as We were when Our Brother and We did. It is how he met his Queen." She indicated the puffy cheek. "Word has come to Our ears that The Royal Princess has bested The Sword Master's very top level."

Chyndra grinned. "We have learned well from all my teachers."

"Teachers?"

"Indeed." She nodded. "The Sword Master, you." Her smiled broadened. "And Seemna, and her witch clan. Some. After all, We were witch raised. The same as Our Brother."

Lurin stared at Seemna. "The witches study the sword art?"

"No," replied Seemna. "But my Uncle, Your King, gave me some special training in his skills. And I taught The Princess some."

Lurin laughed. "So Our Daughter is a surprise to all." And walked over and hugged them both. "We do think, We do, that you do be most ready, most ready indeed." And stepped back. "But not before some filthy young woman is clean and presentable." She nodded. "A great tub of hot water and soap awaits thee."

The tub room was filled with steam and the smell of hot water and strong soap.

Her head bobbed above the bubble froth as she leaned back against the slightly sloped end of the large tub.

The tub was partially sunken into the floor. This brought the very wide, flat lip of the tub to a comfortable distance above the floor for sitting.

"Truly you do wish to come journey with Us?"

Seemna, sitting on one edge of the sunken tub, nodded. "Yessssss."

Chyndra frowned at nothing. "We are not going to clump around the elseplaces in glaring white armor like my mother and my grandmother did."

"It is your custom."

Chyndra grinned at her companion. "We are starting a new one, We are."

"Hum, hum."

Chyndra laughed and explained. "This is what We need to do."

Lurin stared at her daughter.

And at her attire.

She had been absent from The Royal Quarters for a hand of days.

Her daughter was wearing dark brown trousers that flared from the knee and draped ankle length over equally dark brown leather boots. Over a rose colored shirt she wore a vest of soft green material. And over that a leather jacket that ended at her hips. It was also a dark brown color. A great sword rode at an angle on her back, the hilt poking up and over her left shoulder.

Chyndra smiled at her mother and pulled her pant legs up. A knife rode on the outside of each calve-length boot. She released the material and there was no obvious sign of her weapons.

The vest and jacket are special made," she explained as she fingered the edge of her jacket. "Crafted by The Royal Armorer himself. Soft leather hides most cleverly wrought protection. We do shoot battle arrows at close range and hack and flail with all manner of lethal items. While the leather was damaged, nothing could penetrate. These are the second jacket and vest." She smiled into her mother's frown. "Therefore, Most Royal Mother Queen, We do be most armor clad." And grinned. "It is just not obvious." And added, "The rest as well."

"And your weapons?"

"The very best that the Hephira could make. It is a new metal, wonderfully strong, wonderfully sharp."

Lurin nodded. "We will agree. But on one condition."

Chyndra frowned slightly. "What condition? Mother?" It was a very cautious daughter question.

Lurin told her.

Grandeville. Tinker's Place.

Late summer.

Late afternoon.

And all were relaxing, taking it easy.

On the rear deck.

A favorite spot.

"Enter?" asked a voice.

Szart, seated on a bench at one the several large wooden picnic tables on the rear deck, looked up. And nodded.

The air hardened.

Just a little.

Then darkened.

Just a little.

And they stood there. The two of them.

"Hayou, sister," greeted Szart.

"Hayou, sister," responded Seemna. "Where is he?"

Szart indicated the hammock. He was sprawled there. Accompanied by Sha'gar. They were sound asleep. Both visitors looked in that direction.

Seemna nodded at her companion. "He sleeps."

"Who is that wench?" snarled Chyndra. She stomped over and glowered down at the woman lying by his side.

Sha'gar opened one eye and peered past his chest at the glowering young woman. "Be quiet," she hissed. The eye closed.

Chyndra frowned, leaned, reached over, and slapped her.

"NO!" shouted Szart as red flashed.

He bolted upright, starting the hammock into violent motion. "HUH?"

All the rest were suddenly on their feet, eyes darting around, searching for the cause of the sudden commotion.

A glowing red column stood next to the hammock. Over near the deck railing stood Seemna, layered in protection, staring in his direction.

"What is that thing?" He pointed at it.

"Do dark," grumbled Sha'gar.

Szart walked over. "Release her!"

Chyndra stood there, eyes round as round, saw him staring at her, gulped, quickly composed her face, and bowed. "Great King."

"What?" He stared at her.

"Do dark," rumbled Sha'gar, eyes still glowing faint red fire.

Seemna walked over and stood near them. "This is Chyndra."

"Who?" he asked.

"Hum, hum." Then Seemna stated, very clearly, very firmly. "This is The Princess Chyndra!"

"What?" he asked.

"Humble Greetings," intoned Chyndra, looking very puzzled and just a little worried. "From My Mother, Lurin, Queen of The Realm of The Dragon, to Her King."

"Who?" He stared at her, carefully examining her face. "Daughter?"

"This," explained Seemna, beginning to wonder about her Uncle and about her sister's choice in mates, "is the Princess Chyndra, witch raised and warrior trained. We are on wander and quest journey."

Chicken hurried over, smiling broadly. "Welcome, Royal

Daughter. We are The Princess Chicken and his Verra Own First Queen. Do forgive him for he do most slowly awaken." She led Chyndra away and introduced her to all the rest. And then sat her down and began to explain

Fair Morn walked over and handed him a cup of coffee. "Here you go, Daddie."

Szart glowered at Sha'gar, who shrugged and grumbled,. "She was being do dark."

He sipped. "Daughter?"

Seemna nodded.

"Witch raised?"

She nodded again. "She is now nineteen of your cycle count."

Je'leel stepped from the house, looked, walked over and introduced herself to her new half-sister. Then Messenger joined them, a towel wrapped around her head, fresh from the shower. "Oh my gosh! Wait until Chantal hears."

"What?" Chantal clumped down the rear deck toward them, high rubber boots and one-piece coveralls stained and filthy. "I came home early. To get clean." Strong barn odors drifted from her, a hazard known to all veterinarians of large animals. Then she nodded at Smoke. And headed for the house.

Finally, after getting more and more explaining from this one and that one, Chyndra walked over at him. "Mother did not tell. Just that We must visit here first."

He nodded. "Probably figured that you wouldn't believe it." And he grumbled at no-one in particular. "And I didn't get to raise another child."

Chyndra frowned. And nodded back. And smiled. "We would not have believed it." And looked worried at Sha'gar.

"We do beg forgiveness for being so, ummmmm, do dark."

Sha'gar shrugged. "Nobel daughters will be noble daughters." And smiled, a real smile. "It is nice to have another beautiful daughter."

"How long as you staying?" asked Je'leel.

"Some."

"You may share my room. Seemna can share with Szart."

"Most kind."

Je'leel stood. "Come'on. Let me show you where it is." She pointed. "It is way up there." They headed into the house.

Tinker relocated to the large wooden table and sat down and looked at Seemna. "What does some mean?"

She waggled her hand. "Some."

Chicken nudged his shoulder. She was now sitting next to him. "Fret not, t'will be some days."

"Yessssss," hissed Szart, glaring at Seemna.

Seemna glared back. "None told that she was so, hum, hum, uninformed."

"Really really pretty," bubbled Messenger.

"Must be what Lurin looked like when she was younger," suggested Fair Morn.

He refilled his cup. "Certainly a surprise alright. Wonder why Lurin didn't say something first?"

Early Dawn nudged Fair Morn. "Does he get children from every female he meets."

"Nope. Some escape."

"Humbug," he suggested.

Early Dawn began to unbutton her shirt. "Think our offspring will have wings?"

"Knock it off," he snarled.

"You are not fertile," stated Smoke, rolling her eyes at Early Dawn.

"Button your shirt," he grumbled.

Seemna stared at them. Szart poked her with one finger. "He is our's, young witch."

"Nim nip."

"Hum," replied Szart.

"Really?" Early Dawn looked at Fair Morn.

She nodded. "Way we were made, being one time magical jests and all."

Early Dawn frowned. "Maybe we can talk Big Red into doing something. Don't you think that it would be nice to have a child fluttering about?"

"Forget it, forget it, forget it!" He half-turned in their direction. "We are not going to ask Big Red to start making changes to anyone. Ever! For any reason!"

Messenger giggled and played with a spot of water on the tabletop with one fingertip.

And he wondered, once again, about his life and how it had gotten like this.

Fair Morn leaned forward and peered around Early Dawn at him. "May we build a small tower onto one corner of the house?"

"Why? What?"

Fair Morn struggled with both her grin and her laughter, and winked at Early Dawn. "That way she can be the bat in the belfry." And failed, bursting into peals of laughter, lurching to her feet, one hand on Early Dawn's shoulder. "Let's go start dinner, sis."

"Must be the water," he grumbled. "Have'ta get it

tested."

"I am not a bat!" Early Dawn headed toward the kitchen.

"I know," agreed Fair Morn, walking by her side. "Just a small joke."

Seemna leaned very close to her sister and whispered. "None of this was told by mother."

"She knows not," stated Szart.

"Hum."

Szart nodded.

Partnar.

They wandered from the trail and into the smallish town, Aipnir by name. She led him towards the town square, a small open space surrounding a tall statue reported to be the founder of the town.

"There is a small spell shop just there." Reptar pointed at it. It was a small shop with a front wall covered in dark yellow wood vertical planking. The shop was one of many that clustered to one side of the statue. The square, which wasn't exactly a square, being a more or less circular space, was called by the inhabitants of Aipnir, the town square, none the less. "This shop is owned by a Kanikt witch named Uziz I was told."

"Unknown clan," stated Fazbaq.

"It was told that the Kanikt specialize in special spell craft."

"Um um." He looked at her from the corners of his eyes. "Hard to control. But wonderfully vile."

"So it was told."

"So it is." He looked in the front window of the shop. A few wands were on display, nothing else. "Small things."

"Hum." She opened the door and stepped inside. He followed.

The interior of the shop was much brighter than it had appeared from the outside. It was a very neat room with a few display cases, a wall of holes, each hole containing a single scroll. A low railing kept visitors from approaching this wall.

As they stood and looked around the room, the rear door opened and a woman entered, strolled along the space between the railing and the strange wall, carefully inspecting her visitors. She wore baggy trousers of a soft grey material, a white blouse decorated with grey signs. On her feet she wore grey sandals. The blouse opening ran from the corners of her shoulders to her sternum.

"Hum, hum, hum," observed Reptar.

"Um," echoed Fazbaq.

"Name me names," demanded the woman.

"Faan witch Reptar."

"Blue Udaz warlock Fazbaq."

"I am," she responded, "Kanikt witch Wizla." She nodded at them. "Uziz retired."

"Hum," observed Reptar.

"Buy? Sell? Trade?"

"Explain."

Wizla waggled one arm at the room. "Unique wands. One-owner spells."

"Spells?"

Wizla nodded and indicated the ranks of holes containing scrolls. "One-owner spells, each special special."

"How special?" asked Reptar.

Wizla lowered her voice and lightly touched a scroll as

Reptar walked over to look. The scroll soft crackled at her. "Suppose, just suppose, that a certain witch bought this love-touch. That witch would have the only copy, we never make another. The owner may, of course, spell share if she desires to do so. Suppose, just suppose, that a certain witch owned this one and cast on a certain warlock, just suppose." The outer edges of her eyes crinkled. "That certain warlock would be that certain witches to have and to do." She looked slyly at Fazbaq. "This is a quick spell. Few could counter in time."

Reptar frowned darkly at her. "And suppose, just suppose, a certain witch felt great insult at such an offer?"

Wizla shrugged. "Only suppose."

Reptar chewed on the tip of a long silver wand that was suddenly in her hand. "Hum."

Wizla rocked her head from side to side.

"Bargain?"

Wizla lowered her voice even more. "Spell for spell. Or." She licked her upper lip, black eyes fastening on black eyes. "Witch bond mate share."

In one swift move Reptar clamped her hand around Wizla's neck, yanked her over the railing, and dragged her to the floor, fastening her there. Protection crackled around Fazbaq, a long glowing red blade in his hand. His eyes darted everywhere and then at the two witches.

Reptar kicked Wizla in the side and changed wands. The bronze sputtered angry from a blue crystal tip.

"Release me," hissed Wizla.

"Faan witch?" asked Fazbaq.

Reptar bent over and jabbed Wizla with her wand. "This ptar rak tak rar suggested tip ptar!"

Fazbaq frowned at her. He didn't understand most of the Faan sub-dialect, especially when they were Faan excited. He frowned again and growled. "In common!" He changed the knife into a wand.

Reptar called down protection, lifted Wizla by her hair and hung her on the bare wall, using her hair as a rope. "This grey Kanikt witch Wizla suggested a two bond witch mate!"

Fazbaq stared at Wizla. "True?"

"Witch true." Wizla indicated the scroll wall with her eyes. "All come with."

The air settled around Fazbaq as he looked over at the wall. "Many there?"

"Many many," replied Wizla.

Reptar reached out, wand tip to top button. The button sizzled away. Wizla's eyes flew wide. "No harm intended," she stated.

"I am Faan," snarled Reptar. "We do not mate share!"

Wizla stared down past her nose at the wand resting lightly on the next button. "It is told," she murmured, "that a certain Faan witch two bonded, strange bonded, mage and warrior." The button sizzled away. The wand dropped lower. "It is told," she whispered, "that a certain Faan witch multi-shares with a black shape shifter and mythic beings of unusual powers." The button sizzled away. The wand dropped lower.

Fazbaq stepped over and rapped Reptar on the wand holding arm with his wand. He admired the large amount of pale witch skin showing as Wizla's blouse fell open. "Witch true?" he hissed.

Reptar grumbled and growled at him, "Witch true."

"Who?" he demanded.

"My oldest sister. Hacto mage guild and Death Warrior. The clan head's daughter is bonded to The Chosen One and all that one is."

Wizla tried to nod. "Errr att ta! Sooooooo, it was told true that one."

Reptar glowered at her and hissed, "Witch true."

"Release me. I did move wrong not."

"Hum, hum." Reptar tucked her wand into her hair and yanked Wizla's blouse fully open.

"Faan witch Reptar!" gasped Fazbaq. "This is kanpak donar!"

"I would see what is offered." Reptar looked at him. "Not too bad, these Kanikt."

Fazbaq glared at her. "Do war, dotep, andag!"

Reptar nodded. "This witch offered. She can do nothing. Touch taste?"

Fazbaq folded his arms over his chest and glared at both of them. Reptar leaned close, nose almost touching nose, and looked deep into Wizla's eyes. And watched the fire flicker deep down. "Name me all, Wizla."

"I am grey Kanikt witch Wizla spell designer. One of the few few."

"Hum, hum, hum." Reptar lightly stroked lips over lips. "It would be unique. Spell designer."

"Most unique," agreed Wizla.

Reptar leaned back, eyes roving over Wizla's torso. Wizla watched her carefully. With a snap of her fingers, Reptar released her.

Wizla yanked her blouse back into order and ordered the buttons back into existence. "There is a love-touch spell," she whispered. "That was true tell."

"NO!" snapped Reptar. "Anything done must be face done."

Wizla nodded and glanced sideways. Fazbaq was standing a careful distance away from them. "Tall one?"

Fazbaq ordered in a chair and sat, staring from one to the other. "Most strange, most strange."

"Most unique," corrected Wizla.

He looked at Reptar.

"A three bond," she stated. "You appear sturdy enough."

His eyes flickered to the scroll wall and back to them. And began to think, to ponder, to weight and to judge.

"All," whispered Wizla. "And more."

Fazbaq stared elsewhere. And thought that it would be truly rare, Blue Udaz rare.

Reptar touched one side of Wizla's face. "If you die, I will do nothing."

"Worry not, Faan. That one wants greatly."

"Hum, hum."

"A very special sight, very special. You were cloudy, he was clear." She shrugged. "So I dared much."

"Most Faan," suggested Reptar.

"So it is told."

Fazbaq's eyes refocused. And looked at the two of them. Carefully looked at them. "Only if your clan heads agree."

Reptar growled at him. "The Faan choose their own. And ask no-one's permission!"

"Neither do Kanikt!" hissed Wizla. "Udaz?"

"We do as we wish." He stood. "Three link?"

"Yesssssssss," hissed Wizla.

"DONE!" snapped Reptar, coating them in black.

Bahn Duhr Tohr. The Quarters of The Royal Advisors.

Ripple twitched and jerked.

Hanred yanked his hand away.

He was lounging in the couch, his back against one of the large, over-stuffed arms, knees pulled up. She was lounging on him, leaning back against his legs. There were dusty streaks on her skin, left by Handred's dusty fingers. He had been reading one of the tomes of arcana until she decided he needed to be sat upon.

"Not you, husband."

"Ahhhhhhhhhhh?"

"Reptar just cross-linked Faan-Kanikt-Udaz."

"My, my. A surprise."

"Most." She nodded. "We will wait and see what visits." All the Faan brought their's to visit the Clan Head. There had been a number of surprises in the past.

In this case the surprise happened sooner than expected.

"Enter!" demanded a voice.

Ripple waved her blouse on and replied, "Enter!" And nodded at Hanred. "We can wash the dust off later."

"My pleasure, Midnight Delight." He watched them swirl in.

"Hayou, sister."

"Hayou, Reptar." Ripple looked at the others. Both were obviously witch.

Reptar indicated the man. "You remember Blue Udaz Fazbaq. Mine!"

Ripple nodded. She did remember him from her

daughter's training and that Reptar had left to do wander with him.

Reptar indicated the woman. "Grey Kanikt witch Wizla spell designer. Mine!"

Hanred stood and set cups and jugs around the table, then filled the mugs and handed one to Ripple, watching her face carefully.

"Hum, hum, hum." Ripple took a sip and indicated the chairs. "Sit! Speak! Tell!"

Glowering darkly at her sister, mainly due to her tone of voice and the sharp voiced commands, Reptar urged the others to sit. Then she sat, opposite Ripple. And explained.

Quaratab.

They shimmered in, in a glow of black, momentarily frightening the couple that happened to be looking in their direction, not far down the narrow street.

"Where are we?" Chyndra looked up and down the narrow street and watched the startled pair staring at them.

"Quaratab. A place to study special." Seemna tugged her companion in the correct direction. "It is part of my wander."

They started that way when it happened.

She slid from dark shadow, casting dark and under.

Seemna snarled and countered, struggling to reach her wand as the attacker dragged in ugly.

Chyndra's right arm swung up and over her left shoulder as she spun and danced, warrior focused. The golden sword flashed sun bright glitter as it whistled down, a down side stroke.

The attacker fell, splashing gore, as Chyndra whirled

around, checking her companion and everything else in their immediate vicinity.

"Rak rak rak," snarled the witch, the air crackling angry around her as the spell holding her died with its castor. She ordered the gore away and bent over to inspect the deceased's face.

"Who was she?"

"Unknown." The air settled and cleared around Seemna. "Not nice."

Chyndra nodded and looked around for something to clean her blade with. Seemna waved it clean.

"How could anyone know that we were coming here?" She reached up and slid the sword into its sheath.

"Search spell," grumbled the still agitated witch. "Some ptar ptar piz tap seeks me." She cast around them, eyes glittering deep down fire. "The next one stays alive long enough to question."

"As you wish. Which way?"

Seemna led them deeper into the sprawling city. She would find appropriate quarters for them in the place that she sought.

Termion Ianon.

The magician glared at the Quata, a long-time friend. "This is not good, not good at all."

Fula nodded and gurgled wetly. "What do we do?"

"Wait. And wait. If it gets too mixed," he sighed. "Then we shall have to act."

Fula glided into the other room to find something to eat.

New Things

Quaratab.

The three stood in the large and empty room. Two witches and one warrior.

"Erta, erta," said the elderly witch. "One witch and one warrior, both young females. Erta, erta." She pointed at them. "Name me names."

"Princess Chyndra, The Realm of The Dragon, Hahn Dohr Kahn, The New Kingdoms."

"Erta, erta. Such a large title for such a young one. Dragon? Name me a name of this dragon."

"M'Ban, the Great Black."

"Ahhhhhhh, hona. M'Ban! Few would name that name." Her arm swirled wildly. "I am Karna witch Hebtak, trainer."

"Ripple daughter Faan witch Seemna websmith."

Karna stepped close to her. "Erta, erta, one of the few few. Here be training. Hard hard." She leaned close. "That one druzna, your's?"

"NOT!" The air crackled angry around Seemna.

Karna leaped back and away, much easier than one of her apparent years ought to be able to do. The golden blade swished down and around as Chyndra slipped sideways, watching this witch.

Karna tilted her head to one side and studied the pair.

"Erta, erta. Sorry sorry."

The air settled around Seemna as she gave a quick jerk of her head. Karna beckoned to Chyndra. "May I see your weapon, young warrior?"

Seemna nodded. Chyndra walked over and handed it to Karna, the blade lying across outstretched palms.

Karna carefully lifted the weapon and even more closely examined it, her nose almost touching the gleaming metal as she peered intently at it. Then she looked up. "How come you by this? Hephira?"

"Yes. Special made for me. My Brother, the Future King, wed a Princess of their Royal House. My father freed their lands of a terrible evil and rescued The First Princess."

"Your father? The one called Chosen?"

"Yes."

"Erta, erta. May I gift for my, erta, erta, error?"

Seemna gave a quick nod when Chyndra glanced her way. "Yes," said Chyndra. "You may."

Karna tapped the flat of the blade with one finger. The blade flashed yellow fire and relaxed back to golden. She handed it back. "Faster. Lighter. Sharper. Now your thing only."

Chyndra gasped as she clasped the hilt of her sword. The blade had spoken to her. "This is a mighty gift."

"Small thing." Karna shrugged. "For one who travels with this rarity witch. Small thing." She pointed to one side of the room. "In there is a room with a bed. The warrior waits there until the witch is done. Both go there and prepare. The witch exits through the other door." Karna was gone.

"Hum." Seemna walked over, opened the door and stepped into the other room. Chyndra followed and closed the door. It faded away. Now there was only one door in the room, in the far wall. And one large bed.

"What did she say?" Chyndra sat on the edge of the bed and looked at Seemna who was still frowning darkly.

"Vile."

"What?"

"She asked if you were druzna mine!"

"What does that term mean?"

Seemna pushed her over, flat on her back, leaned over, nose touching nose. And ordered Chyndra's vest and shirt open and slid both hands over smooth skin, hands clasping and stroking fire into hard swelling tips.

Chyndra's eyes flew wide as she gasped.

Seemna held her, black eyes staring deep into pale blue eyes. And tightened her grasp. And kissed her. And whispered all harsh tones. "Druzna." And straightened up, released her. "More?"

"No." Chyndra blinked. "Yes." And shook her head. "I do not know." She stared up at Seemna. "Do witches do that?"

Seemna nodded. "A few do. My eldest Aunt took as her's a Death Warrior and a Hacto mage, both females."

"Two?"

"Yessssssss." Seemna's eyes stroked over the sweat glistening skin. "Some would want a taste." She licked her lips.

"Taste?" Chyndra peered down past her nose. "Oh!" And then back up at Seemna. And whispered, "You may, if you wish."

Seemna stepped back and snapped her fingers. And watched as the vest and the shirt wiggled and repaired themselves. "You wait! I train! For you a short time. For me, a long and a hard time." She spun, stepped over, threw open the door and passed through. The door closed itself. The wall became blank and smooth.

Chyndra yanked her sword and scabbard free, crawled higher onto the bed, and sprawled loosely on this extremely comfortable bed, blade by her side.

And fell asleep.

Silca Dergat.

The pair huddled over the corner table and talked in very low tones.

Fasna whispered. "Fazler returned."

Zaruna nodded.

"In two pieces," hissed Fasna.

Zaruna jerked. "That one travels with a rar-dragon? Or a nark-beast? What?"

"Sliced," growled Fasna. "Not ripped. Or chewed."

Zaruna gasped. "How dare she use such a vile spell! That contravenes The Witches Code!" She smiled.

Fasna winced.

"She will be outcast. And we may do as we wish."

Fasna shook her head. "No spell trace."

"You tell some warrior did this?"

Fasna nodded. "Must be so. To do that, it requires a large and mighty warrior. It seems, it does, to me, that the young one beds a dangerous warrior, most like Berserker."

"Ah, umna!" Zaruna nodded. "Those things are hard to control."

"And told spell safe," added Fasna. She frowned at the idea that anything could be spell safe. It was a very disturbing concept for a witch to accept.

"Fazler was careless," suggested Zaruna.

"Young, small experience."

"A sly witch would separate witch from beast."

"I will send Frakna. She has great experience and talent."

"Do." Zaruna ordered two cups and a jug.

Bahn Duhr Tohr. Royal Guest Quarters.

Wizla lifted up and leaned on one elbow, her free hand gliding soft stroke across the hard cords of his stomach and smiled soft witch at Reptar. And leaned over the slow breathing of the deep sleeping Fazbaq. "I will spell share a special rejuvenation cast."

Reptar nodded, hooked a hand around Wizla's head and pulled her closer and kissed her, leaning against Fazbaq. "Hum hum hum."

"Indeed," murmured Wizla as she quiet whispered the code and tickle-touched the pale skin of her bond witch mate share and watched the Faan fire flicker deep in those jet eyes.

Little after much later, they waved in a large nourishing meal and fed special tidbits to Fazbaq. Witches took special care of their mates-for-life. The well being of anyone else, not mate, not clan, not clan-linked, was usually beneath their notice and of little concern.

And later, much much later, as they all sat around the table with Ripple and Hanred, Fazbaq realized that it was true, what he heard whispered ever so carefully to him on his many travels. Whenever Ripple spoke to Hanred or looked at Hanred,

Fazbaq could see the very subtle shift in her bottomless dark eyes. Now that he knew what to look for, he did. And told himself that this was a witch secret none dared speak. Hanred shoved a filled mug over to Fazbaq and winked when no-one was looking his way.

Then the trio stood.

And were gone in a soft puff of black.

"A lethal group," stated Hanred.

"A very pretty," said Ripple, clenching his thigh.

"Faan lovely, of course."

"The soft curved Wizla, lecherous mate."

He nodded. "Seems so. Do you think that your sister would let me do a little comparative work?" He patted her hand. "You could lie side by side while I, ahhh, studied the subject matter."

"Husband, the only subject matter that matters is the matter that you tend to leave dusty hand prints upon."

He reached over and deftly popped the top button of her blouse loose. "Speaking of which, we have had visitors for three days now."

"Hum hum hum. Your fingers are clean," she observed.

"Dark soft love, you haven't interrupted my reading of one of those tomes of arcana this time."

Tir Tir Ta.

He walked along the narrow road connecting one of the small hamlets to another small hamlet and wondered where he was.

He was a rather nondescript person wearing rather nondescript clothes. A loose fitting shirt colored a soft grey near white that was draped over faded green trousers. Good boots, and a small pack on his back. He carried a hiking staff of blue-stained wood.

As he walked along he decided that this was a very nice place to be where ever it was that he might be. He would have to ask someone that question. Perhaps they might even know who he was. He recognized the plants and animals that he saw, and the rocks and the stones. He just didn't know himself. All in all, he thought, it was a rather strange way to be.

Grandeville. Tinker's Place.

He stood in the soft light of late afternoon and looked out one of the large living room windows at winter. It, winter, had arrived as it often did in these parts.

In rush of wind and snow.

All of a sudden.

The blizzard had sailed over the nearby ridge, swirled around the house, then roared past and engulfed Grandeville in soft white as well. The wood stove muttered to the house. The house creaked back. It was their usual conversation during the wood heating season.

Szart leaned against his side, arm around his waist. "They will be fine. Seemna sister is special trained as is our daughter warrior. Time flows a different rate out there."

"I know."

The outside front door banged open and they clumped inside, banging snow from their clothes. Smoke, Chicken, and Chantal.

"Generator's fine, Cowboy. Ready to go."

"Van is buried, MindMate. As well as the back fence."

"Great storm do most bury garage, Me'Lord." Chicken hung her jacket on a peg and dumped her boots on the floor against the wall.

"Stop worrying," ordered Chantal. "It is bothering us." She bent over and began to unlace her boots. "A little."

"Boogle," he grumbled at her.

"That a snide comment about my butt?" She glared around and up at him and began to tug the boot laces loose.

"Nope. Nice butt," he observed.

"Me too, me too." Messenger hurried into the room carrying a large tray which held a pot of steaming cocoa and a number of mugs.

He began to fill the mugs as soon as she set the tray down. "You too, what?" And handed Messenger a filled mug.

She beamed at him. "Nice butt." And plopped a marshmallow from the bag she had dropped on the floor into her mug.

"Merde." He sighed heavily and glowered at them all. "O.K., O.K! Before this topic of conversation can get any further along let me state unequivocally that everyone in the house has a nice butt! Satisfied?"

Fair Morn and Early Dawn strode into the room wearing heavy white robes. They had just come from the shower room. Fair Morn handed Early Dawn a filled mug. "He thinks that you have a nice butt."

Early Dawn took a sip. "How can he tell? He hasn't dragged me into a dark corner and worked his wicked ways upon my barely resisting body, driving me into the throes of ecstasy. Yet!"

"Hold it," he snapped.

Fair Morn dropped a marshmallow into each of their cups. "Perhaps he is making an exception for house guests. This time," she suggested, grinning widely at him.

The very loud, very prolonged sigh, was Tinker. "All right, knock it off."

"See." Fair Morn nudged Early Dawn. "Knew it!"

Early Dawn grinned at him, pointed teeth gleaming white. "Want to check anything else?"

He glowered at them all. "How come she has acquired all your bad habits, every one of them." And looked over at Chantal. "Maybe Raj could check everyone for some weird virus cause you guys seem to be able to infect anyone we come into contact with. He is a pretty knowledgeable Doctor."

Chicken shook her head. "Nay true, Fierce Grumble Lord, thy infection thought."

"Correct," agreed Smoke as she headed for the kitchen to make sandwiches, accompanied by Messenger who was giggling happily.

"Right." Chantal settled on one of large the couches facing the wood stove. And slurped loudly. And leered at him. "You like Big Red creations?"

Fair Morn winked at Early Dawn. "Flip ya, heads or tails, to see who goes first."

"I am not just a creation. At least not any more." Early Dawn glanced at him. "But you can play with me if you wish." And laughed. "There is a small couch in the small living room."

"Lech," grumbled Chantal.

He dropped onto the couch next to her. "What started all this?"

"You were making derogatory remarks about my hind

quarters."

"Merde."

"Bull cheat, Cowboy!" She waggled one hand in front of his face. The large ornate ring glittered in the soft light. It was the scheduling ring. The idea came from their collective minds, minus Tinker who was kept outside that conversation. The ring was passed from one to another using some system that Tinker had never been able to understand or figure out.

"You got it, huh?"

"Heh, heh, heh, heh, heh." She held out her cup. "More cocoa, please?"

Early Dawn filled Chantal's mug, bending over, letting her robe fall open. He was staring at the wood stove.

Chantal nudged him. "Toots want you to admire everything."

"Huh?"

"Ogle, ogle, ogle, ogle," chanted Chantal.

"Oh." He looked up and nodded. "Beautiful, beautiful, beautiful." And growled at the room and its contents. "Don't anyone else start up!"

Chantal leaned against him, after setting her mug on the table top. "How about we just snuggle until it's dinner time?" And closed her eyes and fell asleep as he slid his arm over her shoulders.

A bare foot nudged his leg until he woke up.

"Ummm?"

Early Dawn nudged him again. "Dinner is almost ready."

"Oh. O.K. Thanks."

She nudged him again.

"What?"

"Would you like an appetizer before dinner?" And grinned widely. "Me?"

He reached up, grabbed her wrist, and yanked. She spun around and thumped down onto the couch on his free side.

"Fair Morn said that we ought to tease you because it would keep you from worrying so much," she explained into his frown.

"She said that?"

"Yep."

Chantal stretched and yawned. "Damn right, Cowboy. It is a full time job."

Early Dawn nodded. "She said that we all had to do our part."

He straightened up. "Wait a minute! Now what's going on? Or should I say, what went on while we were sleeping?" He glared at Smoke as she walked in from the dining room. "You didn't? Add another? Not again?"

"Nope. You are safe. Ummmm, so to speak." She leered at him. "She is just being friendly. And attentive."

"And sexy," purred Early Dawn. "Fair Morn said that I should be that also."

"Blabber mouth Moth!" He glared at them all. They ignored him.

Early Dawn nudged him with an elbow. "I am, aren't I?"

"What?"

"Sexy!"

"Sure." His eyes darted to Smoke and back to the questioner. "Pointed teeth and leather are a real turn on," he grumbled.

She frowned at him. "Only my wings are leather." And stood and glared at him.

Chantal stood. "Grumble Butt was making a joke. Sorta. Let's go eat."

She threw her arm around Early Dawn's shoulders as they headed into the dining room. "Don't worry about it. He is just being his usual self. Grumbly, grouchy, and a little slow."

Quaratab.

The door formed and slowly opened and she staggered through. Her hair was matted, tangled. Deep fatigue lines etched her face. The black clothes were tattered and torn, badly stained and filthy. She took two steps and collapsed. The door closed itself. And vanished.

After a few minutes she began a slow crawl toward the bed, trying to speak, making the faintest of faint sounds.

Finally, at the bed, she managed to hoist herself up and crawl over to the deep sleeping figure. Snuggling against her, she sighed and fell asleep.

Chyndra woke, rolled onto her side, and stared at the filthy face of Seemna right next to her's. The witches eyes fluttered open and stared back.

"Hold me, hold me," she mumbled. "Nervous, nervous."

Chyndra did. "What's the matter? Why are you so dirty?"

"Hard work. Spell drained," came the mumbled reply. "Energy drained." She cleared her throat, more cough than throat clearing. "Any witch in this state seeks safety and comfort. Nervous, nervous. Tired, tired." She pressed closer, deeper into Chyndra's arms. And fell asleep.

Chyndra dragged a blanket up and over them and held her friend tightly. And thought that this must be why she had to do quest journey. To learn strange and arcane bits of knowledge not gained in the usual training and study that one did. She certainly hadn't been told all the witch lore during her training that she was rapidly acquiring since coming to this elseplace. She kissed Seemna on the forehead and dropped back asleep.

When her eyes opened again, Chyndra saw Seemna was also awake and looking at her.

"Feeling better?"

"Muchly improved."

Chyndra ran her hand up, unfastening buttons, and slipped gentle fingers over soft skin, and clasped soft warm swelling. "I want to see what it is like to do this."

"Yesssssss." Seemna rolled back, flat, giving Chyndra permission to do as she wished. And sighed.

Chyndra leaned over and peered into those seemingly bottomless dark eyes and whispered. "What else do druzna do?"

Seemna rolled, wrapped one arm around Chyndra's waist, and slid the other lower and lower.

"OH!" Chyndra gasped and hissed, "ST . . . ST . . . STOP, doing that!"

Pushing her companion over, Seemna ran her lips over eyes and lips and caressed down Chyndra's neck to the soft flesh. Then she sat back and looked deep into the pale blue eyes. "That," she rasped, "is what druzna do."

Chyndra swallowed hard. "I see." And smiled. "Lie down. Sleep, witch friend,"

Seemna rolled away and stretched out alongside Chyndra and grumbled at her. "Witches do not have friends."

"You are my friend."

"Hum hum."

"Say it."

Seemna frowned.

"Do it! It won't hurt."

"Friend," mumbled Seemna.

"Still require comforting?"

"Yesssssss."

Chyndra rolled onto her side and wrapped her arms around Seemna. "Safe and comfort, friend. Sleep, sleep, sleep."

And they did.

Both.

Sleep.

Far across town, a tall witch stopped to talk with yet another street vender, one Zata Gooda by name, an elderly woman with sharp eyes.

And finally, Zata Gooda stated firmly, in a do-not-argue-with-me tone of finality, "Naut seen, naut for long moments past, did Berserker Warrior ever be here there. Naut with witch. Ever! Naut them warrior here there now. Naut, naut!"

Frakna slipped two gold coins into the outstretched hand and strolled away. Everyone here had said the same thing. There was no berserker witch pair here. None of the seekers she had released had found them either. They must have twisted elsewhere. She cast sly watch over the town opening, just in case, and headed into the nearby forest. It was time to return and to report. Nothing.

Der Der Tanback.

He lounged behind the desk-like piece of furniture and nodded, more or less wisely, at his number one operator, a faint smile playing over lips just touching the rim of a large glass filled with golden liquid. "It seems that the Faan witch clan have birthed a rarity who even now is doing wander somewhere."

Narl Tra nodded back. "How rare?"

"Websmith."

"Rare indeed."

"And a very egomaniac witch clan is trying to interfere."

Narl Tra cleared his throat. "Which egomaniac witch clan? They all seem to be that way to some degree."

Tzar Maga smiled, and sipped. And set his glass down. "No name yet."

Narl Tra shrugged.

Tzar Maga slumped, just a little. "Rumors say that yet another, ahhh, group has an interest in that rarity."

"Do they want her?"

"Another small problem. No data. Yet."

Narl Tra nodded.

"There is something that we wish. And it takes a certain skill working to accomplish this."

Narl Tra smiled. "In which of the many elseplaces was she last seen? Or last lost in?"

"Quaratab."

Narl Tra stood and headed for the door. Not too fast, not too slow.

"Caution Number One. You would be hard to replace."

Narl Tra laughed and stepped out into the outer hall.

Grandeville. Tinker's Place.

He stepped from his bedroom, one of those on the ground floor of the great space they had labeled *The Atrium*, took two steps, and was knocked sprawling.

She dropped to her knees next to him, brows furrowing with worry. "Did I hurt you?"

He blinked up at her. "Noooo. What hit me?"

A great leather wing curled around and waggled at him. "I was exercising them and didn't hear you step out."

"I thought that your hearing was sharper than most."

She reached up and waggled the earphones at him. "Fair Morn loaned me her player."

"Oh." He rolled onto his side, stood, and rubbed the side of his face. "I'm fine."

She stood close to him, very close, and blinked. "I am really sorry."

He kissed her on the tip of the nose. "Don't worry about it."

"Sure?"

"Sure."

She frowned. "You are not going to rip my clothes off in an angry rage and do terrible things to me?"

"Nope." Then he frowned. "You and Fair Morn have got to expand your choice of literature."

"Why not? I am beautiful."

"No way you couldn't be. Big Red put you together."

Her eyes flicked down to her shirt and back up to his face. "I am not like Fair Morn."

"I think that B. R. toned down, ummmmm, everything." He headed for the kitchen. He had smelled freshly brewed coffee. And started to worry about what ever it was that was going on with them this time.

Quaratab.

The merchant with the pleasant face and the gentle smile wandered from place to place seeking new items for shipment elsewhere. And in the process of discussing this and that piece of business learned several interesting bits of information.

So while he ate a leisurely meal, Narl Tra, wrote a message to Tzar Maga. And told him that a witch named Frakna had been prowling around, seeking a witch berserker pair who certainly hadn't been in this area. He had heard of a witch-warrior pair, both female, both rather young, and hardly what the Quana sought. And no-one had seen these two young women for a number of days.

Plus he had heard a rumor of a messy killing over in one of the smaller streets. No body, just a large bloody stain. He laughed to himself, signed his name, and added one last comment, "And that's the news from exotic Quaratab."

Then he waved over the waiter and ordered another of the local beverages, and sent his message out and away.

He sat.

He sipped.

Then he blinked.

Just there, calmly strolling around the booths out in the large open space that was the middle of town, or something like that, he saw them. Two young women, one dressed in witch black, the other wearing a large sword slung crossways over her back. So, he said to himself, there you are, still in town after all. Dropping a number of gold coins on the table top, he stood and followed them, his curiosity aroused. One rarely saw that combination traveling together. Witches tended to be unpleasant company at best, demanding and narrow in outlook. Then he laughed to himself. That also described most of the warriors he had ever met.

It was early morning, three days later, when he spotted them again. He still hadn't figured out how he had lost them before. But there they were, sitting at a small round table on the cobbled space in front of one of the smaller inns, having an early meal, talking quietly.

So he walked over to them.

And looked into the two pair of eyes that looked up at him. One pair seemed to be bottomless pools of darkness, surround by a face totally devoid of expression. The other pair of eyes, a pale blue, were set in an expression of mild curiosity.

"May I join you?"

"No," grumbled the witch.

"For a short moment," replied the other, eyes flashing to her companion and back. Her companion gave a slight nod.

He sat in the only available chair and cleared his throat. "I am Narl Tra, the Number One of Tzar Maga, Dealer of the Ever Rare, housed in Der Der Tanpack."

"Princess Chyndra, Realm of The Dragon, Hahn Dohr Kahn, The New Kingdoms."

His eyes flew wide. "Princess?"

"Indeed."

He looked at the other.

"Faan witch Seemna," she snapped.

He stared at her, wondering at his luck.

"You have something against witch?" she growled, unhappy with the way he was staring at them.

"Not at all." He waved over a waiter and ordered a local beverage. "Quickly."

It being early morning the waiter did, return quickly.

Narl Tra took a sip and looked at them again, very carefully.

"Speak!" hissed Seemna.

He nodded. "I am not often or easily surprised, young lovelies, but you have managed to do that."

A long black wand tapped the table, suddenly in Seemna's hand. "The short moment is over!" He could feel something changing the air around them.

"Perhaps," said Chyndra, pushing her chair back just a little, "one more short moment." And nodded at Narl Tra. "Explain. Please?"

"The House deals in the Ever Rare. Those items that are truly rare." He waggled one hand at their surroundings. "I came here to seek such." And smiled at them. "But the truly rare are just that. And are very hard to find."

He held up one hand. "But here you are."

Her chair bounced off the cobbles, the golden sword in her hand almost before he saw it move. "Does your house deal in the living? Or only in the dead?" One shining edge lightly touched the edge of his neck.

"Objects! Only objects! Never any being against their will. Never that!"

"Hum," stated Seemna, anchoring him to his chair.

The sword flashed back into its scabbard. Chyndra picked up her chair and sat down. "It would be nice to be told a true tale, Merchant."

He lightly touched his throat and inspected his fingertips. No blood. And looked at Seemna. "What are you, Faan witch Seemna?"

She anchored his chair to the cobblestones. "Websmith."

"Do you know of clan Quana?"

"No."

"Tale!" insisted Chyndra.

He nodded at her. "Some days ago a Quana witch named Frakna wandered here seeking knowledge of a berserker-witch pair. And left disappointed."

"Kapt tip," grumbled Seemna.

He looked from face to face. "She was seeking you two. Her information was flawed."

"And you?" asked Chyndra.

"Websmiths are truly rare." And smiled, a nice, gentle smile at Chyndra. "Princesses are uncommon, but not rare."

She smiled back. "And?"

"I would travel with you and see what truly rare is about."

"Nothing else?"

"For now, no." He glanced at Seemna. She appeared to be deep in thought. Then she looked at him. From the corners of her eyes. One side of her mouth twitched. And he knew that he was about to die. All knew that a smiling witch was right on the edge of doing terrible. He assumed that held true for a witch companion as well.

She looked at Chyndra who looked back. "Where do we wander next?"

He cleared his throat. "May I suggest Lamnar Inzat?

There is a jewel carver there that I would like to visit."

Chyndra picked up her utensils and began to finish her meal. "Sounds interesting."

He tried to stand. And realized what had happened.

Seemna nodded.

And he was released.

Grandeville. The Bowling Palace.

Once again the name of the bowling alley had been changed. It was still the same owner. He just changed the name every once in awhile. No one had ever learned why he did this. It was a topic of conversation among the local folk, especially those that liked bowling.

Janine waggled the deep fried potato chip around in a puddle of catsup on her plate and looked up at her team-mates. "So, how ya doing, Shooter?"

Chantal set down her mug. "All right. Why?"

"We heard about your, umm, injury."

She nodded. "Wanna see my scar?" And grinned at her two long-time friends. "I am doing just fine. But I wish that he would stop being so solicitous."

"Why's that?"

"I think that it bothered him much more than he wants to admit." She glanced down at the bowling lanes where their opponents were just finishing their turn. "It was the loss of the child."

Janine nodded and licked her fingers clean. "Well, being out with the boys might help some." And smiled at the trio walking up to their table. She stood and warned them away from the food. "And leave some for us!"

"Sure thing, babe," rumbled Green, waving at their waitress, rolling his eyes at the red mess on Janine's plate. "Oughta be against the law to do things like that." He sat, overflowing his chair, picked up one of the pitchers and took a drink. He and Red each had their own pitcher. The rest shared the other two.

Red joined him, ordered two more large orders of fries and grabbed a handful from Janine's plate, avoiding the red-stained ones. "Good that you guys could join us, Tinker," he rasped as Tinker sat. It was his normal tone of voice since he had been injured in one of the many college football games when he played with Green. Later in the game his opponent, the one responsible for the injury, had somehow broken both his legs.

Tinker nodded. "Been awhile. Mind if the rest join us at Big Darlene's? When did this place get renamed? Again?"

"Hard to keep track." Green chewed thoughtfully on his hamburger. "Still the same bunch of babes?"

"We have a house guest." Then he explained about Early Dawn's teeth.

"Not a word," agreed Green.

"Right," said Red. "Unless she decides to bite someone. Are they driving in?"

"Nope. Went to a movie." Tinker grabbed some fries from Green's pile. "Promised to behave."

Green smiled. "We'll keep an eye on them after they arrive. Wouldn't want Smoke punching out someone's lights because they decided to get fresh with one of the others."

Red smiled. "Shouldn't happen. The Mauler is back in jail." He remembered when The Mauler had grabbed the Princess and Smoke had smashed his face into the edge of the bar at the Rail, The Railroad Bar and Grill.

"They promised," grumbled Tinker.

Down on the floor loud laughter and hooting broke out.

"Oh, well," sighed Green.

"Beat us again," added Red. He stood. "I'll go pay for everything. Meet you at the truck." His wife headed in his direction as Janine and Chantal joined Green and Tinker.

"Good game," announced Janine, glancing at Green and the few remaining fries.

"We can get some more and chili at Big Darlene's," he stated firmly.

Chantal laughed. "Should have known better, Streak. It takes a lotta calories to fill those two."

Janine wiped her hair back from her face, brushing the thick brown mass with the startling white patch back over one ear. The white patch was the result of a near fatal car wreck and the source of her nickname. And looked up at the big man. Everyone looked up at him. He and Red were a matched pair of gigantic. "You buy the chili!"

"Sure thing, babe." He looked at the counter over the top of her head. "Shall we go?"

Big Darlene's.

They shoved several tables together and shortly thereafter were joined by the movie crowd. Tinker introduced Early Dawn to the others. She sat next to Fair Morn and eyed the chili.

"It's good," said Fair Morn, leaning sideways.

Early Dawn took a tentative spoonful from the large bowl that sat in front of her. And beamed at her. "I like it."

So they sat and talked and ate. Smoke, Fair Morn, and Early Dawn ordered additional servings of the chili as well as the chips that came with it.

Part way through their meal, a large barrel-shaped man walked up behind Smoke, hooked one broad arm around her neck, and growled. "Ready for a rematch?" He released her and massaged the muscles of her shoulders. "You been working out?"

Fair Morn restrained Early Dawn who was about to jump to her feet and punch this person.

Smoke turned her head and smiled at him. "Sure. Care to join us?"

"Nope. Gotta go to work. See ya next week." He turned and headed for the front door.

Fair Morn explained to Early Dawn in a low tone of voice that he was the person who for the last three years in a row was the winner of Big Darlene's Annual Chili Feed, Cookout, and Arm Wrestling Rodeo. He had also won, two years ago, the chili cookout and after beating Smoke in the final arm wrestling match had given her his "secret recipe" after which she promised never to share it with anyone.

He had appreciated her strength, her appetite for eating chili, her willingness to buy beer after losing, and the way she left her shirt unbuttoned almost to her belt buckle during the festivities. In that order.

"May I come also?" asked Early Dawn.

"Sure." Fair Morn carefully explained the rules taking care that no-one could overhear. Tinker had forbidden them from winning as he didn't want to draw too much attention to them. Smoke usually came in second. Fair Morn had come in sixth the last time. So if Early Dawn wanted to participate she had to learn how to lose properly.

Early Dawn leaned closer. "This is really a strange elseplace."

Fair Morn smiled at her. "It is our home."

Early Dawn ordered yet another bowl of chili.

Green winked. "Another large appetite."

"Yep," said Tinker. "Another one."

And then, much later, they all headed in various directions. Red and Green would soon go to work as the late shift of the Grandeville Police Patrol. This month they started close to bar closing time.

Not A Good Idea At All

Lamnar Inzat.

The major city was rather larger than most of the others in this land and of an interesting design. The dwellings sprawled in a loose pattern with acres of garden forest threaded through everything. One constantly passed from dwelling space or shop through grass and trees to dwelling place or shop.

Narl Tra pointed. "The jewel carver's shop is that way. Two green over."

One green over, a tall, thin man dressed in tight pink garb approached the trio, smiling and bowing. "Be any here interested in fine rarity? All hand crafted and often owned?"

Narl Tra crooked a finger at him. "How fine? How rare? How often owned?"

"Fine must be seen. Rare must be touched. Beyond counting."

"Where?"

The man held out a sheet of paper. "Follow, follow." He hurried away as soon as Narl Tra took it from him.

Narl Tra looked at the sheet and scanned their surroundings. And pointed. "That tan building right through there, the one with the yellow roof."

The building was cottage sized, a one story square box. They could see one door and two windows.

He looked at them. "Shall we?"

Seemna shrugged. Chyndra nodded. They headed that way.

They stopped, looked at the building, opened the door and walked in.

And crashed into a heap on the floor.

They stepped from the other door. The one dressed in green and brown handed the one in pink a large sack that clinked gold coin sounds. "Swiftly done."

The one in pink snatched the sack from the outstretched hand. "I am done." And headed for the door.

"Send Bar Nar here." He knelt and rolled the bodies apart carefully, checking the effects of the drop spell.

Bar Nar soon burst through the open doorway.

Ampa pointed. "Deposit him in green six-five." He lifted the limp witch and slung her over his shoulder. "This one is mine. You may sell the toy-warrior for as much as you can wheedle." He stepped through the door and disappeared.

Bar Nar hauled Narl Tra from the room and dumped his burden in the correct patch of green under a thicket of Tarklen shrubs. And ran back to check on the other.

He sat on the floor next to her and carefully searched. And nodded. One gold sword, two gold knives. And nodded to himself again. She had trained. He could feel it in her muscles. Maybe he would keep her for his own enjoyment. He shook his head, extracted a small book from one of his pockets and consulted a certain list on a certain page. He would be able to buy as many as he wished, for any purpose, with the proper sale.

Scooping her into his arms, he walked out the door and

hurried away to arrange a meeting.

His prize mumbled something.

Bar Nar smiled, not realizing that she had responded to her sword.

Termion Ianan.

Fula slid in and sighed agitation.

"What?"

"On Lamnar Inzat was found Narl Tra, mostly dead. Small words say not much. Before that he was seen in company with a young witch and a young female warrior."

"Narl Tra?"

"The same. Dealer in the Ever Rare."

"And the rare?"

"Disappeared. Zim is near Narl Tra. Perhaps he will live to tell."

"It is to be hoped."

Grandeville. Big Darlene's.

This evening the place was packed with happy, boisterous patrons, getting ready for the big event.

Over against one wall leaned Green and Red, dressed in G.P.D. blue. They were on duty and offered a presence to keep life more or less orderly during the festivities. On the wall above their heads hung a great and garish banner of canvas that announced to any and all in glowing red letters what most of the crowd already knew:

Big Darlene's Annual Chili Feed, Cookout, and Arm Wrestling Rodeo.

The arm wrestlers milled about, pushing here and there,

seeking their opponents, the ones wearing the same number as the one pinned on their own shirts.

Early Dawn stood next to Fair Morn, her shirt unbuttoned to the belt buckle. She was, as were all the rest, dressed in blue jeans, cowboy hats, cowboys boots, and cowboy shirts.

Tinker had grumbled and told Chantal and Fair Morn to button up partway at least.

Early Dawn nudged Fair Morn. "I think that he is afraid that you or Chantal might pop out."

"We wouldn't do that." Fair Morn looked around for her opponent. "And he knows that."

A thin nervous young man pushed toward them and stopped in front of them. His number was twenty. So was Early Dawn's.

"R . . . R . . . Ready?" he stammered

Early Dawn smiled. "Sure." It was a thin smile as she was carefully not showing her teeth.

The judges called the first two pair to the only tables not occupied in the establishment. "Number four and number twenty!"

Fair Morn leaned close to Early Dawn. "Remember."

Early Dawn nodded and walked over to the table where her opponent was sitting and waiting.

Smoke eased close and watched.

At the other table the "Champ" and his first opponent were getting ready.

"GO!" shouted one of the judges. The struggles began.

Suddenly at table four there was a loud thump as a hand was mashed flat against the table top.

"Damn," snarled the loser.

"Whimp," laughed the other, banging his opponent a good natured thump on the shoulder. The champ stood and saw Smoke standing, watching, walked over and stood next to her as pair Fifteen settled themselves. Reaching around her, he gave her a friendly pat on rear pocket and laughed. "And that is how it is done. Think you will make it to the main event?"

She smiled at him. "Got a reputation to maintain."

He laughed, pushed away, headed for the kitchen. His chili, the new and very secret recipe, had been one of the six selected for the final balloting.

The pair wearing twenty struggled on. Arms wobbling back and forth, no one gaining an advantage.

Early Dawn watched her opponent's face. It was turning redder and redder, sweat was pouring off the tip of his nose and chin.

The table judge was frowning, beginning to wonder if this pair were faking it. So, he touched each arm with a fingertip. And felt the rock hard tension of muscles struggling to win. "Even match," he mumbled loudly.

And finally, slowly, slowly, Early Dawn's arm tilted further and further over and toward the table top.

"Done!" shouted the table judge, tying a red ribbon around the left biceps of the winner, handing him a new number.

The pair stepped away, making room for the next two.

"Di . . . Di . . . Did I hurt your hand?" He looked very worried and nervous at that thought.

Early Dawn shook her head. "Nope."

"I've ne . . . never won before."

"Really?"

"Yes." He blinked and blushed, flooding his face with red again. "You are a lot stronger than you look. May I buy you a beer?"

"Sure." She watched him push his way into the mob and over toward the bar. Fair Morn bumped up against her. "What took you so long?" The next pair at the table were done and being replaced.

"I didn't want to make it look too easy."

"Why didn't you win? No-one would have been surprised."

"He was trying so hard that I decided to lose."

Fair Morn slipped away. "My turn. I think that I will win. It is just the first rounds. Smoke already did."

Early Dawn's opponent returned with two big mugs. "He . . . here."

"Thanks."

He indicated Fair Morn with his free hand. "Do you know her?"

"Yep."

They watched the match, sipping, now and then. Fair Morn won.

"Wow." He stared at Fair Morn who winked at him.

Early Dawn nodded as Fair Morn got a red ribbon tied on and handed a new number. Her opponent stared at her in disbelief.

"Do . . . do you live in Grandeville?"

"Nope." Early Dawn described where she lived to him.

"Really? No one visits up there. Everyone knows that they don't like visitors. That's what the sign at the base of their driveway says."

"I am a house guest from out of town."

"I am Robert Roberts. My folks had a wicked sense of humor when they named me." He stuck out his hand.

She shook it. "Early Dawn." She stopped a passing waiter. For this event Big Darlene had hired a number of very large men, and ordered another set of mugs. "My treat. Loser buys, right?"

Robert nodded. And blushed.

They stood and watched the matches proceed. And at some point during the matches he ever so carefully slipped his free arm around her waist. So she leaned against him, just a little, and thought about ordering something to eat.

Fair Morn lost in the third round. Everyone of Tinker's mob behaved and enjoyed themselves. And Tinker relaxed and began to enjoy the event.

"Bout time," grumbled Chantal in his ear. "Damn worry wort."

Then, finally, the main event, the last pair. It was, once again, Smoke and last year's champ. The spectators, mostly the usual crowd, had begun to marvel at this.

He grinned at her across the table and set his elbow on it, arm held in the starting position, and winked. "Ready to get your butt whumped?"

She set her arm and grinned back. "Maybe I will just win this time."

The numerous red ribbons tied to their left upper arms fluttered as they readied themselves.

They set their hands and the judge shouted, "GO!"

The place erupted into shouting, catcalls, and general

loud enthusiasm for this last match.

But eventually he won. And laughed loudly. "Damn, almost had me this time." He handed her one of the very large mugs just plunked down on the table. And after taking a long pull from his mug, he nodded at her. "Never met a woman as strong as you." And winked. "If I wasn't happily married and if you wasn't with that guy over there, why I just might suggest we go somewhere else." He shrugged. "But."

"Let's eat some chili, Champ." She yanked him to his feet and headed him toward the food.

Hamal Alma.

This elseplace, far across the universe of universes, was not noted as a place where the strange happened.

And yet.

It did.

Deep down far below something grumbled. And surged upward.

Its presence eventually woke those who taught. They had relocated to this once quiet elseplace.

The four smiled at each other. And withdrew. To decide what it meant. To them. And to the student that they had last trained.

It would take some time. But, eventually, they would know what to do, what must be done.

And when they did. They would act.

Lamnar Inzat.

She strolled across the greens and met a tall, thin man dressed in light pink garb. He handed her a pastel sheet. And was frozen in place. Only his eyes moved. They goggled and stared at her.

"I am Quana witch Frakna and you will do nothing but answer my questions or decorate some of this green with yourself forever." She released the clamp on his throat.

"What do you want, witch?" came out all harsh rasp as his barely functioning vocal cords tried to work.

"I seek a certain witch? Where is she?"

"Know not." He yelped. She held a long silver wand in her hand, the tip just touching his cheek below his left eye.

"Speak tell," she grumbled.

"Know not! All I did was deep sleep drop them."

"Them?"

"One witch, one toy warrior, one man of the merchant type."

"And?"

"Bar Nar," he squeeked. "He knows. I left as soon as they dropped." He indicated with his eyes. "Two that way. Small brown with a yellow roof."

She stalked away and into the next green over. Behind her something made a soft sound.

PUFF!

She cackled.

Piznar Hindo.

The pair, dressed in clothes of grey and black, were sharing a meal and talking low, Nuart and Ninar.

"I have been thinking deep," said Nuart.

"On?"

"Witch clan Occiis and witch clan Faan."

"Ah umm," hissed Ninar.

"We, this clan, owe angry to Occiis."

Ninar nodded.

"None told Faan were so . . . witch!" Nuart lightly touched her cheek with a thick orange rod. "If we learn something Faan useful perhaps they will be in witch debt to us."

Ninar's eyes squinted into thin glittering slits. "Yessssssss."

"I will tell send to the others and then we will travel to, ebb, visit."

Ninar nodded again and smiled a witch smile. It promised terror and chaos.

Lamnar Inzat.

Slowly his eyes focused having just managed to barely open. It had been a long time that they were shut, but he didn't know that. Yet.

Finally, ever so slowly, finally, he could see the room that he was in. It was a rather plain room. What he could see of it while lying flat on his back on a rather firm bed. This room looked healer to him. He slowly looked to one side.

"Who are you?" he asked the tall column of glistening violet that shimmered ever so slightly.

"Zim."

"What are you?"

"Quata."

"Zim the Quata?"

"It is so."

"I do not feel all that well."

"Mostly dead."

"What that means," stated someone else, stepping close to his bed and into his eyesight, "is that you are very weak but are beginning to heal."

The speaker was a woman wearing a silver skirt and a black tunic. "I am," she explained, "Chief Investigator Ban Manot. And I wonder why we found your, ahem, mostly dead self lying on one of my greens?"

"Just me?" Narl Tra watched her face carefully.

"Just you, one almost dead person. Who are you?"

He told her, leaving out this and that, and wondered what had happened to the two young women. Just as he finished his artfully crafted tale someone banged into the room. It was another female dressed in silver and black.

"Teta Bat!" she reported. "Fislap, the Pink Under, has, eeeeeha, died!"

"Calm! Calm!" snapped Ban Manot. "What happened?"

So it was explained. A casual citizen was passing through the edge corner of the green where they had found Narl Tra and saw a witch in deep discussion with the Pink Under. He saw the witch stride off. And just as the Citizen stepped into the next green one step, he heard a soft puff sound.

The Young Investigator sucked in a deep breath. "When the citizen looked in the direction of that sound all that he saw were bits of pink fluttering down." She stared at Ban Manot and swallowed loudly. "All that was left was a large ugly spot in the green."

"A young witch?" asked Narl Tra.

"No. The citizen thought that she looked rather stocky, not too old."

"Better widen our people," suggested Ban Manot, casting

a quick glance at Narl Tra and whisking her Underling from the room.

"I will wait here," gurgled Zim, "until you are mostly not dead."

Fin Bin. The Central City.

It was mid-afternoon. In the shops of the city, it was thronged as usual. Locals and visitors from many elseplaces jostled and wandered, checking, buying, haggling. Most tried not to bump into the witch wearing grey and black as she strode purposefully down the center of the lane. Nor to the other one walking toward her. Jostling witches was not a good thing to do.

She walked up to the woman wearing the flowing pale yellow skirt and yellow blouse with puff sleeves marked with bright red designs.

"Occiis witch?" she asked.

"Occiis witch Zepta to be exact. What want you?"

"You." Ninar, stepping up behind her, striking Zepta behind the ear with a thick brown rod.

Nuart pushed the collapsing figure back in Ninar's arms.

All around them people pushed, shoved, and desperately tried to leave the immediate vicinity.

"Witch war!" screamed someone driving the panic to a much higher level. To be in the area when witches fought was usually lethal for the spectators.

Nuart shifted them away. To their chambers. High in a tower, forty layers above the base. They had three large rooms.

Ninar dumped her burden on the floor.

"Stick her to the wall." Nuart cast quiet over their prize. "We can discuss things when we return. I saw a nice, pleasant place to have a late-day meal."

They disappeared in a soft puff of grey.

Fasback's Delight. A Sunny Day.

She woke and sat up.

She was in the middle of a large and very ornate and very comfortable bed. The four corner posts were very tall, totally carved with symbols and strange faces, all painted in a rainbow of colors, mostly favoring red, green, and blue. Here and there there was a touch of gold gilding.

She looked at her surroundings.

The room was also large, opulent, and decorated lavishly. Light streamed in through floor-to-ceiling double doors with many panes of colored glass. Beyond them she could see a large balcony. Crawling from the bed she stood and inspected her garb. It was a loose fitting smock and pajama outfit of a light green color. On a small table near the bed she found her clothes in a neatly folded stack. They obviously had been cleaned. Her boots were set in front of the table. They had been buffed to a soft gleam.

Tossing the bed garb to one side she dressed in her own clothes and took another look around. Her sword and belt hung on the back of a high-back chair. The knives were still in their sheaths on her boots.

Yanking her blade free, she inspected it and listened to it. Then she swung belt and scabbard in place and popped the blade up and over. All her belongs had not been tampered with as far as she could determine, just cleaned. She walked over to the tall doors, pushed them open, and walked out onto the balcony to see what she could see.

The balcony curved around the corner of the building. It appeared that she was on the top floor of a tall building. Out there was forest and in the distance a single, snow capped grey mountain. Clouds drifted around its top.

It was a nice view, she decided, but where were the others?

She strolled around the corner to find out.

Her boot heals made soft popping sounds on the inlaid wooden designs of light and dark wood.

Niveous Lily.

Ampa dumped his burden on the thick white rug and nodded at the man dressed in a white robe sitting in the large chair.

"Careful," hissed Puartor, "that is precious." He tossed a large sack to Ampa. "The price, as agreed upon. You were careful?"

"Of course. I came down three, two around, one up. None could follow that." Ampa stuffed the sack into a large pocket. "Need anything else?"

"Not a thing, Ampa the Cunnning, not a thing. For the moment. However, if I should desire something, ummm, special, I will send to you."

Ampa nodded. And stepped into the way out.

Puartor stood, walked over, knelt next to her and rolled her onto her back. And stared at her face. And nodded. Definitely Faan witch. A young Faan witch. His information was so out of date. Which witch was this one? He rose to his feet and strolled from the room and issued orders to the waiting servant.

Grandeville. Tinker's Place.

He opened his eyes and stared at the ceiling, then rolled his head and looked at the small alarm sitting on the floor right next to his bed. The bed was set flush with the floor so it was easy to do.

7:00 a.m.

Late. For him. He usually rose early even if it took him quite a while to fully wake up. He looked the other way.

She smiled at him.

"Think we could get Big Red to do something?" he asked. "We could make an exception, just once."

"I like my teeth. I like my body. I like my wings. And everything else." She dragged her arm from under the blanket and waggled her hand at him. The ornate ring glittered in morning light. "And I like you."

He sighed.

"Sha'gar gave it to me."

"Who was that guy?"

"The arm wrestler?"

"Uh huh."

"Robert Roberts. He said that his parents had a weird sense of humor." She kissed the side of his face. "I let him win. He said that he had never won before. Fair Morn told me all about how to behave just like everyone else there." She nudged him. "I saw you ogling the females in the place."

"I wasn't ogling anyone," he grumbled, rolling onto his side, and giving her a little tickle.

Messenger finished setting out the beginnings of breakfast and nudged Sha'gar. "He's got her in his bed."

Sha'gar shrugged. "I gave her the ring."

Messenger looked around the kitchen and whispered, ever so carefully, "Are we adding her?"

"Nope."

Smoke came in from the outside, wiped sweat from her face and began to shed clothes. "Start cooking. I am hungry." She headed for the shower room to wash off after her run.

They did. Sha'gar helped Messenger. Messenger liked to cook. Sha'gar, being a magician, like all magic users, thought it was a waste of time as one could just wave in whatever they wished. But she helped, none the less.

Fair Morn wandered in, peered over the top of Messenger's head, just to see what they were preparing. "Make lots."

"You may help," suggested Messenger. She could feel all the rest of them waking as could Fair Morn and Sha'gar. Sha'gar left to set the dining room table.

Chicken walked in, filled her cup, and looked at Fair Morn. "He do have t'other fair Winged Wench a'bed."

"Sha'gar did it," explained Messenger.

"Passing strange." Chicken headed for the large living room.

"Everyone needs a friendly bat," laughed Fair Morn.

Fasback's Delight. A Sunny Day.

As she stepped around the corner she saw a large man, a rather large stocky man, noticeably overweight, leaning on the balcony railing, gazing out at the view.

Sensing her approach, he turned, smiled broadly, and bowed, as well as he could given his girth. His garb was a light purple. He wore leather shoes dyed a deep grape.

"Ahhhhhhhh, I bow before such beauty that I see before me, such a vision of loveliness." He beamed at her, radiating joy.

She looked him over as he straightened up. "Who are you?"

He threw his arms wide and beamed at her. " I am, the every bit of over-pampered being, Hawlan Fasback."

"Where am I?"

Gesturing grandly, at the building, at the view before them, he grinned. "This elseplace is Fasback's Delight. All mine." He laughed. "As far as the eye can see. And then some."

He waggled one hand at the two chairs and the round table. "Join me for a little refreshment?" He dropped into one of the chairs and filled two clear cups from a tall ceramic vessel. "Local beverage, made just for me."

She sat and took a sip.

"Wonderful, is it not?"

She smiled at him. "So, Fasback, all this is yours?"

"Most true, Vision of Delight."

"Why am I here?"

He looked momentarily puzzled, brows wrinkling. Then he refilled his cup. "Because you are mine."

She set her cup down and shoved her chair back. "No, I am not!"

He nodded. "Of course you are. I bought you. And paid a great sum." He scratched his lower lip. "A very great sum. " He smiled at her. "Worth every gold coin. I have many, many of them."

She frowned. "And who dared do this?"

"Why Bar Nar of course. He deals in, ahh, umm, special

items for those few who can afford the very best." He leaned forward, a little. "Tell me, where did he find you? I think that I would like to have a, umm, matched pair."

Her frown darkened as she pondered chopping off his head.

He blanched and gasped, "Your pardon, your pardon. I fear that I have made a breach of your cultural values asking that." He tried another smile. "Were your quarters adequate? I had your belongings carefully attended to. Did your servant take care of them?" He refilled his cup again.

"Is that who took my clothes off? My servant?"

"Of course, of course. A female, a female." He stared at her. "I would not presume. Never!" And smiled a sly smile. "But one of these days, eh?"

She jumped up, her chair sliding back and away. "Dare to touch me and loose that hand!"

Fasback clapped his hands together and beamed at her. "Wonderful, wonderful. Such character. Such style! Such a delight!" He laughed happily. "One among many."

A woman hurried around the corner and gasped. "There you are!" She was dressed in billowing translucent trousers and blouse, both a soft blue. The deep green eyes watched Chyndra.

"Ah, your servant, Abda," stated Fasback. "Another delight."

Chyndra's eyes darted from Fasbock to Abda and back. "Disgusting."

"Not at all," he replied. "She is a slinth, one of the most rare and the most sensual creatures in all of the universes. I made her your's. A slinth for a toy-warrior. Lovely pairing."

"What did you call me?"

"Toy-warrior, as told by Bar Nar. Two daggers and a golden show sword." He leaned sideways. "Pull up your trouser leg, I would see whether you wear them now."

Abda stepped toward her.

Chyndra sidestepped. "Touch me not, slinth!" She pointed at Fasback. "You! How do I leave this place. I would return to Lamnar Inzat immediately." She glanced up and down the balcony.

"Such fierceness," chortled Fasback, ringing a small bell.

A large man stepped from a side door. "None leave," he stated. And reached for Chyndra.

The flat of the sword slammed into the side of his head, sending him staggering toward the wall.

"Delightful," gurgled Fasback, bouncing in his chair.

Chyndra started for the door. "You! Abda! Come with me!"

Another large man filled the, doorway, holding a large blade in one hand. "Put that ornament down! And behave!"

"Out of my way!"

The man looked at Fasback. He shrugged. "It is only gold coin."

The man lunged. And lost his sword and his sword hand.

Chyndra ran past him as he screamed, and down the corridor. She heard Abda trotting behind her. "Which way is out?" yelled Chyndra.

"Next door and down," replied the slinth.

They hurtled through the door and down and down the stairs.

"Red door," called Abda, gasping for breath as they hit the landing.

Inside the room, Chyndra stopped and stared at the far wall. At the round red spot on the far wall. The surface of the spot shimmered like the surface of a water filled bowl.

"What is that?"

"The way out. The way in."

Chyndra stepped over to it. "What do I do?"

"Tell it the name. And step in."

Chyndra turned around. "Go back to your home."

Abda stared at her. "It is not possible. My home no longer exists."

"Then," stated Chyndra, in her most royal tone of voice, trying to sound as stern as her mother when she was at her most Queen-like royal manner, "you shall come with me."

"I am Fasback's."

"No longer. He gave you to me. And I say we are leaving. Now!"

Abda looked around and stepped close to her. "He did say so, did he not?"

"Most true. He said that he made you mine. Now we are leaving this place."

Chyndra popped her sword into its scabbard, grabbed one of Abda's hands, spoke to the spot on the wall, and stepped through, dragging the startled slinth with her.

Fin Bin. The Central City.

They swirled in, having had a rather leisurely meal, during which they had talked and relaxed, as much as witches ever did, relax that is.

Ninar nodded at the wall and at their captive sticking to it. Her arms were held out to the side. Ninar nodded at her and released the quiet spell. Zepta glared at both of them and hissed, "Release me. Now!"

Nuart stepped over and nodded. "Perhaps. But we would know certain things and you will tell."

"What?" snapped Zepta.

"We would know why Occiis tried to entangle Beris in witch war with Faan."

"Clan secret," hissed Zepta.

"Soon to be shared."

"Never!"

Ninar looked at Nuart who ordered in a chair and sat. "I will watch," said Nuart. Ninar nodded.

"Eh ha," said Ninar, looking once more at Zepta. "Speak tell, witch."

Zepta glared at her.

Ninar took a thin blade from somewhere, inserted it into Zepta's left cuff and slit the sleeve open to her neck. Then she cut the other side.

"Speak tell."

"Pooosga!"

"Occiis vile," observed Ninar as she pulled the remains of Zepta's blouse from her skirt. "Speak tell." She tossed the garment aside.

"This is garnar," snarled Zepta. "Occiis do not show themselves."

"Speak tell." Ninar stepped back and tilted her head to one side, sending the knife away, replacing it with a thin amber wand. She stroked the tip down the outside of a bare rib cage. "The Occiis have a certain loveliness."

"Kiskah!"

Ninar reached out, her hand closing on soft swelling. "Nice pleasant. Shame to loose such."

The wand became a thin-edged blade. She tugged and rested the blade just above her fingertips. "Speak tell, Occiis."

Zepta snarled.

"You have two chances," purred Ninar. She twitched the hand and watched the blood began to ooze down. "I shall cast no-death wish on you. You will have to beg and beg and beg for pity and someone to end it, the ugly maimed witch."

"Stop!"

"Faan?" whispered Ninar.

Zepta swallowed hard and stared downward. "Heal."

Ninar released her and nodded. The knife disappeared. As did the wound.

"The Faan," sighed Zepta, "birthed weird. Clan head Zaruna declared that clan zar zar ghar until the strangeness is no more."

"Name me name."

"Know not."

"True?"

"Witch true."

Ninar looked at Nuart who shrugged.

Ninar leaned close to their captive and whispered ever so softly into one ear, "Did you know, Occiis witch Zepta, that during the great Witch-Demon War that a Beris saved the life of the Chief of the demon mob Kraznar? And that since then to now that we are owed demon debt?"

She slid her hands over the bare torso. "A little lean but the Kraznar never pass up a meal."

Zepta gasped.

"True tell?" asked Ninar, stroking gently.

"Witch true, witch true," sobbed Zepta. "Do not, do not."

Fluttering fingers stroked Zepta's stomach and slipped lower. "Perhaps a male Kraznar, a robust male Kraznar. Just to see what you birth weird?"

"I told, I told." Tears trickled down her cheeks. "Do not."

"What weird?

"Web," gurgled Zepta. "Web wraith."

"No such thing." Nuart leaped to her feet and slammed Zepta with an open hand, banging her head from side to side. "No such witch thing."

"Underdark told," mumbled Zepta.

It appeared.

Zepta screamed.

"Witch," it rasped.

Ninar pointed. "That is Occiis witch Zepta."

The demon poked her with one talon. "Thin pickings."

"No! Safe, safe!"

The monster licked its lips. "No taste?"

Ninar nodded. "No taste. Safe safe. We will want her back. Alive. Unmarked. Healthy." She released the fastenings. Zepta tumbled in a heap and struggled to stand.

"As Beris say, so it is." The demon scouped up Zepta and turned away.

"No tales told by Zepta," said Ninar, heading for the table, ordering in cups and a jug.

She poured and handed a cup to Nuart. "What did the Faan really birth?"

Nuart sipped. "They will share tell."

Far Stirrings

Bahn Duhr Tohr. The Quarters of the Royal Advisors.

He was lounging on the couch, a very large and friendly couch, his back propped up by one of the over-stuffed arms. A very large tome, the lower edge resting on the upper edge of his stomach, was open, and held that way by both of his hands. His knees were drawn up so she could comfortably lean back against them as she slouched at an angle and wiggled one finger, arms curled around the lower outside edge of the book, between the lower two buttons on his shirt.

He pretended to ignore the jet black eyes peering over the upper edge of the volume of the strange and arcane that he had been reading. Finally, he looked up. "Dusky Delight?"

"I am being neglected," she grumbled.

His left hand allowed the book to sag so he could drop that hand to lightly tickle her thigh. "How so?"

"You have been reading one or another of those dust leaking volumes for two days."

He nodded. And smiled over the top edge of the tome at her. "True. But as I recall, Midnight Love, a certain nasty witch asked me to search for a certain kind of information." His hand returned to the book so he could close it and then drop the monster volume to the floor. It made a very heavy thump. Dust billowed up from it in a soft cloud and floated away.

"Nasty?"

He reached out and plucked her blouse loose. "Mostly true."

"Hum hum," she purred.

"My, my," he observed, undoing the upper buttons as she leaned forward so that he could. "Perhaps I have been spending too much time reading when there are other things to attend to."

She sat back and shrugged the blouse from her shoulders. "Things?"

"Indeed, Moon Pale Beauty. Two lovely things." He ran a playful finger here and there, leaving a dusty line. "Are we in a motherly way again?"

"We are not!"

"Well, to my discerning eyes, it does appear that there has been some small increase in circumference." He grinned. "Perhaps you would fetch me my calipers so that I could take a series of measurements just to satisfy my investigatory curiosity."

She grumbled, a little. "Husband, you are not pinching my, hum hum, things with any of your ugly and cold measuring devices."

He shrugged. "I could warm then first."

She kissed him, leaned closer and kissed him again. "Are you up to no good, husband?"

"What a wonderful idea," he murmured, hooking his thumbs inside the waist band of her trousers.

"ENTER!" demanded someone.

"Most inopportune a visitor," he suggested.

"Ptar ptar rak tak," she hissed, lurching upright, her blouse relocating itself, buttoned, neatly tucked in.

"COME!" she ordered, standing, glaring.

They folded in.

Gently.

"You!" she snapped.

"Humble greetings," said Nuart.

"We wish to discuss witch," added Ninar.

Hanred stood, walked to the table and filled four mugs, handing one to Ripple as she walked over, gesturing for the others to sit. He smiled at Ninar and Nuart.

"Witch daring," snarled Ripple, sitting next to him, watching carefully as the two Beris sat across from her. "Speak tell!"

Nuart nodded.

And did.

Lamnar Inzat.

She stepped into the room and looked at the man sitting at the table studying the glossy catalogue spread out on the table top between his outstretched forearms.

He had just finished circling one item and was pondering whether he should select another or not.

"Bar Nar?"

He looked up and over at her. "What want you, witch?"

Freezing his vocal cords. Frakna plunged the thin silver wand down, anchoring his left hand to the table top. "Answers!"

She picked up the catalogue and looked at it. There were a number of pictures on each page, artfully drawn, of females of various classes, with lengthily prose extolling their unique characteristics. In the lower left hand corner of the text was the price. They were very, very expensive. She looked at the cover and read it.

Rare Lovely.
For The Discriminating Owner Who Wants Only The Best!

"Sooooooo," she hissed. "Some person has acquired a large sum and expensive tastes to go along with that large sum. Perhaps some person would like to live in order to do this?"

She slapped the side of his face with another long thin silver wand just to get his attention. He was staring at his left hand and the blood trickling across the table top. "Ready to talk?" He nodded.

She released his vocal cords. "Scream and die!"

Silca Dergat.

They huddled over the corner table and talked in very low tones.

Zaruna said softly and, very, very carefully, "Zepta has disappeared."

Fasna sucked in a quick breath. "Gone far?"

"No. She still lives but is unlocateable."

Fasna shivered. "Strange strange." She, as all witches were able to do, always knew when a clan member died. Not how they died, just that they did. There was just a certain feel to it. "Strange strange," she mumbled.

"Yesssssssssss," agreed Zaruna. "I sent Zirran the Tracker to seek find."

"Was that wise?"

"I am bothered. Your Faslar cut in half and your Frakna

spins away on some unknown thing. Now Zepta is somewhere unknown. None feels Faan to me. Yet since they have birthed weird, things have happened."

"Strange strange," suggested Fasna. Again.

"And correct witches are double sly," stated Zaruna.

"Yesssssss," agreed Fasna.

Magevern. Deep Below the Surface.

She smiled happily, mother to daughter.

They had been practicing subtle all morning, an especially hard skill to master. They had just finished honing a particularly fine point and were now relaxing.

Someone soft knocked on the door, the only door to this room. This chamber, and several others, were special practice areas. One could unleash any spell in here and the many guarded chamber would keep them from leaking out and affecting anyone who happened to be passing down the corridor outside.

One always knocked softly before entering. It gave those practicing time to clear the room.

"Come," said Sa'ar.

Imdar the Healer stepped in and smiled at mother and daughter. "Interesting."

"We are finished here. Let's get refreshments."

The trio walked out, down the corridor and into a room filled with small tables, each with four chairs. Imdar fetched drinks and sat at the chosen table.

"News?" asked Sa'ar.

"Moonda heard on Fin's Table that Faan clan head Ripple birthed a daughter with some rare type of witch." She smiled broadly. "And he and his Queen Lurin birthed a Princess."

Imdar nodded at the young woman. "You have a new sister, Eulin."

Sa'ar laughed. "My husband continues to amaze me. Is she pretty?"

"It is said so. She has ice blue eyes. She was witch raised and warrior trained and now does wander with the Faan young witch."

"Should be safe enough. A witch warrior pair."

"I would like to visit them," said Eulin.

Sa'ar looked at her. "Where are they to be found?"

Eulin held out her hand, forefinger extended, and smiled at the tiny blue-green dragon that appeared, perching on her finger. "The tiny ones can find anything." She told it what to do. It flashed away, seeking her new sister. She stood. "Time to wash practice off." And headed for one of the wash rooms.

Sa'ar winked at Imdar. "Perhaps I should visit him and find out what else he has been doing besides siring a daughter."

"Life is quiet," suggested Imdar.

Sa'ar nodded and stood. "I shall join my daughter in washing off practice. And then visit The Vander Lord." She walked from the room.

Imdar headed for the main lounge to tell all the others.

Tit Tir Ta.

He slowly walked around the town and wondered about himself. And slowly, ever so slowly, he came to the realization. His name was Kanl Ta. He smiled to himself. Well, he thought, that was a good start, knowing your own name.

He checked his jacket pocket, found that there were coins in it, and entered the first food place, took a table, and ordered the first thing that the waitress suggested.

Neither the jacket nor those coins had been there before as far as he remembered. He thought that was interesting. It was almost as interesting as knowing your own name.

He ate his meal, and enjoyed it.

And took rooms.

And went to bed.

Lamnar Inzat.

Narl Tra was sitting up in bed, leaning back against the head board, large pillows strategically placed, and wondering when they would let him leave. It had been sometime and he was feeling mostly healed.

The tall glistening column standing near the bed gurgled, "Mostly alive."

"Thanks, Zim."

The door banged open and Chief Inspector Ban Manot stomped into the room. "Did you meet a one called Bar Nar?"

Narl Tra shook his head. "No, we were just here when whatever happened, happened Who is he?"

"Dead. He was just found. Someone had anchored his left hand to a table top with a long thin silver thing." She held a catalog, one side stained ugly. "This was anchored to his chest. With another long thin silver thing. It also anchored Bar Nar to his chair. Whoever placed those was very unhappy with him. It took him a long time to die."

"Why?"

Ban Manot frowned. "He was, at times, a worker with the

Pink."

"Who is all over your green?"

"The same."

"It would appear," suggested Narl Tra, very carefully, "that the two are somehow involved in what happened to me and my companions."

"Certainly." Ban Manot nodded at him. "Next day you may leave."

"I may return to my elseplace?"

"Certainly. Which?"

"Der Der Tanback."

"If we need, we will come." Ban Manot spun around and thumped from the room.

"The Green Onana will be pleased," gurgled Zim.

Grandeville. Tinker's Place.

They were in her room on the second floor, standing in front of the large sliding glass doors, looking out at the storm swirling white around the house and past the small balcony. She was leaning back against him. His arms were wrapped around her.

"White white," she murmured.

"Probably close the passes again." He blew warmth into the thick lustrous grey hair.

The room flashed violet. And a warm body pressed against his back as her arms wrapped around them. She nuzzled the back of his neck, and said, "So this is what you do on long winter days."

"Sa'ar?"

"You know anyone else that feels this nice?" She laughed.

"Or is that an indelicate question considering what your hands are holding?" She was gone.

Me'Lord, fair Sa'ar do be here.

She had just appeared in the living room where Chicken, Smoke, and Messenger had been rearranging the furniture to take advantage of the radiant heat coming from the large wood stove.

I know, Princess.

Sgenn turned inside his arms and kissed him. "She is very curious about something."

"Now what?" he grumbled. And kissed her back. "Suppose we ought to go down and see."

She smiled, a very soft half-smile, and began to button her shirt. "Yes."

By the time that they walked into the large living room, all the rest had already arrived. It had been quite some time since Sa'ar had last visited them.

Sa'ar stood and bowed her head. "First Greetings to the Vander Lord. First Greetings to The Heart of The Heart." Then she looked up at him, grinned, and fell back into the couch.

"How is it that one finds out from a wandering Vander that I have a new daughter?" She stared pointedly at Szart. "And that you have a new sister?"

"Ahhhh, ummmmmm," he said. "Guess we forget."

"I hear," drawled Sa'ar, "that she is beautiful, a Princess of some sort." And burst into laughter at his expression. "Oh, John, you are so easy to tease." She patted the open spot on the couch next to herself. "Sit, Vander Lord, and talk with me. It has been some time."

    He did. Talk with her.

        Everyone did.

Lamnar Inzat.

    They stepped from the node and were instantly stopped by Inspector Fourth, Ra Tranar, who had insisted, very strongly, very firmly, that they come with her.

    So they did.

    And now, they stood in a large room with a cluttered desk, a number of chairs, and a glowering woman dressed in a silver skirt and a black tunic. She sat in one of the chairs and waved at them to sit. They did.

    "I am Chief Inspector Ban Manot. Tell me who you are and from where you originally came."

    "Chyndra, Princess Royal, Realm of the Dragon, Hahn Dohr Kahn, The New Kingdoms."

    "Abda, Slirna."

    "Why are we here?" asked Chyndra, sitting straight, all Royal Princess.

    "Know you one called Narl Tra?"

    "Yes. Is he here?"

    "No longer. Finally healed, left two days ago."

    "Healed?"

    Ban Manot explained all that had happened And looked from one to the other when she was done. "And what can you tell me?" So Chyndra told her.

    "It would seem, young Princess," stated Ban Manot, "that you are in a very twisted thing. We have only had rumors of this Fasback before. It is too bad that both the Pink and Bar Nar are dead."

She watched them carefully. "Have you thoughts on who or what would use long thin silver things?"

She spun and opened a desk drawer, and took out something and held it out. "Like this?"

Chyndra nodded. "Witch wand. A witch did this."

Ban Manot stared at it. "Witch wand? You know this for sure?"

Chyndra nodded. "I was witch raised."

Ban Manot indicated Abda. "We were told by Narl Tra that he traveled with you and a witch. So where is the witch?"

Chyndra shook her head. "Fasback didn't mention anything like that. When may I leave? I wish to leave, to my home. Her mother will be very upset."

Ban Manot shrugged. "You may leave now. Which of the witch clans?"

Chyndra stood. "Faan."

Ban Manot pointed. "There is a node just that way as you leave our building." And as soon as her visitors left she ordered a search through their files for information on this Faan witch clan.

Outside, on the street, Abda waited for Chyndra to proceed. Chyndra started walking in the opposite direction to that previously indicated by Ban Mallot. "First we shall get you some proper traveling clothes."

Abda hurried after her. "There is nothing wrong with my garb."

"Other than being diaphanous and displaying yourself?"

"Slinth," stated Abda. "Most proper."

"Travel wear." Chyndra turned into the establishment

and beckoned over the first seller she saw. "My companion requires sturdy yet presentable traveling clothes." She pulled a leather sack from a side pocket and dropped it onto the counter top. The sack clinked. "I will pay."

The seller spun and hurried away. He recognized an Upper Level command tone when he heard one. And returned shortly and set the stack of clothes on the counter top next to Abda, and pointed. "Through there. I am sure that you will find everything to be satisfactory. I will fetch proper foot gear."

"Go change," said Chyndra to the frowning slinth.

Abda snatched the clothes and hurried into the changing room.

When she returned she was wearing beige trousers with large patch pockets, a tan shirt, and a soft brown leather jacket.

Chyndra nodded.

The seller rushed up, hustled Abda to a chair, slid soft socks onto her feet, and then the soft leather boots that came halfway to her knees. After quickly lacing them up, he said, "Stand up, please. And wiggle your toes." Abda did. He felt her feet, squeezing the boots here and there. "Very good, very good."

Standing, he nodded to Chyndra. "Tacb beast leather. Soft as a lover's touch yet impervious to almost everything. A specialty of our place."

Chyndra paid the bill and ushered Abda from the shop. "Why were you looking at him like that. It was indecent."

"It was slinth," carefully explained Abda. "He would have happily given us anything that we asked for."

Chyndra halted and glared at her. "I do not buy with my body!"

"Narnko!" snapped Abda. "That person would have gotten nothing but a warm feeling. Slinth do not body trade!"

"Then what are you talking about?"

Abda smiled. "He would have just felt nice toward me and wanted to give me gifts."

Chyndra squinted at her. "You spell cast on him?"

"No. Male creatures feel lust toward us. At times. Some females also." She looked at Chyndra. "If we wish it."

Chyndra jammed her hands on her hips and glared at her companion. "Not while traveling with me you won't. I wish to learn, not cause prurient attacks."

Abda smiled. "Perhaps, Princess, there is something to be learned there also."

Chyndra spun away. "Let's go! We have to visit Narl Tra. Maybe he can help us find my friend. Then I suppose we will have to travel to visit Seemna's mother."

The small blue-green dragon perched on the side of the building watched them. And darted into the node just after the pair stepped in. The small blue-green had no problem, following anything anywhere, even through a node.

Fin Bin. The Central City.

Zirran the Tracker drifted here and there, talking with this one, visiting with that one, and now stood on the spot where many had agreed that witches had tangled.

She stood, feeling the spot, ignoring the press of people around her. Then she sniffed, drawing in a deep breath, deep into her lungs. And exhaled and nodded to herself, Zepta had been here. She could taste her. And two other witches as well.

She looked around. The two witches had to have taken

quarters somewhere. She would locate that place. Eventually.

Termion Ianan.

Aldin Cease, First of the Green Onana mage guild, nodded at Zim and leaned back in his chair.

"So, Narl Tra returned to Der Der Tanback and no one knows what happened to the two young females?"

Zim gurgled agreement. Fula shivered doubt "What?"

"The witch is too important not to know," gurgled Fula.

"I agree. We require a special seeker. There must be a faint trace in Lamnar Inzat. In some way the witch and the warrior are linked. We must find both."

Zim slid from the room to fetch exactly what was needed. The Sadna were exactly what the Green Onana required. They were fast seekers with lethal defenses. And other skills.

Grandeville. Tinker's Place.

Sa'ar smiled at Early Dawn.

"And Messenger freed you the same way she did Fair Morn?"

Early Dawn smiled at Messenger. "She understood, unlike some other person who is slow that way."

Sa'ar nudged him. "Must mean you."

"I wasn't in a collecting mood," he grumbled. "And, before you ask, she is only visiting." He sighed. "Besides, it was a Big Red plot of some kind."

"A homeless waif," intoned Messenger, "sheltering here from the storm while the heartless master of the house, him, plans nefarious and vile deeds mainly directed at dragging a certain alluring visiting female into dark corners where he can finally abuse her."

Sa'ar clucked her tongue at him. "Poor dear."

Him slumped deeper into the couch and frowned at Messenger. "What is this all about? This time?"

"Waifs," stated Messenger firmly.

"She," he announced to one and all in the room, "is not a homeless child!"

Sa'ar laughed, and winked at Early Dawn. "Certainly not a child all right." And slipped an arm around his waist. "You going to keep her?"

He sighed. "Maybe she could go with you?"

"Lovely enough, for starters. But she is not a magic user. We are, after all a mage guild. We do not keep pets."

Early Dawn dropped onto the couch by his free side and stated firmly as she glowered around him at Sa'ar, "I not a pet. I am an alive and real being."

Sa'ar leaned forward and looked past him at her. "Of course. What I meant is just that the Vander do not have non-Vander, non-mage living with them. But!" She grinned widely. "A certain person does."

"Simon Legree," hissed Messenger. She jumped up and headed for the kitchen to make cocoa. Early Dawn bounced to her feet and hurried after her. "I'll help."

"She is nice," stated Sa'ar.

"I know."

Smoke leaned on the back of the couch. "Fair Morn doesn't feel so different with her here."

"You are all different," he stated. And reached out and touched all the minds of the rest of himself. And sighed. A large, long, loud, drawn out sigh of resignation.

"O.K., O.K. You guy's win. Again. I surrender. Again! She can stay."

Sa'ar kissed his cheek. "You are just an old softy, Husband."

"I know," he grumbled softly.

They all came into the room.

And mobbed him.

Sa'ar laughed.

Estur Nal.

The Black Patch Set had been hunting in a new territory and had spoken to a survivor of the small walled dwelling group. What the survivor had told them had sent the Black Patch set hurtling through the opening in a rush. Once on the other side they sent a messenger.

The messenger, a young outer ring fringe female, had been very agile and very fast. She had taken minimal injuries and had given her message to the Core Pair she had been sent to see and to speak with. That Core pair had granted the messenger protection and had sent her back with a reply along with a gift. The gift, to her, was a young outer fringe young male.

Now the Black Patch Set flowed up the valley, headed for the meeting.

The Core Pair of the Green Plain Set watched them approach. All around The Core Pair there was a constant motion as all watched the approaching mass. The Core Pair stood, side by side, occasionally barking orders at a female getting too excited. Behind them, and to either side, guarding the Core Pair, stood the four Prime Males, armed, attack ready.

The Black Patch Set Core Pair strode into the edge of the Green Plain set without hesitation. A path opened before them and closed behind them as they walked with a steady, but unhurried pace, toward the other Core Pair, now sitting on the ground, waiting. They approached and sat, at the correct distance and waited.

Then they were beckoned closer.

To begin the conversation.

Fin Bin. The Central City.

Zirran stood in the room, now empty and swifted delicately.

Unknown witch had been here. Two unknown witches. She relaxed.

She walked, carefully, into the other room. Seeking.

She smelled her. Zepta had been here. She nodded. So, she had found the rooms those unknown witches had used, the place to where they had carried Zepta.

Zirran's eyes flew wide. She smelled great fear in Zepta. What could have affected her so?

Then she knew.

That rank, disgusting taint.

Demon!

In a flash, she was gone.

Grandeville. Tinker's Place.

His eyes opened.

Someone had been shaking his shoulder. For some time.

"Timezit?" he mumbled.

"It is almost 2:00 in the morning," she stated.

"Kinna early," he grumbled, rolling onto his side and sliding an arm in her direction.

She gave him another shake. "Wake up! You have visitors."

He opened one eye and stared through the black in her direction. "We do?"

"Yes."

"Why are you sitting up?"

"Because they are here with us, in your bedroom."

"WHAT!" He thrashed upright and stared. And saw them. Two pair of glowing red eyes staring down at them.

She cast soft light, soft violet light. It flooded the room with just enough light that dark adjusted eyes could easily see.

"Now what's going on?" he grumbled.

"Ah ha," stated Amamaedur.

"Ah ha," echoed Ahamaezur.

They looked at his hands. And saw that he was still wearing the blue ring that they had given him, the one that signified that he was A Prime Male, The Prime Male of The Tark Demons.

"Merde." He smiled at them. "There is no way we can discuss whatever it is that is going on with you two this early. Go somewhere. Visit."

They did.

And settled on the bed.

With him and Sa'ar.

Sa'ar laughed. And tugged the bed clothes back into order. "Very Vander. Lay down, Lord. This bed is certainly big enough. We will sleep till morning." She wiggled closer. "They are certainly warm."

He sighed, and settled down, Sa'ar on one side, Amamaedur on the other. Ahamaezur lay against Sa'ar.

"Yah," he said. "They do radiate heat."

"All right," he grumbled, "turn out the light. And you two lie still and go to sleep." The violet light faded, the room was dark. "And close your eyes," he mumbled. "It's like having night lights in here."

They did.

Amamaedur nuzzled his neck and gave him a few little nips with her razor sharp teeth. But didn't break the skin.

They all fell asleep.

Cabtar. The Gathering Place.

They sat around in the place, it had no real name, and was never mentioned directly, and discussed the compact. It felt good, that owed was already given, and they had liberty to do as they wished.

Four were selected.

All at the gathering finished the ending of beginning.

It was the way of the Sadna to consider those so selected as dead until they returned, their mission over.

One by one, the four slipped out and away.

Over Under. Once A Land of Mines.

Ampa lounged in the restaurant, the remains of some tasty treat on the serving dish, and watched customers coming and going. He ordered another of the local beverages, a particularly interesting orange concoction, with blue specks floating in it. While he was waiting for the waiter to return from the direction that he was watching he didn't see her walk into the establishment.

But he did when she sat across the table from him.

His head jerked. "Witch?"

She nodded. "I wish information. It has taken some to find you."

"Many do not."

She shrugged. And idly scratched the side of her face with a long thin silver wand.

Der Der Tanback.

It was a pleasant town. Lots of green space filled with blooming things, grey-green shrubs and large bluish trees.

They had wandered around, carefully familiarizing themselves with the layout of the town.

At least that is what Chyndra was doing.

Then, after some conversation here and there, they stood in front of the large door of the building, painted a soft rose color. It was a rather large building.

A small wooden sign fastened next to the door told them that they arrived at the correct place.

**TZAR MAGA.
DEALER OF THE EVER RARE.**

Chyndra knocked on the door using the small mallet that hung next to the sign.

The door pulled inward and a startled voice gasped, "You!"

Chyndra nodded. "May we enter, Narl Tra?"

The door opened wider.

"Certainly. Do come in."

He led them deep into the place, a place that was part dwelling, part office, part warehouse, until they entered a large comfortably furnished room. He waved one hand. "Sit. Please. Refreshments will arrive in but a moment." He sat and stared at them, at her, and carefully at Abda.

"Abda," she said, smiling warmly at him.

He felt a strange tingle.

"Stop that!" snapped Chyndra.

The tingle faded away.

"Lovely warrior," he asked. "Who is your companion? This time?"

So Chyndra explained.

And then Narl Tra related everything that had happened to him.

"And no one knows where my friend is?" Chyndra frowned at him.

"No." He shrugged. "Yet." His head jerked. "Did you see that?"

"What?"

"I saw a flash of some small thing." He pointed. "Just there. High on the wall. I think that it was a blue or green color."

She shook her head and looked at Abda who shrugged.

Refreshments arrived and were served by a very silent and efficient servant. He looked at Narl Tra, who nodded. The servant left the room.

Leaning back in her chair, the sword propped against one of the chair's arms, cradling her glass in her hands, Chyndra took a sip and looked over the rim at Narl Tra. "Now, tell us why you were so interested in me and my friend."

He glanced at the sword and then at her. "You will behave?"

"Of course."

"And your, ahh, companion?"

Chyndra nodded.

Abda smiled.

Narl Tra explained.

Discoveries

Grandeville. Tinker's Place.

He was slumped in one of the couches staring vaguely at the wood stove. It showered radiant heat on one and all whether they were staring at it or not.

He was also feeling heat from either side. The three of them held cups of coffee. Amamaedur and Ahamaezur thought that this dark fluid stuff they were drinking was interesting. They had been given some on previous visits.

He was slowly waking up.

Chicken wandered in, ruffled his hair, and smiled at them. "For why, Fair Prince, do these Tark demons come a'visiting?"

"Dun know," he mumbled.

Smoke walked in and sat at one end of the couch.

Ahamaezur smiled at her.

"Very calm," observed Smoke. "What have you been doing to them?"

"Nuthin," he grumbled.

Szart joined them and nodded. "Demons." Even though she knew that they had bonded with him, she still worried. Witches usually attacked any demon that they met and vice versa.

He looked up at her. "You wanna contact Kartz and see

if she would come and talk to them? She understands their language."

Szart nodded and sent to Kartz. Hard. The Nagar was the only one that they knew that understood the Tark language in detail.

Hahn Duhr Tohr. Far Across The Great Sea.

The fleet was anchored.

Not too close to shore.

Not too far from shore.

It had been late in the day when the lookout had shouted and indicated that it looked like something was beginning to appear on the far horizon. And that it looked like land of some kind.

Signals had flashed to the other ships and all had taken in sail and spread out in a wide line and then had slowly approached they knew not what.

Frinda, laughing wildly, had grabbed Sook and wrapped her in his arms. "We have changed the future of all of the kingdoms." And kissed her. And eventually said, "I wonder what we have found."

"Hum hum." She poked him, not too gently in the stomach. Witches were not used to this kind of behavior in front of anyone. They were on deck and the sea folk were watching.

Now it was morning. On all the ships, far-seers were being passed from hand to hand as all wanted to take a look at this new land.

Dense vegetation edged a broad, white sand beach, blocking the view of the interior. The Ship Master of White

Cloud was being rowed over to meet the King and to plan what they should do next.

E'Nilt spoke to her Senior Officers and set them to organizing her warriors for moving onto the dry land. She intended to place two units on the beach. They would punch into the growth, very carefully, and secure an area to built the first camp.

And by mid-day, it was done.

They were ashore and headed inland.

Two grey ships sailed in opposite directions to begin to map the edges of this land and to see what else they might find.

Sea folk were already making wagers with each other as to how large this land was.

The remaining ships were quickly replenishing their water supplies. A small stream had been found, its water, cool, fresh, and quite tasty. All agreed that this was a good sign.

Frinda had climbed as high as he could in his ship's rigging and after some debate with one of the sea folk that had accompanied him, had agreed that it did appear that the interior had some large, rather rounded hills poking up above the vegetation. When they finally returned to the main deck, he threw an arm around his Queen, and said, "Is there anyway you can tell my sister that we have succeeded? Perhaps tell your Mother?"

Sook frowned at him. "My Mother does not run errands for any being."

"Ah well."

"I can send a scroll if you will write one."

He smiled and hurried to their quarters. Returning shortly, he handed her the document, neatly rolled and tied.

Soak took the scroll and poked his side. The scroll disappeared. "It is done, Great King of the new and ever newer lands."

He grinned at her. "If We knew of any way to gift my most clever sister, I would do that twenty times over. If it wasn't for her We would be moldering away in The Old Kingdoms, a Prince in waiting." He waved both arms. "Instead, here we all are doing ever more exciting things."

On shore, the exploring band had followed the stream inland and had walked out into a great open meadow and had quickly sent a runner back to the shore with the news.

Silca Dergat.

They huddled around the corner table and talked in very low tones.

Zeruna nodded at Zirran. "Tell her."

Zirran looked at Fasna and explained how she had followed witch trace and eventually located the rooms where Zepta had been taken by the unknown others. She paused. And cleared her throat. "I feel that all were demon got. The smell was strong and Zepta was terrified, the others strangely calm. The demon was an unknown type to me." She shrugged. "There are so many types."

"Zepta lives, still," stated Zaruna.

"Then dragged deep." Zirran shuddered. "A terrible vile. They will use her endlessly."

Fasna sank in her chair and mumbled, "Now demons. What have the Faan unleashed upon us?"

"That clan," hissed Zeruna, "ought to be banned."

"Tred soft," cautioned Zirran. "Strange tangles here."

Fasna nodded. And wondered why Frakna was so long out there.

Niveous Lily.

She had traveled three down, two over, and two up.

And banged into the witch ward. It felt ice cold and was white as white. Snarling and growling, she gathered in everything that she knew and managed to bang a hole just large enough to hurtle her package through, telling it where to go, before the ward resealed itself.

She whirled away to a safe place to think.

Bahn Duhr Tohr. The Quarters of The Royal Advisors.

"Sooooo," she hissed, "the Occiis and Quana would do harm to my daughter."

The air quivered. Over their heads, where the ceiling ought to be, dark clouds smiled angrily. Red flaming eyes peered down.

Nuart nodded. "So it is told by Occiis witch Zepta."

"And you are truly demon tribe linked?" Ripple rolled a long black wand back and forth between her palms.

"From the times of the Witch-Demon Wars."

"Hum hum." She looked from Nuart to Ninar. "The Faan owe you witch debt! How may we?"

Nuart sat straighter. "The Beris would compact with Faan."

"You would be many linked."

"All to the betterment of Beris."

Ripple tapped the tip of her wand against her chin. "And the Faan would be demon linked. Strange strange."

"Who?" asked Ninar. "Who would we be many linked with?"

"Witch clans Tanpak, Zwar, Grenzanr, Hinta."

Ninar sucked in her breath.

"Mage guilds Vanderlaine and Hacto."

"Mage!" Ninar stared at her. "Mage?"

"It is so," stated Ripple. "The clan learned how to not trigger the mage-witch clash of magic forces."

Nuart stared at her. This type of control was unheard of.

Hanred gently nudged her and said quietly, "Blue Udaz and Kanikt witch clans. And Death Warrior Order."

"Also linked," added Ripple. She nodded at Ninar. "Rumtah will offer for unpleasantness done."

Ninar shrugged. "No need. Witch does witch."

Ripple stood. And cast. Black surged over and across the table. "Faan welcome, Beris." She ordered the dark swirling overhead to go away.

Suti Able.

The air cracked open.

Fasna leaped to her feet and stared at her. This stranger was rather short, dressed all in black.

"Who are you?" Fasna demanded.

"Faan witch Raft," she growled, instantly changing position, and casting. She whispered in Fasna's ear, "You are mine, Quana Head."

Fasna whirled and cast. No one was there. A short wand plunged into the side of her rib cage. She blasted it away.

And was tapped on the shoulder and struck in the chest by another wand, glowing red.

"How?" gasped Fasna as Raft flickered from place to placed, adding wand after wand.

"It is a gift," snarled Raft, standing in front of her, her black eyes staring into black eyes.

Deep down, Fasna could see the red flickering flame in those great dark eyes.

"These," explained Raft, sliding another wand into Fasna's chest, "are spell drain wands. You are spell draining fast fast." She nodded. "Ripple wanted to do vile."

Fasna wobbled, and gasped, "This is vile." Her arms hung limp, refusing her commands.

"This is napta!" snapped Raft. "Name me Quana names! Who yet lives?"

Fasna glared at her. Then felt something pressing against her back. Soft fingers fluttered up and down her sides, then skidded away to elsewhere.

"Kunita Beast," stated Raft. "Now that is vile."

Grandeville. Tinker's Place.

They all sat around the large table in the dining room. Breakfast was just over and people were sipping at cups of coffee or cocoa.

The Core Pair smiled at Tinker, black shark teeth glittering in the morning light, as Kartz finished relating what they had told her.

He slumped in his chair and peered at them over the top of his large cup. "Some kind of demon is holding some kind of witch captive?"

The Core Pair licked their lips.

"Yessssssss," replied Kartz.

He looked at Szart. "I don't understand. Is this important, something that we need to know?"

Szart shrugged. "They said that this witch is not being bad handled. Strange strange."

Amamaedur growled at Szart.

"They will go and look," translated Kartz. "They know of the terror you and them brought to demon tribes past times freeing non-demons. The witch is non-demon."

"That was different. If these demons are guarding her, or whatever it is that they are doing, I don't think that it is anything that we ought to get involved in."

The Core Pair stood, made a hole and stepped in.

Kartz looked at Tinker.

"Thanks Kartz. Say hello to Raj." She stood and swirled away.

And appeared in his office in the hospital. It was almost time to make rounds. The doctor and his nurse. She ordered on her white nurse uniform and smiled at her husband.

Hahn Dohr Kahn. Realm of The Dragon.

The scroll fell from somewhere and landed in the serving bowl, splashing pieces of vegetables and gravy over the beautifully decorated table cloth. The servant leaped away and pressed his back against the wall, staring at the bowl. She stood, leaned forward, and fished the thing out, wiping it clean with her napkin.

Then she sat, turned the small scroll around in her hands, and opened it, read it, and laughed.

The servant hastily fetched her a clean napkin and wondered at his Queen's composure.

"Fetch Bah'n N'der," ordered the Queen.

The servant ran. Moments later, Bah'n strolled in.

The Queen looked at him. "We wish to have posted in both main towns and have runners send to the out towns the news. Our Brother King and the fleet have found new lands." She grinned at him.

"The New Kingdoms have added to themselves. We can use a Fest Day. In two days hence. Ask Our First Lord to come. We have made history."

He hurried away to spread the news.

She stood and walked out of the room to stand on her balcony and to stare out and over her main town. And to marvel at it all. And wished that Her King was here to share the joy that she felt.

Grandeville. Tinker's Place.

They were on the rear deck shoveling the snow off. Everyone was hard at it. That way it would only take a short while. Sa'ar had joined them, arguing that, after all, she had grown up, in a manner of speaking, in Grandeville, and that she certainly knew how to shovel snow.

And it worked.

With that many shovelers, the deck was quickly cleared. Stacking all the shovels along one wall, they trooped inside to shed many layers and to warm up.

Messenger, Fair Morn, and Chicken hurried toward the kitchen to make pots of cocoa.

The rest settled in the large living room on the several couches and poked a few more pieces of wood into the stove.

Sa'ar winked at him. "Like my underwear?" She was in

dark blue, skin tight, thermal underwear, having shed everything else. "Borrowed it from Smoke."

"Comfortable?"

"Sure is." She settled next to him.

"Certainly shows off your body," stated Early Dawn, as she settled by his other side. And nudged him. "She is pretty nice, huh?"

He sighed, and grumbled, "Don't start that up."

Szart hissed. Sha'gar jerked.

"What?" He looked from one to the other.

"Ptar ptar rak nar par," snarled Szart.

"Sure. Perfectly clear. What?" he demanded, frowning at her.

"Mother!" snapped Szart.

"Has declared witch war," explained Sa'ar. "She just contacted every Faan linked Clan and Guild Head and named the targets."

Sha'gar looked over, red glow pulsating in her eyes.

Deep down something rumbled. Sgenn looked at Szart.

"My mother," stated Szart, fingering a long black wand, "has named the witch clans Occiis and Quana. They have entered compact to trap Seemna."

"Merde," he grumbled.

"Damn witches," agreed Chantal. "We are not going out there."

"No need," said Sa'ar. "The witch clans are doing all the hunting. The rest only if they need more, um, help."

He frowned at Szart. "Exactly what is going on? You guys are out there killing people?"

"Paz kar," she growled at him. "They will all be held,

and, eh, . . . talked with."

"Talk?" He slipped upward and sat straighter. "That a euphemism for something?"

Szart stomped over to him and banged his knee with the wand she held. "Lap!" she demanded.

And sat.

On him.

"They will be dissuaded from future bothering," she stated firmly.

"And," he said carefully. "We will not get involved."

"Yesssssssss." She leaned against his chest. "No need."

He kissed her cheek. "O.K., witch little. Good to know that."

"Probably," she added.

Silca Dergat.

She sat at the table and searched the room. Then she ordered a jug and two mugs and decided to wait for some short time.

And after some time, she watched as a slim witch slide into the room and glide toward her corner of the room.

This stranger settled across the table from her. Zarna gasped. This one was obviously Faan. Large black eyes, high cheek bones, that certain exotic look.

"Speak! Faan!"

She nodded. And answered, her voice the soft caress of the shadows of the night. "I am Faan witch Reep, often called The Silent One. You will come with me."

Zarna gasped, blanched, her skin becoming whiter than was normal for a witch. "The Silent One is child scare Faan tale."

Reep looked at her with eyes that seemed to grow larger and larger.

Zarna felt her life draining away. "Stop," she gasped. "Sssssssssssstop!"

Reep blinked, stood, and crooked one finger at her. "Come," sighed the night. "Ripple wishes to speak with you."

Zarna lurched to her feet.

They faded away.

Paslar Morm.

They faded into the room, the three of them.

Zarla leaped to her feet, a gleaming green wand suddenly in her hand. "How dare you!"

"Be still," snapped the witch, batting the cast to one side. "I am in no mood for this."

Zarla layered on protection. "Name me names."

"I am," hissed the witch, "Faan witch Ranna. This is Hacto mage Adarlak, and Death Warrior Anjan Trap Zahan. Come with me, slurz napta."

"Slurz napta!" screamed Zarla as she slashing at Ranna with her wand. It was deflected by a many-edged glittering thing colored orange and blue. It had suddenly appeared in Anjan's hand. The magemace smashed into the side of Zarla's head, dropping her where she stood.

"Not in the mood for conversation," grumbled Adarlak.

Anjan bent and slung the inert form over one shoulder.

Ranna twisted them away.

Trash Din Pit.

"I am Zwar witch Surlindar," stated the tall woman just

after halting the other. The many rings on her hands glittered with an inward light.

"I am Occiis witch Ferder," came the angry reply. "Out of my way! I have none with Zwar."

"Not true," stated Surlindar, enclosing her in crystal clear wrap tight. "Faan witch Ripple wants you." She took her prize away.

Der Der Tanback.

Long after a late meal, they returned to their room.

The single bed was enormous. It didn't appear all that large as the room dwarfed everything in it. A number of tables and ornate chests were scattered here and there.

Abda sat back against the head board, pillow shoved behind her back, legs straight out, and smiled at her. "Very comfortable. Nice meal. Very luxurious living for a warrior Princess."

Chyndra hung her sword and belt over the back of a chair sitting near the side of the bed. "Warriors do not only sleep on rocks and dirt." She sat on the edge of the bed, and began to remove her boots. "So enjoy it. We travel early tomorrow."

She stood, made a neat stack of her clothes and crawled onto and under the covers on the bed. "Make room. One side or the other. Not in the middle."

Abda rolled to one side and sat on that edge of the bed. She dumped her clothes in a heap and slipped under the covers. Then she worked her way toward the center and upward, her head popping out not far from Chyndra's. "Room for many."

Chyndra yawned. "Go to sleep."

Abda nodded, rolled onto her side, and kissed the side of

Chyndra's face.

Chyndra snapped up right. "What are you doing?"

"Slinth custom, toy-warrior."

"Go to sleep."

Abda nodded, sprawled flat, and closed her eyes.

Chyndra lay back, rearranged the covers, and wondered about her new companion.

The tiny blue-green dragon hung from the ceiling and watched them. Then it disappeared.

Bahn Dohr Tohr. A Large Room.

Ripple sat in a chair set against one wall.

Hanred stood next to her chair, one hand resting lightly on the high back, and watched them arrive.

This room had been selected from among the many many in a little used, mostly closed wing of the castle.

They entered the room in as many varieties of witch entrance as there were witches arriving. Each deposited their prize and walked to one side after nodding greetings to Ripple.

She nodded in return and told each name to Hanred who would remember them for later. Later she would pay witch debt.

Soon along the stone back wall, across the bare stone floor, across the floor from Ripple, stood a number of very very unhappy witches, all Occiis and Quana.

Raft flashed in and dumped a staggering woman in front of Ripple. "Quana witch Clan head Fasna," she announced, waving away all the wands, coating her catch in healing, slow healing.

Raft stood by Hanred's side. "Hayou, Hanred." She

popped up and kissed him on one cheek.

"Hayou, Raft. Where's your's? The cat-folk healer."

"On Dan Wittle. Small outbreak of Nip Rasp." She stood in front of Ripple. "Call. If need." She was gone.

Ripple looked at Fasna. "Are all Quana here?"

Fasna slowly turned. She scanned the angry looking faces, turned back. "No."

"Who?"

"Frakna."

"Where?"

"Know not. She went fast wander. Sudden sudden."

"Hum hum." Ripple fingered a yellow wand.

"Clan heads do not control," grumbled Fasna, carefully watching that wand.

Ripple pointed. "There stand!"

"Enter?" whispered the passing breeze.

"Enter," replied Ripple in a most non-witch gentle tone of voice, startling many of the witches present.

Reep folded in with another witch who carefully did not look at her.

"Occiis witch Clan head Zarna," sighed soft shadow as Reep glided up to Ripple, bending close and kissing her on the forehead. Straightening up, she nodded and drifted over to stand next to Hanred. "Hayou, Hanred," whispered the night.

He smiled at her. "Hayou, Silent One. Stay some?"

She nodded. "Mine is working. There is time." She looked around the room. Witches tried not to jerk and twitch, but all averted their eyes. Those who did not recognize her had heard Hanred's greeting. The Silent One, the slim witch standing so still next to him, so quiet, was legend, the deadliest legend. If she looked at it, and wished it so, if it was alive, it would die. If it was anything else, it would crumble to dust. No being would deliberately make that one unhappy. All wondered how it was that Zarna had survived.

Ripple pointed. "There stand!" She waited while Zarna carefully placed herself next to Fasna who wouldn't look at her.

Slowly she stood did Ripple and looked from witch face to witch face until all the snarling and unhappy witches had quieted down, as much as witches ever did.

"Occiis clan thought to bring harm to Faan using witch debt clans Quana and Beris." She pointed to one side. "Now Beris is Faan linked."

One finger crooked and beckoned at the group standing along the side wall. "Clan heads Tanpak, Zwar, Grenzanr, Hinto, Beris, Blue Udaz, Kanikt, all linked to Faan."

She sat on the floor and waited while the others joined her, forming a tight circle. It was a ring of black with exceptions: the Kelly Green of the Grenzanr, the Power Blue with dark trim of the Blue Udaz, the grey and white of the Kanikt.

Ripple looked from blank face to blank face and nodded. "We are many linked." Her eyes flicked over to her eldest sister, Ranna, who stood flanked by her's. "I did ask none but witch to do this thing."

The ring facing her nodded, silently agreeing that witch insult was answered by witch action. While all were linked to mage guilds and the Death Warrior Order, no witch felt completely at ease with them.

Ranna shrugged.

Ripple's eyes flicked toward the other cluster, all the Occiis and Quana. Deep red fire flickered in her enormous black eyes. "Quana owe witch debt to Occiis. Occiis have strange beliefs. What shall we do with our toys?"

Occiis and Quana gasped.

The Quana moved themselves into a separate cluster of worry.

Dark Lakar. The Lands of the Kraznar.

They stood just below the crest of the small ridge, surrounded by the mass of the Tark Green Plain Set. Ahamaezur smiled at him and licked her lips. He could feel the heat radiating from them, the Core Pair, as they stood very close to him. All around, the Set vibrated with the uprising energy of the hunt.

He threw an arm around each waist. They were exactly where they appeared to me, unlike their usual attack mode of indirection. "Everything lives. We need to find out what is going on." He had been talked into this operation by Szart.

They nuzzled his neck and stepped away. And barked orders. The Set flowed in two directions and raced over the top of the ridge to surround the small encampment just beyond. Scouts had found this place. The place where the witch was being held captive.

The Core Pair and the four Prime Males ran to the top, to watch and to bark orders.

Tinker and the rest trotted after them. To stand and to watch.

He looked at Szart. "O.K., now what? This was your idea."

She growled, deep in her throat, "Witches are not held by demons."

Just below them they could see the small encampment now completely surrounded by Tark. Weapons glittered in the early morning light.

Amamaedur pointed. They could see someone, not demon, standing in the center of the encampment, dressed in pale yellow.

"Yellow," gurgled Szart. "Not known."

"You sure that is a witch?"

She nodded.

He sighed. "O.K., let's go down there and see if we can do anything."

Accompanied by the Core Pair and their four Prime Males, they walked down and into the encampment. Sha'gar, Messenger, Fair Morn shifted sideways, weapons ready, a clear space between them and the demon horde.

As they stepped close to the encampment they were met by a large male demon.

Chantal, having joined Szart and Tinker, looked up at it. "Damn ugly," observed Chantal.

"Most kind," it gurgled. It stared down at Szart, and growled, "Small witch, leave! Take these with you."

She kicked it on the front of one crooked leg. "Why are you keeping that witch?"

Baring warped fangs, it leaned over her. "Very ill mannered. It is our duty." Red eyes glanced sideways at Tinker. "This small taste your's?"

"Yep."

"Trade?" It held up four claws. "Tarkle slabs?"

"Nope."

It held up six claws.

"Nope."

The demon straightened and grunted. "Tough pista taste probabably."

Szart kicked the demon again. "I am not tough pista taste!"

Dat walked up, having been wandering around, looking at things. She had been watching the demon conversation and had decided to join them. She had persuaded Tinker to take her along, big. Normally, she was a very tiny figure who slept inside her ornate ring. She had never explained to Tinker how that was possible. Other than the fact that an injinn could do whatever she wished to do. She had come along as she felt that she might be able to help them in any demon interactions that they might have. Demons always talked to indjinns.

"Great Master?"

"Go ahead." He yanked Szart back and glared down at her. "And don't growl at me, either."

Sgenn stood quietly, arms tucked inside the baggy sleeves of her grey robe. Dark things lurked just below the surface of the ground, ready to react. She had called them up from the deep below.

Dat rubbed one hand over the demon's chest. "Most handsome."

It sniffed and stared at her. "Indjinn?"

"Indeed."

"Lovely eyes. Beautiful claws."

She smiled, showing her long canines. "Why do you have that strange witch in your encampment?"

The demon sucked in a deep breath, expanding his chest. Scales crackled and popped. "Demon pledge."

"Most unusual. Tell me of this pledge."

The demon nodded as it gently ran a glistening talon over her torso. "Long long long many past during the Great Witch-Demon Wars, the tribe was near finished. A witch saved the few and today the Kraznar are. The pledge to that witch and to that clan holds forever. They gave us that thin taste. To keep unharmed until called for." He pointed one warped talon at Szart. "That unpleasant thing is not one of them." The demon's gaze shifted to the surrounding Tark. "We will take many."

Dat rubbed the demon's round belly. "What clan are you pledged to? We would speak with them.

"Ooooooo," moaned the demon as her hand slid here and there. "Beris."

Szart yanked her hand free from Tinker's grasp and stomped over. "I am Faan witch Szart, ugly lump! We are clan linked Faan Beris.

The demon licked its lips. He had been drooling. And nodded at her. "I am. Most kind." And tapped the short witch on top of the head with one splintered talon. "Why didn't you say so? First?" It looked at Dat and indicated Szart. "This little taste is untrained taught."

Tinker hurried over and wrapped his arms around Szart before she could do anything. "Hold it!" he hissed at her.

He looked up at the demon "We came for her, that witch that you hold. The cross link means that this one may ask you to do that, correct?"

The demon nodded. "You may take it. It was very bothersome listening to it crying and sobbing every all time and day." It spun and barked something.

An even larger demon grabbed the witch in yellow and

carried her over and handed her to Tinker.

He hastily grabbed the body as it was thrust at him.

Smoke stepped over and lifted the witch from his arms, set her on her feet, and stared into her eyes. "Frightened. Confused."

Szart touched the witch and shuddered. "Spell drained."

"Untouched," rumbled the demon.

"Let's go home," suggested Tinker, heading back the way that they had come.

The Core Pair looked around, barked orders. The Tark Set flowed up and over the edge of the ridge toward the hole that they had poured through. As the Set milled around Tinker, he thanked the Core Pair, got his neck nuzzled and nipped gently, and watched as they made ready to depart this demon elseplace.

He looked at Szart. "Can you take us home from here?"

Szart grabbed one of Sha'gar's hands and nodded.

The demons watched the Tark leave and the others swirl away in a puff of black. They told each other that they hoped that the little nasty taste never visited or asked them for anything else, ever again.

Learning Things

Der Der Tanback.

Her eyes popped open. The soft light told her that it was early morning. She could feel someone in their room. She felt it, a definite presence. Lurching upright she quickly looked from the chair where her sword hung to the chair where their visitor sat. Smiling at her.

"Who are you?" she snapped.

"Eulin. Your sister." She stood, walked over and sat on the edge of the bed and nodded at the still sleeping figure of Abda. "Most Vander."

"Sister?"

Eulin nodded. "Same father. Different mothers."

She bowed her head. "First Greetings to the daughter of The Vander Lord." She smiled. "Mother told me of you." She held up her hand, forefinger extended. A tiny blue-green dragon flew down and perched on it. "I sent him to find you." With her other hand she scratched the tiny dragon on top of the head.

"Well done, tiny one. You may return home." It chirped and flashed away.

"You do not look witch." Her sister was dressed in garments of a soft purple hue.

Eulin smiled again. "I am not witch. I am the Future Heart of the Vanderlaine Mage guild, trained as Dragon

Master." Her eyes slid sideways. "And I see that you are a warrior. I met your mother, Father's Queen Lurin, and your brother and his princess as well."

Chyndra slid from the bed and began to dress. "Mother didn't mention you. Neither did father."

"He tends to forget things like that." She watched Chyndra as she yanked on her boots.

"There are others you know."

"Others? Besides Frahn and you?"

"Rorx. Je'leel."

"I met her."

"And Sedeem."

"Rorx and Sedeem?"

"One brother, one sister." Eulin indicated Abda. "Who is your, ummmm, companion?"

"Abda. We are traveling together."

"Very nice."

Chyndra frowned at her. "We are only traveling together. Nothing else." She walked around the bed, leaned in, and shook the sleeping form. "Up, up, up, up, up, up, up, up!"

Abda woke, smiled, stretched, and yawned. "It is early." Then smiled warmly at Eulin. "Lovely," she purred and nodded at Chyndra who glowered at her.

"NO!" snapped Chyndra. "This is Eulin, my sister." And wondered why everyone was always jumping to the wrong conclusion.

Abda sat up, eyes roving over Eulin. "Warm touch, Eulin, warm touch."

Eulin stood, walked back to her chair, sat and watched Abda as she crawled from the bed and dressed. "What is she?"

"Slinth," answered Chyndra and Abda.

Eulin looked at Abda. "True?"

"I am." Abda buttoned the last button on her shirt. "You?"

"Vander."

"Eh ah. One of them." She stepped closer to Chyndra. "I am your sister's. Touch me not!"

Brows furrowing, Eulin stood and stared at her, at them.

"She was given to me as a servant," explained Chyndra, watching Eulin carefully, "by a person I should have hacked into small bits."

Abda smiled. "She rescued me."

"Perhaps," suggested Eulin, "we could go get something to eat and you can explain what my sister has been doing." She was really curious. Slinth were so rare that most folk felt they were nothing but child tell-tales. But she knew better. One of the first Vanderlaine, one of the founders of the guild, had been slinth. The Vander owed much of the foundations of their body magic and spells to that slinth. It would be very interesting to talk with this one, this real one. She followed Chyndra and Abda out, down the hall, and outside and across the open space to the nearby inn.

Termion Ianan.

The Sardna stood and delivered its report.

Aldin Cease nodded. "Keep searching." He watched the small creature stride from the room. "It is very strange that no trace track can be found. Someone, or something, most powerful must be involved."

Fula gurgled agreement. Zim shimmered.

Aldin Cease picked up a small globe and peered in. "Word comes that the Faan witch clan have taken both the Occiis and Quana witch clans from their elseplaces. Were all removed?"

Fula shimmered silver. "Occiis Zepta and Quana Frakna are not held. The Faan many link are greatly agitated." Everyone in the room knew that greatly agitated witches were flash lethal.

"Except the clan Beris. They are calm."

"Can something safe speak with the Faan clan head?"

"All linked gather in a guarded space," gurgled Zim. "None would dare attempt approach."

Aldin Cease nodded. "How did Narl Tra manage to lose her?"

Der Der Tanback.

Narl Tra told everything he had heard to Tzar Maga. The live jewel he had set among the other gems on her scabbard had activated as soon as she had exited the building. So far the only interesting information was that the warrior was sitting in front of the inn over there talking with her sister.

The surprise was the sister. Both of them wondered how the sister had found the sister.

Narl Tra touched the live gem on his left ear lob. Its twin was listening on her scabbard. "Nothing said so far explains the sister. The conversation mostly concerns the past and, ummmm, recent adventures."

"It will work all places?"

"Yes. Wherever they go."

Tzar Maga smiled. "A good thing. It is bothersome that the other remains lost."

Narl Tra agreed and went upstairs to peer, ever so carefully across the street, through a window and to listen.

Grandeville. Tinker's Place.

They were all settled in the large living room.

Chicken and Szart were talking softly to Zepta, and, aided by Smoke slowly bringing the witch from deep inside where she had retreated.

Sha'gar had managed to nudge him into a corner of one couch.

"So?" he asked, slipping his arm around her. "What's going on? This time?"

"Not much," she grumbled, making sure that he could see the ornate ring she wore on one finger. Chantal had handed it to her as soon as they had arrived back from the demon lands.

"With her," he grumbled back.

"Witch ptar nap," she mumbled.

Smoke looked over at them. "A few days of rest."

He nodded. And sighed. He really didn't like having a stray witch hanging around. Things always seemed to happen when they did.

Chantal and Messenger handed around mugs while Fair Morn and Early Dawn poured coffee or cocoa. Dat had gone upstairs to visit with her daughter, Je'leel. Chicken headed for the kitchen to start dinner, aided by Sgenn, leaving Szart with Zepta.

Zepta carefully looked around the room and at the people in it. "Where am I?"

"Safe safe," murmured Szart. She knew that a spell drained witch would be very nervous and frightened. When

Zepta recovered some more then they would ask her why those demons had been holding her. Szart floated more heal over her and watched the nervousness settle just a little more.

Niveous Lily.

She sat in the chair where she had been placed. She could barely feel her arms and her legs but they wouldn't work. Neither would her vocal cords. He had told her that it was because he didn't want her to cast spells. He was being much more careful and cautious than had been his brother.

So, she had sat, waiting, and had watched the package sail gently into the room from somewhere and settle to the floor, right in the middle of the ornate rug.

And, long time after, he entered the room, ice white robes whirling around him, ice white with a faint undertone of blue. He stopped and stared. "What is this?" And glowered at her. "Did you do this?"

She slowly wobbled her head.

He laughed. "Of course not, of course. You can hardly do anything. You are my very own black clad thing to do with as I choose." He walked over and peered down at the package. "So what can this be? And how came it to be here?"

Calling in a servant, he ordered her to open it. She knelt next to the thing, a many sided box, and untied the gleaming golden ribbon twined around it. Then she unfolded the top pedals, and leaped back, crashing into a chair. "Ahhhhhhhh booo dab ta!"

The pale face stared up at them. It was a head, not too neatly separated from its body.

He peered down at it. "Ehhhhhh. Sooooo, Ampa, who

did you make so angry?"

The head didn't answer. It had been dead too long. After ordering the servant to dispose of the box and its contents, he hurried from the room to carefully inspect the ward. And, eventually, he found it. A small spot, once damaged, now self-repaired, just large enough for that grizzly package to enter. Nothing should have been able to do that. Well, he said to himself, almost nothing. It must be time to relocate. Someone knew where he was. And what he had. The delivery of Ampa's head had told him that.

Bahn Duhr Tohr. A Large Room.

Ripple said something and the tight circle shuffled and made two open spaces, one on either side of her, just big enough for someone to sit down. She looked over and beckoned. "Zarna, here. Fasna, there."

The pair carefully walked over to the indicated spots and sat. They made sure that their faces were totally blank and would give nothing away to all those staring eyes.

"Sooooo," hissed Ripple. "Tell why Quana would do this."

Fasna carefully looked at the bare floor in the center of this tight circle of witches. "We owe great witch debt." She paused. "And we believed that spoken by Occiis." She blinked. "I would spare the rest of the Quana. The clan head is followed. The clan head is believed. The clan head will take all."

"Hum hum hum." Ripple looked around the circle and tapped Fasna sharply on one knee. Fasna jerked. "What think the Quana now?"

"We were ill-informed. This witch sees many witch clans,

each unlike the other. Some as different as Quana to Occiis."

"Hum." Ripple nodded. "If the Quana live?"

Fasna stared at her, then quickly recovered her poise. "Witch debt!" She looked up, eyes gliding from impassive face to impassive face, then she turned, body partially twisted around, and looked into those great black Faan eyes. "To all."

Ripple nodded. "The circle agrees. There is no flare between Faan and Quana from this moment." She snapped her fingers and Fasna felt the spells dissipate and heard the low murmurs of her clan members as they felt themselves come free.

"Say," said Fasna, "and it shall so be."

"Frakna!"

Fasna jerked. "Know not! She went wilding. None know where. None!"

"Hum," mumbled Ripple. She nodded. "Stay or go, as Quana wish."

Fasna looked past her at Zarna. "Stay."

Ripple nodded. She scanned the circle again. "Sooooo ," she hissed, "tell why Occiis would do this?"

Zarna shuddered. "Long before long before one always told one that Occiis were true witch. The true witch. And few few were. The Faan birthed strange . . . different. Word came and came again. Faan many linked." She cleared her throat and rasped, "Even mage linked. Even non-users linked. Long before long before one always told one that true witch remained pure, stayed pure." Her eyes darted around the circle. "Not like this, not."

She struggled to contain her reaction. Then she bent forward, back bowing over, staring at the floor. "Not since before the Great Witch-Demon Wars have Occiis bowed to any.

And since, Occiis would not!" She jerked upright, eyes flaring. "I would have the clan survive," she growled as she yanked a long wand from her sleeve and plunged it into her chest.

Witches snapped multi-layers of protection everywhere as Ripple leaped up, snarling, smashing Zarna flat onto her back, yanking the wand free. She beckoned to Reep.

Round Habna.

It was a rather pleasant, but small meadow, edged on one side by a vertical cliff. A gentle breeze floated through the surrounding brush and tickled the tall grass-like vegetation that coated the meadow in deep green.

She stood in the center of the meadow facing the cliff and the dark splotch that marked the mouth of the opening into a vast interior space. It was not a space that one ventured into. One waited, outside, patiently.

So, there she stood, waiting, patiently, more or less. After all, she was a witch and witches were not noted for being very patient.

But, eventually, it slithered out into the sunshine, blinking great orange green eyes. The head lifted, towered high above, and then it asked why she had come.

She answered, using the precise, correct phrases that kept one alive, and that began the learning process.

That is what Frakna hoped to do.

Learn. Not die.

Niveous Lily.

He hurried into the room, ice white robes swirling around him, and jabbed one finger at her, and snarled at the servants,

"Pick her up! Time to travel."

The servants did as ordered, picked her up, chair and all.

He nodded. And in a flash of cold, they were gone. But he left the ward in place. Just as a safety measure.

Termion Ianan.

Aldin Cease nodded, and sighed, as the Sardna finished its report.

"I see," he said, more to himself than to anything else. "One is an ugly mark in some grassy spot, one was stabbed to death, one lost his head."

"It is so."

"And this effectively erased the trail?"

"It is so. Almost."

"Almost?"

"We found faint witch trace intersecting all three events. It is being hunted."

"This witch might lead us to that which we seek?"

"Unknown."

"Do not stop. I shall add to the amount paid."

"It is good," stated the strange being as it hurried away.

"Strangely twisted," gurgled Fula.

Zim shimmered agreement.

Aldin Cease leaned back in his chair. "To quote our short hunter, it is so."

Der Der Tanback.

"And you have no idea what happened or who was responsible?"

"No, not really." Chyndra frowned at the tabletop. "But

someone killed the two men who were involved."

"Do the witches know that Seemna is missing?"

Chyndra shook her head. "I don't think so. I have no way to speak to them."

"I could send a message to Ripple." Eulin picked up and slowly chewed on the last fragment of her meal. "I had better stay with you two until this is settled. The witches can get very angry, which is a very mild term for the state they will be in when they find out." She cast protection over Chyndra and Abda. And then sent the message.

Across the open way, upstairs, peering at them through a narrow crack, Narl Tra went very pale, and lurched away to lean against the nearby wall. Rampaging, barely in control, witches were about the worse thing that he could imagine.

Grandeville. Tinker's Place.

"Well," he observed, after all had finished breakfast, "it has been about a week." He nodded at her. "How are you doing?"

"I am healthy," replied Zepta.

"Very witch," added Szart.

He nodded. And decided that if that were the case then he could ask. So he did. In a manner of speaking. "Tell us why those demons were holding you."

Zepta jerked, stared around the table at all those watching eyes, nodded, and did.

Bahn Duhr Tohr. A Large Room.

Reep slammed her hand into the middle of Zarna's chest and watched her eyes pop open.

Ripple jerked and snarled. Szart had sent. Hard. And angry. She didn't explain, just demanded to know of her youngest sister.

Leaning back on her legs, Ripple watched the Occiis witch slowly sit up. "My daughter," she hissed at Zarna. "Just sent hard and angry. She found out about the Occiis and their false beliefs. My daughter, like all my daughters, are witch, very witch, and are very, very hard to control."

Zarna nodded. "Most sorry sorry." She sat straighter. "We did nothing. That daughter could not be located." She stared deep into Ripple's eyes. "Could not." She leaned forward and hissed at Ripple, "Something else must be involved."

Ripple stared back. And blinked. "What would you?"

"Witch debt," stated Zarna. "Great witch debt to all links." She leaner closer. "Something not-witch to seek the newest daughter. Know you something?"

"Hum hum." Ripple's eyes half-closed as she thought. Then they popped open. She crooked one finger and said to Nuart, "Would certain demons do this?"

Zarna gasped and snarled at the Beris clan head, "You! You took Zepta with demons?"

Nuart shrugged. "She will be returned." And sent the call. Asking for Zepta, and said to Zarna, "In few few."

The demon popped in. Every witch in the room threw protection as wands and other devices appeared in their hands. It ignored them all and looked at Nuart. "No have. Taken by a small taste, a small very unpleasant taste and a group of very strange accompanied by a great gobmob of horrid Tark." It swivelled and snarled at Ripple, "That unpleasant taste was one of your smell."

The air crackled around Ripple. The demon eyed her and licked its lips.

"Which witch?" she demanded of the monster.

"This size." The demon held one hand about where it thought the top of the head would be. "This size."

"And others were with her?"

The demon nodded, great ears flopping back and forth.

"Who?"

It began to drool, and hastily wiped its mouth with a large fragment of leather yanked from a back pocket. "A beautiful indjinn. Lovely purple eyes, nice fangs, but she clipped her claws."

"Ptar rak ptar par," snarled Ripple. She looked over at Zarna. "My daughter, Szart, took her from these things."

"Your daughter?"

"Yesssssssss," hissed Ripple. She sent to Szart. And turned her attention back to the demon and Nuart. "Ask!"

Nuart began to talk with the demon after making it lower its head so she could speak low into one great ear, bending one great ear tip over and down. She finished, and released the ear.

The demon licked its lips. "May we eat everything we find, except?"

"NO! We will decide after."

"You are hard hard," it spat as it swirled and disappeared.

Nuart nodded at Ripple. "They will seek."

Grandeville. Tinker's Place.

Szart leaped to her feet, snarling and growling. And

glared at Zepta. "My sister is missing. Did you do this?" A long black wand crackled in her hand.

Zepta layered on protection. "No! None did. We were seeking. But not finding."

Szart stalked around and kicked him, not too gently, on the side of one foot, and stared at him until he drew up his legs making a lap so she could sit there, grumbling low in her throat.

"Now what's going on?"

"Damn witches," grumbled Chantal in their general direction. "What is going on is that they are always a pain in the butt." She looked over at Zepta whose mouth was open as she stared at Chantal. "And not a word from you either!" She stomped from the room. "Gonna go clean my gun."

Chicken looked at Smoke who nodded. They left, taking Fair Morn and Early Dawn with them. It was time to pack their travel gear. They all felt it.

Wrapping both arms around her, he nodded. "So, short stuff, what do we know, if anything?"

"Dip dip ptar," she grumbled.

"Sure. What else?"

"Mother feels a certain vague with Seemna. No send works. She must be missing, magic bound missing."

"Un huh. So?"

"You are being rak tak!"

"You are being more than vague if not obscure and totally unclear."

She growled.

So he tickled her. "Tell me something that we can do. She was with Chyndra. Now she isn't?"

"Know not."

"Ah ha."

Sgenn, sitting in the overstuffed chair, quietly watching them, nodded, and sent something to find out.

He ticked a handy rib. "Is Chyndra in trouble? Danger? What?"

"Know not," grumbled Szart.

"We will know. Soon," said Sgenn in a gentle, calm tone of voice.

Heads snapped around to stare at Sgenn. She smiled a soft half-smile at Tinker. "Soon."

He nodded. "O.K., we will wait. And see." And kissed Szart on the check. "And you, calm down. And try and find out something useful."

"Yesssssssssss." Szart looked at Zcpta. "Your clan head wants you!" And threw her out in a soft puff of darkness.

Niveous Lily.

She stood and gently tested the ward with a cautious fingertip. Nodding to herself, she stepped back, drew down the power and blasted a gaping hole in it. And stepped through.

And began to search through the vast structure for the one that she sought. And smiled to herself as she thought what she would do to the one responsible for the agitation that she felt.

Fir Ter In.

He jerked and glared in her direction. Somehow it must be her fault. He couldn't understand how it could be, but it just must be. Although she didn't appear capable of doing anything that he could detect.

But he had felt it. Someone, something, had punched a hole in the ward that he had ever so carefully constructed around Niveous Lily. He would have to add something new to this place, something wonderfully unpleasant.

The great black eyes watched him from that carefully controlled expressionless face. He nodded at her and laughed. Whatever it was that she was thinking about, it would do her no good.

In a swirl of white, ice cold white, he hurried from the room to add to the ward that protected this place, a place that he wished to keep as safe as possible.

She looked down at her limp right arm and at the right hand lying so loosely in her lap. And watched her index finger make a very slight twitch. Leaning her head back against the high back of the chair she watched the only door to the room and concentrated on her task.

Bahn Duhr Tohr. A Large Room.

She thumped down in a swirl of yellow with crimson streaks encased in black. She stared at the circle sitting there, gasped, and called down all the protection that she knew.

"Stop that!" hissed a tall witch dressed all in black.

"You are safe," said Zarna. "Come, sit here. We must talk, Zepta. This is Ripple." She indicated the witch that had hissed at her.

Zepta jerked. And cautiously, very cautiously sat near Zarna. Then they talked.

Der Der Tanback.

Their meal was done and they sat, relaxed, and talked,

Chyndra and Eulin. Abda listened.

Suddenly Chyndra's head snapped around. Something dark, mostly shadow, all bent, twisted angles, appeared. And disappeared. "What was that?"

Eulin laughed. "Our Father must be worried about you."

Chyndra stared at her, mouth failing open. "That thing was . . . Father? My Father?"

"No. That was a, ummmmm, servant from the deep down of Sgenn's, one of your, ahh, mothers. Just checking, I suppose."

"Sgenn? My Mother? Sent that?"

Eulin nodded. "Guess they didn't explain much, did they?"

Chyndra sat straighter. "No, they did not! I shall certainly speak to them about things like that!" It was a very Princess Royal pronouncement.

"Allow me." Eulin waved over a waiter, ordered some new refreshments, and began.

Across the street, Narl Tra went pale, lurched backwards, and fell into a handy chair. What he was hearing was almost beyond belief. Almost. But he had traveled widely. And in traveling widely he had heard tales in many elseplaces, tales which he had discounted as some sort of fantasy story told by strange populations.

Now what he was hearing, ever so casually told, indicated that it was no fantasy tale that he had heard, here and there, and that this Princess Warrior and her sister were related to those beings that he had heard about.

As Eulin continued her explanation of what she called the mothers to her sister, Narl Tra began to wonder whether it might not be a very smart thing to do to forget trying to find that witch and move on to other endeavors. He wished to live to a very old age.

"Perhaps they can find Seemna?" asked Chyndra.

"No need to bother them." Eulin held up her hand, forefinger extended. And there it perched, a tiny blue-green dragon. "Here." She extended her hand and arm over the table to Chyndra. "Tell him all about where you and Seemna were lost."

Chyndra carefully reached out her hand, finger extended, and watched. The tiny dragon hopped onto her finger and peered at her from one glittering yellow eye. She told it. It disappeared.

"Well," asked Eulin. "Shall we go now?"

Chyndra shrugged.

Eulin stood. "Allow me." And as soon as Chyndra and Abda stood next to her, she took them out. In a soft puff of violet mist.

Across the street Narl Tra heaved himself to his feet and stumbled downstairs to relate all that he had heard and to argue with Tzar Maga. This time he intended to win the argument.

Grandeville. Tinker's Place.

They were sitting, lying, and sprawling, in the large living room. In chairs, on couches, and the floor. It was evening and they were relaxing, each in their own fashion.

Tinker was reading a book.

Sgenn was using his lap for a pillow, her legs kicked over one arm of the couch. One of the cats, curled into a ball, was using her stomach as a resting place.

"Chyndra," she stated softly, interrupting his reading. "Is eating breakfast and talking with Eulin. And accompanied by another person, a very pretty female person. All are relaxed and healthy. Seemna is not with them."

"Ummmmm," he replied, not exactly interrupted.

Szart stomped over and glared down at Sgenn. "My sister was not there?"

"She was not there. They were very calm. If Seemna was in danger would they be so calm?"

"Unlike a certain short witch." said Tinker, now interrupted.

"Rak tak!" snapped Szart, glaring at him.

"Witch coarse," observed Sha'gar from one of the other couches.

"Nice expression." Tinker frowned into Szart's frown.

"Witches all need to get their butts kicked," grumbled Chantal from the dining room. She had completely disassembled her revolver, and was carefully cleaning and oiling every part. Now she began to put it back together. And then to stack boxes of ammunition next to the holster and the ready to go weapon. Reloading the revolver she stuffed it into the holster, stood, and swung the wide belt around her hips. The ammunition was special loads with heavy slugs.

When she shot something, she intended that it would feel real pain.

"Well, short and agitated," he asked. "What do we know? Anything more than this afternoon? About Seemna? Chyndra is certainly in no trouble and is perfectly safe with Eulin around."

"Ptar rip dir," grumbled Szart. "No. But something is not witch well. And mother is not telling."

"Can we assume that your Mother knows what she is doing?"

"Poo tak!" she suggested, dropping into the couch by his free side.

"I'll take that as a big uh-huh." He opened his book, freeing his finger, and went back to the action, and slipped his free arm around her shoulders.

She didn't like detective stories so she didn't mind-share. Instead she began to mentally rehearse one of the banned spells that her Aunt R-Bar had taught her. This one was perfectly vile. It was a very pleasant thought. For a witch. She smiled.

Grandeville. The Greater Downtown Area.

Red and Green were strolling down the sidewalk in the late evening, maintaining the peace and quiet of Greater Downtown Grandeville. They had just left *Big Darlene's* and were headed over to *The Railroad Bar and Grill,* and were just passing *Chen's Chinese.*

"It's been a month since the chili feed arm wresting at B.D.'s," observed Red.

"Uh huh," agreed Green, nudging his partner toward the door of the *Dough To Go,* one of the two doughnut shops in town. The other one was on the other side of the block.

"Maybe," said Red, pointing out his selection to the young woman behind the counter, "we ought to ask Tinker to take Chicken and Smoke bar hopping. He could unleash them and they could find someone to beat up."

Green indicated his choices and told the startled counter girl. "Just kidding. Right, partner?"

"Sure thing, partner." Red paid for everything and handed Green a large cup of coffee.

As they stood outside, Red took a loud sip from his coffee cup. "Wonder why the denizens are being so well behaved?"

"Beat's me." Green ate half of one of his doughnuts and indicated one of the figures walking along across the street. "There's always hope."

Red looked and nodded. "Slick Willie Warter. My, my, my. He must have been released from the county lockup."

So they wandered along in the same direction that Slick Willie was taking.

"Think Tinker and Chantal will come bowling with us next Saturday?"

"Sure." Green took another sip from his cup.

Findings

Fer Ter In.

The servant, a rather pleasant woman with an unhappy expression on her face, carried in a flat bronze tray. It was the late-in-the-day meal for the witch. She brought two meals a day and gently and carefully fed the captive. And massaged her limbs to keep them firm and supple. The massages were not part of her assigned duties. It was just something that she did. Anything to aid the prisoner that would not draw undue attention from the magician. She hated that one with a deep burning anger.

"I am," she whispered carefully, many, many days after they had arrived to this place, "Barla." She spooned in the second course and gently wiped Seemna's chin. "If I could free you, I would. If I could kill him, I would."

She looked into those great black eyes, seeing the glittering fire points deep down, and nodded. "Someday I will find a way." She sighed, "But he is very careful. Very."

Seemna smiled. And her right hand, now freed, moved.

Barla nodded. And quickly gathered up everything as he hurried into the room, just to check that his guest had, once again, been properly fed.

Niveous Lily.

The Sadna slipped through the hole punched in the ward

and carefully began to search.

Two rooms deeper, it paused, jerked, and turned away and out. This was not a safe place to be.

It had felt the wildness in the air, witch rage. Nothing with any sense wished to be near a witch at that flash point.

Deeper inside the vast structure the tiny blue-green peeked from a small hole that it had made in a wall and watched the snarling and growling witch as she carefully searched every inch of the place. It flickered away, following the trace.

Termion Ianan.

The Sadna made its report. And stated that they would go no further.

Aldin Cease nodded and agreed. And paid the full price. Again. It was always a smart thing to do to keep in the good graces of The Sadna.

After the searcher left, he asked, "Who would know about Niveous Lily?"

Fula shimmered gentle. "Ron Tum."

Zim slid away to visit this individual.

Bahn Duhr Tohr. A Large Room.

There was a soft puff of violet mist. The scroll thumped to the floor in front of Ripple.

Witches jerked and hissed.

Ripple picked it up and read the message. "Hum hum. The daughter Chyndra visits with a sister, One of the Vander mage, and knows not what happened to Seemna. The Vander also search."

She rolled a long, black wand back and forth between her

palms. All held their breath as they watched her deep think. The mere thought that magicians were involved was unsettling to the gathered witches and witch clan heads. Even if they were linked. Ripple blinked, and looked across the circle at the slight, still figure, patient as death. "Reep sister, go speak with him. Ask the Grey One to help." She was being deliberately elliptic. She didn't want the rest to know what she was asking for.

Reep nodded.

And was gone.

Just a soft puff of black.

Grandeville. The Bowl and Burger.

They were in the last few frames of the third game, Red and Sandy, Green and Janine, Tinker and Chantal.

The "girls" were bowling, the "boys" were watching. They were tied one game to one game, but it looked like the guys were about to lose the third game in spite of their best effort.

Red drained his pitcher. "Next time."

Green nodded. "Let's go to The Rail this time."

"We could," agreed Tinker. "The chili is all right."

"Slick Willie hangs out there," explained Red.

"We've been keeping an eye on him for the past three weeks," added Green.

They stood and watched their opponents coming up from the alleys, laughing and chattering happily.

"Might as well concede the game," stated Janine, smiling up at Green.

"We always play to the end of the game," he rumbled back. "Right, partner?"

"You betcha," stated Red. He stepped around his wife, Sandy, and gave her a gentle pat in passing. "Might just win. It's close."

"You guys leave anything to drink." Chantal scanned the table.

"We can get more at The Rail," suggested Tinker.

The game was close.

But the guys lost.

So they paid.

And then they headed for their next stop. Tinker and Chantal followed Green's truck in their van.

And they all wondered why the name of the only bowling alley in town kept changing its name.

Grandeville. Tinker's Place.

She faded in, soft shadow, into the middle of the large living room.

Sha'gar looked up. "Hayou, Mother."

"Strong daughter," sighed the darkness. "Where is your's?"

"In town with Chantal."

"And my other daughter?"

"Upstairs."

"I will wait. For him to return." She drifted over and settled on the couch next to Sha'gar. And began to talk with her, telling her everything that had happened and all that she knew concerning Seemna and the witch gathering.

Grandeville. The Railroad Bar and Grill.

"I think that B.D.'s makes better chili." Chantal dumped

hot sauce over her serving.

"They use Smoke's arm wresting buddy's recipe." Tinker wondered whether he ought to order another bowl or not.

Chantal nudged Green in the side with her elbow. She was sitting between him and Tinker. "Who's the sleaze at the bar that keeps staring at my shirt?"

"Not your shirt," said Tinker, reaching for the crackers. "It is the shirt filling."

"Slick Willie," rumbled Green, nudging Janine.

"What?" she asked.

"Nice shirt."

"Who's?" she snarled.

"Your's."

"Pervert!"

He looked over at Red. "Just no pleasing them, is there?"

Red shrugged. And gently laid a massive arm over Sandy's shoulders. "I take the fifth on accounta I don't wanna incriminate myself."

"Smart move, copper," she replied.

"Thought so, counselor."

"Nothing perverted about admiring your shirt!" Green refilled Janine's mug and his. "Pretty nice."

"Well?" she said. "Think so?"

"Uh huh. Always liked plaid."

She looked at him from the corners of her eyes. "Just the shirt, huh?"

"Right." He smiled at her. "What else were we talking about?"

Red quickly suppressed his smile as Sandy kicked the side of his foot.

"We were talking about Chantal's . . . "

"Hold it!" snapped Chantal. "Just because that sleaze over there is staring over here is no reason for this conversation to go any further in that direction than it has already gone."

"Right," agreed Tinker. He drained his mug. "Time for us to head for home, anyhow. See ya, later."

They all headed up and out and went their separate ways.

Inside the bar, Slick Willie looked disappointed.

Doth Lamex. A Place of Healing and Relaxation.

They lounged in the thick grass, having just finished their noon meal, specially ordered.

"A strange place," observed Chyndra.

"This is the safest and most private place in all the universe of universes as well as a healing environment," explained Eulin. She held out her hand. "May I see your sword? And scabbard?"

Chyndra shrugged them off and handed them to her. "Be careful, it is very sharp."

Eulin carefully examined the ornate scabbard and the sword hilt. "Hephira."

"Special made," explained Chyndra. "I asked for plain but the Armorer insisted. He stated quite firmly that this design was the ancient and only proper one for a Princess." She grinned. "So, I agreed."

Eulin nodded. "This blade has been magic'd. Who did that?"

Chyndra stared at her. "Magic'd?"

"Certainly. Haven't you noticed?"

"I thought that I was imagining things." Her brows furrowed. "It must have been that witch teacher, the one that taught Seemna." She stared into the distance. "Before . . . everything happened."

Eulin ran one fingertip gently over a portion of the exposed blade, she had slid it partially out. "Yes. Feels like witch." Shoving the blade back in, she plucked a small gem from the scabbard side.

Chyndra gasped. "Don't do that!"

Eulin held it out, the jewel, still pinched between thumb and forefinger. "Someone, not Hephira, but knowledgeable, put this on your scabbard." She peered at the thing. "This is a live gem. Some nosy person has been spying on you, on us."

She smiled. "Nasty, nasty." And tossed it into the air where it flashed in a small gout of flame. And was gone.

"Narl Tra," suggested Chyndra.

"Probably," agreed Eulin, thinking over all that her sister had told her of that person.

"I like it here." Abda smiled, a very happy smile, not an effect smile.

Eulin stood. "I think that we need to visit your elseplace and ask a certain being for help." She nodded at Chyndra.

Hahn Dohr Kahn. The Realm of the Dragon.

The first tendrils of ice-touched wind tickled over the land and out to sea. And all knew that Ice Time was near.

One of the sea folk fast ships tied up at The Great Quay and discharged a last shipload from the Old Kingdoms for this season. After relocating their ships to the Ice Time Yard where they would soon be hauled ashore, a number of excited sea folk hurried into town and into their inn. And the word spread rapidly.

The fleet had been sighted tacking into the ice wind, headed for home. Runners raced across to their sister town and another up to the Royal's House. Prince Frahn and Irinl, his Princess, had not all that long past returned from their mapping expedition in the interior land of their kingdom's portion of this great island. It would be great news for one and all.

Crowds swarmed around the quay, watching and waiting, anxious to hear what, if anything, had occurred. Little word had been sent by Frinda's Queen, the witch Sook.

Lurin, the Queen, stood, wearing the Royal Colors, white cloak thrown over her shoulders, holding in the excitement that she felt. Frahn and Irinl stood next to her. The trio was surrounded by The Queen's Own, her men-at-arms, and sea folk who had sailed with their Queen on her original trip to seek these lands and later during her coastal exploration voyage.

Her Ship Master squinted at the far horizon and said. "There are only five returning, Majesty. I see one white, one black, and three grey." And even though he had kept his voice low pitched, the soft murmuring rippling outward told all that the news was spreading. People quieted down, all wondering what had happened to that one ship that was not in the returning fleet.

Grandeville. Tinker's Place.

They banged into the house, Tinker and Chantal, and headed for the large living room to see why Reep was visiting. As soon as they were close enough, Smoke had told them that Reep was visiting.

He flopped into his chair and watched Chantal drag another chair around. "Hi, Reep. What's up?"

"The clan," whispered dark shadows, "asks for your help. We, so far, have not been able to locate the missing Seemna. None of the witch links have. Ripple asked me to come."

Szart stared at her Aunt. It was unheard of for a witch or a witch clan to ask for help. It was especially true if that witch happened to be her mother, Ripple, the most rangle of witches.

Tinker sighed and began to worry, a whole bunch. "How?"

"We would ask Sgenn to help . . . search. None else."

"Just search?"

Reep looked at him for long moments, great bottomless eyes swallowing up the light in the room. "Yesssssssss. Just find. We will do anything else." She blinked. The room returned to normal.

Sgenn looked over at him and then at her mother, a soft half-smile on her face.

"What? Mother?" she asked.

"Find your cousin, strange daughter . . . Please?"

Szart gasped.

Deep down, things rumbled and surged upward. "Yes, Mother." Sgenn told them what she wished. The sounds faded away.

Reep stood and drifted soft silent over, bent, and kissed Sgenn's forehead. "Ripple will owe witch debt to all." And faded away.

Chantal stood and crooked one finger at Tinker. "Come'on, Lover. You can tuck me into my beddie." And winked, a slow lecherous wink.

Der Der Tanback.

The argument had been growing louder and louder. It had been going on for quite some time.

Narl Tra was standing, walking back and forth, gesturing wildly. Tzar Maga sat, and glared at him. And so far neither had yielded.

Narl Tra stopped hiking back and forth, stepped close to Tzar Maga, and leaned over, face close to face. "One final comment. Then it is your decision!"

Tzar Maga nodded, forehead almost banging into forehead.

Narl Tra nodded in return. "And then I will decide whether it is time for me to retire or not." He began to whisper very, very softly, the one final piece of information. And straightened up.

"True?" gasped Tzar Maga.

Narl Tra dropped into a nearby chair. "Yes. Most true."

"Then." Tzar Maga cleared his throat. "Then we are no longer interested in that particular young woman." He stood. "Allow me to buy you a great meal and as much liquid as we can stand at the finest establishment."

Hahn Dohr Kahn. The Realm of the Dragon. Deep In the Interior.

The stood in a narrow valley that headed straight into the flank of the enormous mountain, a cone shaped ancient volcano.

"Mount M'Ban," stated Eulin. She pointed at the dark shadow mouth of a large cave. "That way." She started walking up the slight slope and inside.

Casting light, she led them a twisting and turning path, deeper and deeper into the heart of the rock mass.

Abda stayed very close to Chyndra and stared at their surroundings, what little that they could see of them in the soft violet light hovering around Eulin.

They turned a sharp corner and entered a vast cavern, a vast hollow space, that was mostly black on black. Seen from high above, the trio was a mere dot of violet light slowly traversing the smooth floor. Far to one side, deep red glowed from a crevice in the floor.

Eulin stopped. "I will talk with her. First. Stay calm. You are safe." She waggled one hand. "Stay here." She walked off in the direction of a hill rising shadow vague from the stone floor. "Wake up," she called. "You have visitors." As she stepped closer to the hill, a wide, green disk appeared, close to the floor.

Abda grabbed Chyndra's arm. "It is an eye."

"It is wider than my sword is long," observed Chyndra.

"Who disturbs my sleep," hissed something large.

"Eulin."

They all could hear the sniffing sound. "Ahhhhhhh, it is The Dragon Master. And two others." The other eye appeared. "A warrior," observed the deep voice. "And a slinth. Thought that they had all disappeared."

"I would like your help," said Eulin.

"You ask? Not command?"

"Yes. Ask."

"Most strange. For a Dragon Master." A foreleg reached past her and snatched Chyndra and Abda off the floor and lifted them up and up, close to the monsters's head now towering high above Eulin.

"A dragon," gasped Abda.

"I am M'Ban. Who are you?"

"Abda."

"Chyndra, Princess."

M'Ban huffed laughter. "Griz, griz, griz. You, Chyndra Princess, smell like the Queen, my Queen Lurin."

"My Mother."

"Please to meet you, Princess Chyndra. I am your Mother's Royal Dragon. Thus I am your Royal Dragon as well. You wear my emblem on your shirt. Do you require help as well?"

Chyndra nodded. "Yes. It is as my sister stated."

M'Ban gurgled. The sound rumbled off walls and ceiling, echoed back from distant chambers. "It has been a long time since I aided anyone other than that grumpy Hephira, Princess E'Nilt." She sat back on her haunches and picked up Eulin, holding her near the others. "Sooooo, how may I aid you sisters?"

Eulin explained. Chyndra added details here and there.

Eventually M'Ban set them down and followed them outside.

Bazzle. Trico Town.

Zim oozed into existence in the well tended garden. "Ron Tum," it gurgled.

The short, wide, thick, and rather short man looked at the shimmering column. "What kind of visitor are you?"

"Fula."

"Eeee a ha! A Fula." He sat on the stone bench. "Something?"

"I am Zim."

"Zim. What?"

"What kind of thing owns Niveous Lily?"

"A magician. Crazed. Bent strange. Powerful."

"Name?"

"Puartor. A White. Last of the three brothers."

"Three?"

"Parquar witch tangled and was done horrible after stealing one. Nartor vanished."

"What witch clan did he steal from?"

"Faan. Now the most tangled, coursing in new directions."

Zim shimmered. "Puartor. It seems he does as his brother."

Ron Tum nodded. "If so, then he is soon to be no more. Clever beings would stay far clear of that magician. Angry witches freeing one of their own tend to not discriminate." He leaned forward and lowered his voice to a more confidential tone. "It is heard that one of the Faan read the Book of Banned Spells. And that the clan head has a vast library of arcana, some spells in that collection are almost beyond control."

Zim oozed away.

Fer Ter In.

Barla set the last dish on the small table and smiled at Seemna. "I use special ingredients. These foods will raise your energy level. If you break free, kill him!"

Seemna nodded.

With a low earth rumble it rose from deep down, all odd angles, darker than a nightmare. Empty eye sockets stared at them.

Barla shook, barely able to stand. "He sent it to kill us."

Slowly, Seemna shook her head.

Barla grabbed one her arms. "No? Who could send such a thing?"

He raced into the room, the air crackling around him, and leaped back out of the room, screaming.

It sank down and into. Barla collapsed.

Puartor peered around one edge of the doorway. "How did that thing get in here?" He stalked into the room and glared at Barla. "SPEAK!"

She struggled to her feet and pointed, one quivering finger. "It just came up, passing through the tiles." She stared at the unbroken floor and then at him. "What was it?"

His hand snapped out and clamped around her neck. "That thing was from deep down. Why are you still alive?" And released her.

Gasping for breath, she shook her head. "It just stared. At us. And went down."

"Must have eaten someone else," he mumbled, leaning forward and yanking Seemna's blouse open. "Guess you are getting enough to eat."

Seemna slowly nodded.

"Good." He looked at Barla. "Good work. Maybe I will let you sleep with me. You can be second." He smiled, an oily, sly smile. "After I enjoy the limp witch."

He pointed. "In two days, bathe her. Use the special oils and lotions. I think that it is time that I enjoy what I have been feeding and caring, for ever so long. Wonder if she is fertile?" He swirled around and hurried from the room. To his study. To think. There had to be some way to seal the floors.

Grandeville. Tinker's Place.

She slipped into his room, soft and silent, a grey shadow. It had been six days since Reep had visited.

Two green spots appeared in the dark. "Oh," said Messenger. The green spots blinked. "Is something the matter?" To her the room was as bright as day.

Sgenn walked over and knelt next to him, next to the king-sized bed set flush to the floor. "No. I know where Seemna is." She nudged a large lump under the covers, not too gently.

And eventually was successful.

His head poked out. "Ummm?"

She gave him another heavy shaking.

He slid further out and up and back, to lean against the wall. "Well? What?"

Messenger rummaged around in the bed and found her pajama top and slipped it on.

"I found Seemna," stated Sgenn. "She is with another female and is being held by a magician dressed in white."

"White?" He remembered their involvement with Parquor the White. "Another one?"

"Yes," agreed Sgenn. "Another one."

The door banged open and Sha'gar hurried inside and knelt next to Sgenn.

"I called her," explained Sgenn.

Messenger finally found and yanked on her pajama bottoms. And stood. "I'll start the coffee makers." She headed for the kitchen.

"I called Mother." Sha'gar cast light, soft red glow, not to bright, easy on eyes that had been staring into the darkness. It was almost 3:00 a.m.

He glowered at them. "Couldn't this have waited until morning?"

Sgenn handed him his pajamas. "It is morning."

"Normal morning," he grumbled.

"Ummmmm," said Sgenn.

"No," replied Sha'gar. "Our cousin has been held for weeks, many many."

"That magician needs killing," added Sgenn, smiling a soft half-smile.

"Tell Reep to wait in the living room," he growled, yanking on his pajamas and standing. "Too crowded in here already."

"Heh," said Sha'gar.

"Heh heh," agreed Sgenn as they followed him from the bedroom

Sha'gar leaned close to her sister. "I will give Messenger my turn. For the interruption."

"Hum hum," observed Sgenn.

"Hum," agreed Sha'gar.

The silent, slim, absolutely still figure waited for them in the large living room. She was dressed all in black, black robe with the hood thrown back. Several of the lamps were on. The great black eyes looked at them. "Daughters?"

Messenger hurried in with a tray bearing cups and a steaming coffee pot. She served.

Sgenn began to explain all that she had found out and how to exactly find the elseplace where Seemna was being held.

"Witch debt," sighed the night. "Ask Ripple for anything." Reep faded away in a wisp of black.

Messenger stared at them eyes wide and round. "Oh, my!

Do we need anything?"

"No!" snapped Tinker, dropping into one of the couches, beckoning to Messenger. She settled by his side. "No," he repeated and glowered at the other two. "Right?"

Sha'gar shrugged.

Sgenn shrugged.

Chantal wandered in, more asleep than awake, eyes narrow slits, crashed down by his other side, and leaned heavily against him. "Damn early for this kind of stuff," she mumbled, holding out one hand.

Sha'gar handed her a cup. Sgenn filled it. Then she refilled his cup and sat in a chair, setting the pot on a small table. Sha'gar sat in another chair.

And slowly, the rest of them filtered into the room.

And eventually, breakfast was prepared and all watched the sun rise above the mountain range on the far eastern edge of the valley.

Bahn Duhr Tohr. A Large Room.

She faded in, silent shadow.

And drifted through and around clusters of witches, to stop in front of her older sister.

"Your daughter has been located," sighed soft shadow to Ripple.

Ripple shocked most of the witches in the large room. She hugged Reep and kissed her on the forehead, in public. "They may ask for anything."

"I told them that," breathed the night. And then Reep told her everything that Sgenn had related.

When she finished her tale, Ripple spun away and began

to tell the gathered witches exactly how they would proceed.

It would take them some time to prepare.

Hahn Dohr Kahn. Realm of the Dragon.

They stood in a large open meadow.

The four of them.

Three people and one dragon.

M'Ban filled most of the meadow, her head propped on her foreleg. "Tell me, Princess Warrior, what you have been doing to lose your friend, the witch, this way. And then I wish to hear from the slinth."

Eulin hoped up and onto one great paw. "Do it. Dragons are very curious, enjoy such tales, and won't budge until they are satisfied" She grinned at the others. "Dragons have a different sense of time."

Chyndra jumped up and sat next to Eulin and waited until Abda had joined them. Then she began to tell M'Ban her tale.

As she started, Eulin cast a barrier around them to keep out the ice cold wind.

Fer Ter In.

Seemna smiled at Barla. Her facial muscles were fully functioning now. Of course the smile was very not-witch.

Barla gasped. And hastily set out the early day meal. "What?" she whispered.

Slowly, carefully, Seemna formed the words with lips long unused for speaking.

"They are coming?" Barla stared at her. "They are coming? Here?"

Seemna nodded.

Barla fed her another small morsel and leaned close to wipe her lips. "Who?" she whispered. "Who is coming?"

Seemna smiled. This time it was a pure witch smile.

Barla nodded, and laughed. She understood that smile, a pure witch smile, a smile that indicated sudden, or prolonged, horrible death. A smile like that could empty a very large town as all fled to save themselves from the chaos about to be delivered. "He doesn't know?"

Seemna's eyes slid from side to side.

"Good!" She smiled and opened another food container. "Whatever happens, I want to watch." She spooned out a chosen morsel. "I prepared this special special. Chew it well."

As Seemna did, Barla began to run her hands up and down the witch's legs and thighs. "Good tone," she mumbled as she worked.

She picked up her charge and gently laid her on the bed, pulling the serving table over. She slipped another morsel into the witch's mouth. And began to massage her stomach and lower torso. "You are in good shape. When this spell is released you will be stiff but you will not be feeble." She reached up and slid her hand here and there. "Forgive me, witch. But I had to know."

Sitting Seemna in a chair Barla leaned close and whispered ever so softly, "When we are freed you may beat me for taking such liberties." She slowly buttoned the open shirt. "Perhaps you could use a faithful and loyal servant?"

Through the rest of the meal Barla's eyes never looked into Seemna's.

Bahn Duhr Tohr. The Quarters of the Royal Advisors.

Ripple stood in the middle of the room in their private quarters and stared into the eyes of her mate-for-life. He stared back. And cleared his throat.

"Well?" she asked.

"Midnight Delight. I believe that what you want is in a certain volume in there with the rest of those dusty tomes." He kissed her.

"What?"

"That book has never been opened. I have never heard of anyone ever opening that thing. Terrible terrible is inscribed inside."

"Show me this book."

"You will be careful. More careful than you have ever been?"

"Of course."

"I have heard you say that before."

"I am still here."

He turned, walked over, and opened the door to the storeroom where all those things resided. He pointed at a large volume that sat by itself. "That one."

She stepped close and touched it with one tenuous fingertip. "Hum hum."

"Ripple witch!" he snapped.

She looked at him, red flare flicking deep in her large black eyes.

"I do not want to lose you."

"I am in no danger."

He looked doubtful.

"It is true. Witches know. You saw it in R-Bar. She felt her end coming and carefully trained Szart."

He eased up to her side. "I know that."

"I will take that thing, that tome, to a private as private very guarded space and work there." She brushed a finger over his cheek. "Want to know what I feel in my immediate future?"

He blanched, and gasped, "What?"

"A large bed with a certain illusionist."

He sighed. "I will patiently abide my time."

"Not with any of The Queen's Handmaidens."

He shrugged. "You are my only."

She nodded. And faded in a puff of black, taking the book with her. "I know," said a disembodied voice.

He walked into the other room, grabbed a tall jug and a mug from the table, sprawled on the couch, filled the mug, set the jug on the floor, and took a long swallow, and worried.

Surprise!

Hahn Dohr Kahn. The Realm of The Dragon.

The fleet was tied up along the Great Quay. One vessel, blazing white, another jet black were tied along one side of the it. Two grey vessels were tied along the opposite side. At the end, the last vessel, grey, was moored.

Lurin beckoned to her First Lord and murmured to him, "It appears that we require additional facilities to handle all our ships."

He nodded. "Indeed." And strolled off to whisper to the Ship Master. Tomorrow they would begin plans to add to their facilities. The planning and preparing would occur during Ice Time so everything would be ready to start as soon as possible once the Warm Time arrived.

The crowd sighed and murmured as they turned toward the jet black vessel. Frinda and Sook had stepped up onto the gangway. Frinda was grinning broadly. He swung one arm over his Queen's shoulder and waved gaily to one and to all with the other arm.

Then looking down at the crowd, he stated in loud, rolling tones, "The New Kingdoms have new lands, new resources, and soon, a new seaport."

He waved grandly at the Great Quay and the five ships. "The sixth ship we left behind and a number of the folk to prepare for Ice Time there." He strolled down the gangway, his arm still around Sook, and walked over to his sister.

"Mighty Queen, it is good to be a King in these times and to behome." He laughed happily, released his Queen, bowed formally, and made his report, speaking loudly enough that the massed folk could overhear.

"Our folk and the Hephira labor long and hard to prepare a new town for Ice Time. We have maps to add to the Kingdom Map so all may see what we have found and what we have accomplished." He hugged her. "Sister, I am ready to sit and to relax and to share our news."

"Brother, the sea folk have set a table in their inn just for us to do so. Come, but be prepared to be jostled and toasted for We did declare a Two Fest Day, as We heard of your approach, starting this day."

They headed down the quay and into the inn, *The Wet Way*, on the corner where quay met land, the hangout of the sea folk.

Two tables had been shoved together in the middle of the room crowded with sea folk and ship masters. Lurin, Frahn, Irinl, Frinda, and Sook were seated there, an island of calm in the middle of a very boisterous crowd.

Frinda sat next to Lurin and began to tell her all that had happened. Then he asked for news of events while he was gone. And gasped. "A daughter?"

She smiled at him. "A beautiful Princess, Chyndra by name, who even now does quest journey with the newest offspring of Our Mother's Dark Advisor witch Ripple." She kissed his cheek. "You will like her, she is very warrior trained."

He frowned. "She does quest? Is she safe?"

"She travels with a witch. What could be safer?"

Sook stared at them. And decided that this was not the time to tell them all that she had been told about the strange magic swirling around her sister, Seemna, and the Princess. That could come later. After the Fest was over. She hadn't told her King either.

Somewhere in The Castle. A Safe as Safe Place.

The crumpled form, dressed in black, rolled onto her side and slowly heaved herself to her feet. Black fumes, and something else still seeped from the large tome lying on the table top. The book was closed, Next to it sat a small black ball. Its surface glistened oil soft slick.

She nodded and cast healing over herself. And waited, not very patiently, until she had the strength to go elsewhere.

Fer Ter In.

The great black dragon dropped into the garden, smashing into the ground all the carefully arranged plants, benches, fountains, and statuary. She carefully set down the three individuals she was carrying in one massive front paw.

"Please wait for us," asked Eulin, eyeing the large white structure before them.

"Shall I open it up?" asked M'Ban.

"No. We do not know exactly where she is." Eulin cast multi-layers of protection over them. Except for the dragon. M'Ban didn't require it. Eulin looked at Abda. "You could stay here. M'Ban will protect you."

"You could sit inside my mouth. Perfectly safe." The

great jaws yawned wide, just to demonstrate how much room there was. And snapped shut. "Lots of space for a small person." Great black dragons thought that all people were small.

"I will stay with Chyndra." Abda stepped sideways. "Close."

"On my left," ordered Chyndra, reaching up and yanking her great golden sword down. It glittered in the sunlight and whispered to her.

"We must be careful." Eulin started for the entry door. "This magician feels powerful. And unstable."

Inside, as they walked down the wide corridor, a horse-sized golden dragon materialized and huffed unhappy at Eulin. He didn't like being left behind.

She laughed. "This is Anamaxtor. He was a gift from Sha'gar."

"True?" Chyndra stared at the dragon who rolled one eye at her.

"Most," replied Eulin. "You must revisit the Mothers and have them explain in some detail, themselves."

Chyndra nodded. "That We will do!" And pointed at a staircase. "Up there. I feel that she is up there."

Eulin smiled. "Must be a link of some kind." A long violet wand appeared in her hand.

They started up the staircase followed by Anamaxtor.

Outside, clusters of witches swirled in, clan by clan, some distance from the blazing white edifice.

Ripple stared at the building, wondered about the large black hill that she could see, rolling a small ball from hand to hand, and snarled, "Ptar rak ptar. He has built a multi-layer witch ward."

Spinning to one side, she issued instructions and watched the clans scatter until they formed a long line around the structure and the ward. Then they began to build the container, designed by the Tanpak, the crystal adepts. Whatever was hidden inside there would not be able to escape. As soon as the container was in place they would begin disrupting the witch ward.

M'Ban wondered why all these witches were standing around in such an agitated condition. Then she thought that it was just the usual witch behavior, nothing to be all that considered about. Those inside the structure could take care of whatever the problem was.

She puffed in, in a burst of angry black. And stomped over to Ripple, the air snapping and crackling around her. "Make room," she growled. "I must get inside."

Fasna came running from one side. "FRAKNA! Where have you been?"

Frakna looked at her clan head. "Humble greetings?" And pointed. "Who is that?"

"Calm, calm. I will explain. There are many witch clans here."

Fasna told her all that had occurred since Frakna had gone wilding. Frakna gasped.

Grandeville. Tinker's Place.

"Yum yum yum."

She wiggled into a slightly more comfortable position and nodded agreement They were sprawling on one of the couches watching a movie, Sha'gar and Tinker. It had been his observation.

Actually, everyone was sprawling, lying, reclining, and in general being very relaxed, all around the large living room watching the movie.

"Don't drool on her," grumbled Chantal from another of the couches.

"He doesn't drool," giggled Messenger. "He just sorta licks."

The loud sigh was Tinker, wondering whether they would finish watching this movie or not.

"Just one of Doctor Pavlov's misplaced dogs," suggested Fair Morn. She and Early Dawn were sharing another of the couches.

"Think so?" asked Early Dawn.

"Nope. But we have probably conditioned his salivary glands." She grinned. "That is what Chantal thinks."

"Quiet!" He doubted that they would be, but there was always hope.

"Because we let him open our shirts?"

"Yep. It is all that beauty."

"Most true," stated Chicken from the floor. She was reclining against a couch, a number of pillows tucked here and there.

"What is?" asked Smoke. She was lying next to Chicken.

"The proclivity of Our Fair Prince for to rip Our Fair apparel asunder."

"Merde," he grumbled.

"When?" asked Sha'gar.

"What?" he asked in return.

"Are you going to rip my apparel asunder?"

"Never! I am taking a vow."

"Gosh," gasped Messenger, lurching upright. She had been slumped in one of the large overstuffed chairs. "We had better feed him lots of vitamins and minerals, just lots and lots. And toast soaked in milk!"

"Thought that we were watching a movie," he mumbled.

Sha'gar shoved her hand inside his shirt. "Is the hero going to rip her apparel asunder?"

"Nope. This is a PG-13 movie. More or less. Wholesome entertainment. Fit for children. That is all you guys."

Messenger bounced to her feet, stomped over, and glared down at him and Sha'gar. "Pervert! Evil corrupter!"

He frowned up at her. "Now what?"

Chicken joined Messenger. "'Tis most true a'fact. Be we children, then thee do be most foul abuser of youth." She pointed dramatically at Sha'gar. "Unhand that long, luscious, lanky child, foul fiend!"

"Yah!" added Messenger "I bet he really left fingerprints on her . . . "

" . . . fatty deposits," finished Fair Morn.

Szart walked over and peered over the back of the couch at its occupants. "The linked clans surround the one who took Seemna. He will not escape." She smiled.

"Witch nasty," observed Sha'gar, recognizing what that smile meant.

"Yessssssssss," agreed Szart.

"And we are not getting involved, right?" he asked.

"Witch true," stated Szart. "You may return to abusing that magician."

"He hasn't started yet," grumbled Sha'gar.

"Anyone else want to watch this flick?" he asked.

A chorus of agreement came from all directions.

Szart walked over and rewound the tape to the spot it had been when all this discussion had started.

Everyone settled back into their chosen viewing spots.

They actually watched the movie to the end without further interruptions.

Much to his surprise.

Fer Ter In.

He ran into the room, white swirling around him, snarling angrily. And grabbed her by the throat with one hand, wrenching her head back so he could glare into her eyes. "There are hordes of them out there! How did you do that?"

The long and heavy wooden leg, snapped from a table in the storage room, smashed into the back of his head just where neck joined skull. He dropped into a loose heap.

Barla kicked him in the side. "Doesn't always take magic to do things." And smashed the side of his head with the thick end of her improvised club. Then she hooked the fingers of her free hand into his robe and dragged the body to one side.

For the first time in ever so long Seemna felt her arms and her legs and her vocal cords freed as the magician's bind spell began to fade away. She cleared her throat and rasped, "Witch debt, Barla, witch debt."

"Always before," stated Barla, indicating the body, "he had been too guarded, too focused." She set her club on the table next to the bed and looked at Seemna. "He was correct. There are large numbers of witches all around this place. And someone put a great black hill right in the middle of the main garden, ruining it."

The door banged opened, bounced against the wall, and she stalked in, golden sword in her hand. "Release her! NOW!"

"Chyndra." Seemna coughed. "This is Barla, a, hum hum, friend." She stared at the others. "Who are they?"

Eulin was kneeling next to the body, examining it.

Chyndra laughed. And pointed. "My sister Eulin, a Vander, and Abda, a slinth."

Barla gasped, lurched away from them, grabbed up her gore drenched table leg, making warding off signs with her free hand. "Stay away slinth! Touch me not!"

Abda stepped from behind Chyndra and peered past her. "Eeeee chi ti! She is a cadta!"

"A what?" Chyndra kept her sword between herself and Barla.

"Cadta," repeated Abda.

Eulin stood and walked over to them. "Dead. Who killed him?" Then she noticed the blood covered table leg. "You? Did that?" She nodded. "Very brave. He was a seven-level mage. Amazing that you could do that."

"He was distracted," explained Barla.

"What's a Cadta?" asked Chyndra.

"Witch licta," whispered Abda.

"False tale!" hissed Barla.

"They ensa witches and play with their bodies," hissed Abda.

"Slinth vile tales!" snarled Barla, stepping toward them.

The sword flashed and half the table leg tumbled to the floor. "Stay!" commanded Chyndra.

Seemna looked at Barla. "Ahhhhh . . ."

"We do not!" stated Barla. She pointed a quivering finger at Abda. "Ever since the Sevnar, the slinth have lied."

Eulin laughed. "Now I understand what they are saying about each other." She looked from Seemna to Chyndra. "In our archives I read a very old document about the Sevnar. They split into two factions, two different populations and became the Slinth and the Cadta."

She laughed again. "These two are, ahhhh, cousins."

Seemna looked from Barla to Abda. "The same? Just different names?"

"Yes." Eulin smiled at the pair staring at her. "More or less."

"I am not the same as her," grumbled Abda. "She is ermat!"

"Pakga!" snapped Barla. "Ensrir slinth!"

"QUIET!" Seemna sat down and looked at Barla. "What does ermat mean?"

Glowering darkly at Abda, stepping carefully away from the golden blade, she said, "That is a vile slinth word. It implies that we trick witches into a, ermmmmm, emotional state in order to take advantage of their, ermmmmmm, physical charms."

Seemna nodded. "Like, for instance, running their hands over a witch's torso and, hum hum, physical charms."

"Yes," whispered Barla. "Like that. Because the witch wants it. Unbearably so."

"A charm spell?"

Yes. That is what that pakga meant." She glowered at Abda again.

"Hum hum." Seemna looked at Chyndra. "Cousin, you

have been traveling with a slinth for some?"

"True." Chyndra continued to watch Barla and her weapon.

"Has that slinth ever body charmed you?"

"Never!"

"I would not do that!" snapped Abda. "She rescued me."

"Barla," said Seemna. "Get rid of that table leg." The leg bounced and rattled on the floor.

The golden sword flickered back into its sheath.

The witch's dark eyes shifted to Eulin. "Cousin, what say you, a Vander?"

Eulin crossed her arms over her chest and looked from Abda to Barla, appraising, judging, deep gazing.

Barla gasped. Abda slipped to the other side of Chyndra.

Eulin nodded as she looked at Seemna. "They are similar but different. Probably due to the long ago split." She folded her arms and waggled one hand. "Mildly talented. Good enough for most beings. I doubt one of the trained would be affected." She grinned at Chyndra. "Including warrior trained, ahhhhh, at your level."

"Hum hum hum." Seemna nodded. "It appears that we are safe from having our, hum hum hum, physical charms, hum hum, played with."

"Most true," stated Eulin. Then she stared at Seemna. "Cousin witch Seemna, why are you so calm. Your, ahhhh, companion just bashed that mage into the other worlds and you have been missing long long."

One corner of Seemna's mouth twitched as the outer edges of her eyes crinkled. "Because it was bound to happen." She stood and walked over to the window to peer out.

"Although I have no idea what caused a great black hill to grow just there."

Eulin laughed and stepped up to her side. "We brought her, in a manner of speaking."

The great head reared up and up on the long sinuous neck until one great, green eye filled the window.

"A dragon?" Seemna froze in place.

"A great black," replied Eulin. "Rare and few and the most powerful of the dragon folk. M'Ban, this is Faan witch Seemna, one of my many cousins."

"Pleased to meet you," said M'Ban. "Do you want that body over there?"

"Witch debt, mighty M'Ban." Seemna shook her head. "We have no need for that dead magician. It is your's, if you wish."

Eulin stepped sideways and threw open the doors framing the small balcony.

A large taloned forepaw scrapped through the opening and plucked the body from the floor and withdrew. M'Ban chewed thoughtfully. "A certain sharp taste. He must have been very unpleasant."

"I thought so," said Seemna.

A witch raced into the room, a mace crackling angry in her hand. "I am here!" She had burst through the witch ward which had resealed behind her.

Seemna turned and nodded. "Most welcome, Frakna." She made a small gesture. "You are released."

Eulin looked at her sharply.

"I am a websmith. The now dead Puartor would have soon understood the folly of his actions." She stepped over and kissed Chyndra on the forehead. "Sorry, sorry, cousin, you were also pulled to me."

"Websmith," murmured Eulin. "More rare than a great black."

Outside, from all sides, something screamed agony. The witch ward had just died. And in moments she stalked in, the air snarling around her.

"Hayou, Mother," greeted Seemna, being witch proper.

"Daughter, where is that ptar ptar tak do?" growled Ripple. She bounced the small black ball in one hand. "I have something to give to him."

There was a loud burp that came from outside the window.

"Gone," replied Seemna. "Forever."

Ripple cast lightly.

"I am well," replied Seemna.

"So I see." Ripple looked at the others. And nodded greetings to Chyndra and Eulin and pointed. "Who are these two nar tipt?"

Abda shifted to the other side of Chyndra. Barla looked at Seemna.

"This one," stated Seemna, "is Cadta Barla. She killed Puartor the White, the rak tak ptar nar nar that held me."

Ripple nodded. "Wonderfully vile," she observed at her daughter's description of the dead problem, witch pride in a witch talented daughter.

"And that one is Slinth Abda, rescued from somewhere by Chyndra."

"Hum hum hum," suggested Ripple.

"Mother!" gasped Seemna.

"You did say Cadta and Slinth?"

"Yesssssssss. But they have been, hum, well behaved."

Ripple's eyes darted to Barla. "Witch debt, Cadta Barla, witch oath."

Barla sat heavily on the edge of the bed and stared at Ripple. "You owe me witch debt?"

"The Faan," stated Ripple. "And the Tanpak, Zwar, Grenzanr, Hinta, Beris, Blue Udaz, Kanikt, and Quana."

Eulin grinned at the stunned Cadta. "Also the Vander, who some call The Purple Mage. It appears, Barla, that you could probably ask for anything and receive it."

Anamaxtor shoved his big head through the open door and huffed nervous at Eulin. Dragons did not tend to associate with witches and he was getting apprehensive. They were everywhere.

"We are fine." Eulin looked at the others. "Are we not?"

"Witch true," stated Seemna. She stepped over to Chyndra. "Shall we continue our wander?"

Chyndra nodded. "Abda will come also. We have some unfinished business."

Seemna looked at Barla.

"If it is permissible." Barla stood.

Seemna nodded and stepped close to Ripple. "The Clan head has been busy. You have many more linked."

"Yesssssssss." Ripple kissed Seemna on the forehead. "Visit when you are done. Your father misses you." She touched her on the forehead with one fingertip. "Witch proud, Daughter, witch true."

Seemna nodded.

Stepped over to Chyndra and Abda.

And beckoned Barla to stand close.

They swirled out.

Eulin stepped to the open window. "Many thanks, great M'Ban. We are done."

"Farewell," came the answering rumble as the great shape leaped into the air, wings open and beating. She soared up and away.

Eulin looked at Ripple. "Time for me to return home, Aunt. Mother will be most interested in what my sister has been doing."

"Wait," ordered Ripple.

"Aunt?"

"My daughter neglected to tell of that warrior Princess. He is responsible?"

Eulin smiled. "And Queen Lurin."

"Well well, niece."

Eulin nodded. She explained all that she knew. And faded into violet mist.

Taking Anamaxtor.

Ripple tossed the small ball onto the bed and stalked from the room followed by Frakna. Outside, she gathered all the clans together. "This elseplace is soon not to be. I would meet with the Clan heads in the safe place. All are debt released."

The air snapped. Dark black

She was gone.

The rest, each in their own fashion, left.

As the last twisted out, the small ball popped open.

And ate the elseplace.

Folded into itself, and disappeared.

Fer Ter In became only a name in an oft told tale.

Some Things To Do.

Grandeville. Tinker's Place.

She sat on his stomach and peered down into his face.

He had been lying flat on the floor in the large living room, looking at the ceiling, thinking about a new book, requested by his publisher, listening to music, his head cushioned on Smoke's stomach. She was also sprawled flat on the floor.

It was several hours after dinner and everyone was relaxing.

His eyes popped open as the weight dropped onto his mid-section. "OOOF!" He stared up into the large black eyes staring down at him. "What?"

"Mother says that all is resolved and that Seemna and Chyndra have decided to continue doing wander."

"Good." His eyes closed.

She jabbed him with one finger.

"What? Now?" His eyes reopened.

"They travel with a Cadta and a Slinth."

"O.K."

"Cadta and Slinth cast body magic spells."

"Huh?"

So she explained. Then added that neither Seemna nor Chyndra need worry about that.

He sighed. "Witch little, is there any reason why you seem so determined to interrupt my work?"

"Keeping my stomach warm?" asked Smoke.

"Eh?" asked Szart.

"Thinking," he stated. "About a new book. My editor is complaining."

"Piffle," firmly suggested Chicken, sitting on the couch near them. She reached out with one bare foot. And poked Smoke and began to rub her foot back and forth.

"Those are not piffles you are messing with," grumbled Smoke at her.

"T'was mere comment small pon Our Prince scribe agent."

"What does that have to do with erotic toes?" Smoke grabbed her ankle.

"Naught." Chicken yanked her foot back. Unsuccessfully.

"Merde," he grumbled, knowing that all hopes for relaxation and contemplation had just ended.

"DESIST!" ordered Chicken as Smoke slowly dragged her from the couch.

"Pesky poke Queen," replied Smoke.

Messenger sat on the floor near them. "I thought that was his job."

"Huh?" He rolled his eyes in her direction.

"Poke." She nodded vigorously and giggled as Chicken thumped to the floor.

"Vile wench," snarled Chicken at Smoke.

Chantal joined the group. "I don't think she was referring to your toes, Cowboy."

"Chicken?"

"Messenger."

He decided to that it was time to bail out of this conversation. So he closed his eyes.

"Stud," added Fair Morn as she and Early Dawn sat on the floor near him. Fair Morn gave him a little jab in the side.

He jerked. His eyes popped open. "Stop that!" And glowered up at Szart. "Somehow, in some manner beyond all human understanding, I think you started this."

She frowned back. "It was the Princess. Rubbing her foot on Smoke's br . . . "

"Fatty deposits," interrupted Fair Morn. "I think that she has a foot fetish. A very strange foot fetish."

"Piffle!" suggested Chicken again.

He sighed loudly, and grumbled at one and all, "It never stops." He admired the ceiling, and wondered, once again, what had started them up this time.

Sgenn and Sha'gar walked in from the kitchen where they had been checking what kinds of ice cream were in the inside freezer, and joined the group, on the floor.

"Your mother," hissed Sha'gar at Szart, "released vile above vile and removed that elseplace."

"Deserved it," grumbled Szart. "That ptar ptar nak tak held Seemna and was going to do untap!"

"What?" he asked.

"Untap!" hissed Szart.

"Sure," he said. "What?"

"Body vile prowl use take. Against her want!"

"Oh."

"It could have been done," stated Sgenn, "without witch vile."

Szart shrugged. There certainly was nothing wrong with witch vile. Not in her mind, there wasn't.

Je'leel came in, cup of cocoa in hand, book held in her other hand, one finger clamping inside, marking her place, stopped and looked down at group. "Father, what are you doing to them?" She laughed.

"I," he stated firmly, "am not doing anything. To them. They are, as per usual, intent on doing something to me." He sighed very dramatically. "And I have no idea, either."

"Damn grump," grumbled Chantal, at him. "Studying?" she asked Je'leel.

"Test tomorrow."

"Need any help on your test?" asked Smoke.

"Nope."

Dat leaned on the back of the couch and peered down at them. "My daughter is indjinn clever."

"Night," said Je'leel, heading for the hall and her room in the far upper corner of the house.

"Great Master?"

"What?"

"Shall I do something to your houris so they will behave correctly as benefits your exhalted station?"

"Nope. But thanks. For the recognition." He reached up and tickled Szart. "O.K., witch little, what is going on? This time?"

"Eh?" asked Szart.

"Eh?" echoed Sgenn and Sha'gar.

"Triple merde," he mumbled. "Get off," he growled at Szart.

"I like sitting on your stomach," she stated firmly as only

a witch could. And bounced, just a little to emphasize her point.

"OOOOOOF! Stop that!"

"Fair Prince?"

"Princess?"

"Tis naught but fair distraction for to most cleverly a'bringen relaxation to thy mind which do be most concerned with fair Princess, Our Daughter Chyndra, and Szart's fair sister witch, Seemna."

"I was relaxed," he grumbled.

"Hum buggy do do," suggested Messenger.

He sighed.

"Right," agreed Chantal. "And bull cheat, also."

"Well," he conceded, "maybe just a little." He smiled at them.

They mobbed him.

He, of course, wound up on the bottom.

Niveous Lily.

They faded in, from a black puff of night.

Seemna had been given that effect by Reep.

"I wanted to get a few things," explained Barla to Chyndra and Abda. She hurried out a door.

"This was Puartor's before he moved everyone to Fer Ter In." Seemna looked around the room where she had been held for so long.

"It is empty?"

"Yessssssssss."

"Someone should use it."

Chyndra looked at Abda. "You could have it."

Abda wobbled her head from side to side. "No need." She

smiled. "I like to be around others."

"Hum hum," observed Seemna.

Barla returned. Her trousers were bright orange, wide flared cuffs ending at mid-calve just below the tops of her dark brown boots. The blouse was a soft blue topped by a green vest. She carried a sturdy black hiking staff in one hand. Bright gold ferrules decorated either end. A brown pouch dangled from her wide purple belt. "I am ready."

"Very subtle," observed Abda.

"Rupa!" suggested Barla. Then she turned and held the staff in her outstretched palms toward Seemna.

"Eh?"

Barla bowed her head. "As I did say. You may beat me for that which I did."

"No need. It was understood." Seemna nodded. "Remember, we owe witch debt." She looked at Chyndra. "Where?"

Chyndra told her. And why.

Seemna smiled, a true witch smile full of the promise of chaos and terror.

Abda gasped.

Barla shuddered.

Chyndra nodded.

Fasback's Delight.

They stood before the ornate entry door to the immense structure towering above them.

Chyndra tugged on the handle. Then she thumped on the door with the pommel of her sword.

A small portal eventually opened. "Go away."

"Let me in."

"'No."

Abda nudged Chyndra aside and smiled in at the guard. And purred, "I would be soooo pleased if you would allow us to come inside." Her smile shifted, ever so subtly.

They heard the latches being shifted. Then the door swung in.

"That," said Abda to Barla, "is how it is done."

"Rupa," suggested Barla.

The guard watched Abda as she seemed to flow inside and past him, her fingers tickling lightly across his face. "Stay here. I will return."

His face flushed. He nodded.

The four headed up the staircase.

Moonikta.

She stormed into the establishment followed by her assistants and thumped her fist on the middle of the wide counter top, demanding attention. The counter top creaked under the assault.

The man behind the counter jerked his eyes away from one of the others, an attractive female with the strangest eyes he had ever seen. They were multifaceted and glittered dozens of reflections.

"Who are you?" he demanded of the loud but nice to look upon female wearing the rather severe military-cut gold-yellow uniform looking garb.

"I, dumbkopf," she stated, "am Chief Investigator Mirf, Monetary Control. Send your boss out here! Now! Machen schnell!" She thumped her fist on the counter top again, just for fun. "Go, go, go, go, go, go, go!" The counter top creaked louder, small cracks appearing from edge to edge.

He hurried away. His boss would take care of this unpleasant person, probably throw her out the door and across the street.

"I'll bet," Mirf said to her assistants, "that they will not listen to reason, not even a bisel bit." She carved a design in the counter top with her thumbnail. A habit, an attribute, left over from her hob-goblin days as were her fingernails.

Her assistants waited, fingering weapons obvious and not so obvious. With Mirf one had to be prepared for anything. Which usually happened.

Fasback's Delight.

She banged the door open and stomped inside. The guards merely smiled with a rather vague but pleased look. Barla nodded at Abda as they followed Chyndra into the room. Seemna stopped just inside the door and watched. Everything.

Fasback smiled happily, clapped his hands, and bounced in his chair. "It is the Toy Warrior, returned with my slinth, and two others. Wonderful, wonderful."

He pushed a small pot across the table at her. "Join me in some delightful beverage?"

In one smooth flash of gold, Chyndra drew her sword and sliced the table in half. The two pieces toppled sideways. The pot bounced off the floor at Fasback's feet.

"Astonishing," he bubbled. "Even better. A real treasure." He beamed at her.

She stepped closer and frowned at him. "I am not your treasure. Not now, not ever!"

"Of course you are." He smiled at her. "I purchased you, fair and square."

She gently prodded the large swelling that was his stomach with the tip of her blade. "Perhaps this needs to be sliced open before you will understand?"

He nodded. "I see. That under dealer, Gerbast, has somehow made you an even greater offer." He winked at her. "Makes not a terpit! I will offer more than any. Name your price!"

She winked back at him. "So be it!" And smiled even broader. "Do I have your word? On the price?"

He smiled back. "Instantly. Name it!"

"Freedom, Fasback, freedom is the price."

Fasback laughed and beamed at her. "Beautiful! I have been bumbled by my very own words." He stood and held his arms out. "So be it." Then he wiped one eye and looked as sorrowful as he could. "But I will miss you."

His eyes and demeanor returned to normal. "Are you taking my slinth as well?"

"Yes. She does not wish to be anyone's object. And, if you will remember, you did give her to me."

He sighed. "I will be so lonely. Have you no pity?"

Chyndra shook her head. "In this case, no." She glowered at him. "And I would suggest, most strongly, that you collect treasures that are not alive. It might be safer."

He shrugged. "Perhaps you are correct. Would it be permissible to receive a farewell hug?"

"All right." Chyndra held her sword out to one side and allowed herself to be wrapped inside his thick arms. Then he stepped back and bowed.

"Farewell, Fasback. Be well, Be careful."

He laughed. "Oh, I will, I will." He dropped back into his chair and watched them as they walked away. And thought that it was a true pity that they were leaving.

Moonikta.

"Why are we here?"

Chyndra looked at the buildings, varying heights, varying materials, lining the street and then at her cousin.

"It is said that Moonikta is an elseplace where things may be found," explained Seemna.

"What sort of things?"

"Magical things." Seemna looked at her from the corners of her eyes. "Anything that one would want."

"And what do we want?"

"Perhaps," Seemna turned, glanced up at the building, constructed of red brick, poking up behind them, "a better understanding of that weapon you carry."

Chyndra thought a long moment and nodded. "Where?"

"We shall have to search. A little."

And, in a little, not more than a lot, the four of them walked through an intersection, turned left, and started down a street named *Hildle Street*. As they approached the middle of a long block of shops and other businesses, it happened.

A large wooden door burst outwards, scattering pieces of itself across the street, startling all the folk nearby. The cause of the door behaving in such a strange manner bounced and rolled before coming at rest against the front of a shop selling hats.

Seemna hissed. Chyndra's sword flashed into her hand, singing softly. Barla and Abda leaped back and behind them.

"DUMBKOPF!" snarled someone as she angrily stomped out of the shattered doorway and over to the now moaning man trying to sit up amongst the wreckage . "When I want to play word games with someone, you it wouldn't be." She leaned over and glared into his now open eyes. "So, do I have your attention or do I have your attention?"

He twitched. "Yes, yes, yes," he gasped.

She straightened up. "Good, good, good. That is one good for each yes, in case you miscounted."

Yanking him to his feet, she asked sweetly, at least to her it was sweetly, she thought so. "Shall we return to your house of ill repute and continue our little conversation?"

"Release him!" Chyndra stepped close to this pair, but not too close, the golden blade in front and ready.

The woman shook the man, not too gently. "This chickeedoodle one of your's?"

"No." Chyndra had no idea what a chickeedoodle was, but it was no to that question in any case.

The strange eyes looked at her. "So do me a favor and go wave that gold sticker at someone else. This nogoodnik and I have to settle some business. Then if you should want to talk, make an appointment."

Seemna stepped up to Chyndra's side and stared at this woman. "Hob-goblin eyes."

The woman shrugged. "So I had a little accident. Ho boy, such an understatement that is. Go away, witch."

"Hum hum." The air crackled around Seemna.

The woman gasped and dropped the man back onto the street. "Oi vay, not another hummer! Tell me it isn't so! You're not another of those Faan schicksas."

Both stared at her.

The air around Seemna did strange things.

The woman pointed at her. "So stop that already. I know Ripple. You got that same look, that same sulky look."

"Mother," stated Seemna.

"So," the woman asked no one in particular, "why me? Did I do something wrong in another life?" Then she took a careful look at the pair facing her. "Don't answer that! Who are you two? Four?"

"Ripple daughter Faan websmith Seemna."

"Princess Chyndra, Realm of the Dragon."

"Barla."

"Abda."

She smiled at them. It was ghastly. "Mirf, Monetary Control." She waved an arm that seemed strangely disjointed, at the four standing slightly behind her. "My assistants, Fred, Quan, Rema, Nema."

Then she peered at Chyndra, eyes narrow slits. "Ho ha, that face I've seen before also. Your father run around with a bunch of babes?"

"Yes."

"My, my, my, my, my, my, that boy never stops. So, honey bunch, I buy dinner. In a minute after business."

Mirf grabbed the man by the collar and dragged him across the street and heaved him back inside his establishment. "Don't go away." She watched him bounce. "I'll be back!" She spun around, laughed loudly. "So an Arnold I'm not, but he'll understand."

She pointed. "Just down there is a nice, expensive restaurant. M.C. is buying. So don't stand there gawking, let's give a go, head for dinner."

Mirf was correct. The restaurant was very nice and the food was also very good. During the several courses of dinner, Chyndra told Mirf about her traveling companions. Then Mirf explained, over dessert, her companions. She smiled at Seemna and Chyndra, frightening a couple sitting one table away, and asked, "So, tell me, Honey Buns, what are you chickees up to, here in this elseplace?"

Seemna frowned at her. It was no business of anyone what a witch might be doing.

Chyndra smiled at Mirf. "Did you know Mirf, that you have the most absolutely ghastly smile that I have ever seen?"

"Really?" Mirf smiled again, even broader. "Better?" It was worse.

Chyndra laughed.

Mirf shrugged. "So, it'sa me. Tell me, what are you and the hummer up to?"

"My sword has been magic'd by a witch and Seemna thought that we might be able to find someone here to tell us exactly what was done to it."

"Someone didn't like you?"

"Oh no. It was done to help. She just didn't explain what it was that she did to it."

Mirf glanced sideways. "And you are Ripple's newest daughter?"

"Yesssssssssss," hissed Seemna.

She waggled one loosely connected hand, it appeared that way, at the others. "So, what do you do? What can you do?"

Abda and Barla told her.

"HO BOY!" Mirf looked back. "Sooooo, as you cuties are

sitting, here, looking innocent, eating my dinner, maybe I can ask a something? You wanna do me a favor? A big favor? A big biz favor? A super colossal favor?"

"Well," said Chyndra.

"For you and the dark cloud sitting with you, I'll give anything?" She shrugged. "Well, almost anything."

"And?"

"Oi," sighed Mirf. "What we have here is a one word bargainer." She grinned. "So hookey, just for you, today's special, never to be repeated, not never again, double negatives and all!" She gestured grandly. "I will make these two slinky bods part of my office staff. Fancy shirts, high pay, paid vacations, and I won't work them too hard. As long as they agree to not seduce all the males in Monetary Control Headquarters."

She winked lewdly. "One or two, that's hooky-dooky, but not the whole bunch." She leaned back and grabbed her mug and took a long drink from it.

"So, it's a deal?"

"No," stated Abda.

"Im ip piz," mumbled Barla. "Doing what?"

"Oh," said Mirf, trying to sound innocent, failing totally. "Just use your, ummm, talents, now and then. Just being yourself."

"Doing what?" demanded Chyndra.

"Wheedling information from this nogoodnik or that nogoodnik." She waved a hand at Barla and Abda. "For these two warm smiles it should be like breathing."

"Could they get hurt?"

"So who hurts what they love?" Mirf wiped her hand

over her face. "So, wrong thought." She filled her mug and bellowed at a passing waiter to bring some more. And leaned forward again.

"All right! I will get them their very own associates, mean and nasty associates. But oh so innocent looking." She laughed. "They can pick who." And whispered, a real whisper, "I will even bring the slinth upstairs from the Record Section to join them."

She laughed at all their expressions. "Knew what she was, just didn't know what she was." Setting her mug down, she rubbed her hands together. "Such a team this will be!" Her eyes glittered, hob-goblin delight.

Sometime later, they stood before a building constructed of dark stone, of deep grey dark stone blocks. The structure loomed over the street and seemed to frown at the folk passing by. Most walked just a little faster for that short distance that was the front of the place.

"Here?" Chyndra looked up.

"Inside." Seemna pushed open the narrow door and led them in.

Inside was a surprise. The hall was wide, wood paneled, bright, and very pleasant. At the far end, stairs headed upward, splitting and turning in two directions.

"Two up." Seemna strode for the far end and the stairs going up. "Bir Indict dwells two up."

As they walked upward and upward, Barla and Abda glanced from side to side. This place didn't feel bright and pleasant to them.

"AHM." He looked from one to the other, a rather wide man dressed in an orange smock and deep red trousers. He was Randa clan, a clan that specialized in thing magic. Thing magic, as its name implied, was magic that applied to things.

Seemna had guided them to this set of rooms.

"We," stated Chyndra, "would like to know about this blade." She reached up and down, holding it lightly in her grasp. "A witch magic'd it. We would like to know what she did and what it means."

"Ummmm, ahh." He pointed. "Let it there lay. Pay or debt?"

"Pay!" snapped Seemna.

Abda smiled at him.

Barla glanced at Seemna who shook her head.

Chyndra nudged Abda with her elbow. "No!"

His eyes danced from face to face. "Name me names."

Seemna handed him a leather pouch. "I am Faan witch Seemna."

"Chyndra, Princess, Realm of The Dragon."

"Abda."

"Barla."

"Randa warlock Dema. Bir Indict is no longer here." He bent over and stared at the golden sword and then carefully touched it with one cautious fingertip. "Ummmmm, ahh, Kazmir sharp spell."

He looked sideways at Chyndra. "Be careful warrior one. This blade cuts all." He carefully touched the weapon again. "Um, ah, Ddabdar in-dwell spell."

Straightening up, he stepped back, just far enough. "It is occupied by a Ddabdar and knows only the owner. Never give your weapon to another."

"Is it safe?"

"For you, warrior one, for you." He shrugged. "For anyone else most probably fatal." He picked up the pouch and dropped it into a large side pocket. "You have been gifted much. Use it wisely."

Chyndra looked from him to Seemna. "What's a Ddabdar? And what is it doing inside my sword?"

Seemna nodded at the warlock. "Explain, Randa." Something witch subtle in her pronunciation of his clan name caused the warlock's eyes to dance and stare at her.

He cleared his throat. "It is a wraith of sly death that is now your weapon, Princess Warrior. This in-dweller makes your skills, how ever great, even greater. Using this blade you will become legend." He looked at Seemna. "The witch who did this must have held your companion in very high regard as she cast Kazmir on the cutting edge."

Chyndra held the sword close to her face and peered at it. "Can it be taken out?"

"No," whispered the sword only to her. "My Warrior Princess of Legend."

"No." Randa patted the pouch in his side pocket. "Is there something else you wish to understand?" He cleared his throat and watched Seemna carefully.

"No." She headed for the door, stopped, turned and squinted at him. "Hum."

"What?" He jerked, took a step back.

"Have you things for sale?"

Randa waggled one hand. "Some few. Of?"

"Protection for them." Seemna indicated Abda and Barla.

"From?"

"Much much."

"Um zuba." He nodded and held out his hand. Two blue rings lay in the palm of his hand. "For them, these." He watched the pair each take a ring and slip it on a finger.

Seemna handed him another pouch and turned back toward the door. Then she stopped, spun, and stared at Dema.

"We require one more of those rings."

As they walked along the narrow side street, Barla wiped at one eye with her sleeve.

"I owe debt," grumbled Seemna. "Say nothing."

Abda nudged Chyndra.

"Shhh," whispered Chyndra.

Several streets over, well on their way to meet Mirf at the chosen place that she had suggested, they turned into a narrow passage which would lead them there.

A few of the local folk wandered past, unconcerned, unbothered by the dim light and rather cluttered walkway. Three large men turned from the bright patch of light at the far end into the passage, wandered toward them. As they approached they fanned out and blocked the way.

The quartet stopped and looked at them.

The middle man spoke to them. "I am Narzop, Toll Taker." He smiled a gap toothed grimace and gurgled, "That means, dears, that you hand over all of your gold coins."

Chyndra waved her left hand. "Make way!"

Abda looked at Barla who nodded.

The air hummed soft menace around Seemna.

"Gently," said Narzop. "Or roughly. Makes not a tret to us."

Chyndra stepped back, just a little, just to make a small amount of extra space before she attacked, her right hand sliding up to grasp her sword hilt.

And then.

To everyone's surprise.

It happened.

From one side, from a dark shadow patch, he leaped between the two groups, announcing in rolling tones that echoed off the walls of the narrow space, "The Bold and Dashing Prince Dumar leaps to the rescue of the Fair and Innocent Maidens!"

"Who are you?" gasped Chyndra and Narzop.

"I am not innocent," growled Seemna, bristling angry. It was not nice to call a witch innocent.

"The Handsome and Ever So Noble Prince Dumar, of The House of Hagon, House of Mnab, House of Contan, stands before you, ready to defend and protect all ladies in peril." He took a heroic stand, feet wide, one hand on a hip, smiling broadly at one and all, the staff held vertical in the other hand.

"This zek tak better watch his mouth," snarled Seemna. Witches hated being called ladies. It was worse than being called innocent.

Chyndra waggled her left hand at him, frowning mostly at him. "Stand aside, Dumar, we have no need of such assistance. We can easily handle this minor problem.

"Stand aside child," gurgled Narzop. "Or do you wish to pay toll as well?"

Dumar stared at him. "Do what?"

Chyndra stepped up and shoved Dumar to one side. "Get out of the way!"

"Din dodag," agreed Narzop, heaving Dumar further away.

Gold flashed, Narzop staggered sideways. Chyndra had banged the flat of her weapon off the side of his head.

Dumar leaped further away and stared to her.

Shaking his head, Narzop peered at his companions who were standing and smiling soft smiles at Abda and Barla,

"What did you do?" growled Narzop at Chyndra.

"Left your head attached to your shoulders. Leave us!" She glared to one side. "You, Dumar, stay where you are!"

Narzog grabbed each of his helpers by an arm and tugged them away, headed for the far entrance to the narrow way. "Come, come, come, come, come." They grinned happy at him.

Dumar glared at the rapidly departing trio. "DEPART, EVIL DOERS!" He whirled and glared at Chyndra. "Fair and Innocent Maidens do not assault Handsome and Daring Princes during their rescue!"

"Perhaps," stated Chyndra, rapping him on the sternum with the hilt of her blade, "it is because I am neither fair nor innocent? Or perhaps it is because we did not require a self-struck Prince of some sort getting in our way? So, are you really a Prince? Or just some large child playing at a tell tale you wish to live inside?"

Dumar stared her, mouth hanging open, as she slid her weapon back into its sheath.

"Your mouth is open, Dumar."

He snapped it shut and stood straighter. "Of course I am

a Prince! As anyone with discerning eyes can see!" He frowned royally at her.

Chyndra looked over at Seemna who shrugged.

Abda nudged Barla. "He is pretty." And asked Dumar, "Is that how one can tell?"

"No!" He crossed his arms over his chest, leaned his staff on one shoulder, held his head a little higher. "It is my Noble Bearing, Great Courage, and Impeccable Manners!" He dropped his arms and looked from face to face. "As you can see." Then he bowed, quite elegantly. "Prince Dumar, at your service." And hastily grabbed his staff.

Chyndra bowed in return. "Princess Chyndra, The Realm of The Dragon, Hahn Dohr Kahn, The New Kingdoms." She waved one hand. "Ripple daughter Seemna web smith. Slinth Abda. Cadta Barla."

He stared at her.

"Your mouth is hanging open. Again."

"A sword wielding Princess?"

"I am witch raised and warrior trained, Dumar. And have no need for a posturing Court Crawler."

"Most ill-mannered for a Princess." He wondered what kind of thing a Court Crawler was.

"We speak direct We do. Not great inflations."

"Our Court Staff instructed Us to do so."

"Your Court Staff is grossly ill informed. Have you been doing that in many elseplaces?" She wondered how he could have survived if he had.

Dumar shook his head. "I have just started My Great Adventure, not one day past. How is it that a Princess travels with these?" He waggled one hand at the others.

"These are friends and my cousin. In My Kingdom none dare look down upon any kind as a lessor person as each are valued for their skills and position."

"A different place. What is your lineage? If I may ask, Princess?"

"My Mother, The Queen, is also known as The White Warrior as was her Mother. My Father, The King, has many titles: Lord John Tinker and The Chosen One being the two most commonly heard here, there, and elseplace."

Dumar lurched backward.

"Your mouth is once again flopping open. Do you have trouble breathing, Dumar? Try breathing through your nose."

"Your Father is him. That one?"

"Most true."

He dropped to one knee and bowed his head.

Abda nudged Chyndra. "Perhaps you hit him too hard."

"Rise!" snapped Chyndra. "And go away!"

Seemna stepped to her side. "Where shall I send him? Bog Nar Gapo is wonderfully vile." She smiled.

Barla shook her head. "No need for that. He will be very happy to go away." She smiled at him.

"Stop!" Chyndra looked from Barla to Abda. "Do not! He is just badly told, most badly."

"Most Noble and Fair Princess Chyndra," intoned Dumar, lurching to his feet. "I beg a boon, Court to Court."

"What? Now?" She was frowning royally.

"I would travel with your Royal Party. As a lessor minion."

"What?" She stared at him.

"To learn. To travel. To see."

"He is nice faced," observed Abda.

"Well muscled," added Barla.

"Hum hum." Seemna looked at Chyndra. "Do we need his tall company?"

"Most so?" offered Dumar.

"Rid yourself of all that good for nothing Court talk," ordered Chyndra.

"Instantly."

"Titles and all."

"Absolutely."

"Are you trained? In anything?"

Dumar held out the tall staff of dark polished wood. "I am warrior trained." He sighed. "As The Third Prince there was nothing else for me to do but train." He smiled, a small smile. "So I sought something in the elsewheres. And first day thought to do my duty." He rubbed the side of his face. "I did not expect to be beat for doing it, however."

Chyndra nodded and looked at Seemna. "He could aid us in doing that favor for Mirf."

"Mirf?" Dumar stared at her, brows furrowing, wondering how this Princess knew those sort of folk. "The Mirf? Monetary Control?"

"Where is your kingdom, open mouthed Dumar?"

"Gasta Pleesa."

"Hum."

"What?" asked Chyndra.

"Far over, one down," stated Seemna. "A small corner."

Dumar cleared his throat. "Please?"

Chyndra nodded and walked off with Seemna. Abda and Barla each grabbed one of Dumar's arms and tugged the startled

Prince into motion. He gasped.

Hahn Dohr Tohr. The Realm of The Dragon.

It was Warm Time again.

They had been walking due east.

From the town of Wurm.

For many days.

Frahn, Irinl, and one troop of Silver Rangers. They were exploring from Wurm into the eastern portion of the Kingdom.

The two map makers were kept busy sketching everything that they saw as well as making a map of all they passed through. So far it was mostly a passage through open grassland as the forest edge appeared to remain just to the south of the line they were traveling.

The area they were covering was unknown. The maps made during the Queen's sea exploration up the south and east coasts indicated that there were three rivers somewhere out there. The party expected to find the first one and follow it down to its mouth.

It was hoped that the river was wide and deep enough that sea folk vessels could sail up and into the interior to a place suitable for a small town and an anchorage.

In front of them, on the far horizon, there appeared to be a mountain sticking up. When they got closer they would decide what to do about that.

Grandeville. Tinker's Place.

He finished.

Dropped the last page of his manuscript into the box.

He leaned back and took a sip from his cup.

And looked around, just taking a quick peek.

He was seated at one of the wooden benches at one of the large wooden tables on the rear deck. It was late afternoon. It was late in a fine summer day, one of those perfect temperature days. To him, everyone and everything appeared relaxed and quiet. It was wonderful.

Bodies lay here and there as they enjoyed this part of the day as well. Some floated on mats in the swimming pool. Some lay on the deck near the swimming pool. Chantal sprawled in the hammock with an assortment of professional journals and other literature of interest to a hard working veterinarian.

Fair Morn and Early Dawn walked from the general direction of the kitchen carrying large trays containing glasses and pitchers of lemonade. Slowly everyone gathered around the appropriate table, yawning, stretching, and pouring themselves a full glass.

Je'leel joined them, sitting across the table from him.

"Three of my friends," she announced, "are having a Before The Start of School dinner party."

"Uh huh," he said.

"Here." Chantal reached past him and handed her car keys to Je'leel. "Have fun."

"Thanks, Mom." She stood and headed for the parking space next to the house. And then all heard the small sports car head down their driveway.

Sgenn pushed into the space between him and Messenger who was refilling her glass and his.

"Hi, Quiet," he said as he reached for his glass and took a sip.

"I have been told to come," she said.

"What?" He gasped and cleared his throat several times.

"Calm down," growled Chantal, thumping him on the back.

He had mis-swallowed.

"Oh my?" Messenger peered at her. "What is wrong?"

Sgenn shrugged.

He wiped his chin with a napkin. "Honk, honk."

"Eh?" Sgenn twisted around to stare at him.

"Wild goose sounds," he grumbled. "Do we hafta?"

Sgenn nodded.

"Um, O.K. We will pack and leave in the morning. And we will be careful, right?"

"Absolutely, Our Prince." Chicken nodded at him. "Nary a chance will betaken a'Us."

"You betcha," agreed Fair Morn. "Shoot first. Talk to the survivors later."

He sighed.

Sgenn stood. "I must talk with Mother." Sha'gar stepped over and they faded in a swirl of black.

"Now what?" he mumbled.

Chantal banged him on a shoulder. "Start worrying when we get there. Tonight you are entertaining a bat."

"Really?" Early Dawn grinned, sharp teeth glistening in the sunlight.

"Sho nuff," said Smoke. "Just don't bite him."

"I don't do that." Early Dawn laughed. "He does."

The loud sigh was Tinker.

Moonikta.

"Ho boy! So who's doing the collecting?"

Mirf stared at the group as they walked up to her, her eyes jumping from face to face.

"No one." Chyndra indicated the newest member of the group. "This is Prince Dumar."

Mirf stepped close to him and stared into his eyes. "So, bubbe, are you a real prince or you just trying to impress the chickees?"

He stared at her.

"BOO!" Mirf spun around, waggling one seemingly disconnected arm. "O.K., O.K., O.K. already, gather around and we will discuss the plan, such as it is."

She began to explain what she wanted each of them to do. Then she threw a comradely arm around Chyndra's shoulders. "So do me a favor and don't tell your Father about this. He tends to get excited about things like this."

"And?" Chyndra smiled at her.

"OI! So I already promised you the world, so what else do you want? Vat?"

"When we finish, Abda and Barla go with you? Back to your office?"

"Absolutely! I take the two beauty bods and set up a new office right next to mine. All three of them. These two and the one from downstairs." She kissed Chyndra on the forehead. "So don't worry, be happy! They will be safe." Mirf stepped back and shrugged. "Well, as safe as anyone can be working for me." She grinned widely. "Did you know that your sister, Sedeem, worked for me, once?"

"No."

Mirf nodded, her head wobbled loosely. "But she snatched this moose meat Silver Ranger off the street and married him." Mirf leaned closer and whispered. For Mirf it was a whisper. For everyone else it sounded pretty much like a normal speaking voice, "You gonna grab that Prince, or whatever he claims to be and do . . . things?"

Chyndra whispered back, a real whisper, "Do you think that I should?"

Mirf shrugged. "So don't ask me, I am not one of your Mothers."

Chyndra laughed.

So did Mirf. "Nuff chit chat. Let's get this show on the road! We have some real nogoodniks to take care of." She charged down the street toward their destination.

Doth Lamex. A Place of Relaxation and Healing.

They were finishing their lunch in their selected spot.

It was a small meadow surrounded by tall trees. The sky was blue, the grass green, and the air temperature was just right. This was Doth Lamex after all.

"Why are we here? And why are you glaring?" Dumar frowned at her.

Seemna waved her eating utensil. "This is Doth Lamex, the safest and most comfortable elseplace in the universe of universes. It is a good spot to visit."

Dumar frowned at his dish and then glowered up at Chyndra. "A Princess does not do that!"

She looked at the leg of whatever animal it had been that she was holding and took a bite. "It is quite tasty." She smiled at him. "This Princess may use Our fingers if We so choose to do so."

"Not that! What you, what we, did. For that Mirf person."

"We did not do much." She took another bite.

"It was crunar!"

"We suppose."

Seemna looked at him from the corners of her eyes.

"No," said Chyndra.

"Can't here," replied Seemna. She shrugged. "Not allowed."

"What?" asked Dumar.

"You have two older brothers?" asked Chyndra.

Dumar nodded. "Mardu and Ardum. The soon to be King and the soon to be Prince of Hanldan, the Lessor Kingdom."

"And you?"

"The Prince of vast amounts of nothing."

"Sisters?"

He nodded again. "One! Ragla, the Overbearing. Married Casnap, the Round, now King of Oapa."

"You could always marry one of your folk's fair Princesses and gain lands that way."

Dumar sagged and poked at his food with the tip of his knife. "I would rather attach with a quarta demon."

"Hum," observed Seemna.

"So, Prince Dumar, for what reason do you travel? The real reason."

He sighed and tried a smile, a rather weak smile. "I thought to find somewhere a kingdom, an elseplace, where this Prince of no resources might settle and be just me."

"Hum hum." Seemna took another look at him, a much closer look.

"So you seek to wed your way into a kingdom and live

off your wife's lands and treasure?" asked Chyndra.

He jerked, straightened up, and glowered at her.

"What? Dumar of the Open Mouth?"

"How can someone who claims to be a Princess be so crude?"

A grey wand appeared in Seemna's hand.

"WARNING! WARNING!" boomed a voice from somewhere.

Seemna hastily sent the wand away.

Dumar leaped to his feet, seeking this new thing.

"SIT!" snapped Seemna. "That was a Doth Lamex guardian. No violence is permitted here." She looked at Chyndra. "Sorry sorry. But this ptar nik needs to be taught much much." Her expression suggested that the teaching might be wonderfully painful.

"Please sit, Prince," said Chyndra. "And calm yourself as well. We did but wish to understand your quest and your purpose. And do forgive Our manner as the folk of Our Kingdom do speak straight and may appear much too blunt to the folk elseplace." She was using as much of her Mother's royal tone and court manner as she could remember.

He sat. "Humble apologies, Princess. We did react without proper thought." He watched her face. "But We would never expect to be some soft appendage to another's lands. This Prince expects to make his lands, if he ever has any, happy and prosperous."

"Even if it means working side by side in the heavy and dirty chores with the folk of those lands?"

He shrugged. "If the land requires such, such it will be. The Prince must work harder and better than any." He held his hands out and looked at them. "Although these hands are ill-trained for such but fighting and other warrior skills."

"A mighty problem, Prince." Chyndra refilled her cup. Then looked at Seemna. "Where from here?"

"Toos Tok has a minor foregather."

Chyndra nodded and stood. "Coming, Prince?"

He stood. "Yes."

Hahn Dohr Kahn. The Realm of The Dragon.

They skirted around the southern edge of the great isolated peak and ran into it.

The river.

The river curled around the eastern edge of the slope of the mountain. Its origin appeared to be somewhere in a general northerly direction into the grass lands. To the south it flowed just along the edge of the forest.

Scrambling up the slope they could see that the river seemed to curve off to the east.

They camped in a flat space near the bank of the water course to allow the map makers to have all the time that they required to record all that they had found including the enormous conical mountain, the river, and anything else that the map makers felt needed to be drawn and recorded.

Irinl pointed at the jagged peak piercing the apparently permanent cloud layer and said to Prince Frahn and the map makers, "Cloud Spire is a good name, don't you think?"

The three nodded and the mountain was named. Frahn sent two of the Silver Rangers off to explore some of the lower slopes. He was curious to see whether they might find a tunnel entrance. And wondered whether there might be another great

dragon dwelling in a lair inside this peak.
So they camped for two days.
And swam in the river.
And caught and ate the fish.
But only after the fish were properly recorded.

New Places, New Thoughts

Far Dark. A Strange Place.

Sgenn stopped them at the inner door.

"From here I must go alone. To speak with them. The Four Who Teach." She kissed his cheek. "Not long, not short." She opened the door and stepped through.

All the rest could see before the door closed was a soft golden glow.

Deep below they heard things starting to growl.

He looked around, walked over, sat on the floor and leaned back against the wall.

Chantal joined him. "We know, Lover. We can all feel it." She leaned, just a little, against him. "So relax. Sgenn is very calm."

"She always is," he grumbled. "Doesn't mean anything."

Fair Morn sat by his other side, cradling her weapon in her arms. "Szart and Sha'gar don't think that their magic will work very well here or have much of an effect although Szart thinks one or two of the banned spells might." She grinned. "I set it to high power. I doubt anything could withstand that."

"Wonderful," he mumbled. "Just no firing unless absolutely necessary. All right?"

"Sho nuff," she mumbled. And winked at him.

Early Dawn sat next to Fair Morn. "What do I do with

this thing?" She wore a holster on her belt with a large handgun stuffed into it.

"Nothing," he said.

"Just in case," stated Fair Morn. She smiled. "If we are outside, just gain altitude and shoot anything not us."

He sighed, heavily. And really began to worry.

"Worry wort," grumbled Chantal.

Toos Tok.

It was a small foregather as foregathers go. It was, as Seemna had said, a rather minor foregather.

The booths, displays, and spell spots were scattered in four directions along the main streets of the place from the central square of this small town, Tumil by name.

"Witches," gasped Dumar after they had swirled in.

"Of course," stated Seemna. Everyone knew that a foregather was a Witch Fair. But it seemed that some isolated far corners did not. Like the one Dumar came from. She headed for and into the lodgings tent, made arrangements, and aimed them in the correct direction. Their inn was a short two blocks down the street called Zisint.

They were almost there when a rather short witch approached them. She, unlike most, wore clothes of a deep green color. Baggy trousers and an equally baggy smock. As she stepped in front of Seemna and stopped, all could see the small orange dot appear on the left cheek of each witch.

"Grenzanr witch Mbarta," she stated. "Clan linked."

Seemna nodded. "Faan websmith Seemna. Clan linked."

Mbarta indicated Dumar with her eyes. "Your's? Her's?"

"None."

"Sooooo."

"He does wander with us."

"One witch, two warriors. Strange group."

Seemna shrugged.

Chyndra eyed this witch in green.

Seemna touched Chyndra's arm. "One cousin." And indicated Dumar. "Newly wander joined. Where?"

Mbata pointed at the inn. "Dril Inn. One up."

Seemna consulted something. "We are two up."

Mbarta nodded. "This is First Night. Join?"

Seemna nodded, pointed at a nearby food booth, and then led Chyndra and Dumar inside *The Dril Inn*. There she said something to the inn keeper, received the door patch, and headed up the stairs, two up.

At the end of the hall she threw open a brown door and stepped into the barren room.

"Here?" Chyndra stared at the large, empty space.

Seemna yanked in a green wand, said something, and pointed at the right hand door in the wall that had just appeared. "Dumar there." She opened the other door and stepped inside followed by Chyndra.

The room was a large, furnished bedroom of rather plain furniture. Chyndra sat on the large bed and decided that it felt comfortable.

"We must rest now," said Seemna as she crawled onto the bed. "This is First Night. All events at a foregather occur after sunset and run until sunrise. This is a minor foregather of three nights."

"What do we do here?" She dropped her sword, sheath,

and belt to the floor next to the bed, and sprawled flat.

"Meet. Visit. Look. Maybe buy. Spell learn. Listen for strange." Seemna stretched, yawned, and fell asleep

As Chyndra fell asleep she thought that this was just one more new thing to learn about witches during her wander.

Hahn Dohr Kahn. The Realm of The Dragon.

Days passed. The Silver Rangers returned and reported that they had found no trace or indication of a tunnel opening.

The group spent the rest of the day resting, finishing maps, and then set off along the south bank of the wide river.

The map makers felt that this was the first river that The Queen had found during her coastal exploration. They had brought along a small scale map of the eastern edge of the land and added to it in quick sketches what their large map in the central city contained in detail.

It was another two days when they found it.

It was not exactly what they had hoped to find.

They had been walking along a game trail that wandered along the edge of the river but just inside the forest that crowded the water's edge.

At first it appeared that the river had taken another bent to the south in a wide sweeping curve. Then they realized that they faced a small lake. Here and there they could see small currents roil the surface while bubbles popped and burst. One of the Silver Rangers plunged his arm into a similar spot next to the shore.

"Warm! Most warm!"

Everyone joined him in testing the water.

"This is the same as Spa," said Frahn. "Only this is many

times larger. Spa is but three small springs bubbling to the surface, But this," he waved one arm, "is large enough to anchor a dozen of the sea folk's medium vessels." He threw an arm around Princess Irinl. "If this river is like this to the sea, I would say that here is a good place for a small town and port."

"Why build here?" Irinl looked at the forest, the water, and the bubbling springs. "I see nothing that is not already available closer to the Royal Town."

He nodded. And pointed to a small bump of land poking out into the lake. "Let us camp there and carefully map this place. If the maps are accurate it would be two days swift sail from the coast to here."

The map makers looked indignant at their Prince but agreed that it would be two days if the wind was right.

The place was named Talking Water after a comment made by one of the Silver Rangers.

One day later it happened.

The totally unexpected.

One of the sea folk fast vessels appeared, tacking toward their camp.

The Ship Master delivered a message scroll to Frahn, who read it, handed it back, and whirled away.

"Sook directed them to here. Break camp! Everyone on board! We are commanded back to the Royal Towns. Mother and Uncle are off to the Royal City and order me to stand in their stead. Until they return, I am The King of The New Kingdoms." He nodded to the Ship Master. "Once we are away we will speak on this. It seems Mother utilized Queen Sook's talent for the ship to find us.""

In rapid order, the sea folk and the Silver Rangers had

everything stowed on board and the vessel headed downstream as fast as was deemed prudent.

Bahn Dohr Tohr. The Royal City.

Lurin banged through the door and strode across the large meeting room to the large table, startling most of those present.

Frinda strolled in behind her, smiling broadly at their parents, Toucan and Willawa, The King and Queen of Bahn Dohr Tohr, the King and Queen of The Old Kingdoms and The New Kingdoms.

Behind Frinda walked the New Kingdoms First Lords and a few others all carrying large cloth bags.

Lurin wore her kingdom's Royal Garb along with a wide leather belt from which hung her great two-handed white sword. She clenched the hilt with her left hand. Her expression suggested that someone was close to being hacked into small pieces. She stopped and turned.

"Hail Queen. Hail King. Your dutiful and obedience daughter Lurin, Queen of Hahn Dohr Tohr, The Realm of The Dragon, stands before you, as ordered. As do King Frinda." She bowed to them. As she straightened up, she murmured, "Are these," she barely acknowledged the rest seated at the table, "those who would dare nothing, but would claim much?"

Lords began to sputter. They were cut off by The Queen of All Kingdoms.

"Sit down, Highness," she said to her daughter, looking Royally stern but with a small smile tugging at one corner of her mouth.

"You also, Noble Sea King. And the court of each. We

have serious matters to discuss and weighty problems to resolve."

Lurin dropped into a chair and stared at those across the table from her. She didn't recognize any of them.

Frinda took a chair next to her, grabbed a jug, filled his mug, then his sister's, took a sip, and laughed happily. Then he nodded at those others.

"Why do you feel that We should give you anything? It was my sister's drive, passion, and courage, and her, and mine, coinage, that did find the New Lands, now called The New Kingdoms." He decided not to mention what the fleet had not long ago found. This would only be shared with their parents.

A heavy set man wearing the orange and brown colors of his kingdom, cleared his throat. "The Far Fringe Kingdoms have always occupied the slivers that none wished from many, many long ago. Our people are few, our fortunes few. We heard, even there, of the voyage of Queen Lurin and King Frinda and of their success that none would support." His eyes jumped to the other Royal Pair. "Other than the Central City. Thus we do understand that none may claim support share."

Frinda stood. "Then why are We here? Why are We here, dragged from pressing matters in Our own lands?" He leaned forward. "Do any wish to dispute Our claim, Our right, to that which, We alone do find, supply, and even now build?"

"SIT!" The Queen reached out and touched his arm and waited until he did. Then she smiled around the table and at her son and daughter. "None would dare contest your claims, either in Our Court or on the field of battle."

Lurin unhooked her sword and laid it on the table, point aiming across the table, hilt close to her right hand. "Then?"

The Queen leaned back and nodded at the King of Kahn Cahn Tahn.

He looked from His Queen to Lurin and Frinda, and stood. And bowed formally to the pair.

"Our Kingdom will willingly transfer all our holdings, with certain exceptions, to The New Kingdoms, providing that those New Kingdoms will deed us comparable lands plus a Knight's Share. For this, with your assistance, we shall transport all of Our people who will follow their Royal Family into this endeavor."

He unhooked his battle sword, heavily worn and scarred, and placed it on the table. Then he leaned and gently pushed it across to Lurin. "We also do pledge to be forever and forever One Step Down."

He swayed slightly from the tension and battle nerves he felt. All the tales had come to him about Queen Lurin. He had sent seekers to find out all that they could before he had made his plans and had traveled to The Central City to propose what he had just said. He knew that if great insult were taken now, he could well lose all as could the two other Fringe Kingdoms that he had convinced to join with him. Sweat trickled down his face and into his beard.

Lurin looked at the others, then turned to her brother. "Great King, what say you? Have we need of such?" She had used a carefully selected choice of words, had couched her question to raise ire in those listening and asking.

The dull thump was the King of Kahn Cahn Tahn dropping heavily into his chair, face going pale. She was even more difficult than anything he had been told. In two short sentences she had demolished all his hoped for plans and had insulted them as well.

Frinda stared into somewhere for long moments while all at the table held their breath. They knew that he was more impulsive than his sister. Then Frinda smiled at his sister and waggled one arm, beckoning his First Map Maker forward.

"Let us look at Our Kingdom Map showing all we know of The New Kingdoms, and see if there is anything We might discuss." He stood and looked across the table. "Will the three Kings join us?"

Carefully controlling their surprise the three hurried around the table to stare at the map now covering most of the table top. On side tables the King and Queen ordered food and drink to be placed.

The King leaned close to his Queen and whispered carefully so only she could hear, "Our children would frighten even the stoutest of hearts. What do you think they will do?"

"Bargain shrewdly. If these three can persuade them that they have something to offer. And, My King, we must quickly make our own plans if we wish to have some small portion of the New Lands as well."

He stood, leaned, and kissed her. "We will begin." He excused himself as the conversations at the table began with five people all gesturing at the great map.

Two days later, after many hours of discussion, some quiet, some loud and contentious, the agreements were made.

Kahn Cahn Tahn became part of Lurin's kingdom. Rahn Rahn Tahn joined with Frinda. Vahn Uban Dahn withdrew, declaring that the New Kingdom's social rules were too radical for them.

Rahn Rahn Tahn enhanced Frinda's metal crafting guilds while Kahn Cahn Tahn added their valuable wood and jewelry crafting guilds to those already in Lurin's holdings.

Frinda laughed and smiled at his mother and watched as the three Kings left the room. When the door was firmly closed, he said, "Now, Mother Great Queen, let us tell you Our news and what we think ought to be done."

Toos Tok.

Seemna sat up and shook Chyndra. "Rise. It is First Night."

"What?" She yawned widely.

"First Night. We will eat and then enjoy the foregather. The Grenzanr and that Prince will be downstairs, waiting." She stood and ordered on their clothes, and headed for the door, and down and outside to the food booth.

Dumar and Mbarta looked up at the pair approached. "May I?" asked Mbarta. Seemna nodded and the green ordered their food and beverages. As they ate, Mbarta explained that this foregather was a three dark foregather as this elseplace had no moons or other night illumination.

"How do we see?" asked Dumar.

"Witch glow," said Mbarta, smiling a slow witch smile.

"Hum hum hum," replied Seemna.

"What?" asked Chyndra and Dumar.

Seemna looked across the table and stared hard at Dumar. "You will promise, here and to her, to behave in your most Princely manner and to control, most strongly, your baser male impulses!"

"What?" He stared at her, not sure if he had been insulted

or not.

"I could cast nip pa," offered Mbarta.

Seemna gave a quick shake of her head.

"Seemna?" Chyndra looked from witch to witch. From her training she could feel-sense the witch under-emotions.

Seemna sat straighter and stared into the pale blue eyes. "Princess, it is witch custom during any dark night of any foregather, great or minor, to dress in a certain proscribed manner."

Chyndra nodded. She knew that the witches had a great number of special customs.

Mbarta's eyes glittered soft amusement as she watched the non-witch faces as Seemna explained.

Chyndra's face darkened, her eyes closing into mere slits. The others could feel the tension radiating from her and a soft hint of mayhem building. Two witches, one booth over, cast protection and hurried away. All knew that arguments between warriors and witches could often become quite bloody to all for some distance around.

"We are creatures of the night, Daughters of The Moon," stated Seemna. "Moonglow is preferred."

"A Princess does not expose herself so," stated Dumar. He cleared his throat. "As far as I know of other elseplaces."

Chyndra looked at the witch pair. "This is often done?"

"At a dark night foregather," stated Mbarta. "None else."

Chyndra glared at Dumar. "To touch is to die."

"Horribly," gurgled Mbarta. Then she nodded at Chyndra. "Unless invited."

"Hap tak!" snapped Seemna.

Mbarta shrugged. "Unless invited."

Chyndra chewed on one corner of her mouth and stared out and past Seemna. Then she refocused. "We are on quest journey."

"Most true," agreed Seemna.

"A time to learn much new."

Mbarta nodded. "Much much."

"It is proper?"

"Witch true," said Seemna.

"Witch true," echoed Mbarta.

"Then We will do this thing," stated Chyndra, all Royal tone.

"Male and female," added Mbarta.

Dumar squirmed in his seat, his face flushed.

Chyndra tapped his arm with one fingertip. "You are on quest?"

He nodded.

"Then," she stated in her best command tone of voice, "you will do as all do. And behave most proper!"

He nodded again. And mumbled, "Witches are strange. A Prince is always proper."

"Pik tik," suggested Seemna.

Mbarta smiled agreement at her. It was a wonderfully vile suggestion.

First Night.

Soon it was dark, the start of the Foregather.

Here and there could be seen soft clouds of gentle witch glow as witches drifted from spot to spot, as witches wandered from booth to booth, to this display of things and paraphernalia for sale, or to that demonstration of magic practice.

They stepped from the booth and Mbarta cast soft glow. She was bathed in a gentle green.

Chyndra suddenly felt warm air brush over bare skin as Seemna sent all their upper garments to their rooms. She cackled softly as Dumar tried not to look in their direction. "Heh heh heh heh heh."

"Eh eh eh eh eh eh," agreed Mbarta.

By the second booth Chyndra no longer felt uncomfortable and by the fourth booth Dumar finally relaxed.

Chyndra leaned close to Seemna, sipping some beverage that they had just purchased, and whispered in her ear, "This is very comfortable."

"Hum," replied Seemna. "He does look warrior trained. Nicely muscled."

"Then his tale was true," said Chyndra. "That is a nasty scar." A long jagged line ran down the left side of Dumar's chest and disappeared into his trousers.

Mbarta jabbed him in the side. "What cause?"

He looked at her, jerked, blushed, and then realized that she was staring at his scar. "Oh! A minor Prince sought to take land which he did not own. I held the center of the line and removed that Prince but his First Warrior did that as the greedy Prince went to the land of shadow."

"Near fatal?" asked Mbarta.

He nodded.

"Sooooo," she hissed. "Do you like that which you observe?"

He jerked. And nodded. "Are all witches like this?"

She frowned at him.

"Ah um, lovely?"

"Witch nature. Most true in witch light."

"I did not know this."

"Few do other than those at foregather. Of course, our Mates-for-life know. For them we are always willing. None else."

He glanced at Chyndra who was walking on the far side of Seemna. "You were correct, Princess. One does learn much new on a Great Adventure."

"Eh eh eh eh eh," cackled Mbarta. She halted them at a display of dark blue fog foam. It grinned at them.

Finally, not all that long before sunrise, as the four wended their unsteady way toward their lodging, unsteady due to the fact that Mbarta had insisted on ordering another round of Squeeking Orange Kak, they were stopped by a tall man who was leaning heavily to one side. He nodded at the group and stared at Mbarta's chest.

"Oza warlock Hudz," he mumbled. "Pale blue and green Oza."

"Granzanr witch Mbarta," she hissed at him.

"Faan websmith Seemna."

"Princess Chyndra."

"Prince Dumar," he mumbled. Something seemed to have numbed his tongue. He squinted up at this man and took another sip from the beverage container that he held. And shrugged.

"A lovely Princess," said Hudz, running one finger over her.

A sudden flash of light and the Nakle Beast pulled Hudz

to the pavement. On all sides witches hastily backed away

"Hudz," snarled Mbarta, "the only reason that you keep your face is that we are at foregather. Deep apology and nazta payment are due to this Princess. Unless she wishes to take some piece of you home with her."

Chyndra blinked, her eyes were trying to not focus. "No. This person is of no concern." She squinted at Seemna. "Is it correct behavior to chop off his head during the day?"

"No, Princess, it is not. All during foregather we are sworn to witch truce." She kicked Hudz in the side. "You are fortunate Oza warlock Hudz."

"She is not-witch," he mumbled.

Seemna kicked him again. "No cause for itchy fingers to be so free. Stand!"

Mbata sent the beast away and yanked the warlock to his feet.

Hudz bowed in Chyndra's direction, more or less, and after three attempts snapped his fingers. A black ring appeared on Chyndra's right thumb.

Mbata nodded and sent him to the far end of the foregather and grumbled, "There is always one in every foregather."

They popped up just one block from their lodgings. The inn keeper watched them as they stumbled up the stairs and decided not to challenge them having a large lump of dark blue foam fog going with them. As they sprawled on the bed sinking toward sleep, Chyndra said, "He likes what he sh'ees."

"That horrid warlock needs a piece missing," grumbled Seemna.

"Prince Dum'l," slurred Chyndra.

"Dumar?"

"Something new on quest," mumbled Chyndra.

As the pair fell asleep, the blue foam fog slowly faded into nowhere.

Second Night.

They were gathered around a table in one of the food booths, relaxing over the end of their meal.

Chyndra indicated a witch, here and there, wandering about. Their upper garments were open and flopping loose. "It appears that some start early."

"Brazen intaps," said a deep voice.

All turned to see who had spoken to them.

He was somewhat shorter than any of them with very broad shoulders.

"Hum hum," said Seemna.

"Witches," he said. "Non-witches. May I share Second Night with this group?"

"Most polite," observed Mbarta.

He flicked his shirt with a fingertip. "Deep brown Brakal warlock Mirdata." He nodded at them. "But I am Mir to witch antak."

"Granzanr witch Mbarta." She nodded at him.

"Faan websmith Seemna."

"Princess Chyndra."

"Prince Dumar."

Mbarta ordered a chair over. "Beverage? Mir?"

"Witch true." He waved in five tall glasses of foaming pink. "From Uta Under Cloud." And waited until Mbarta took a sip. Then he sat.

"It is said that a certain warlock came near to going far from doing nik tar. It is said on a non-witch." He glanced at Chyndra.

"Hum," said Seemna.

"Sooooo," hissed Mbarta.

Mir shrugged. "Some warlock ought suffer much much." He stared at the ring on Chyndra's thumb. "Ah hap ta!"

"Yessssss," hissed Mbarta.

He took a sip and cleared his throat. "It is told that Faan are many linked."

Seemna nodded as did Mbarta.

"Faan Grenzanr?"

"Witch true," stated Seemna.

"My older brother mated her older sister," said Mbarta.

"May one know?"

"They may, polite Mir. Mantara and Shitar."

"Ahhhhh, ata! One does hear tales, here and there, of Shitar of the Faan."

"Sooooo?" hissed Seemna.

Mir shrugged. "Witches do witch." He ordered another set of beverages. "We have time before dark night."

Eventually the group set off into the darkness of Second Night.

"How is it, warlock Mir, that one has such muscles?"

"It is a small vice."

"Yesssssssss?"

"I enjoy hard manual labor." He looked somewhat embarrassed, about as embarrassed as a warlock ever was, which was not much.

"A strange warlock," suggested Mbarta.

"Some might say that." The air soft crackled around Mir.

"Pleasant strange," suggested Mbarta. "Not strange strange."

Seemna nudged him with her wand, a short thick bronze. "Shhhhh."

Mir nodded. The air settled. But he watched her from the corners of his eyes until she sent that wand somewhere.

Dumar spoke softly to Chyndra. "One does learn much on a Great Adventure."

She laughed gently. "That is the purpose, to learn, and to understand. Necessary skills for those who would rule over any. Think you not?"

He nodded. "Now I agree. Two days past I would not have."

"Then there may be some small skills developing, perhaps?"

"I have many skills," he grumbled at her.

"Indeed?"

"Most true."

"Oh?"

"Most true." He glared at her.

She frowned back at him. "I haven't noticed much in the way of true Courtly manner not inflated mannerisms, staring Dumar. Perhaps a Third Prince has no need."

"A Third Prince has greater need than a King."

"Oh?"

"Most true."

"When does it start?"

"What?"

"All that Courtly manner?"

"I do not understand."

Chyndra suppressed her grin. "You have yet to compliment Us."

Dumar, frowned, squinted, and stared. "For what? On what?"

"On the obvious beauty that your Princely eyes have been ever so slyly caressing." She laughed. "Or should We say, beauties? Perhaps this Prince prefers witch?"

His face flushed red, obvious even in the faint witch glow. Jerking to a halt he glared at her. "This is not a proper way for a Princess to behave! Any kind of Princess! I do not believe that you are really a Princess! Flaunting your, ahh, errr, self like a back street low wench." He twisted away and stomped off to walk alongside Mir, mumbling to himself.

Seemna, in three long strides, walked up to his free side, and wacked Dumar on the side of the head with a long silver wand. "Cretin!"

"OUCH!" He snatched the wand from her hand and struck her with it. "Stop that!"

The air crackled anger as she stuck him to the pavement. Red flared in her eyes. On all sides, witches cast protection. Mir shoved Mbarta behind himself and layered protection over them both. She shoved him aside, green pulsating around her. "Faan witch," she cautioned. "This is a foregather."

Seemna whirled in her direction, black swirling over her head, and hissed, "Thisssss ptar ptar kak tak thinks to freely insult my Princess! None may do so. None!"

Dumar stared at his feet, then at each witch in turn. He looked at Chyndra, who was carefully holding her face in a neutral look. He cleared his throat. "Princess Chyndra, the Prince Dumar begs forgiveness for my insult or any error made." He looked at Seemna. "If you will tell this creature to release my feet, I shall depart your company and proceed elsewhere."

"Creature?" snarled Seemna. "Dumb pis pak!"

Chyndra looked at him. "A grave insult?"

Dumar sighed. "It would seem so."

"Then We may request special recompense. True?"

"Ask and it shall be done, Princess."

Standing tall, she stated, all Royal Command. "Then, Third Prince Dumar, you shall accompany us until We do give you Our Leave to go. Release him, cousin, We have much of Second Night to enjoy."

Sooooo, they strolled off and wandered from booth to booth. Sometime after each witch had purchased a new spell from a booth whose banner read **ARCANE THINGS**, they stopped for refreshments, and then at a booth selling rings, where they pushed and shoved things from pile to pile.

Dumar found a narrow band of red with a yellow strip meandering snake-like around the exterior. He handed the vendor the price and stepped next to Chyndra, held the ring out, pinched between two of his fingers. "A small token from the ever so humble Dumar to the beautiful princess Chyndra."

She took the ring and slipped it on her left hand. "Most kind, dutiful Prince Dumar." She yanked the black ring from her thumb, grabbed his right hand, and jabbed the ring on his second finger. "A gift for a gift."

"Nooooooo," gurgled Seemna.

"Am ta do pa!" hissed Mbarta.

"What?" asked Dumar and Chyndra.

Mir held a whispered conversation with Mbarta who then spoke low tone to Seemna.

"Ptar ptar nar!" snapped Seemna. "We have to find an Esta witch!"

"What!" demanded Chyndra.

Seemna pointed. "That ring was nazta payment from that rak tak Oza warlock. If something activates that ring while he wears it, Dumar will be lucky if he only loses that hand."

Dumar blanched and tugged at the ring. "It will not come off."

"Mir agrees," said Mbarta. "One of the Esta clan might be able to free it."

"Then we must find one." Chyndra peered into the darkness. "How do we do that?"

"Tomorrow, after first meal, we will seek at the Lodging Booth, see if any are here visiting." Seemna looked grumpy at Chyndra.

"I think," stated Chyndra, "that witches ought explain things before, rather than after." She looked at Dumar. "Truly sorry, Prince."

He looked at Seemna. "What activates this thing?"

Mir stepped close. "It is a defensive ring. Sudden magic attacks."

"Then I should be all right."

"Don't anger any and you are mostly correct." Mbarta nudged Mir. "Most learned."

He shrugged. "One tries." He glanced at the brightening edge of night. "Might a certain warlock walk a certain witch to her lodgings?"

"This witch," she purred, "thinks that it would be a safe thing to do."

Third Night.

Immediately after a hurried meal, they entered the Lodging Booth and stood along the narrow counter.

Seemna frowned at the person behind the counter and tapped a glittering yellow wand on the hard surface. "We would know whether any Esta did here come?"

"Most bothering," stated the thin witch.

Mbarta flicked a gold coin to her.

The clerk hauled a ledger from somewhere, laid it on the counter, and cast a minor seek spell. She watched, arms folded, while the book opened and pages began to flick over, one by one. Somewhere, near the middle, the book lay still, an entry glowed soft blue.

The clerk leaned close and intoned, "Esta witch Nunderla, sub-order Mataca." She straightened up and pointed. "Three down, floor four." And sent the ledger away.

They hurried in that direction, turned into the inn, and stopped by the entry desk.

"Esta witch Nunderla," stated Mbarta.

"Flickered out early," replied the inn keeper.

"Ptar ptar tak!" snarled Seemna.

The inn keeper winced. He knew agitated witches were one step from doing mayhem and awful to anyone handy.

"To where?" she grumbled.

He hastily checked his book. "Far wander," he said. "To Pazel Pearl."

"Hum hum." Seemna cast soft know and waited. Mir and Mbarta backed away. Whatever she had done, it felt strangely bent to them. Then Seemna nodded. "We will travel after Third Night."

The group left the inn and headed for a spell intark Mbarta had heard mentioned.

Seemna walked by Chyndra's side. "Be warned, Princess. On last dark night some witches tend to do loose behavior. Many find their's at foregather."

"Loose behavior?"

"Druzna," hissed Seemna.

"Oh?" Chyndra blushed.

"What?" asked Dumar.

"Ask her." Chyndra flushed even brighter.

During the spell intark, Seemna leaned close and whispered in Dumar's ear, who gasped, and wiped the sweat from his face. "Just don't anger any," she reminded him.

At the end of the demonstration, they strolled to a booth of wands and one owner rings. Two booths away, Mir and Mbarta pawed through a table of ancient spell scrolls. Now and then, Mbarta showed one to Mir who shrugged.

Then the group headed for a bright yellow glowing refreshment booth.

Mir leaned close and said, "It is said that Grenzanr are few and are hard to deal with."

Mbarta shrugged. "We are few. The rest is to see."

He nodded. "I see lovely and talented witch."

She stopped, turned, the green glow around her fading to soft soft. "Would one handle what one sees?"

He looked at her. "One would prefer life."

She nodded. "It is told that Deep brown Brakal are twice twisted sly."

He shrugged. "Some might so tell."

She stepped close. "This witch would not mind a certain warlock with a small nice who touched ever so gently but firm." She spun and leaned back against him. And exhaled. "With ever so warm hands."

"Witch smooth," he murmured. "Witch smooth."

"Beverage." She headed them that way. Followed by Chyndra and Dumar.

They walked to the beverage booth she had pointed at and waited as she ordered for them a drink with red flashes, a tall slender witch surrounded with soft pink glow stepped from the edge where she had been leaning and approached them.

"So so so," she breathed, a very crooked grin on her face. "A broad shouldered warlock." Handing her beverage container to Chyndra she leaned toward Mir. "With non-witch company." She licked her lips. "Soft pink is finger tingle delight."

"MINE!" snapped Mbarta.

The witch stared at Mir. "True?"

His eyes flicked sideways and back. "Witch true." He nodded at her.

"Kaz kaz," she grumbled, turned away, snatched her beverage container from Chyndra, and saw Dumar ordering something else from the harried booth owner who was mixing and shoving tall glasses to the folk crowding around the front of the booth. She stepped over and jabbed him in the side. "Turn this way, battle scarred one, I feel lonely."

Chyndra stepped close and snarled at her, "Mine!" and carefully watched the witch as she walked away grumbling darkly to herself.

"What?" Dumar stared at Chyndra.

"Just fending off a witch," she stated.

"Hum hum hum," said Seemna.

"Behave," growled Chyndra.

"Eh eh eh," cackled Mbarta. Then she whispered to Mir, "I think that his fingers just itch to hold those."

"Shhhhh," he replied.

She pinched his side, just to calm him down a little. "We must visit the clan head, my brother Mantara. The clan head must approve."

"Now?"

She nodded.

Chyndra, Dumar, and Seemna watched the pair disappear in a green puff of mist.

Seemna nudged Chyndra. "It is as I said. Some find their's at foregather." She stroked her upper lip with a fingertip. "Now Faan are linked through Grenzanr to Brakal."

Their orders arrived and the trio wandered into the night sipping from their tall containers. Somehow, after a display of laughing fire, Dumar and Chyndra became separated from Seemna.

Staring into the dark, she could see something pale sorta blurred standing nearby. "That you, Dumar?"

"Indeed, Noble Primsech, We are here." He touched his face with a finger. "As far as I can tell." He leaned to one side and blinked. "Why do you lean schum?"

"Step closer, I cannot see you clearly. Did a fog settle here?"

"Nup." His nose bumped her's. "Touch," he muttered.

"That you?" He reached out. "Oh!"

She lurched away, spun. And crashed back against him. "None can see us in this dark of night. For this moment We do be a pair of most brazen witch folk. Treat us so, besotten knave."

"You are puddle brained," he muttered into her hair, arms encircling her.

"Nay! We are over celebrated." She laughed, a soft gentle laugh. "For such a hard warrior, you have a most gentle touch."

"Smooth pleasure."

"A Prince tells every maiden that."

"Not trush. Schum of little honor do schush. Nop I, Pinsch Chimum."

"Dumar," she sighed. "Release me."

"Mosht hard an order to obey, but We do obey We do dee done." He spun her around and peered into her eyes, forehead bumping into forehead. "I, Dumar, wilp do any deed put upon me self, I, umm, to demonstrate my worthiness to your Noble Parents. Any deed! Pon my honor!" He had worked slowly and carefully to get that sentence clearly stated, more or less. He hiccuped.

"Then the first deed, Our Warrior Most Bold, is to find our lodgings. Our very eyes refuse to obey Our orders."

Light popped around them.

She grinned crookedly at him. "Well done, Dumar!"

"Chyndra," growled Seemna, "why did you come this way?"

"Seeking lodgings, thesh way, umm road," mumbled Dumar, canting dangerously to one side, squinting at her.

"Hum hum hum hum," observed Seemna as she led the pair in the correct direction.

"Of corseh nop," slurred Chyndra. "Perpec't Primce."

Once at their lodgings, Seemna shoved Dumar at his door and tugged the badly tilting Princess into their room and the bed.

Ordering the lights and their clothes off, she hissed, "What did you do, Princess?"

"Nothing mumpsch," came the mumbled reply. "Played wipsch."

"Zip tik!" Tiny spots of color exploded against the ceiling. "He wears that ring and you allowed him to fondle you?"

"Just a little."

Seemna cast deep sleep and cast a ward to remove the ring body control spell. If they couldn't locate that Esta witch she would kill him.

Dol Spar. Monetary Control Headquarters.

"HO BOY!"

Mirf laughed loudly and beamed at Fred, the female suk-dragon, and her husband, Quan. She had sent the sisters, Rema and Nema, to search the file for information on certain subjects just presented to her in a message from The General.

"Such an agitation this is becoming." She grinned broadly. "Maybe I will take over M.C." She banged a certain spot on her desk top. "Such a messuggener thought that is! I would be buried up to my tukus in beaurocrap!"

"Yes," oozed an oily voice from her desk top.

"I have permanently borrowed the office next door for my new staff. Send someone up there to take measurements and to deliver the proper clothes. And send that green-eyed slinky bod up from Third Floor Records to join them. All three, count 'em, are henceforth Agents dash Undercover, and work only for me. GOT THAT!"

"Yes, Special Investigator."

"Hurry hurry hurry," gurgled Mirf, breaking the connection. "Fred, you're a female, check 'em out. As soon as they get dressed we will feast! In the nearest expensive restaurant. M.C. pays." She leaned back and rubbed her hands together, eyes glittering in hob-goblin delight.

Deep Happa.

They arrived in a swirl of black.

And stood and looked around.

On one side, pale sand rising in soft swells to the far horizon. On the other side, an azure sea with low curling waves sliding up the beach almost to their feet.

"Nice beach." He looked up and down the shore line. "Now what?"

Sgenn pointed.

The group hiked that way, staying on the hard packed sand, toward a large lump of grey-red rock hill, all jumbled and tumbled in a strange heap.

"Why here?

"The Four said that deep below said that a force had opened into between here and the Trantil Layer. This end must be closed before they pour forth."

He nodded. "Sure. Perfectly clear. Before what pours forth from what?"

"The Trantil Layer. The Place of the Unspeakable."

"And how do we do that?"

Sgenn shrugged.

"Merde."

She shrugged again. "It must be done."

He grabbed one of her hands. "But carefully, right?"

"You betcha," said Fair Morn who was walking right behind them.

Sha'gar nudged Szart. She had never heard of the Trantil Layer. Szart shook her head and sent a message to her Aunt, Reep. Of all the clan, she had wandered the most widely. Perhaps she knew something.

The group slowly walked down the beach and finally arrived at the base of a strange hill just as the sun was setting.

Sgenn pointed at a symbol carved into the rock. "There leads to the entrance."

"Guess we camp here." He looked from ocean to sand to rock jumble. "Smoke?"

"Nothing that matters." She sat on a rock. "Let's eat before it gets dark."

Szart waved in mats, sleeping gear, a table, and chairs.

Sha'gar waved in food.

Chantal sat next to him and began to eat. "So far, so good."

"Uh huh. Wonder what's going on this time."

"Strange that Quiet was told so little."

He sighed. "Do you think that this is some strange ploy of B.G.'s?"

"Makes even less sense than his usual plot." She laughed. "No babes."

When all were finished with their meal, Szart and Sha'gar cast protection, layer after layer.

And all went to sleep.

Termion Ianna.

Zim slid into the room and shimmered soft excitement. "They were at a minor foregather on Toos Tok."

Aldin Cease nodded. "The rare and her associate?"

"True. And some young Prince."

"Does he guard her?"

"Unknown."

"Watch carefully."

"They left. An innkeeper thought that they sought an Esta witch on Pazel Pearl."

"Esta witch?"

"True. Unexplained."

"A twisted thing. I thought that she would have gone home after that mage and his elseplace were removed."

Zim shimmered agreement. "That witch clan have added more links. They have threads scattered wide."

Aldin Cease stood and stared out a window. "Perhaps it is time for a more direct approach?"

Zim gurgled warning.

"I understand, Zim." He stepped over and out.

Deep Happa.

Shortly after sunrise, Smoke began to rouse all from sleep.

Fair Morn shook Early Dawn awake.

In short order their breakfast was eaten, the camp was gone, and they began to follow the carved symbols deep into the rock jumble, and found it.

It was a tunnel carved deep into the rock, the far end was

dark and out of sight, even for Messenger for whom there was no dark. It was a rather wide, very straight, very long, dark tunnel.

He halted the group as he swung down his great sword. "O.K., anything that moves in there, kill it. Right?"

"Absolutely, My Lord." Chicken swished her blade back and forth.

"Deader than dead," agreed Messenger, yanking her long black wand from her hair where she had stuffed it right after breakfast.

"All right by me." Chantal spun the cylinder of her long-barreled revolver and stuffed it back into its holster.

Szart nodded and cast light ahead of them into the tunnel.

They slowly walked in and followed the light as it led them deeper and deeper. And not all that soon, they walked around the first bend, a sharp right-hand turn, and stopped. To stare. A large spot on the rock wall glowed faint blue and shimmered.

"Reminds me of Big Red's portal," he grumbled. "Now what?"

Smoke leaned closer to it. "Can't see anything on the other side."

He leaned against the rock wall. "I do not like the idea of us just blindly stepping through that thing. There is no way to know what it lurking on the other side."

Early Dawn walked over and poked one finger in and out of the blue. "I will go."

"Nope." He shook his head. "Bad idea."

"I have very fast reaction time. I am not part of you. So,

I will do it."

"Ummmm."

"Just in and back," she said. "No standing around."

"I don't like it."

Fair Morn joined them, yanked her weapon free, quickly set the levers, and handed the Space Cannon to Early Dawn. "One step in, and one step back out. If you see anything, point and fire." She grinned at Early Dawn. "I set it for wide and powerful. You can't miss." She showed her how to handle the weapon. "Be careful, sis."

"Ummm?"

"What Fair Prince do mean this thy um?"

"What happens if she doesn't return?"

"Waaaaaal, Cowboy," drawled Chantal. "I suppose we will just have to jump through and shoot everything in sight."

Szart nodded and began to call in one of the Banned Spells that her Aunt, R-Bar, had taught her.

Sha'gar yanked in a flaming red wand.

He sighed. "Still don't like it."

"Quick in and quick out," stated Early Dawn as she took one step in.

They waited.

And waited.

And waited.

"So, how much longer do we wait?" He looked at the rest of himself.

"Five more minutes," suggested Chantal, checking her watch, and rechecking her revolver.

"Fair Morn?"

She blinked and stared at the flickering blue glow. "One

step in, one step out." She gasped, "She must be dead."

He threw an arm around her shoulders. "We don't know that. We don't know anything."

"It has been too long."

"On my mark," intoned Chantal.

They readied themselves.

Pazel Pearl.

Aldin Cease stepped out and looked around.

The street was narrow, the buildings neat and tidy. The few people that he saw didn't look concerned at his sudden appearance. So he started to walk down the narrow street. And pondered how he was going to find that Esta witch.

The best way was usually the most direct way.

So he found an inn, took rooms, ate a meal, and sent a seek spell.

And waited.

Hahn Dohr Kahn. The Realm of The Dragon.

They swirled into the Royal Chambers, Lurin, Frinda, Sook, and the rest of their small party.

Lurin had carefully kept this mode of travel, witch travel, a secret from the folk of her kingdom as well as from those in the Old Kingdom. Although the servants did gossip about her sudden disappearance, now and then.

"Hail, Prince King! We return with great news and even greater business to plan." She laughed at her son's expression. "How goes your short reign?"

He laughed with her. "To be honest, Great Queen Mother, I find exploring ever more enjoyable than holding court hearings, listening to petitions, and overseeing this and that." He waggled one hand loosely.

Frinda laughed, walked over and clapped him on the back. "In that, we share much." He pointed at the great map being unrolled on a large table by the map makers.

"Come look. We have made a great bargain to develop some of the wild regions. State your opinions and search our plans for errors. We have some days before they descend upon our ports and quays."

They all gathered around the maps.

Fast beast riders were sent to fetch E'Nilt and her First Lord. And Frinda's Master Armorer. Others were sent to gather in every free beast and wagon available.

Dol Spar. Monetary Control Headquarters.

Mirf burst into the room and boomed, "Glad that you are dressed, we are going to dinner."

The three stared at her. Then Abda smiled.

"Careful," hissed Mirf at her. "I am hungry, I don't require stimulation."

Abda's smile broadened as she threw an arm around the slightly taller green-eyed woman standing next to her. "This is Dama, my thought lost sister. She tells me that she has been working here long time. We are both very happy."

Mirf watched the pair. "Is it safe?"

Dama frowned as Abda laughed. Abda was getting used to Mirf. "Safe as safe."

"Vunderbar." Mirf twirled one finger in the air. "So spin around. I want to see what you sleek shapes are doing to my uniforms."

The trio did.

Mirf laughed happily. "So you will only cause traffic jams." She laughed even louder. "And you work for me. Ho boy, such a team this is going to be." She threw open the door and charged into the hall, shouting back over her shoulder, "So what's all the standing around for, let's go eat!"

They were shortly joined by the Special Assistants that Mirf had promised Chyndra the slinth and Cadta would have.

Farnar's Star.

They had been prowling The Tna Bazaar in the main town of Herebe, spell browsing, Shitar and Mantara.

Now they sat, enjoying the local beverage at a table outside a refreshment stall.

His clothes were a deep forest green while her's were jet black with one exception, The exception was the green belt she wore around a rather narrow waist. His cape was draped over the back of his chair.

They had found a few spells of small interest but the owners had asked too much, so the pair had acquired little. But they both felt that a return visit was warranted, now and then.

So they sat, and sipped, and watched a rather slim woman in billowing pink garb drifting from place to place. Shitar thought witch. Mantara shrugged. She was definitely a magic user but he wasn't sure what type. Perhaps some mage guild or other.

He suggested that he could go talk with her and find out. Shitar grumbled at that suggestion.

So they sat and watched her as she drifted from place to place.

A small green tendril materialized and gently tickled his ear.

"Visit," purred a silken soft voice.

"Enter," said Mantara. "Sister."

They did.

In a gentle puff of green.

She waved a chair over and sat, nodding for the man with her to do the same thing. Then she looked across the table at them.

"Humble greetings, Brother. Never met before, witch. I am Grenzanr witch Mbarta. This is mine, Deep Brown Brakal warlock Mirdata, who you may address as Mir, if my brother, the clan head, approves?"

Mantarar nodded approval. "Warm welcome, Mir. One has heard some of the Brakal."

"We prefer quiet business," replied Mir, watching Mantara's companion who was chewing on the tip of a long thin wand. "Humble greetings, witch."

"I am Ripple daughter Faan witch Shitar," she grumbled. "Mantara is mine." Her eyes indicated the woman in pink. "What think?"

Mir and Mbarata looked. Mir laughed. "It is that dotap from the foregather that was fast seeking."

"Witch," stated Shitar, giving Mantara a gentle nudge in the ribs with her elbow, just to let him know that she had been correct.

"Fast seeking?" Mantara watched the pink witch drifting here and there. She appeared to be ever so slowly approaching their table.

"She tried Mir," growled Mbarta. "At the refreshment

booth."

"Ptar rak," snapped Shitar.

"Moments too late," suggested Mir, slipping an arm around Mbarta's shoulders. "Then she tried the non-witch Prince with a dazed expression."

"Non-witch?" Mantara frowned. "A Prince at a foregather?"

"He," explained Mbarta, "was apparently doing wander with a nicely formed Princess. It was dark night."

"Two Royals at a foregather? Most strange."

"Traveling," added Mbarta, "with Faan witch Seemna."

Shitar sat straighter. "That must have been Princess Chyndra. Dark night? Hum hum hum."

"Very nicely formed," purred Mbarta. She nudged Mir.

He nodded. "Very nice." He tickled Mbarta's ear. "For a non-witch." She ordered refreshments for all.

"She comes this way," hissed Mantara. "The pink."

She swirled up, fog soft billowing pink garments, ordered over a chair, waved in a refreshment, and sat. "Soooooo, two green, a brown, a black. Very interesting."

"Name!" Shitar tapped the table top in front of this person with her wand.

"Puz puz, witch." The wand was flicked away with one finger.

Black began to gather around them as Shitar stared at this irritating person. Mantara ever so gently slipped his arm over Shitar's shoulder and ran an equally gentle finger up and down the back of her neck.

"Control that black nukna," snapped the woman at Mantara. "Before she becomes dopa bits!"

Shitar hissed and the thing began to form. Large, black, ugly.

Something long, green, and eager wiggled down from somewhere, slithered past the face of the witch in pink and slipped past her neck into her garment.

Her eyes popped wide as she thrashed and cursed and rent the air with dancing pink affect. To no avail. "Stop!" she demanded.

"Apologize," purred Mantara. "Tasty pink."

"Sorry sorry," she gasped. "Most sorry sorry."

The thing vanished. She slumped and glared at Mbarta. "That was puk puk vile."

"Name," suggested Mbarta.

"Rose Batl witch Soona."

"Grenzanr witch Mbarta."

"Deep Brown Brakal warlock Mirdata."

"Grenzanr warlock Mantara."

"Ripple daughter Faan witch Shitar," growled Shitar. She waved one hand. "Go away irritating pink!"

"What want you?" Mantara filled Shitar's glass.

"Faan?" Soona stared at her. "The many linked clan?"

"Yesssssss." Shitar sipped and wondered what spell she ought to use on this witch. She thought that the one Mbarta had used looked wonderfully vile.

Soona nodded. "I saw these at foregather with a show proud non-witch female who snarled."

"Show proud?" Shitar looked at Mbarta.

"Many witch beverages," explained Mbarta. "Third Night dark night."

"Hum hum." Shitar frowned, just a little. "Snarled?"

Mbarta nodded. "This Soona wanted free play with the very dazed Prince and was ordered off."

"By my cousin? The Princess? Ordered a witch off?"

"She told witch raised and warrior trained." Mbarta watched Soona carefully.

"Haz nap na," mumbled Soona. "A witch raised non-witch Warrior Princess."

Mbarta leaned forward and tapped the table top in front of Soona with one fingertip. Small puffs of green smoke echoed each tap. "What want you, Soona witch?"

Soona ordered the green smoke away. "There is a Three Moon foregather on One Star Over. I seek travel with." She indicated Mbarta. "She did quick find. I would need learn this."

Soona glared around the table and cast a cone of silence over them. Staring at the table, she whispered witch soft, "Witch need. Ever stronger. Sister Sunl birthed some ago." Looking up, she looked from face to face. "Witch debt is offered. Even two ask."

Shitar and Mbarta sucked in quick breaths. Soona must be near flash to make such an offer.

Mantara slowly rubbed the green jewel on a ring on the other hand.

"Hum hum hum hum." Shitar recognized the deep thought look on his face.

He looked at Soona. "If this black heart wishes to do so, we will witch travel. My sister, just found, has other activities planned."

"For some time," purred Mbarta, nodding at Mantara. "If the clan head gives."

Mantara nodded at Mir. "Grenzanr welcome."

The pair stood and disappeared in a soft puff of green.

Shitar elbowed him, not too gently. "None told clan head."

He shrugged. "None asked."

"Hum." She looked at Soona and nodded.

The trio were gone.

Shitar had left a gold coin on the table top.

One Star Over.

She leaned on the railing in the Housing Tent, smiled at the clerk, and demanded, "Rooms! Two!"

The clerk recast protection and pawed through the ledger. A witch that smiled like that promised vile terror.

"Behave," murmured Mantara. It would not do to have a clerk panic in The Housing Tent.

"Hum hum," suggested Shitar.

He reached around and patted one witch hip. "Here? You? Soona?"

"Cretin," she grumbled happily, and snatched the room slip from the clerk. "Follow," she snapped at Soona.

One door over at a tall yellow inn, she shoved the slip at the inn keeper, who pointed. "Grey door, blue door."

"Grey," said Mantara as they walked down the hall.

Soona shoved open the blue door and turned to face them. "This is First Night. Slow Yellow Moon with dark start." She spun inside. The door shut itself.

Inside their room, Shitar quickly ordered it to her taste and then shoved Mantara onto a large, plush couch, and sprawled on him. "A two ask requires much thought."

"Explain." He wiggled them into a more comfortable

position.

"A rarely offered, never told witch thing."

"Yessssssssss."

"Ask all, never denied." Shitar frowned. "She gave a two ask."

"Even?"

"However you would ask." She tapped him on the forehead with one fingertip. "The Faan are fiercely protective, Husband."

Tugging her blouse loose, he nodded. "None else required, Faan love."

Deep Happa.

She stepped out, grinning broadly. "I'm back!" And stared at them. "What's wrong?"

"Where have you been?" He glowered at her.

"Nowhere. One step in, one step out. I didn't see anything at all. Just rolling hills and grass."

"You were gone for thirty minutes." Fair Morn took her cannon back and hung it in its holster.

"But I only took one step, looked around, and came right back."

He now glowered at the shimmering spot on the wall. "Now what?"

"Tis a puzzlement, My Lord." Chicken carefully checked Early Dawn for damages.

"John," said Chantal. "Everyone says that time runs differently out here. It must be something like that."

He sighed. "I suppose. That's all you saw, grass and hills?"

Early Dawn nodded. "Yep."

"I don't like it."

"Why?" asked Messenger.

"Do grass covered hills sound like a place that is called The Place of The Unspeakable?"

"The Trantil Layer," corrected Sgenn.

"Nope," said Messenger.

"Maybe," suggested Smoke, "the name refers to the inhabitants rather than their environment."

He sighed. "Even worse. Perhaps. Sgenn?"

She shrugged. "Unknown."

He nodded, mostly to himself. "Just like always. We don't know what we are doing. O.K., here is what we do. We step through and wait before doing anything else. But! The same rules apply. If it is going to cause us harm, maximum reaction. No messing around."

Everyone readied whatever weapon they preferred.

They all stepped through.

Pazel Pearl.

Seemna took them downstairs into the dining area where they had a leisurely meal. As they tried one of the local beverages, Seemna nodded.

Dumar looked at his mug. "This stuff looks like those pink giggling drinks. My eyes still hurt and I am not sure what we did after that purple magic tower display."

Chyndra blushed and quickly took a sip. "Tastes safer."

A witch carefully approached their table and bowed to them.

"I am Esta witch sub-clan Mataca witch Nunderla.

Humble Greetings. May some witch table share?" She wore a full skirt of midnight blue and a long shirt of pale grey with pale blue cuffs.

Seemna ordered over a chair. "Some polite witch may do that." After Nunderla had seated herself, Seemna stated, "Faan websmith Seemna." She had pulled Nunderla to them although she didn't feel like explaining that to this witch. Yet.

Nunderla sucked in a quick breath. "One of the rare of the rare." And looked at the others.

"Princess Chyndra, The Realm of The Dragon."

"Prince Dumar."

"Odata! A witch-warrior group. I feel need. What could such need?"

Seemna leaned sideways and began whispering very low so only Nunderla could hear.

Nunderla nodded. "A complicated thing."

"Can?"

"Much work."

Seemna set a stack of gold coins on the table.

"Need not." Nunderla shoved them back.

"What?"

Nunderla licked her lips.

"What?"

"From her some little."

"And," hissed Seemna.

"From him much much. I hear tell tale and wish to opportunity grab deep debt."

"Hum hum hum." Seemna looked from Nunderla into somewhere, then snapped, "Start!"

"Now?"

"Yesssssssssss."

Nunderla took them out with a loud pop.

Standing in the street, staring at the building, Aldin Cease looked at it carefully. The seek spell was very clear up to the entry door. Then it became confused. He strode over and silently slipped inside.

Deep Under Two.

In a soft swirl, a soft pop, they entered the large comfortable room.

Nunderla pointed. "That room for the female. That room for the male. The dark one in there. That one is mine. The red door is to be opened not. The room beyond is layered nine deep and twelve twisted."

She cast a sly glance at Dumar. "From that room no magic will leak, no sound escape. A special room for special purpose."

Her eyes flicked from face to face. "Shall we begin?" And licked her lips.

Seemna nodded and looked at Chyndra, who said, "Yes." Dumar swallowed loudly. "Of course."

Nunderla nodded. "The male remains here or in that room." She pointed at it again. "The female with me there. Dark may stay or come."

"Come," said Chyndra.

Seemna nodded.

Hahn Dohr Kahn. The Realm of The Dragon.

Vessels had been arriving and departing for days. The unloading went as fast as the quays, greatly augmented, could handle. The Queen's Own Guard and Frinda's Royal Black kept everything organized and sent parties and supplies, wagons and animals, men, women, and children, in the correct directions, down the correct roads.

Lurin took the Lord of Kahn Cahn Tohn and his Royal family to her quarters so she and the Lord could discuss in greater detail all that had to be accomplished in so short a time. Frinda did the same, taking the Lord of Rahn Rahn Tahn and his Royal family across the Great Bridge so they could organize and plan this new sub-kingdom.

At the large table, cluttered with maps, Lurin ran a fingertip along a line. "This road, newly constructed, runs from the town of Wurm to E'Nilt's Town. From here many are already at work building a narrow track to this area near these great mountains to the spot where clear waters pour forth. It was thought to be a fine spot for a new settlement, if you wish. During the next Warm Time we propose to build a small port town down here, called Talking Waters, and a road trace up to this proposed settlement spot. All this land here is probably forest and this grassland area looks to be suitable for crops and beast support. Here, in these fierce crags is unknown territory."

She turned and looked at the new Royals. "Our folk are all agreed. During the next Two Ice Times, they will take in all your folk, or as many as quickly built housing up there can not support. This should be sufficient time for everything you will need to be established in your new homes."

E'Nilt smiled at the gathering and emptied a small sack on the table in front of the new Lords. "First gift, Great Lord, from this your neighbor, Daish a'an'Nald ca E'Nilt, Royal Princess of the court of The White Warrior, Queen and Princess

Lurin, Realm of The Dragon." She stirred the gems with a finger. "We bargain hard and expect the same."

The Lord bowed to her. "We are humbled by your gift, And ennobled as well."

Frahn smiled and bowed to him. "We are Prince Frahn and Princess Irinil, Second Princess of the Hephira, Noble Wive, and cousin to Princess E'Nilt."

The Lord returned to bow. "We had heard accounts, but none were accurate as to the nature of Hephira beauty."

Lurin smiled at the Lord. "My daughter, Princess Chyndra, now does quest journey out there. She will visit at sometime." She laughed." We have ordered a grand banquet in order to display Our New Royalty in the Great Square."

The Lord laughed with her. "Else your folk would grumble."

"As well The Lord do know." She bowed. "Shall we proceed?"

Deep Under Two.

Nunderla peered at Chyndra and walked over to her. "Have you mated yet?"

Chyndra blushed and looked at Seemna who gave a quick nod of assurance.

"No!" snapped Chyndra.

Nunderla stepped in front of her, reached out, and squeezed. "Have these had male taste?"

Chyndra jerked, her arm flying up. The sword flashed gold light as it swung down, the edge just resting at the junction of Nunderla's neck and shoulder. "You almost became headless, gutter wench! Explain fast!"

Nunderla moved only her eyes, cleared her throat, and whispered, "It is the price to remove that ring. A certain small essence is required by a certain mage for a certain rare spell. The Dark One may guard but you must willingly agree,"

Seemna rolled a crackling bronze wand between her palms and watched Chyndra.

The golden sword flashed back up and into its sheath. "I agree," said Chyndra.

From somewhere Nunderla fetched a tiny vail. "This small amount, none more."

"Proceed."

"No jacket, no shirt," ordered Nunderla. "Then sit." She ordered over a chair.

As soon as Chyndra was seated, Nunderla handed the vial to Seemna, and opened a jar of white cream paste. "Now answer my questions."

Chyndra blushed. "No. And no."

"Not mated? Not male tasted?"

"True."

"Do not move." Nunderla quickly rubbed on the cream paste and watched Chyndra's face flush even brighter. Then she snatched the vial from Seemna and finished the process.

"Done," snapped Nunderla as she quickly stoppered the tiny vial. "As I said, from this one very little." She dropped the vial into a pocket and stepped to the door. "The next step takes some subtle. I will ask help soon." She stepped through and left them.

"Princess?" Seemna handed over her shirt.

"Uninjured." She looked up. "Was that druzna?"

Seemna nodded.

"Will this wear off? I feel tingle strange."

Seemna cast and watched Chyndra's flush fade away. "Better?"

Chyndra took the shirt and wiped her chest. "Much." She slipped on the garment. "Do witches do things like this much?"

Seemna shook her head. "I think that this Esta is twisted."

One Star Over.

They strolled in the dark of First Night waiting for Moon Rise, visiting this booth and that booth. Soona, eyes glittering wildly, approached male after male.

Shitar whispered to Mantara, "She is flash ready. That witch will not make another foregather. By this mid-moon, if she hasn't found one, dramatic must happen. That clan must be bent very strange." She had been casting calm over Soona with no apparent affect.

"What do you propose," he whispered back.

"If I cast bind, you cast quick hold. Then we have a hard decision to make."

Mantara nodded and began to cast layers of protection over them using every spell that he knew.

The grey popped and puffed around from them, taking Soona. Snarling angrily, Shitar leaped, grabbed something, and quickly attached it to her wand. "Some rak tar tak tar cast quick grab at this foregather." Witches ran, clearing the immediate area around the pair, spells flashing in all directions.

Mantara jumped to Shitar's side. "Quick grab?"

"Yessssssss. I snatched a magic strand, a skill from my Aunt. It will take some, but we will be able to follow it and visit that ptar ptar zik tik." She smiled. More witches ran.

Deep Under Two.

The door banged open and Nunderla hurried in, cackling softly. "Now for the rest." She gestured them from the room and pointed at Dumar. "He must be willing." She stared at him. "Are you willing?"

"To do what?" demanded Chyndra before Dumar could reply.

"Yessssssssssss?" hissed Seemna.

Dumar stared from face to face. "What? Do what?"

Nunderla explained. Chyndra blushed. Dumar glowed bright red, his eyes refusing to look anywhere near Chyndra.

He held his hand toward Chyndra. "Lend me your weapon. This person suggests low purka!"

"Only way," chanted Nunderla. "Only way. When her energies release, that ring will crumble into dust. Only way. Only way."

Chyndra glared at her and flushed. Dumar stood and stalked toward Nunderla.

"Stop!" Seemna halted him. "No harm, no harm."

"Witch true," snapped Nunderla. "Nothing done yet. To the male. Soooooooooo?"

Dumar glanced at Chyndra, then down at the ring and tugged at it. It stayed firmly in place. Making a fist he held out only that finger and looked at Chyndra. "Princess, chop it off. One quick blow."

She shook her head. "I will not!"

"Many warriors lose parts. It is better than what this, this, this . . . person, wants."

"Not me. Not me. Not me." Nunderla stomped her feet

and pointed at the ring. "The one in the next room wants, not me." She sidled close to him. "Prince, that one in that ring will die horrid ugly when you do this deed. A life saved for some pleasant, eh eh eh, work? Is that so wrong for such a strong warrior?"

Dumar pushed her away and looked at Chyndra. "Princess," he rasped, "what do I do?"

She tugged her shirt down, fingers fiddling with her jacket lapels, and then replied, using her most Royal tone of voice, "Prince Dumar, a life, your life, is in peril as well as one other. What would you do if it was some of your folk that had this need?"

He nodded at her, gulped, blushed, and gestured. "Open that door!"

Nunderla did and waved him inside and pointed at the door. "None open that door. Yet."

Beckoning in beverages, chairs, and a table, Seemna sat and poured. "Wait in comfort. He looks sturdy enough." She took a sip from one of the cups. So did Chyndra and Nunderla. Nunderla firmly closed the door after Dumar entered.

By the time that the second jug had been emptied, Chyndra was beginning to worry about what ever it was that they were doing.

The closed door shuddered, tore the hinges loose, and fell into the room.

Chyndra and Seemna leaped to their feet. Nunderla stood and stared.

She strolled through the opening, ordering on new garb as she looked at the three seated there.

"I am," she stated to one and all, "Rose Batl witch Soona."

She jabbed one finger at the opening and the other room. "That male in there, quick recovering, is declared Special, and is to be treated as such. I see two witches. Which one am I witch debt to?"

Nunderla cackled. "To this one. And the two ask as well."

"NOT!" snarled Soona. "I gave him the two ask."

Nunderla growled and yanked in a flaming red wand. "Mine!"

"Late!" snapped Soona. "That male had already asked twice."

"Vile, vile, vile," chanted Nunderla. "Cheat, cheat, cheat."

"Not so, nameless witch. I still owe witch debt."

Nunderla grumbled, "Esta witch sub-clan Mataca witch Nunderla."

"Ripple daughter Faan websmith Seemna."

Soona stared at her. "Faan and websmith?"

"Witch true."

"Powerful setting."

"Witch true." Seemna stood and stepped close to Soona, the orange wand gurgling angry sound. "What was asked? If harm or vile comes to the Princess, two will die ugly."

Soona nodded. "The vigorous and Noble Prince, for so he told after this, and after that, and some other, asked unusual."

"What?" hissed Seemna. "Speak tell!"

"Both asks were for that Princess."

Seemna growled and began to call it in. "Calm calm," hissed Soona. "He asked, for her, great protection. And so it is. He asked, for her, even greater protection. And so it is."

Shoving Seemna to one side, she stepped over to Chyndra, crossed her arms over her chest, and intoned, "The

Princess Chyndra may refuse this offer, those protection offers, offered only once. Rose Batl witch Soona, protection spell weaver, places herself and her offspring into your service."

Her eyes glittered with happiness. "My daughter is named Tuvilna." She whispered softly, "It seems to this witch that the honor of the Prince would be greatly shamed if his twice ask was refused."

Chyndra nodded. "It would be most unkind to refuse such a gift and bring shame to Dumar. We are honored, Rose Batl witch Soona, protection spell weaver, for what you have done and for your offer of service. And We will so say to your daughter Tuvilna at the appropriate time."

She hugged Soona, startling the witch. Folk just did not hug witches. Chyndra stepped back and gestured. "This is my friend, Seemna. We are doing wander and quest journey with Dumar. Will you come? Or do you wish to proceed to Our Kingdom? Seemna can give you directions and I can write a scroll for my Mother, The Queen."

Soona stared at her, then at Seemna. "Friend?"

Seemna nodded. "This Princess is different."

"Mam nat ta," agreed Soona.

Then she turned and handed Nunderla a small stone. "Witch debt. Use it well."

Then she waved them out and away, yanking Dumar along.

One Star Over.

With a soft sigh of faint pink, they were there.

Soona looked around and nodded to herself. "This is Second Night. Most half way over. Would my Princess enjoy or seek our rooms?"

Chyndra peered around, at the booths, and clusters of witches coming and going here and there. "Enjoy."

So they walked from display to display. Dumar trailed along after the trio. It seemed to him that every witch here knew about what he had done and brushed against him more than the passing through a crowd required.

Soona looked at Chyndra. "This witch must need explain past happenings so a certain witch and a certain Princess and a certain Prince will not poor think."

"If you wish."

Soona led them to a refreshment booth and ordered for all, tall glasses of Giggling Pink. Dumar eyed his beverage warily and took a careful small sip, his eyes never leaving the counter top.

"Among some witch clans," began Soona, "but not all it happens this way." She told them of the name grade members becoming actively fertile when one of that name grade group did. In some clans it only happened to those having mates-for-life. In a few clans not at all.

But among the Batl clan it was a terrible thing. All clan members, mated or not, without offspring, had a great must. It became stronger and stronger and stronger, until all energies, magical or otherwise, became focused only on one thing, the need to reproduce. Some who could not find willing partners could, and some did, use force. Frequently these died as most folk considered using force like that to be vile and tore that witch apart. If not quenched the massive energy building would lash out and destroy the witch.

"So, my princess, that noble Prince did save this one from

vile actions as this witch was near craze and flash danger." She nodded, as a soft very not-witch smile flickered on and off. "Now this witch is mother bound and alive and ever safe as that Batl urge is a one time thing, although more offspring are possible."

Chyndra stepped over and hugged her, which startled Soona again.

"Princess?" she mumbled. Folk just did not hug witches.

"Thank you for explaining." Chyndra sat in her chair, took a sip from her beverage, and frowned at Dumar. "Frown not, Prince, for quest journey is a time to learn much and to experience much. To rule well one must understand others as they understand themselves." She smiled as he looked up at her. "And no-one need know what or when or how that knowledge was acquired." Setting her empty glass down she looked at Soona, who reordered.

Two glasses later, Soona ordered food for all, protecting her Princess.

Chyndra was crunching loudly on the last lump of whatever it was when a tall woman dressed in black stomped up to their table accompanied by a much calmer male dressed in green.

This female person ordered over a chair, dropped into it, and grabbed one of the beverages that had also just appeared. "Soona! Sister?"

"Hayou, Shitar." Seemna sat as witch proper as she could and nodded at him. "Hayou, Mantara. Not met since training."

"Sister?" Chyndra looked from face to face and saw the similarity there.

"I am well," stated Soona, "as these three did save a

certain witch."

Shitar frowned at Dumar. "You?"

"Sister," cautioned Seemna, flicking her eyes from Chyndra to Dumar and back.

"Hum hum hum," said Shitar.

"Hum hum," replied Seemna.

"Greetings, Seemna," said Mantara. He looked at Soona. "Most healthy."

Chyndra sat straighter. "We are Chyndra, We are. Princess Royal, Realm of The Dragon, Hahn Dohr Kahn." She banged Dumar in the side with her elbow.

"Dumar," he slurred.

"He is a Noble Prince from Gasta Pleesa," added Chyndra, thumping him on one shoulder. "A doer of mighty deeds did he do some did." She laughed.

Shitar watched her from the corners of her eyes. So did Seemna. Soona cast lightly over Chyndra, protecting her Princess. Mantara nodded, admiring her skill.

Chyndra blinked and straightened up. She had been tilting heavily in Dumar's direction. She peered into her glass. "Interesting."

Dumar nodded. "Musht," he mumbled.

Shitar glowered at him, leaned across the table, and tapped him in the center of the forehead with one fingertip.

He leaned back in his chair and nodded at her. "Thanks. These are dangerous drinks."

"Hum." Shitar looked at Soona. "We travel elsewhere, Batl witch, as none is required here."

Soona reached over and handed her a stone that was glowing soft red. "A gift of interest, witch to witch."

Shitar took the stone, peered at it, and handed it to Mantara. "Keep." He dropped it into a pocket and nodded at Soona. The pair stood and swirled away in a puff of black tinged green.

Soona looked around at the group. "Second Night ends. Come, we have rooms." She took them to the appropriate lodging place and shoved Dumar into one of the rooms after rearranging each room to the correct state of being.

In their room Chyndra crawled into the large bed and collapsed flat on her back. "Witch foregathers are hard."

"Hum." Seemna joined her, sitting up, and looked at her.

"What?"

"Checking."

"What?"

"That twisted Esta is not trust. I would make sure that none else was done."

"What!" Chyndra snapped upright.

Seemna pushed her flat. "Contain yourself. I must check." She began to pat gentle hands here and there.

"OH!"

Seemna growled and stroked.

"OOOOOO!"

"That ptar rak tak nar must need vile ugly." Seemna snatched in a long silver wand.

"What?" sighed Chyndra.

"She thought to corrupt you with touch tangle." The wand plunged down and anchored Chyndra to the bed as Seemna cast hard and heavy. She watched the flush fade. Yanking the wand free, she leaped from the bed and stepped from the room.

Far over and one up, as Nunderla was deal working with a certain mage for the small vial that she held between two fingers, the bolt blasted in, taking the vial, the Esta witch, and that certain mage into nowhere.

Seemna came back into the room, crawled into the bed, tugged a blanket up and over them, and cackled softly to herself. As she listened to the slow sleep breathing of the Princess, she fell asleep.

Third Night.

Seemna woke, sat up, and carefully reached out.

Soona was outside, eating, at the closest food booth.

Dumar was stirring, rubbing sleep heavy eyes.

Seemna nodded, tugged the blanket aside, rolled, and wrapped Chyndra in her arms.

"What?" mumbled Chyndra.

"Lovely Princess, it is time for us to go our own ways. I have much yet to study and must do so alone."

Chyndra turned her head and peered into the great black eyes. "True?"

"Witch true." Seemna kissed her and held her tight.

"Uhhhhh?"

Slowly releasing her, Seemna sighed. "We are now skin sisters, witch glow delight. You must be careful around males."

"What?"

Stroking gentle fingers over smooth skin, Seemna murmured into Chyndra's ear, "Royal Princess, this wander quest and the things done, and learned, have made subtle changes. Any witch will see and understand. Most will quick guard their mates-for-life and dance nervous."

"I don't understand."

Seemna sat up. "You may have any male that you wish to have. Just beckon with a slight certain smile." Leaning over, she brushed feather lips here and there.

"Choose well, Princess Chyndra, Realm of The Dragon. Your mate would fight the Great Black Dragon for you. Charm none in your lands else all the females will come to hate you."

Seemna sat up and smiled at her, a true witch smile. "But obstinate Lords of other kingdoms will be of little." She jumped from the bed and waved on their clothes. "Meal time."

They joined Soona at her table and watched Dumar approach.

Chyndra nodded at him. "How feels your head?"

"Most well and clear." He sat and began to eat, then looked up at her. "What?"

"Nothing, Fair Prince."

"Oh. I thought that you had said something."

Seemna lightly touched Chyndra's thigh under the table.

Chyndra nodded.

Soona glared at her and frowned dark.

Chyndra ducked her head and finished her meal.

Then the group prowled foregather.

As the moon set, Seemna kissed Chyndra on her forehead. "I will visit." She began to fade. "Friend," she whispered. And was gone.

Chyndra looked at Dumar. "She has much to study and learn alone. My quest journey is done. What do you now, Dumar?"

He shrugged. "More Great Adventure, I suppose." He

sighed. "I have little to return to. Third Prince Court Duties are dull and tedious."

"This Prince craves more?"

"Indeed he does." He looked at her. "Chyndra, let us do more. Together."

She shook her head. "My Mother Queen's Kingdom is vast and requires much work. It is time for me to return and aid in this. There is more than My Brother, the King To Be and his Princess can handle."

He jerked. "You Mother, the Queen, would allow Her Princess to do this? Work?"

She laughed. "Not allow, Dumar. Expect! There is ever so much to be accomplished. It is a New Kingdom."

He sighed, shoulders slumping, and stared into somewhere. "Would that I had such a problem."

Ever so carefully she nudged him and said ever so softly, "Would The Noble Prince Dumar wish to come visit? For some short time?"

Hastily clearing his throat, he gasped, then grinned. "I would indeed!" He cleared his throat again. "If it would be allowed. And if it was deemed proper in your Royal Parent's eyes."

Chyndra twisted in her chair. "Soona, can you do this?"

"Yessssssss. Dark Seemna told where. Now?"

"Indeed."

All around that space, witches jerked. It was strange to leave so early before the end of a foregather.

Hahn Dohr Kahn. The Realm of The Dragon.

In a soft rose glow they appeared.

In the large room.

The great table was covered with maps, charts, orders, and lists of this and that.

The woman standing there finished her instructions to the two burly men standing next to her, looked over, and smiled warmly.

"Welcome, Daughter. Welcome, muchly changed Daughter. Is your quest journey over?"

"Hail, Great Queen." Chyndra used as formal a tone as she could manage. Then she ran to her mother and was hugged and kissed. "Yes. Over. We learned much, and learned ever so much more."

Twisting in her mother's arms, she gestured. "This is Third Prince Dumar of The House of Hagen, House of Mnab, House of Conta of Gasta Peelsa, and Rose Batl witch Soona who has placed herself in Our Service."

Dumar bowed. Soona stared.

"This," smiled Chyndra, "is Our Mother, Queen Lurin of The New Kingdom, Hahn Dohr Kahn, The Realm of The Dragon. She is also called, here and there, The White Warrior."

Releasing her daughter, Lurin smiled at them. "Warm welcome to Our Kingdom, prince Dumar, witch Soona. But We are called Lurin in any place other than formal court occasions." Throwing one arm over her daughter's shoulders, she tugged her closer to the table and pointed at the clutter.

"Great changes have We made while Our Daughter was on quest journey. Prince, do come here. We would know your thoughts as well." Then Lurin began to explain everything, shoving maps, charts, and lists around as required.

In the midst of all this explanation, a door banged open.

Two very dust stained and dirty folk walked in.

Dumar jerked. Soona, stared at the female, cast protection, and hissed, "A nak nabl!"

"Sister?" asked the man.

"Chyndra and guests," stated Lurin. "This is Our Son, Frahn, King To Be, and The Second Princess of the Hephira, his Princess wife, Irinl. Hard journey, Prince?"

"Indeed!" He handed her a thick map scroll. "The Lord sends this rough sketch of the new town. Houses rise quickly and many will spend Ice Time there."

And then, much later, Lurin said, "Dirty son and Princess, go bathe. Daughter, your quarters are there. Prince Dumar, your guest quarters are that way."

Servants hurried away to prepare baths, rooms, and to lead Chyndra and Dumar and Soona in the appropriate directions.

"Soona stays with Us." Chyndra pointed at an adjoining set of rooms and told the servant, "In there. Unless Mother calls for Us we wish to eat and rest here until next day."

The servant bowed and left them, anxious to tell the news of the Queen's daughter and her strange companions. He also had much to relate about the conversation over the map cluttered table. All the folk knew that events were occurring faster than the Criers could speak to all. The folk, high and low, were anxious to know every detail.

While Chyndra and Soona rested and relaxed, Chyndra much and Soona as much as a witch ever did, which was not much, Lurin ordered Dumar to attend her on her private balcony to talk.

She pointed to various of the features of the Royal Town

easily seen from this top floor balcony, seven flights above The Great Square.

"There is The Great Quay and Our Fleet, Our's and Mine Brothers. There The Great Span connects both kingdoms. Everyone, everywhere, are building as we need to do, but there is ever so much more to do. This is a New Kingdom, starting anew. All the folk, high and low, Royalty and all, work hard, as hard as the lowest carpenters and rock breaker, for this is what we all must do. In these New Kingdoms We have changed some behaviors, We have."

Dumar nodded and cleared his throat.

"Prince?"

"Might there be some small thing that I might do?"

Lurin laughed. "Prince, We do not treat Our guests so."

"Your pardon, Majesty."

"Lurin," she corrected.

"Oh! Lurin."

"You did quest journey with Chyndra?"

"Some. She had been traveling long before we met."

"Learn much?"

"Indeed!"

"Are We somehow threatening?"

"Nay."

"Then why, Prince Dumar, do you seen ever so much nervous to this Queen?"

"Dumar, please."

"So it shall be, Dumar. Why?"

He cleared his throat. "Chyndra is very attractive."

"Yes?"

"I know your Court Customs not."

"And?"

"How may I plead my case?"

"You seek a boon from Us?"

"Oh, no!"

"What, then?"

"I am only a Third Prince of no lands and of no standing and of no chance of ever gaining some."

"So?"

"So, I would plead my case for your daughter's hand, or however your folk attend to such matters."

"Our lands attract you, do they?"

He snapped upright and spun in her direction. "Majesty, not so! I wished for Chyndra long ever before we did come here. On our journey she was a Warrior Princess from unknown lands. Although she did speak of her parents, some."

"We do see." Lurin smiled a soft smile. "But We cannot aid you in this, Prince."

"Oh." He sagged and leaned heavily on the railing, turning, staring out over the nearby town and out at the open sea beyond.

Lurin thumped him on the back, a heavy warrior's thump. "Prince, here in Our Kingdom, and My Brother's as well, you must speak directly to the one you seek, high or low. It is their decision to make. Royalty or other, it is all the same. We do not interfere. Mostly."

She turned and headed for the door. "Come! Join us for dinner. You may there speak of your lands."

The Trantil Layer.

"So," he said, "here we are. Now what?"

Chicken looked at their surroundings. "Most pleasant a'place?"

It was.

Soft rolling hills covered with grass. A few clouds puffing along in an otherwise clear blue sky. Here and there, small clumps of trees and shrubs. Behind them, the shear cliff, a part of the rock mass soaring up and to the sides. A spot shimmered and glowed in the rock face. It was the entrance spot.

He pointed at it. "O.K., Killer Moth, blow it away."

Everyone hurried back, giving Fair Morn all the room that she required.

"Hold it!" He looked at Szart and Sha'gar. "Can you guys take us somewhere from here?"

Szart nudged Sha'gar who thought some and then nodded.

He stepped further back. "Fire when ready, Gridley."

Fair Morn quickly set the levers on her weapon and did.

No sound.

No explosion.

There was just a faint hiss as a large section of the cliff vanished, leaving behind a smooth polished surface in the deep concavity.

"Too easy," he grumbled.

Chantal frowned at him and grumbled, "Damn worry butt!"

"Damn right." He glowered at her and watched as the group scattered and began to examine their surroundings.

Early Dawn walked with Fair Morn. "Where did you get that thing?"

"From Macabre. He thought that we needed it. Wonder

who lives here?"

"I could just fly up and take a look. I don't see a road or a trail, do you?"

"Nope."

"Well?"

"Go ahead."

With a soft pop, Early Dawn unfurled her great bat wings, gave one pump, and lifted into the sky.

"Hey!" He ran over to Fair Morn. "What do you guys think you are doing?"

"Taking a look," Early Dawn called down. And spiraled higher and higher and higher. Soon she was coasting just below the few clouds, swooping back and forth, obviously enjoying herself. Suddenly she pulled in her wings and plunged toward them. The wings snapped out and she lightly touched down next to Fair Morn. "Nice day for flying." The wings popped back and disappeared.

"See anything, sis?"

Early Dawn pointed. "That way there is a small cluster of buildings, right on top of one of the hills."

"Well," he said, "it is a nice day for a hike."

They headed for the buildings that Early Dawn had seen.

Doth Lamex. A Place of Healing and Relaxation.

She sat in her picnic spot, some time after finishing her meal, and sipped at the beverage.

It had been, for her, four long years of deep travel and hard training. There was a small cresent shaped scar on her left cheek, barely noticeable most of the time, a small reminder of some slight error during one of the many training sessions. But now she was done, her powers at their greatest. She waited for him to turn up.

She had chosen this spot carefully during her conversation with the gate guardian. She wondered who he was, this person that had been tracking her for so long a time.

So she sipped. And waited.

She knew that he would have to come. He had no choice. It was the way of a websmith. Those came that were called. Few ever knew why they did this.

So she sipped. And waited.

And saw him enter her chosen spot, stepping from behind the tree that was the entrance.

He approached very carefully and stood a proper and cautious distance from her. "I am," he said softly, "Aldin Cease, Green Onana mage Guild."

She nodded. "Sit."

He did. "I have searched far and wide. You leave a twisted hard path."

She nodded. And sipped. And waited.

He cleared his throat.

She sipped. And waited.

"You are the rare among the rare. Hardly ever does one appear among the witch clans. A deep seeker in the Guild felt you come into being and from that moment I have searched. By the time that I found you the witch clans had swarmed and you were freed and gone again. Now here we are."

"Yessssssssss."

"Few witches do wander with warriors."

"True."

"Why?"

"A cousin."

"Eh ta, a cousin. One that can persuade a large dealer like Fasback?"

"Just so."

He nodded. "The Green Onana are few, less than one hand's fingers. The Faan clan, known far and far as the most vile and most dangerous, are large, many linked."

She shrugged, And sipped. And waited.

"The rare of the rare are often sought by those who want too much and who would deal vile."

"Like Puartor the White."

He hissed. "That Guild ought to have been ended long long before."

"Hum," observed Seemna.

"The Faan are known beautiful."

"Yesssssssssssss."

"Perhaps a mage of the few might journey with a witch of the rare as careful protection?"

"Perhaps it might be allowed." She ordered a beverage for him.

"It is told that the Faan know how to touch a mage without destruction of magic clash."

"A special talent urh-witch given."

"True?" He sipped.

"Witch true." She patted the grass by her side.

He carefully relocated and sat.

"One might gentle touch."

He cautiously, carefully, reached over with one finger and touched her shoulder. And gasped. Nothing had happened.

She laughed.

He leaped away. Laughing witches were lethal. He listened. No warning came from the Doth Lamex Guardians that controlled anything that might cause upset or violence in this elseplace. "What?"

"Merriment. Learned from my cousin."

He sat, near her.

"Most not-witch."

She shrugged. "One learns interesting on wander."

He nodded. "True."

"What want you, Green Onana?"

"If a certain mage replied to a certain witch would it be safe?"

"This is Doth Lamex."

"Devious reply."

"Devious mage."

He nodded. "True. Where go you from here?"

"I journey next to visit with my cousin. You may come, if you wish."

He nodded. And stood.

They walked to the entry plaza and gateway.

Hahn Dohr Kahn. The Realm of The Dragon.

She knocked him stumbling into the wall and watched carefully.

Lurching upright, he charged, twisted strangely and knocked her legs out from under her.

She hit, rolled, spun, and jumped. The heavy stave crashed across his mid-section.

"OOOOF!" He landed on his back and bounced a little. And grinned up at her. "A Warrior Princess."

Offering him her hand, she hauled him to his feet. "A Warrior Prince."

"Chyndra?"

"Dumar?"

"It has been two hands of days and all that I do is practice train with you when you have time."

"We have much to do."

"I know. I talked with your Mother."

"So?"

"Put your weapon away."

She walked away and set the stave in the practice weapon rack and walked back.

"Step further away."

She did.

He positioned himself carefully. "Your Mother said to talk to you."

"And?"

"I want to know what I must do, ah umm, to speak, umm ah, for your hand."

"You want to, Third Prince Dumar," she said as she leaned forward, "to be My Prince, oath bound, wedded, and bedded?"

He flushed. And nodded. Watching carefully.

She leaped.

And bowled him over in a great puff of training area dust. Sitting on his stomach, she looked down at him. "This Kingdom has much work, hard physical work to do, and a long deep labor for all in it."

"Your Mother told me."

"The Prince for this Princess gains as an equal in work not

as a Court Decoration."

"Your Mother told me."

"I will never rule this land as my Brother will be King."

"Your Mother told me."

"We may build a vast holding of open plain or dense forest."

"I like forest."

"The Prince for this Princess has only and ever this Princess and no Court Ladies or Wenches for sly arrangement."

"Your Mother told me."

"Your hands are holding my waist."

"It is a very nice waist."

"So this Prince noticed?"

"Hard not to at foregather."

"Did you tell Mother that?"

"Never."

"Only a nice waist?"

He blushed.

She grinned. And stood and held out her hand. "Come, Prince, we have a Queen to visit."

Lurin looked up, then down, signed the order and dumped it into the small box. "Most dust coated a pair of Royalty."

"Warrior practice," explained Chyndra.

"Did she beat you badly?" asked Lurin, smiling at him.

"Mostly." Dumar grinned. "Very warrior trained."

"Mother?"

"Daughter?"

Chyndra pouted dramatically and pointed. "This Prince!"

"What?" Lurin stared at him. Dumar blanched. It was a hard Warrior Queen stare.

"Wishes to marry one of our folk."

"Oh?" Lurin shrugged. "He needs not Our permission. Do We know?"

"Indeed." Chyndra grinned at her. "Us."

"Our Daughter!"

Dumar hastily backed up as the Queen called for a servant. "Take this dirty Prince to his quarters and keep him away from the Princess for . . . ?" she looked at Chyndra.

"A hand of days?" suggested Chyndra.

"Two!" stated the Queen. "Two hands of days. With all the turmoil it will take that long to arrange everything. Both Kingdoms must be notified, to the furthest town."

Dumar stared at them, mouth open.

"It is Our custom," explained Lurin. "From this time until the Grand Ceremony, the Prince may not cast eyes on the Princess." She waved one hand. "Take him away!"

The servant quickly led Dumar to his quarters and started preparing the deep bath. And wondered how this Prince had gotten so filthy.

"Go clean thyself. Daughter. We have work to do."

Chyndra, soap foam up to her chin, tilted her head back. Soona poured water over her head and hair. "Is this Prince so worthy?"

"We do think so." Chyndra wiped the water from her face with one hand.

"If this Prince, by word or deed, by gesture or tone of voice, injures or threatens you, I will kill him."

"Fierce Soona, We have no fear of that. Can you contact

my Father?"

"It will be hard. I know nothing of them."

"Sook knows."

"Your Uncle's Queen?"

"Yes."

Soona nodded. Sook appeared, looking very witch unhappy. "Who dares?"

Soona nodded. "The Princess wishes to contact her Father."

Chyndra reached out an arm and gently touched Sook. "We will not wed until my Father, The King of these lands, can attend. Please, Aunt? Can you contact them and tell them of Our wish?"

Sook nodded.

Sent to Szart.

And disappeared.

The Trantil Layer.

They were approaching the small cluster of buildings when Szart suddenly jerked and snarled.

Weapons leaped into hands. Sha'gar layered on protection.

"What?" He stared at the buildings and then their surroundings, very, very carefully.

"Sook sent," she grumbled. "Hard!"

"Oh. Now what?"

"Your daughter will not be wed until you can attend."

"Je'leel?"

"Chyndra, Princess Royal, and the Prince Dumar."

He nodded. "Um, wonder who he is. O.K., but we finish

here first. I assume that the amount of time that we spent here won't really matter."

Szart shrugged. "It is a big event."

"Most true." Chicken nodded. She remembered being told of the event when her brother, Toucan, married Willawa. The entire Royal City and most of the surrounding kingdoms had celebrated. "What think you, My Lord?"

"I think that we ought to worry about here and now. And try to figure what is going on here."

The buildings that they stood near were all constructed from stacked stone. Each roof was conical and covered with sod growing grass. The doorways were short and wide. Windows dotted the walls in some sort of pattern. All around them was piece and quiet. They stepped to one side and peered down a narrow road that twisted its way into the town.

"Ready?" He checked the rest.

All nodded. Fair Morn quickly pushed Early Dawn behind herself. "Remember what I said?"

"You betcha!" She yanked her pistol free and cocked it.

He leaned forward, sucked in a deep breath, and bellowed, "HELLO! ANYONE HOME?"

A short, wide man waddled from the nearest structure, glaring at them. "Stop yelling! Stop all that yelling! Explain what sort of cause spell is that hello thing. And why are you stabbing it at us? Who are you group anyhap?"

Tinker looked at Sgenn. "You sure that this is really the correct place?"

She nodded. "So told."

He waggled one hand at the man and their surroundings. "This is Unspeakable?"

She shrugged.

"Merde," he mumbled.

"Na ta da!" stated the man. "Here we be Uerde. What are you?"

"Avon Polymorph," stated Chantal, deciding that the name given by them in the demon layers was as good as any.

The man scratched his chin. "Did I ever hear of that? Somewhere?" He shook his head. "What do you here? There is little trade."

"Just a little information," said Tinker. "Is this The Trantil Layer?"

"Boo tat ta!" He waved one hand. "Everywhere."

"So far so good," grumbled Tinker.

"Na ta da! This be Berta Top."

Tinker sighed. He dreaded asking, but he did. "Is this The Place of The Unspeakable?"

Uerde stared at him. "Who do tell clap?"

"Guess it is not," sighed Tinker.

"Driven down deep." Uerde stomped his foot. "Deep!"

"True?" Sgenn stepped closer.

Uerde stared at her, then snapped angrily, "Leave them down!" He spun and ran into his building, then hurtled out, brandishing a strange twisted weapon at her. "Leave down!"

Sgenn nodded.

Uerde swung. And was hurtled back against a wall of his structure by Sha'gar's cast.

"He must be a special warrior," mumbled Sgenn as she sagged sideways, looking down at the rip in her robe and the spreading stain.

The great black sword danced in Tinker's hand, Sgenn

being attacked and hurt had triggered his rage. The warrior berserk of the entity that was his weapon merged with that rage and sang blood lust that roared through his being. The emotions poured through the rest of them.

Chantal grabbed Szart by the shoulder and yelled at her, "Take us out of here before he loses control."

Szart grabbed Sha'gar's hand and ripped them away.

Soft black drifted across the landscape.

Hahn Dohr Kahn. The Realm of The Dragon.

They spilled into the room, rolling and tumbling.

Tinker lunged to his feet, sword clipping an arm from a nearby chair.

Chantal heaved herself up and began to dump the contents of her pack on the floor. She ripped open their medical supplies, then Sgenn's robe. After pouring disinfectant everywhere, she began to tear open bandage packets.

"Not too bad. Those floppy robes took care of most of the cut. Creased her ribs, missed her gut, sliced right below those two beauties. All in all, not too bad."

She wiped the wound clean and began to apply the bandages, and winked at Sgenn. "Just have to stay out of his bed for a week or so."

He peered over Chantal's head. "You sure?" He was calming down.

"Think so. You will just have to sleep with the rest of us."

"Not what I meant," he growled in her ear.

"Just fine," said Sgenn.

"How come your information is so bad?"

She shrugged. And winced.

"See?" said Chantal to her.

She nodded.

Two servants raced into the room followed by a woman wielding a large two-handed white sword. "WHO DARES FIGHT IN OUR QUARTERS?" she demanded, a battle loud bellow. And slid to a halt. "Great King?"

He straightened up and flapped the black sword onto his back. "Hi! We, ummm, had an accident elseplace. Szart yanked us to here."

Lurin strode over and looked down. "How fare you?"

"Just fine."

Lurin pointed. "Help her up. And prepare a large soft bed. In the King's Quarters. Hurry, hurry." The servants hurried. New arrivals scurried away to prepare the bed and to air out The King's Quarters.

"Come!" Lurin led them into an adjoining room. After all had settled into chairs, she said, mostly to Tinker, "Our Daughter delays the Royal Joining until her Father, The King, can attend. The folk are beginning to grumble and to mumble."

"We came as soon as we could," he grumbled at her.

"If Our King does agree, tomorrow at High Sun?"

"Sure. Why not?"

Someone charged into the room, carrying a wicked looking golden sword. She slid to a halt and looked as Royal Daughter proper as she could. "Hail, Great Father King!"

He looked over. "Holy Cow!"

"A strange oath," observed Lurin.

"He means," explained Chantal, "that she has become a real beauty."

"We do think so," agreed Lurin.

He stood and smiled. "Hi, daughter. Congratulations. Who is the lucky guy?" And wrapped her in his arms as she crashed into him.

"Most Royal Prince Dumar."

He looked past her head. "Who's that?"

Chyndra pulled free and turned. "Rose Batl witch Soona, my guardian."

"Huh? I meant Dumar.""

Soona looked from face to face and then back at him. "You are The One of legend and these are your's?"

He sighed.

"They are, he is," said Chantal. Then she introduced Soona to each one.

Szart nudged Sha'gar. "That witch will soon birth."

Messenger stepped close to Szart. "A guardian?"

Szart nodded. "It is told that Rose Batl are protection weavers. In some way that daughter has bound one to her." She waved her wand away. "Our daughter has little to fear, ever."

Chicken stepped close to Lurin. "From which of the kingdoms comes this Dumar?"

"Elseplace, elsewhere. She met him on her quest journey. We do think that it is a good match." She kissed Chicken on the cheek. "All will meet him, next light. We shall declare a Two Day Fest at first light next, now that all are attending.

"Oh boy," gurgled Messenger. "Two days."

By the time that he was awake, leaning on the balcony, sipping at his coffee that Sha'gar had produced, the Great Square, seven stories below, was filling with crowds of spectators, all swirling around the high, ornate platform on top of which the Royal Ceremony would take place when the sun was directly overhead,

Merchants had already set up tables around the edge of the vast opening, and the folk of the two New Kingdoms had begun to enjoy The Two Day Fest. It was a welcome break in the hectic pace to settle entire sub-kingdoms before Ice Time arrived, not all that far off.

She bumped against his back. "First Light, Great King. We have ordered Our Royal Garb for all." She stepped around and leaned against his side, sliding an arm around his waist, and took a sip from his proffered cup.

"We are greatly pleased that thee and thine have arrived. Our headstrong daughter refused for to wed unless Our King was attending which caused some consternation among the folk and most great worry for her Prince."

He sighed.

"Our message from Chyndra was Sook sent. It do be three hands of days past the chosen time afore thee do appear sudden and bloody."

He slipped her arm free and turned. "Sorry."

Far below and close to where the Great Quay joined land at Front Road, one of the sea folk peered up the narrow and straight road toward the Royal Quarters with a far-seer

"Fair galoon," he snapped to himself. "Our Queen do be grappled by Our King afore most folk weight anchor."

He rolled into *The Wet Way*, the inn of the sea folk, and bellowed the news to one an all. All those present agreed that the Queen was indeed one of them and told each other that this had been true since the first historic sea voyage that had founded the New Kingdoms.

In the Great Square, as the sun crept to directly overhead, the guests climbed up into the high wooden platform and waited.

Frinda and Sook, Lurin and Tinker, Frahn and Irinl, and all the rest of Tinker's group, as well as the new Lords of the new sub-kingdoms and their families, stood there.

The sun hit its mark, directly overhead. A solitary trumpet sounded a long note, and silence rolled across the gathered throngs.

Then Chyndra stood where all could see her, elegant in the one-time ceremonial robes, face composed and solemn, attended by Lurin's First Lord and his wife. Frahn stepped to her free side and gave her a slight elbow nudge that those below could not see.

Dumar stepped up and joined them as the First Lord stepped away.

The First Lord spoke to the crowds, briefly, turned and thumped the Prince and Princess on their shoulders with the ornate ceremonial sword and intoned, voice echoing from the Royal Quarters high wall, "AND NOW DOES CHYNDRA, PRINCESS, JOIN DUMAR, PRINCE, FOREVER AND FOREVER AND FOREVER!"

The crowds erupted, the sound roared and bellowed over all as the Two Day Fest exploded into the normal riot of celebration.

Sometime, this day or next, all hoped to meet and greet one of the Royals, as all mingled and wandered the two main towns, back and forth across the Great Span. The Royals would celebrate as hard as any. It was an ancient and grand tradition.

On the seventh floor of the Royal Quarters they swirled in, Seemna and Aldin Cease, they swirled in.

The pair stared at the large table cluttered with maps and other documents.

On the platform, Sook leaned close, whispered to Frinda, and disappeared.

Szart spoke to Smoke and took Sha'gar and Sgenn up, leaving a small trace of black.

They all arrived in various styles. Aldin Cease stared at them, at Seemna, and wondered what was going to happen to himself with all these witches swirling in.

Seemna nodded at him. "These are my name grade sisters and cousins." More arrived. She named each in the room, slowly filling.

"Faan witch Shitar, sister, and her's, Grenzanr warlock Mantara."

"Faan witch Santar, sister, and Faan witch Sepanix the Wild, sister."

"Faan witch Sook, sister, her's is Frinda the King."

"Faan witch Szart, sister, her's is The Chosen One and King."

"Faan witch Szaifeh, cousin, her's is Vander warlock Rorx."

"Faan mage Sha'gar, cousin, and Faan theurgist Sgenn, cousin."

She waggled her hand at him. "This is Green Onana mage Aldin Cease. This one has been tracking me for long long and claims no harm but an intent to protect me. What say you all to this claim?"

He waved a chair over and sat, heavily he sat. This was

beyond any tell tale that he had heard or gathered. He felt the magic soft crackling here and there as all those eyes watched him. He knew that the Faan clan had been birthing strange and raising successful.

He looked again at Sepanix and could feel the wild magic nestling around her. Those he had heard tales of that had been born with wild magic had been ripped apart by it. Yet, there she stood, grey black eyes peering caution at him.

Then Szaifeh looked him with death staring out, learned from her mother, Reep, and a special trainer. He could feel a slight tug. The slight pull on his life, ever so gentle. And she had cross-mated with a mage, a thing rarely done without disastrous results. To a Vander mage. He had heard that the Vander Guild could control any male with but a passing glance.

The short witch, Szart, eyed him like a specimen kept in a jar while standing next to her sister, Sgenn. The grey haired, grey clad theurgist stood as still as still, a calm silence. He had never heard of that skill and wondered what is was that she did or could do. That much calm was unsettling.

Shitar looked at him and chewed on the tip of a long black wand. "Sooooo, Green Onana, you would offer protection, would you? Think you, mage, that there is such required?" Vague began to hover behind her.

"No," he whispered into the soft feel of death beckoning him from all directions. "No, I do not. I did, but no longer."

Shitar stepped closer. "Hum hum hum. Much more to tell, mage, much more. Seemna sister?"

"The White took me. This one did nothing. The fat Fasback took our cousin Princess. This one did nothing. The Green Onana play devious! With Fula creatures!"

He saw the red flare in Sha'gar's eyes. The one in grey stepped close, a soft half-smile on her face and she said, ever so gently, to him, "Green Onana and the Fula could become no more."

Aldin Cease managed to maintain control, but barely. Her voice had been so calm, so matter of fact, as she offered, ever so casually, that suggestion.

He managed to wobble to his feet, as she stepped away, and clear his throat, several times. "Listen close to my tale. Long long past long, a wizard of strange released into the universe of universes a being, vague and unfilled. That wizard, twisted strange, saw the survival of the Faan clan from their unknown beginnings and saw the arrival of Faan websmith Seemna."

He waggled one hand, "Out there, his creature comes aware. To pluck away the rarest of the rare, a websmith. His creature is to do this. The Green Onana, long Fula linked, for long long have gathered small tales, small words, and felt this strange creature appear. We sought to stop the one and keep the other."

"Keep?" hissed Shitar.

"Alive! None else."

Sgenn leaned and spoke to Szart. Szart, Sgenn, and Sha'gar were gone.

Sook swirled away.

Shitar said something soft. Santar and Sepanix banged out taking Aldin Cease with them.

The rest gathered around to talk and to discuss.

Sook stepped from somewhere and took her King's arm and leaned against him. He smiled. "That wasn't long."

"Long enough," she murmured.

Szart, Sgenn, and Sha'gar stepped from a shadow heavy space between two buildings and joined the others as they slowly made their way through the Fest throngs. The three Faan once again wore their Royal garb. Smoke had kept Tinker from knowing of their short absence.

They pushed inside *The Wet Way* and joined the Royal group, Lurin and Tinker, Frahn and Irinl, Chyndra and Dumar. Dumar was already looking somewhat dazed.

Chyndra held one of arms tightly locked to her's. "It is an historic custom of great meaning," she said into his ear, leaning close so he could hear over the din.

"Two days?"

Smiling broadly, she nodded. "The Queen did so order. Thus it will be."

The Queen, one arm around her King's waist, hoisted a mug with her free hand and toasted the sea folk.

The sea folk roared their approval and those standing close thumped Dumar on the shoulders and on the back and winked lewdly at Chyndra.

Dumar was slowly getting use to this behavior, all the people of the kingdom treating their Royal's as no more than stout neighbors and hearty drinking companions. In his lands none would have dared such familiarity. But he noticed that there was a certain special character to it, all subtle ritual and casual formality. He hoped that they would get something to eat soon.

So did Tinker. He remembered that last Fest that he had attended, He leaned closed and spoke into Lurin's ear, "FOOD!"

The Queen's First Ship Master saw the word and bellowed at the inn keeper in a voice that could cut through the roar of a storm at sea.

Tables were hastily cleared and food hustled from the kitchens and served. It was plain sea folk fare served in large bowls and on large platters. All began to eat. Tinker smiled at Lurin.

Two blocks away, the rest, now separated from Tinker and the Royals, wandered. Smoke reported to her group Tinker's progress and ordered something to eat from a street vender, some sort of cooked sea creature. Fair Morn and Early Dawn had already started on their order.

In *The Wet Way*, Lurin spoke into Frahn's ear and then Chyndra's and tugged her King up and from the inn. Lurin and Tinker had to pay a visit to the inn where The Queen's Own Guard visited. It was always the next stop after spending time with the sea folk at their inn during a Fest Day.

The Queen's Guard celebrated quietly but no less heavily. Many of them recognized her King from the last Fest time and saluted him and their Queen with their mugs.

Tickling his ribs, she murmured, "Let us cross The Great Span and wander Our Brother's First Town."

Outside, she headed them in the correct direction.

They stood in the center of the great bridge, leaning on the railing and staring down at the water. Her arm was hooked around his waist, his arm over her shoulders.

"Nice bridge."

"Most so. A great hard labor it was."

People flowing in both directions left them some small space as they appeared to be immersed in some private conversation. They thought that it was good to see their Royals engaged in such mundane activities and enjoying a quiet moment during the Fest.

"Still being careful?"

"Indeed. But We do work no less hard than those less well positioned."

She pinched his side as he mumbled something. "Our King, there was some small miss event pon the land side wing roof of Our Great House of Royals."

His head snapped around. "WHAT?"

"One worker do stumble and fall."

"From the roof?"

She nodded. "Most true. But We do but break one leg." She laughed. "The fall was into not off. All floors were finished but not the roof, then."

He glowered at her, then kissed the tip of her nose. "Let's go look at your brother's town."

She yanked him into motion. "We do hear that *The Armored Fist* do have most fine a beverage."

Those that saw them enter that establishment waggled their eyebrows at friends. That place had a reputation for rowdy behavior. Not proper for Royals. It was where the metal workers spent time.

The pair leaned on the bar, a long metal thing, hand-crafted by the denizens of the place as a show piece. Everything was metal, including the serving mugs.

"Most fine," said Lurin to the burly man behind the bar

as she took a swallow from her mug.

"Strong," gasped Tinker.

"Cross-water?" asked the bar tender, plunking down two more filled mugs.

"Yep." Tinker grabbed one of the mugs.

"Most so." Lurin dropped a coin in a puddle on the bar top and took a long swallow from her mug and set it down.

The bar tender stared at her shirt as she arched her back and rubbed the small of her back.

"Do We besmear Ourself?" She looked down at her shirt.

"Neat and clean," he said. "There be rich lodes."

She smiled. "Most kind."

"Be they native materials or enhanced."

Lurin laughed. "Entirely native to us."

He leaned forward and grabbed her with one large hand.

And staggered backward. She had smashed her mug against the side of his head, snarling, "You rope crawler, wharf dreg, offspring of a sea wart. Think you We do be some corner wench wiggling for sea quail stub sport?"

As he straightened up, she bounced the empty mug and then the other two off his forehead in three quick over-hand throws.

The barman reached under the bar and yanked out a thick rod.

"OUTSIDE!" yelled Lurin, spinning and stomping for the door, kicking two tables over as she passed, scattering utensils and customers, slamming the door against the outside wall.

In the street, she whirled around and stood ready and grinned at Tinker. "Fear not, Our King." She beckoned over a vender who was pushing a small cart that had two long handles.

"Fried hartl," he said.

Lurin handed him two coins and wrenched one long push pole from his cart. The vendor stared at her as she waited, the long handle held down and to one side. Anyone not angry or confused would have recognized her stance. This was obviously a warrior holding a great two-handed sword in a ready position.

The bar man hurtled from the inn and charged.

She stepped lightly, dancing warrior steps, and chopped his legs out from under him. As he rolled, she wacked him on the side of the head. Turning back, she handed the pole to the cart owner, smiling sweetly at the wide eyed stare. "Many thanks. We would have two fried hartl." She paid for their purchases and then added some more for the use of the pole, selected her choices, and handed one to Tinker. "Fried hartl, Our King?" This was said very loudly.

Tinker took the food, some sort of fish coated in red batter. "Did you kill him?"

"We think not." She crunched loudly. "But We do believe some thick skull do learn most painful a lesson. Let us see what else do reside in Our Brother's town."

Metal workers heaved the wobbly man to his feet, handed him large wads of cloth, and told him who that woman must be.

He blanched, staggered to one side of the street, and lost an earlier meal into an empty barrel. They told him that if her brother heard of this he would probably never see the light of day again.

He wobbled inside and wrote a note to his wife telling her what to do and seriously though of fleeing to one of the Old

Kingdoms and then decided that would not be any better. He wondered where a Queen had learned such language.

As they admired a storefront display of fancy garments, he nudged her with one elbow. "Guess you haven't been over here before?"

"Most so." She turned and purchased two large mugs from a vender who waited until they emptied them and handed them back. She stared into Tinker's face.

"What?"

"Think thee that We do appear artificially enhanced?"

He laughed. "Not to me."

"Perhaps thee would care to prospect these lodes?"

"Lurin!"

"Small jest." She tugged him into motion.

By the time the story of her encounter with the barman crossed over the river the tale had become more and more dramatic. When someone told one of her guards of the event, the anecdote had become even grander. Two large soldiers heaved themselves from behind a small table and drifted out and then across the river, just to investigate.

As the pair wandered and held small conversation, here and there, they met a pair of soldiers dressed in black and white and held a whispered conversation with them.

The four wandered to *The Armored Fist*, walked inside. Three blocked the exit while one of their member strolled over to talk to the battered looking barman, who blanched and knew that he was about to die, or perhaps something worse than that. His imagination was working overtime. After the soft conversation was finished, the four walked back outside onto the main street and laughed, banged each other on the shoulder, and went their separate ways. Lurin's soldiers wandered back across the river and into their gathering place to regale their fellows about the latest thing that their Queen had done.

It was very late when the Royal pair wandered, not quite aimlessly, toward the Great Span. All the shops were closed. Most of the inhabitants had retired while their more determined celebrants still enjoyed the first day of Fest. The inns still roared boisterous noise into the mostly emptied streets, a thing allowed to happen only during Fest days.

Their shirts had long ago become untucked and were mostly unbuttoned, mainly to cool off. Lurin's hand was firmly anchored to his belt. Standing in the middle of the Great Span, they leaned on the railing and stared out at the sea past the mouth of the great river. All the anchored vessels at the Great Quay sported lighted lanterns.

"A pretty sight," he observed.

She handed him the bottle that she clenched by the long neck in her free hand. "Have some, Noble King. Your Queen commands it!"

"Sure." He did and handed it back, and winked at her. "Pretty sight."

"Ah ha!"

"Huh?"

"Thee has inspected our native materials." She peered down her nose. "Some enhanced."

"What?"

"Two offspring do add some, they did."

"Oh." He waved a loose arm. "Let's get going. That stuff we have been drinking is trying to dissolve my legs."

"We will steer thee to most safe harbor, We will." She tugged him into motion.

She did. Over and down the Great Span. She, towing him along, crashed through the front door of *The Wet Way*, and were greeted by the rowdier of the sea folk still hard at their celebration.

After the required toasts and a few suggestive songs and comments, Lurin shoved him in the right direction, down a side hall, and into a large room with a large bed. "Safe harbor," she announced giving him a hard shove.

In the main room of the inn the sea folk agreed that their Queen was certainly one of them. Many suggested that was true for her King as well but couldn't understand why they saw so little of him. Some wondered how that could be given that the Queen was certainly a very attractive woman. Someone got thumped heavily for making lewd comments about the Queen. Then someone suggested, a designer of ships, that it weren't really lewd, it weren't, but merely a learned observation on the general overall structural design and ornamentation of that particular vessel.

Bright sunlight streamed through an open window and woke him up. Perhaps it had been the slamming of the door. His eyes popped open.

She set the large tray, heavily laden, on the bed. "First meal." She had a blanket swung over one shoulder toga fashion, the rest wrapped around herself. "The Master of the inn has provided a most hardy meal." She piled both plates with this and that.

He sat up, took a mug, and sipped. "You wandering around like that?"

She nodded.

"Do Queens do things like that?"

"We do." She laughed. "All those rope crawlers will stare at thee with new eyes."

"You did that deliberately."

She shoved more food from a platter onto his plate. "Some." She grinned. "It do Our Folk good for to see Us as being more like them than as Royalty far removed from the people."

When they had both finished the meal, she piled everything on the tray, pushed it out into the hall with one foot and bellowed, "DONE!" Then she crawled onto the bed. "A sunny day and a splendid meal. Good start for the second Fest day. But, for now, we must wait for washed and dried attire to arrive." She poked him with one finger. "We are most happy that thee could Our Own Daughter's Ceremony attend. Now attend to this, thy Royal Queen."

The Princess gently patted one cheek of her Prince. "Most sunny day, Dumar."

He looked up at her, eyes more or less focused. "Your people are certainly different. Does this happen? Often?" He frowned. He didn't think that he could survive Fest if it occurred frequently.

She shook her head and set the tray down. "Fest are only declared on great ceremonial occasions, such as a Royal wedding, or some very special event, or if The Queen decides that the folk do require some great relaxation."

He struggled back until he could lean against the head board. "Good!"

She smiled broadly. "Our folk's saying do be: Fest hard, labor harder."

He nodded and smiled happily and warmly at her.

"Eat!" she commanded. "We have Ourselves one Fest day yet to enjoy."

"What?"

"Eat and cloth thyself, Dumar. It do be Our Duty to see and to mingle and to hear from our people."

"Among my people newly wed Royalty have a day or two for themselves not bothered by anyone or anything."

"Have We not said that this, Our Kingdom, follows different ways. The Fest do be a time for the folk for to see for themselves what We have taken as Our Very Own. It do be an ancient custom, dating into the early time of the first Kingdoms. Thus, having mingled with Our folk, when orders are given, bills issued, all do feel less directed and more a part of that action. There do be a great closeness between those who labor on scale small and those such as Us, charged for to labor for all who do reside herein."

They ate their meal, he yanked on his clothes and tugged up his boots, and stood. "Fest day or not, I wish to hold My Princess in my arms."

She laughed and kissed him as he did. "You may do so as we wander about and the folk will see and approve Our Selection as good." She tugged him down the hall, down the stairs, and out into the streets which were rapidly filling with celebrants.

Smoke nudged Chicken as they were finishing their breakfast sitting at a table in the main room of the inn they had selected. "No new kittens. That Queen is not in her fertile time."

"Shall We cross to other side and see what lies yonder?"

Smoke stood. "We will be close enough."

The group pushed outside, watched by many careful eyes. Many wondered who these Royal females were. They were all wearing the Royal garb provided to them by Lurin before the wedding.

In the main room of the inn, Lurin greeted Ship Masters and crews. Some of these wore a small black dragon patch on their left sleeve. This indicated to all that they had served on her vessel, during the first discovery voyage across uncharted seas.

Others wore colored scarfs loosely knotted around their necks. These were the sea folk who had sailed with her on the first coastal expedition. She told her King, loudly, that while these were indications of past deeds that none of this made any one of them any better than any other rope crawler.

There were small smiles and controlled expressions as all tried to not appear too proud at her comment. *Rope crawler* was a grave insult and usually caused not a small amount of damage to the speaker unless you happened to be one of the sea folk. As far as all of them were concerned, she was certainly one of them. They had already heard and discussed many times the events that had occurred across the river. She had certainly been as rowdy as any tall mastman, or mastwoman, yesterday.

Outside, on the street, she grabbed his hand and towed

him out onto the Great Quay and to her Royal Vessel, gleaming white, newly repainted white.

"We would show Our maps few have yet seen." Inside the main cabin, she spread them over the table. "These are Our new lands, found by Our Brother during his sea search."

His fingers slid up her backbone as she leaned forward and pointed out various features on the maps. "You are certainly building quite an empire."

She jerked upright. "Not so! It is not only Our's, but part of the New Kingdoms and the Old Kingdoms. We are deeding some portion of this to the Hephira. Sook sent Princess E'Nilt to speak with her First Pair to gently work out all the appropriate details with a matching set of maps. We feel it do be to all a benefit to bring the two peoples, Hephira and Us, closer together."

Winl Fzar. The Hephira Land.

She was glaring and contemplating separating his head from his shoulders as she stood, leaned forward, and glared across the table. "You pizgak!"

The object of her glare and rather unkind and rather uncouth comment glanced nervous eyes at The First Prince, who was struggling not to smile.

"I believe," stated The First Prince, nodding at his Princess *cousin*, "that the Princess E'Nilt is suggesting that The Trade Guild House is being, perhaps, just a little unreasonable. After all, she does speak for the rightful owner of those lands who have most generously offered this, Our Land, a rather large share in whatever wealth and material we might acquire from that region."

E'Nilt dropped heavily into her chair, her glower lightening a bit. "Our First Prince speaks plain and true. The Trade Guild House may kizna this opportunity into the dung heap!"

The Trade Guild House Spokesman stared at her and wondered how and where a Royal princess had learned such vulgar expressions. Then he thought that it was probably from the soldiers she was known to train with, and to lead, if necessary. So he carefully slid a different written suggestion across the table for her inspection.

Finally The First Prince stood. Everyone filed from the room to begin to organize this new project.

"Nandau and I would like to talk with Our Princess E'Nilt and hear all the news," he said.

E'Nilt stood and bowed. "Of course."

Grandeville. Not All That Far From Town.

The two large men stood on the edge of the small river, or large creek, depending upon your point of view, fishing poles in hand.

"Well, partner," rasped Red. "What'da ya think?"

"I think," replied Green, "that we have drowned enough bait for one day."

Red nodded. "That is a big uh huh."

The pair had decided to go fishing as their babes, Red's wife and her secretary, were off doing something of special interest to them and before leaving had suggested pointedly that Red and Green should find something else to do other than to tag along.

Red reeled in his line and inspected what came up. "I

think that the way we fish is even worse than the way that we bowl."

Green began to pack their gear. "Let's go get some chili at Big Darlene's. It is a couple of hours until dinner."

"Sounds good to me." Red grabbed his stuff and walked over and dropped everything into the back of Green's pickup.

And soon they were bouncing their way down the wheel ruts to the road that led back to town. Later they would stop at the grocery store and buy some fresh fish for dinner.

Hahn Dohr Kahn. The Realm of The Dragon.

She drifted through the crowds, munching on a round Trila fruit and sat next to Chyndra.

"Our daughter has arrived and will be witch-raised by my clan. Sisters Spolit, Sfoka, and Safir have also birthed daughters. Sisters Sthat and Santil went far as did almost this witch." She leaned forward and stared past Chyndra at Dumar. "This witch owes great debt to the Prince and to the Princess for allowing us such." She sat back and watched the swirling crowds with witch careful eyes.

Chyndra threw an arm around Soona's shoulders and hugged her. "Does this happen often?"

"Noooooo," she hissed. "First cycle only for the name-grade. Spolit and Sfoka had mated before." She hid her eyes with one hand and whispered ever so softly, "Safir swift took a Circle Twift. Strange strange strange." She stood. "I will return in two of your times." And faded away in a soft pink glow.

Chyndra rose to her feet and tugged Dumar up. "Let us wander across the river. We want to look at that inn where Mother knocked around that bar person."

Dumar nodded. "Does she do that often?"

"We do not," stated Chyndra firmly, all Royal tone, "allow untoward behavior at any level. He treated her like a dark shadow woman. We would, We would, go see whether this person has learned some."

And eventually, after a number of starts and stops, to talk and mingle with Fest goers, the pair walked into *The Armored Fist,* stepped up to the bar, and ordered two mugs from a man wearing black and blue bruises and a large bandage on one side of his face.

The bar man looked at their garb, jerked, hastily served them, and quickly walked to the other end of the bar, hunching his shoulders protectively.

Chyndra took a sip. "Pears so."

"Wonder what he did?"

She leaned close and whispered into his ear.

Dumar's face flushed. His hand snapped to the hilt of his sword.

"Our Queen do all that required doing, Fierce Prince."

He took a swallow and grumbled at her, "A different land."

She emptied her mug and tugged him toward the door and outside. Numbers of careful eyes watched them go.

Three shops down the street, they stood and inspected the display of shirts in the window.

A man stepped from the throngs and hugged her. And laughed happily.

"Uncle," she said. "Queen Aunt." She turned to Dumar. "This is King Frinda and Queen Sook."

Frinda grinned at them both. "We met at your ceremony." And bowed to Dumar. He laughed again. "We have heard the most interesting tale from some of Our soldiers about Lurin thumping one of our bar keepers. Think that We ought speak with his person?"

"No." She smiled at him. "Mother told him all he required."

"Black and blue," added Dumar.

Frinda laughed again. "Then We shall bother him not. Although do We ever hear of such behavior again, that one will shortly thereafter dwell in one of the Old Kingdoms." He bowed to Chyndra and Dumar and walked off, Sook at his side. Frinda smiled and beamed at everyone and everything. He thought that Fest days were ever so much more fun than the normal duties of being King.

"Exile?"

"Of a sort," said Chyndra. "Let us seek some unique thing for My Father."

"Thee do be some sly," said Lurin.

They stood on the high rear deck of her vessel, leaning against the waterside railing, watching the flying sea creatures wheel and dart about.

"Me?"

"Just so," she laughed. "Unless Our very Own shirt do be magic'd and do by its same self crawl free allowing Our King's hand to wander pon skin bare."

"Um," he replied, running his fingers gently over her ribs. Suddenly his hand jerked away as he spun and glowered at her. "What did you do? This time? Ahhhhhhh, that time?"

She frowned back at him. "King Dark Glower?"

"I don't remember that scar."

"Scar?"

He spun her around, yanked her shirt up, and tapped her left side. "This one?"

She laughed. "Be this some rope crawler desire to gaze pon our natural deposits?"

"Don't avoid the question!"

She tugged her shirt back into some semblance of order. "Some small thing."

"Not small," he growled.

One Royal finger tapped him sharply in the center of his chest. "We will not be snarled at!" She leaned close. "Fret not, t'was but a most minor accident. We were swinging some cargo aboard when hanger do snap and large load do pour forth. Errant timber do pluck Our shirt away and some small amount of Our skin."

He sighed and cupped her face in his hands. "You could have been killed."

She blinked. "We do know that and now thee do know as well. But tell not Our children for We would not have them fretting about Us in protective manner." She held his hands. "We do no less than Our Own folk."

He nodded and grumbled softly, "Don't like it. Anyway."

"Come to sea with Us on the morrow. We would view the Sea Edge Road progress from a small fast vessel."

"They all have to come."

She nodded. "The sea folk will be most well mannered." And grinned broadly. "For them."

"Not them I'd worry about. Let's go get something to

eat."

"Great King?"

"What?"

"We shall have to first reorder our upper garb or will thee have Our folk mumbling about their disheveled Queen?"

"Bad as the rest," he mumbled as she buttoned and tucked her shirt into place and grinned at him.

Smoke nudged Chicken and winked at her. "Might as well. One day, more or less, shouldn't matter to do what Sgenn wants to do. And he is very relaxed. It is good for him. And for us."

Chicken drained her beverage container and headed the group down the street. She had heard someone mention a store selling clothes and she thought that they all ought to purchase something as a souvenir of Chyndra's wedding.

Soon, they were inside the appropriate store, inspecting everything, shirts, blouses, and smocks, for the proper color and cut.

Fair Morn held up a pale rose blouse with a deep and wide opening bordered with two rows of some kind of green vines. "I like this one."

Messenger spun around and gasped. "Gosh!" She shook her head. "He will never let you wear that outside the house!"

"It is pretty."

"And shows an awful large amount of you. Really really."

"It is supposed to do that."

Messenger shrugged, turned, and began to inspect a number of shirts with fancy carved fastenings running down their front.

Early Dawn nudged Fair Morn with an elbow. "I think that she is correct." And was handed the garment accompanied by the grumbled comment. "Here. You can wear it."

Early Dawn glanced around the shop, nodded, yanked off her shirt and yanked the new one into place. "Well?"

Messenger glanced around and giggled. "It is very pretty."

The shop keeper peered down an aisle and stared at them. Royal Ladies just did not walk into her shop, yank off their clothes, and put on one of her wares.

Early Dawn shrugged at her. "There were no males in here or peering through the window."

And in rapid succession they all did the same. Then they decided that they ought to buy two new garments. So they did.

Their purchases would be delivered.

Mount M'Ban.

She eased her way through the twisting tunnels she had made deep inside the great volcanic mountain and outside into the narrow valley. She walked to a broader spot, unfolded her wings, gave one pump, and soared up and over the tree tops. It was time to visit the queen.

Ran Far Bar. A Seldom Visited Place.

He felt the tug and knew what he needed to do. The awareness came slowly but sure. He had known who he was for some long time. Now he understood why he was, the very reason for his existence. And with that came strength, building and building and building.

Hahn Dohr Kahn. The Realm of The Dragon.

The fast vessel sailed parallel to and not far off the coast just beyond the swells of beginning waves heading ashore to crash and foam against cliff and beach.

Periodically Lurin took one of the far-seers and checked the road located just above the high storm line. It was The Sea Edge Road, a major project planned to connect her main Royal Town with the eastern edge of this gigantic island.

They had been sailing for two days and all of Tinker's group had shed their boots and socks and joined the vessels crew in bare-footed freedom.

Fair Morn and Early Dawn had startled the crew when they had crawled high into the rigging and had perched on various of the high points.

Lurin had leaned close to Tinker, pointed up at them, and had told him that the pair were receiving openly admiring looks from the sea folk more from this activity than their being beautiful women of her Court.

Both were now standing at the top of the highest mast holding a conversation with the watch men up there. They saw her gesture and waved happily.

"So," he asked, "how's the road project?"

"Well done."

"Why?"

"What?"

"A road along the coast?"

She pointed in the direction that they were sailing. "In yet one day there is a great cove which could make a fine harbor for fast vessels. The First Lord is there studying it for suitability. The weather just prior to Ice Time becomes unpredictable and Our sea folk do require more than one safe harbor. Last Warm Time, late, We lost two vessels in a sudden storm. We seek to provide our sea folk with some additional safety."

She led him over to the map anchored to a table and pointed. "Here is that cove and this do be the road." She dragged her finger along a dotted line and then up and inland. "Here is a large river and here is Talking Water, a place much like Spa but grander. It will become another safe port and eventually accessibly by road to Our new Sub-Kingdom located far to the north just there."

"Hope that they are a hardy group."

"They were one of the Fringe Old Kingdoms and are a very hardy folk even now building small towns here and here and here. Next Warm Time fields will stretched all along here mostly in support of their people."

She indicated a section of the forest where they would build a road under the direction of her First Green Guard, a newly created sub-section of the Wood Guild who wished to protect their resource.

"A small fee paid by the user pays for The Green Guard. We shall adjust the fee as required to ensure that each is satisfied." She laughed. "A chore for The First Lord."

Later in the day the fast vessel anchored in the cove, a large dent in the coast. The crew rapidly set up tents on the bench above the steep beach.

The Map Makers rapidly set to work while Lurin pushed inland to inspect the road work. Construction had pushed east beyond this point. Tinker walked with her while the rest of himself scattered about with Smoke maintaining contact with all.

"Well?" He watched as she knelt and ran her hand over the tightly packed rock surface.

"Most well done." She stood, wiped her hand on her trousers, and peered down the road. Inland the forest was dense. Seaward they could see the sea sparkling beyond the sparse brush and scattered trees. "The First Lord pushes faster than We do think."

She grinned at him and waved one hand toward the tents that they could see billowing softly in the gently sea breeze. "We do smell cooking, We do." She bowed slightly. "Our King."

He took one of her hands as they headed for their mid-day meal.

Far around the curve of the cove Smoke suddenly grabbed Chicken and shoved her off the bench to the beach and jumped down to land lightly beside the sprawling figure frowning darkly up at her.

"Wench!" Chicken heaved herself upright and looked at the debris for something suitable to hit her with.

"Sssssssh!" Smoke clamped one hand over Chicken's mouth and spoke into her mind. *Quiet. And be still, perfectly still.*

Dark One?

Smoke slipped the image into Chicken's mind. It was a large beast, thick fur colored a deep brown, that slipped westward through the forest making not a sound. It was hunting one of the large forest grazers.

What be that?

Hunter. An animal native to these forests.

When the beast was far enough away Smoke began to

brush sand from Chicken's clothes. "We had better talk with Lurin. She doesn't know that those hunters live here."

After crawling back up onto the bench they jogged toward the tent camp. The breeze drifted smoke and fumes out to sea.

While they all ate, Smoke told Lurin about what she had seen.

Lurin hooked one finger at a Map Maker. "Bring drawing materials." She looked at Smoke. "Describe this thing."

Slowly slowly, under Smoke's guidance, the image took shape.

Lurin gasped. "We did see drawings of these things in old volumes in the Royal Archives. Many long ago, warriors hunted them in acts of daring. In the Old Kingdoms those beasts have been gone for many reigns. Now We do wonder what else still lives in Our Lands long not seen by any."

Taking up the sheet with the drawing of the hunting beast, she began to write. When she was finished, she handed it to the Map Maker. "One copy." She stood and told the Ship Master. "Break camp! Ready the vessel! We must sail as soon as possible." She strode off, giving orders here and there.

It didn't take long. The vessel, healed well over, every sail set, headed east. Lurin leaned on a railing and scanned the coast with a far-seer and spoke softly with the Ship Master.

The sea folk swarmed and soon had great side sails out, dramatically increasing the speed of the ship.

"We will," she said to Tinker standing by her side, "sail all night if necessary for We do wish Our First Lord and the builders of Our Road to be fully aware of those great hunting beasts."

They did.

The sun was barely above the horizon when the sails were hauled in and anchors dropped. A cluster of tents on the shore bench indicated the road builders camp. Lurin and Tinker were rowed ashore and were met by The First Lord. He carefully watched his Queen and her King approach and walked to them as they clambered up onto the bench.

"Highness?"

Lurin handed him a scroll. "Something to be aware of that prowls these forests."

The First Lord carefully unrolled the scroll. "This? Lives in the forest?"

"Most true. And this is Our Word, soon to be known to all who do dwell in our lands. Leave these beasts to themselves. They are not to be hunted for mere sport of warriors or excitement of youth." She smiled at his puzzled expression. "But do set your camps in such a manner as to not attract untoward attention. As We do know nothing of their habits We do urge great caution. Perhaps We should sent a great vessel so all may live there rather than on land?"

He nodded and looked at the image again. "Large for a camp pet." He waved one hand. "Visit our endeavors."

"Lead us." She grabbed Tinker's arm as they followed her First Lord to inspect the camp, the road edge, and to speak with the builders who were enjoying their first meal.

She questioned all about their tools and spent some time being shown exactly how to set the road surface properly.

Finally they headed back toward the shore

Tinker jerked.

"Our King?"

"Sgenn wants us to leave. Now!" He turned toward her. "It is some unfinished business. Are we gonna disturb them if we suddenly disappear?"

She tugged him close. "We will explain to all. Be safe! The Kingdom do require its King as do its Queen."

He hugged her. "We know. And we will be."

And then.

She held empty air.

Szart and Sha'gar had taken them out.

Alicar Plae Nar.

They swirled in, billowing black mist, and thumped down into the heavily churned soil.

"Huh?" He stared at his feet, the soil, and then at their surroundings.

The place, where they stood, sloped down toward a heavily wooded area. Something, mostly hidden, could be seen inside all that growth. In the other direction, uphill from where they stood, stood a walled town, the large battered gate closed.

"Nak tak plak!" snapped Szart.

Sha'gar nodded. "Ptar ptar nar!"

"Gosh!" Messenger stared at their surrounding and then at the two grumbling magic users.

"Certainly doesn't look like the place where we were before." Chantal yanked her revolver free and looked at Szart. "Is it?"

Sgenn shook her head. "No." She stepped close to Szart and Sha'gar. "Why are we here?"

Szart growled at her. "Some nik to tak pulled us sideways."

"Hum," replied Sgenn.

"Most true." Sha'gar nodded at her sister. "Something strange strange. I felt the pull."

"Hum hum."

Under their feet they heard low rumbling.

"Gosh." Messenger stepped closer to Tinker.

"What?"

"I think that it was the wand." She nodded. "Really really."

He nodded at her. "Sure." And looked at the wand tucked in her hair and at the ones held be Szart and Sha'gar. "Which wand?"

Messenger yanked another wand from her hip pocket. "This one." She held it up before her face and said to it, "Naughty naughty."

The loud sigh was Tinker. "Now what's going on?"

They all heard the loud clicks as Fair Morn set the levers on her weapon. "Taking no chances, One."

Early Dawn yanked the pistol from her shoulder holster, cocked it, and leaned very close to Fair Morn, and whispered, "Think that I will get to shoot something?"

Chicken stepped over to Szart and Sha'gar, blade swishing back and forth. "Know thee what place this do be?"

Sha'gar shrugged, Szart growled.

"Witch?"

"Alicar Plae Nar, a small elseplace mainly occupied by Slba, a strange folk that do strange."

Chicken pointed with her sword at the dark figures beginning to edge from the dense growth downslope, dark figures beginning to gather in groups and to stare up at them.

"Be those Slba?"

"Noooooo," hissed Szart, staring at the wide and thick beings clad in soft glitter armor. "Those are not Slba."

"Well," said Chantal as she joined them in staring downhill, "if they just stand there and stare, there's nothing to worry about, is there?"

From behind them the gate of the town made thumps and grinding sounds, rasping, screeching metallic sounds. They fanned out and watched carefully, weapons of all kinds of lethal held in hands. The gate slowly opened, just enough, a narrow slot one person wide. Something moved back there. And then stepped out.

"Holy cow!" gasped Tinker.

"Dad?" She charged down the slope, grabbed and hugged him. "What are you doing here?"

He hugged her in return and grumbled, "That is what I asked?"

Farth stepped out and stood a proper distance back. "Mighty King, Greetings."

As Sedeem stepped free to be overwhelmed by her mothers, hugs and kisses from her mothers, Tinker walked up to the Silver Ranger. "Just you two?"

"No. We camp out of sight of those." Farth pointed at the groups forming down below. "The Qzar Horde."

Then he explained why the Silver Rangers had come to this elseplace and what the Qzar Horde leader had told him and then what the Slba had said.

He shook his head. "The Slba told us that the Qzar seek an object that was long long ago lost, taken by thieves unknown and unseen. The Slba stated that the Qzar do not believe this and have decided to break into the town."

He fingered the hilt of the great silver sword hung on his belt. "Many will die before this day ends."

Sedeem, finally freed from her mothers greetings, joined her father and her husband. "The Qzar are somewhat dull witted. But very determined. They came here to retrieve their relic from the Slba. For some reason the Slba refused to talk with them. The Slba and the Qzar do not like each other. So the Qzar decided the simplest solution to the problem was just to kill all the Slba and then search the town. The Slba called for help and here we are, a troop of Silver Rangers."

She grinned at her father. "Right in the middle." She poked her nine-ring wand into the roll of hair at the back of her head. "So why are you here? Certainly not doing noble deeds to protect folk?"

Farth fizzled, and was glad that none of his officers were around to hear his wife's comments.

"Beat's me. We were headed somewhere else and just sorta popped out here."

Messenger walked over to them and held out the strange wand. "I think that this wand did it."

Sedeem stared at the wand. "Mom?"

So Messenger told her.

"Hum." Sedeem nodded. "I think that we ought to show that wand to the Slba." She headed for the gate, beckoning Messenger to come along. "Farth can stay outside and visit. It is perfectly safe."

The pair slipped through the narrow opening and into the town. Farth looked unhappy but remained with Tinker.

Tinker pointed at the churned up ground under foot.

"You guys do this?"

"A mighty battle," stated Farth. He stared down at the ever gathering Qzar. "We had to kill some to make them stop their assault." One foot kicked at the battered soil. "We have until nightfall to find a way to stop this."

Fair Morn strolled up to them cradling her space cannon in her arms. "Could just remove the problem."

Farth fizzled and Tinker frowned at her. "Cool it, Killer Moth. We are not removing anything." He nodded at her. "For now."

Then they all stood around talking quietly.

Szart wandered off to one side, fingering a jet black wand, and thought about one of the Banned Spells. The wand grumbled at her.

Sha'gar walked down the slope, plunged a flaming red wand into the soil, and walked back, leaving it there. Her eyes glittered fire.

Fair Morn, accompanied by Early Dawn, walked up to the town and sat down and leaned back against the stone wall.

Chicken stood and talked quietly with Smoke who was trying to read the Qzar thoughts.

Chantal pulled autoloaders from her pack and stuffed the patch pockets of her shirt full, and mumbled to herself, "That ought to do it, for starters."

Hahn Dohr Kahn. The Realm of The Dragon.

After Lurin had explained the sudden disappearance of her King and his "Guard," she gathered around her staff to discuss building the road toward Talking Waters.

Camp had been relocated back to the cove and close to

the Queen's fast vessel.

Once the plans were finalized, Lurin ordered everything packed and taken on board her ship. At First Light she would head back to the First Town. Everyone was ordered to spend the remainder of the day resting and relaxing. So all did and enjoyed the kegs of beverages that had been stored below deck for just such a occasion.

Sea folk and road builders sat intermingled and talked and jested back and forth and all agreed that their Queen was a wonder.

A dark shadow covered the group, the space where they sat, and much of their surroundings. The gigantic form glided overhead and slowly settled into the cove. Waves surged almost to the feet of the folk staring at their visitor. Sea folk called from their vessel assuring all that they were well and truly anchored and in no danger.

Once the wings were settled properly, she sank a bit deeper in the water and looked at Lurin, stretching out her long neck until her head was not too far away, not to close to cause discomfort to the others. "Griz, griz, griz," she laughed. "This is a nice spot."

Lurin, now standing as were all the others, bowed formally. "Greetings, Great M'Ban. What brings Our Royal Dragon to this place? Be this your wash basin?"

Rolling the large eye peering at Lurin, M'Ban snorted a small puff of smoke. "Griz, griz, griz. Long ago did I dig this small hole to enjoy the warm waters of summer. But if My Queen wishes to make use of it I can make another. Some year or other." Her head lifted high into the sky as she scanned the faces peering up at her. "Where is he?"

"Our King?"

"Yesssssssssssssssssss."

"He travels elsewhere."

"Into great danger, Queen of The Realm of The Dragon." The great wings unfurled and stretched out and out and out as the immense breast stood dwarfing all, people and sea vessel. She reached toward Lurin with a front foot, palm side up. "Shall we go?"

"Great M'Ban?"

"To help your mate!" Dragons always helped their mates whenever they might be in danger, especially when they were in danger.

Lurin spun around and issued orders to her First Lord and the Ship Master, spun back and clambered into the still outstretched foot.

Ebony talons slowly curled around forming a safe cage for Lurin. The great wings gave a sudden pump and the great black dragon soared upward. A wing tip brushed a spar on the sea folk vessel, snapping it into pieces as she sailed past.

"Most sorry," she hissed as she dwindled into a dot high above just before she slipped inbetween.

Bahn Duhr Tohr. The Quarters of The Royal Advisors.

They were in the large tub, surrounded by heaps of green foam.

The green foam came from a potion he had persuaded her to allow him to pour some into their hot water. She grumbled, but agreed. So he did, pour some, explaining as he did, and as he swirled the water into heaps of green foam, that it was just a little something he had found in a small shop down a narrow side way not too far from the Royal Castle.

Now he was, ever so gently, scrubbing this and that with a large soft cloth. She was leaning back against his chest, eyes shut, relaxing as much as she ever would. She really was getting better at it, this relaxing thing. But relaxing was not a very well developed skill for a witch, especially one of her magnitude.

"ENTER!" demanded a disembodied voice from overhead.

Her eyes popped open. "Pak ptar tak!"

"Vile nasty," purred that voice from somewhere.

"In the main room," she snapped. "And wait."

"Heh heh heh heh heh," cackled that voice from overhead and then from the main room.

"Oh well." He squeezed warm water from the cloth over her head, washing away the green foam.

She snapped her fingers.

They stood next to the tub, dry and properly dressed for visitors. She waved the tub empty and clean and headed for the main room.

Ranna, Anjan, and Adarlak sat around the table, mugs in hands, sipping. Waiting. Two mugs, just filled sat in front of the two empty chairs. They were also waiting.

"Hayou, Ripple," greeted Ranna. Her eyes flickered at Hanred and back as she purred, "Were we interrupting? Something?"

Ripple frowned and grumbled, "Hayou, Ranna." She sat, grabbed a mug, took a sip, and hissed, "Don't be rak dak!"

Ranna shrugged.

Hanred smiled at the trio. "All look healthy and well."

Ranna nodded. "Where is that Rekel? And her's?"

Ripple shrugged.

Anjan refilled Ranna's cup, her own.

"Enter?" asked someone.

"Do!" snapped Ripple.

She popped in, kissed Hanred on the cheek, and sat next to Ranna as another chair appeared. "Hayou, sisters?"

Then she brought in her's. Mrrinar, the cat-folk, stood behind her, his tail curled casually over one crooked arm. "Magic ones," he purred and smiled, carefully keeping his fangs covered. It was a very polite thing to do.

"Hayou, Raft," Ranna ordered in another jug and two more mugs.

"Hayou, Raft," grumbled Ripple. "Greetings, Cat Folk."

Hanred smiled at Raft and refilled Ripple's mug.

Ranna nodded. "Will all come?"

Ripple shrugged. "Sisters will be sisters."

"Enter?" whispered the sky.

"Of course," replied Ripple in a most not-witch gentle tone of voice.

A shadow thickened as she faded in with a soft swirl of dark. She was wearing a black robe, hood thrown back.

"Hayou, sisters," sighed the darkness.

"Welcome, Reep. Come sit by us," said Ripple.

She drifted wraith silent and settled in a chair next to Hanred. "Hayou, Hanred," whispered a shadow.

"Hayou, Reep. Where is your's?"

"Working," murmured dark night.

The Trantil Layer.

He stood and stared at the rock face. And wondered who

had done that.

A large concavity, walls polished mirror smooth, reflected images of him staring into the hole where the opening should have been.

He walked away and sat on the grass facing the cliff face and thought about it. It would take some time.

Deep deep down they stirred.

Alicar Plae Nar.

Dull thumps and rust grinding screech of metal caused all to spin and look at the great battered gate as it slowly opened outward.

Three figures slipped from the just wide enough space and walked down to the waiting group staring up at them.

Walking between Messenger and Sedeem came a tall man dressed in a severely cut costume of silver and blue material. The three stopped near Farth.

"The Slba agree to return the relic to the Qzar," said Sedeem.

"Now that it has been returned," stated the man, holding both arms out, his palms up, cradling the strange wand across his hands.

"That?" Tinker stared at the wand.

"Yep." Messenger nodded her head.

The man cleared his throat. "The Wand of Cation Guisin Ombor, the long before now Haxar of the Qzar placed their relic into our Pnln until there was a great necessity. Now time is that."

He crashed to his knees. "Many before it was taken. Now all goes Xaratum to Qzar." A long drawn out musical note whistled from his throat. The gate to the town swung wide.

From down below the horde rushed upward and stopped just below the small group.

Sha'gar's wand flickered red fire.

The man stood as the spokesman of the Qzar stomped up to him and began to hold a conversation of wild arm swinging and shouts with the Slba.

Then the pair stood quiet, banged each other heavily in the center of the chest, and spun toward Messenger. Both leaned until their faces were very close to her's.

"What?" Her eyes jerked from face to face.

The Qzar dropped a loop of fine chain over her head. The Slba grabbed it and fastened a small black globe to it and dropped it to hang in the hollow at the base of her neck. Both stepped back as Messenger lifted the globe and peered at it.

"Thank you," she said. "It is a very nice gift." She smiled at them.

The Qzar hurried away and rejoined the horde which ran down the slope into the forest and to the place where they had come through.

The Slba bowed to Messenger, then to Farth. "All is restored, all is correct. It is natda." He turned and walked back up to and through the town gate.

Sedeem looked at him. "Dad?"

He sighed. "Things just keep happening to us. Messenger found that wand, that relic, in *Rachael's Thing Shop* in Grandeville among a bunch of stuff. Rachael had no idea what it was. She thought it was just another of the decorative wands that she sells."

He smiled at her. "By the way, your sister Chyndra just got married to a Prince named Dumar."

She grinned. "We will have to visit, take her a wedding present." She nudged Farth. "After we return the Silver Rangers to their town. We can always come for a inspection of the Wing stationed in Wurm while we are visiting. They would probably like that." She hugged her father. "Take care and be careful."

"Sure," he grumbled. He watched as she and Farth walked up the gate where the Silver Rangers were streaming out. He nodded at Szart. "O.K., want to try it again?"

The Trantil Layer.

They swirled in, soft black mist, not far from a small collection of structures.

He spun and glowered at them all. "O.K., here's the drill! If anyone, or anything, looks like trouble, kill it, or him, or her, or whatever. Questions?"

"Nope," they all said.

"Sounds worse than The Mob," suggested Chantal.

He pointed at Sgenn. "She isn't even healed and here we are back here again. Next guy that runs at us with anything gets thumped badly."

Someone charged from a nearby building, a long glittering thing held in his arms.

Tinker stepped forward. The great black sword, his weaponkin, flashed outward as Tinker spun. The flat of the blade drove the man backward as it smashed into his midsection. He bent double gasping for breath. The sword bounced off the side of his head, rolling him down and on his side. And very still and very quiet.

Chantal eased the hammer of her revolver back down, stepped over and knelt, inspecting who ever it was. "Well, still alive."

"Coulda been in two pieces," grumbled Tinker.

"We just got here." He looked around. "What caused that? We haven't had time to cause trouble."

Off to one side there was a soft puff of black fog.

"Hayou Uncle, Aunts, Cousins, Sister." Seemna walked over and looked down at the crumpled form. "Hum hum."

"Now what?" He looked from Seemna to Szart.

Szart stepped over and looked up at her tall, younger sister. "What?" she demanded.

"Here," Seemna gestured at their surroundings with one arm, "lives a twisted happen that bothers all."

Black snarled nearby, and they appeared. Santar and Sepanix stood on either side of a surprised looking man.

Seemna waved her hand at them. "There stands Aldin Cease, a mage of The Green Onana. He is also part of the twisted happen. He doesn't know that."

Aldin Cease glared at everyone. "What is the meaning of this?"

Seemna waggled a cautioning finger at him and cast lightly on the figure lying on the ground.

His eyes popped open. He sat up and reached for his weapon.

Tinker stepped on it. "Don't even think about it."

Sgenn walked over and looked down at him. "Why are you attacking us?"

He leaped to his feet and staggered away from her. "Don't touch! Don't touch!"

"Maybe I hit him too hard," mumbled Tinker.

"Not in the mood for this," growled Chantal, stomping past them, leaning forward, grabbing that person by the front of his garment, shoving the front of the revolver barrel into his cheek just under his eye, and cocking the hammer. "Exactly what is your problem? Speak! Or I will blow the back of your head off!"

He stared up at her with no idea of whatever it was that she held, but he understood her tone of voice, and pointed. "He makes an opening to let them out. There. At the cliff range. You help. This must not be allowed. They must not be released."

She yanked the revolver away, released him, tucked her revolver in its holster, and punched him with her left hand, rocking him backward. "Damn dumb! We are here to stop it!" She straightened up and looked at Tinker.

"Damn rough on the natives, Cowgirl." He nodded. "Let's go."

Szart grabbed one of Seemna's hands. And yanked them away.

She settled gently to the ground on three legs, great wings arched up and back. For her it was a very gentle landing.

The ground undulated in long waves. A part of the nearby cliff cracked and tumbled into a large mound.

When the dust had settled, slowly drifting away on the slight breeze, her held her clenched foot near the ground and uncurled the talons.

Lurin landed on her feet, snatching her great white sword free, ready to do battle. As she scanned their surroundings, all appeared to be empty. "Whither?"

One long finger pointed. "That way."

Lurin started in that direction followed by what appeared to be a great black hill.

In a sharp crack of black they were there.

They stared at the man standing there, staring at the polished cavity and the soft spot shimmering deep inside.

"Remove that spot," snapped Tinker at Fair Morn.

She stepped sideways and fired. The spot, the concavity, and another large portion of the cliff face disappeared.

The man turned and frowned puzzlement at them. "Why did you do that? Now I shall have redo all that work." He spun back to face the gap in the cliff.

Seemna walked over and tapped Aldin Cease on the chest with a long black wand. "You must help."

"Do what?"

She gestured. "With him."

"Who is he?"

"Long before before and before that, a Green Onana released him, a nar rah creature. Your ancestor wanted to shatter the hold on the never to be seen, which are now very close to being released." She pointed straight down. "For him it was curiosity. For all rest, disaster."

Fair Morn fired again, removing the soft shimmering beginning to form again on the rock face.

The man turned and flicker her away, tumbling and rolling almost to the far distant tree clump.

Chantal fired, and was hurtled backwards, crashing into Early Dawn, Smoke, and Messenger.

Sha'gar and Szart cast.

He shrugged the spells away, turned and stared at the polished stone.

Tinker charged, the great black sword singing angry blood lust as it flashed in a downward two-handed cut. The blade clanged and bounced back, the shock twisting Tinker around. "Merde!" He spun and lurched back. "What is he?"

Sgenn stepped over, a soft half-smile on her face. Something black reared up and reached. Claws and clenching hands passed through the figure standing so calmly. "Take them away," he said to her. "I cannot be touched by the deep down." Sgenn nodded. Her strange companion sank away.

The ground shuddered. Rocks tumbled and bounced from above.

"Now what?" Tinker looked from face to face and upward.

Everyone looked at everyone else.

"Know not," growled Szart.

Aldine Cease stepped over, grabbed the man's shoulder and yanked him around. "Stop this!"

"You may not!"

"I say stop!"

"Not to be so."

Green leaped from the wand clenched in the hand of Aldin Cease. "Then die!"

The bolt flashed out, blowing the magician across the ground crashing into Santar. They sprawled in a limp tangle of limbs. The green flame vanished.

The ground thumped again.

Tinker scanned their surroundings. He looked, rubbed his eyes, and stared even harder at what he saw. It was. A black hill.

Coming toward them. "Oh, oh." He ran to where Chicken sat on the ground, cradling Fair Morn's head in her lap.

Chicken looked up. "She do arouse not. Most strange."

He knelt next to them. "We are in big trouble. We don't seem to be able to do anything to that guy. And something else, something really really big is headed in our direction."

Gently allowing Fair Morn to settle flat on the ground, she stood and looked. "Do pear most large, My Lord."

"Uh huh. Any ideas?"

"Nary a one. Be there more we might call upon?"

He shook his head. "I doubt that Macabre could get here in time."

Wild black swirled around Sepanix as she stalked toward the man who ignored her approach. Her spell struck. And ruffled his hair. Snarling, she leaped and plunged her wand into his back. The wand exploded. She blew backward and rolled in a dazed loose limb heap.

Szart stood to one side carefully constructing the spell. It was a three-locked one from The Book of Banned Spells that her Aunt R-Bar had taught her. She began. On all sides, time and space began to bend. In the far distance, the hill lifted into the air.

"Run for it!" shouted Tinker. "That thing is coming at us." He ran over, grabbed Szart by an arm and tugged her into motion. The spell folded into itself.

Chicken raced past them, sword in hand.

Messenger ran after them. "Stop! Stop! Stop! Stop! Stop!" She managed to grab the back of his shirt and yanked hard. "STOP!"

They did.

Messenger pointed. They could see the great wings beating.

"What?" he gasped, "is it?"

"Dragon!" gasped Chicken.

Messenger nodded, sucking in deep breaths. "M'Ban."

He stared. "M'Ban?"

Messenger nodded. "Yep."

Smoke charged over to them as the monstrous shape thudded down sending shock waves through the ground. She staggered to a halt. "Who called her?"

"Beats me." He watched as the great dragon reached forward and opened her clenched foot. Someone tumbled out, sword flashing as she raced toward them, eyes dancing, seeking enemies.

He stared and growled, "What are you doing here?"

"To aid Our Great King," she snapped. "Where do be the foe?"

He glared at her. "Who? Where's your armor?"

"No time!" She spun and looked around. "Some casualties." And nodded at Chicken. "Great Queen, where do be they?"

Chicken pointed. "That one." And grabbed Lurin by a shoulder as she stepped forward. "Pears most immune to weapons, Fierce Warrior Queen. Our Lord's blade do naught but bounce away."

"I see armor not."

"We do feel he do be a'magic'd being of some sort."

"Then," demanded Lurin, "how do we kill him?"

Seemna stepped close. "Not a him. It is a nar rah creature cast from something outside most by a long before long before

Green Onana mage and released." She pointed at the soft shimmer on the polished rock. "Soon there will be an opening and those forced forever below will pour into the elseplaces."

"Griz, griz, griz." The immense head dropped to their level. One huge eye, glowing dragon green, peered at them. "So that is his thing. Always wondered what he did with it."

Lurin looked up. "You know of that thing?"

"I told that mage that he ought to be more careful. I even gave him a little dragon blood for his studies. Griz, griz, griz."

"This is not to laugh about," snapped Seemna.

"Would Our Royal Dragon aid us?" asked Lurin.

"A Royal command?" M'Ban puffed smoke, momentarily covering the group.

"A Royal request," coughed Lurin.

"What do you wish, Queen of The Realm of The Dragon?" She gently blew the smoke cloud away, tumbling them over. But it did clear the air.

They scrambled to their feet.

"Rid us of that creature. Forever and forever."

The great eye blinked. "That long?"

"Indeed," stated Lurin, Queen firm.

"My Queen," hissed M'Ban, "you will have to move them all back and away."

Lurin urged them back and helped Tinker and Smoke and Early Dawn shift those lying limply here and there.

M'Ban watched them. Then she turned away.

"Stop!" she hissed at the creature still constructing the opening in the cliff face.

It ignored her.

M'Ban looked back at Lurin, who nodded. Turning her

head, the great black dragon, one of the primal forces in the universe of universes, sucked in a long, long breath, unfurled her wings and curled them forward.

Then she blew.

Dragon fire spewed forth, splashed up the cliff face and to all sides, cascading back at the rock from her cupped wings.

The blast seemed, to those watching, to go on and on and on as the rock glowed and slumped.

Then the fire went out. Steam and a little smoke curled up as the rock cooled and crackled.

M'Ban turned her head and peered at Lurin. "Shall I fly you home?"

Lurin hooked her free arm around his, watching the great sword he held very carefully. "Nay, Great Dragon, We shall stay some with Our King. Many thanks, Most Royal of Dragons. How may we gift thee?"

She puffed surprise. Then quickly blew the orange fumes away. "A gift?"

Lurin nodded.

One green eye rolled as she licked her lips. "Perhaps one of those witch tastes?"

Lurin gasped.

"Griz, griz, griz. Dragon joke." She sprang into the air, gave a single pump of her wings, and soared up, dwindling into a speck which suddenly disappeared.

Tinker freed his arm, swung his arm up and around, flopping his sword into its usual place on his back and curled one arm around Lurin. "Let's go check."

They walked over and stared at the scorched, once molten area, heat radiating over them. There was no trace of the creature or the opening.

"Good thing that she was on our side," he mumbled.

"Most so." She kissed his cheek and turned him around. "Pears most do survive."

Fair Morn was standing, one arm thrown over Early Dawn's shoulders. Early Dawn had an arm curled around Fair Morn's waist.

Sepanix, Santar's arm swung around her neck, talked quietly with Seemna.

The crumbled body of Aldin Cease lay nearby.

Seemna spun away and joined Tinker and Lurin.

Tinker pointed. "Who was he?"

"Aldin Cease. He was trying to help." Seemna nodded. "I think that I will visit my cousin and her new mate." A very not-witch smile tugged at the side of her mouth. "I knew that she would choose him." She was gone in a soft sigh of black mist.

Sepanix pointed and watched the body fade into the ground. Then she took Santar out.

He looked around and nodded at Szart and asked Lurin, "Where?"

She smiled slyly and plucked at her clothes, heavily stained from the road construction site, "Our Very Own Royal Quarters. A great soak in large tub does seem most suitable. What say thee, Great King?"

Szart grabbed Sha'gar's hand.

They splashed waves of water over the floor.
"WHAT?"
Lurin laughed as she began to peel off waterlogged

clothes.

They were standing in her tub, already filled with steaming water covered with heaps of soap foam.

"Your witch is very understanding," she purred as he began to help her.

"Sometimes," he grumbled. "Sometimes."

The rest of himself sat around the great table in the dining room, ate, and laughed.

They now wore selections from the clothes hastily delivered some time past by the shop that they had visited.

Individuals Of Note

Grandeville.

Tinker's Place.
John Tinker -- the individual used as an intermediary by Big Red in his ongoing activities to maintain the balance of the universes. During his initial time on Mirk Wild Weald, Tinker was told by The Thought that he is The Chosen One of legend. Now merged telepathically into an entity with the rest following the cultural values of Smoke's people.
Smoke of the Velvetmist - a gigantic, telepathic carnivore, now transformed into a human shape by Big Red. She was selected from her home, a hidden and never visited elseplace, to be one of the original companions to aid and journey with John Tinker. Now MindMate to Tinker, Chicken and the rest.
Princess Chicken - an Easter Season fluffy chicken toy from an Easter basket, transformed by Big Red and placed as a traveling companion and aid for John Tinker.
Messenger - Once "The Messenger" of her people but joined with Tinker and the rest when she began to fold inside herself believing Tinker and crew were monsters and demons from her folk's mythology come alive.
Fair Morn - a one-time mythological jest created by the magical force, Big Red. Messenger severed her magical bonds changing Fair Morn from a jest into a real person.

Ferrelden - of the Risshar, a Night Runner from Zhorndar'h. (Deceased).

Flar - one time owner of a Magical Items Shop. (Deceased.)

R-Bar - a witch of The Faan clan, joined into the polyorganism of Tinker and the rest by Smoke. (Deceased).

>**Sedeem** - her daughter, a magician.

>>**Farth** - Sedeem's mate-for-life, a Silver Ranger.

Chantal Baire - a Veterinarian with a clinic near Grandeville.

Ranfer - witch of the Tanpak clan. Preferred to be called Ran. (Deceased).

Sha'gar - Faan magician, daughter of Reep and J.C.

Sgenn - Faan theurgist, daughter of Reep and J.C.

Dat - an indjinn, gifted to Tinker when the group bought a ring, The Eye of Dat.

>**Je'leel** - her daughter by Tinker.

Szart - Faan witch - chosen by R-Bar to be Tinker's mate-for-life.

Early Dawn - a one-time mythological jest created by the magical force, Big Red. Messenger severed her magical bonds changing Early Dawn from a jest into a real person - visiting Tinker and Fair Morn.

Chantal's Friends

Frederica Hensler - "Freddie" - lives in Portland.

>**Ralph Andervante** - her husband

Sandrew Sherl Sandermeyer now Anderson - "Sandy" - Tinker's Attorney.

>**Red** - her husband, a member of the Grandeville Police Department.

Janine Teacate - "Streak" - Sandy's secretary.

Chen's Chinese - The Building.
Adam Lieu Chen - Master Chen owns and operates Chen's Chinese, a restaurant located in Greater Downtown Grandeville. He also trains Tinker in the martial arts.

Dragon Ranch - not far from Tinker's Place.
Prince Goose - a windup plastic toy transformed by Big Red into a traveling companion for John Tinker. He is a brother of Chicken.
Chen Gum Lung - The Golden Dragon of the House of Chen. A sometimes amulet gifted to Tinker by Master Chen, now the consort of Goose.

Doc's Home.
Kappa "Doc" Heckmann - anthropologist and adventurer. A friend and neighbor of John Tinker's.
J. C. Smith - one of Tinker's close friends. He works for Doc in many capacities.
> **Reep** - of the Faan witch clan, married to J. C.
>> **Szaifeh** - daughter, a witch.
>> **Sha'gar** - daughter, a magician.
>> **Sgenn** - daughter, a theurgist.

Membrane - one of Doc's "associates." He run Doc's stores, Cactus Spine, specializing in cacti and succulents.
Badnews Treefalls - another of Doc's "associates." He is Doc's constant companion.

The Hardcastle Residence.
Alandale Fredrico Hardcastle IV, known as "Hard" by all his

friends.

> **Ramp** - of the Faan witch clan, a magician, his wife.
>> **Sa'ar** - twin daughter, a magician.
>> **Shem** - twin son, a magician, also known by his parents and grandparents as Alandale Fredrico Hardcastle V.
>>> **Tajaar** - his wife.

Grandeville Police Department (GPD)

Red and Green - two very large men who once played football together on the local college team. They function, usually, as the late night patrol. They are good friends of Tinker, J. C., and Hard.

The Elseplaces

Paradise.

Big Red - a pure force of magic personified. He is primarily concerned with maintaining the balance and order of the universe of universes. And, more often than not, has some influence over the events that plague Tinker.

> **Dancing-All-The-Day** - Big Red's wife.
>> **Silly-All-The-Day** - son.
>>> **Treena** - wife of Silly.
>> **Ianna "Sun Song"** - daughter

Various - depending upon mood.

Dram - an individual often called The Evil One. He began life on

Murk Wild Weald as a magician-in-training. But after long and secretive study in The Library of Arcana he slowly was transformed by his knowledge and his ambitions into one of the few pure forces in the universe of universes. Dram has a tendency to work at living up to his title.

Stumpf.
The-Mountain-That-Walks - an individual most often addressed as Mountain by his traveling companions. He is one of the original companions selected to aid John Tinker.

A Place Unnamed.
Macabre - who specializes in killing things. He is usually accompanied by his pets: The Vipers, and the Sparkling Tigers.
Gyre - his female companion, created by his vessel, Gyreship.

The Six Lands.
Sorrowful Mistidings - a professional Teller of Tales, selected from The Six Lands, as one of the original companions to aid John Tinker. He lived with his wife and sons. Now deceased.
Tears Trimblechin - his grandson, a growing Teller of Tales, trained by his grandfather.

Clear Bandler - The Land of Magicians
The $1.98 Magician - trained by Big Red and told to aid Tinker in whatever manner he could.
Plum Duff - a magician and consort to $1.98.

The Old Lands - Bahn Duhr Tohr.

Willawa, The White Warrior, Queen of all the lands, New and Old.

Toucan, The King - he is the brother of Prince Goose and Princess Chicken and once was Tinker's advisor.

Hanred, Ripple's mate-for-life - he is a Master Illusionist who once traveled widely through the universe of universes and is also known by many of the folk as "Old Hanred."

Ripple, Advisor to the Royals - she is the Clan Head of the Faan witch clan.

The New Lands - Aahn Duhr Tohr

> **Frinda** - son of Willawa and Toucan, now King of Bahn Aahn Tohr.
>> **Sook** - a Faan witch, now his Queen.
> **Lurin** - daughter of Willawa and Toucan, now Queen of Hahn Dohr Kahn, The Realm of The Dragon.
>> **Frahn** - her son by Tinker.
>>> **Nadarl ca Irinl** - his wife.
>> **Chyndra** - her daughter by Tinker.
>>> **Prince Dumar** - her husband.
> **Daish a'an'Nald ca E'Nilt**, The Swordpoint of the Victorious.

Dol Spar - Headquarters of The Monetary Control and Mirf's home.

Mirf - The Special Chief First Inspector, often sent on special assignments by The General, the overall director of The Monetary Control and her boss.

Fred - a female suk-dragon, her Assistant.

Quan - Fred's mate - Mirf's Assistant.

Rema and **Nema** - her clerks (sisters).

Abda, Dama - slith; **Barla** - Cadta.

Magevern - home of the Vander mage Guild.

Sa'ar - the Heart of the Vander, who made Tinker The Lord of The Vander.

Clans, Guilds, and Other

Organizations.

(known individuals listed)

Anaza sorcerer Phylota - located in Far Corner.
> Netanada -- Elixa (Clan Head), Sorceress.
> Abadoda -- Three Rank Sorceress.
> Hatopa -- Three Rank Sorcerer.
> Important Artifacts.
>> The Ancient Book of Songs.

The Divineal of Thantala - located in Murklan Obscuratan. A Place Never Visited.
> Lady Grimtouch - The Glimmer (Clan Head) of The Divineal of Thantala.
> Lady Fairdeath - traveling with Sluba mage Ransapal.
> Lady Dawnmort
> Lady Softtouch
> Lady Nightreaper
> Lady Final Kiss
> Lady Lastgift
> Clan robe color - forest green almost black; carry a short gold staff.
> Important Artifacts
>> The Book of Death.

Potri witch Clan
Turintor
Clan robe colors - grape and green design.

Faan witch Clan - scattered widely throughout the universe of universes.
Ranna - The First Born
Anjan - mate-for-life, Death Warrior
Adarlak - mate-for-life, Hacto mage.
Riz - The Second Born.
Rekel - The Third Born.
Ap Kar - Hinta warlock, mate-for-life.
Rbat - The Fourth Born. At one time thought by many to have gone far.
Ripple - Clan Head - The fifth Born.
Hanred, the Illusionist, Mate-For-Life.
Shitar - daughter, a witch.
Mantara - Grenzanr warlock, mate-for-life.
Santar - daughter, a witch.
Sook - daughter, a witch married to Frinda, King in The New Lands.
Sepanix - daughter, a witch, wild magic.
Szart - daughter, a witch - mated to Tinker.
Seemna - daughter, a witch, websmith.
Reptar - The Sixth Born.
Fazbaq, Blue Udaz warlock, mate-for-life.
Wizla, Kanikt witch, spell designer, mate-for-life.
Rumtah - The Seventh Born, The Lucky One.

Reep - The Eighth Born, The Silent One.
    Married to J. C. - mate-for-life.
        Szaifeh - daughter, a witch.
        Sha'gar - daughter, a magician.
        Sgenn - daughter, a theurgist.
Rotak - The Ninth Born.
Raft - The Tenth Born. Known as The Fast.
    Mrrinar - a Catfolk Healer, her mate.
R-Bar - The Eleventh Born. (Deceased).
    Tinker - her Mate-For-Life
        Sedeem, daughter, a magician.
Ramp - The Twelfth Born. A Magician.
    Married to Hard.
        Sa'ar, daughter, a magician.
        Shem, son, a magician.
Important artifacts - held by Ripple and Hanred.
    An immense collection of volumes dealing with
    the arcane collected by Hanred during his many
    travels through the universe of universes.

Talair witch Clan - located on Tanadra.
    Motaiss - a warlock
    Mendurra - a witch.
    Clothes colors - black with just a hint of faint grey in an
    ornate design that runs down the outside of each sleeve.

Sluba mage Guild, one member located in Three Trees Town.
    Ransapal- studied the Dark Under and ancient witch
    history. Traveling with Lady Fairdeath.

Vander mage Guild - located in Magevern.

    Sa'ar - the Heart of the Vander.

        Eulin Dragon Force - daughter by Tinker, a mage and Dragon Master.

    Tobtz - the Soul of the Vander.

    Cazor - mage warrior.

    Moonda

    Aada

    Bant

    Andovar - the Farseer.

    Imdar - the Healer.

        Rorx - Vander warlock - son by Tinker.

        Szaifeh - a witch, Mate-For-Life.

    Imten - the Artificer.

    Tinlee - the Adept.

    Xanx - Apprentice Healer.

    Marl - the Seeker.

    Galron - The Bent.

    Zulan - The Brave.

    Arboc - The Sensitive.

    Clothes color - they are always dressed in garb of the faintest purple. It is from the color of their garments that folk often call them "The Purple Magicians."

The Wood With - located in Newlar, relocated from Blurratha. Hidden. In Plain Sight.

    Fairlan - Cluster Head

    Ringlan - Cluster Head

    Clearlar - Cluster Head

    Faerlar - Cluster Head

Flerlan - The Observer
The Wood With are always accompanied by their beast. When the Wood With are present one might notice the smell of blooming flowers on the air.

The Garden Gnomes - located in Growing Green.
Phineas Grass
Hiram Toadstoll
Franny Waxflower
Franelken Vetch
Tiny Rosebud - the emissary
Rose Perrywinkle

Monetary Control - located on Dol Spar.
The General - Head of Monetary Control.
Mirf - Head of the Special Investigations Office.
Fred - a female suk-dragon - First Assistant.
Quan - Fred's mate - First Assistant.
Rema - First Clerk.
Nema - First Clerk.
Special Staff: Abda, Dama - slinth; Barla - Cadta.

The Nagar
Kartz - Head
Raj - a Medical Doctor - mate-for-life.
Reslar - youngest sister.

The Silver Rangers - located on Fandor's Dan.
Farth - Tindar (General) of the Silver Rangers.
Sedeem - Faan magiwitch - his wife.

The Wizards of Trefil - located in The Guarded Lands.

Ragnok - grandfather

Bizl - grandmother

Braidna Chin Lee, Lyral Princess, The Enchanter
- their granddaughter.

Bits and Pieces of Cultural Data

(From the files of Monetary Control)

The Garden Gnomes.

The Garden Gnomes are a small folk, perhaps the smallest of all the folk. As their name implies they are fascinated by gardening and frequently visit those gardens that they recognize as being above the average in terms of arrangement and care, whether ornamental or functional.

At some point, in their past, one of them had been seen while visiting a particularly well designed ornamental garden. This kind of happening was not something that they liked to happen nor did they like to talk about it. This garden, as things seem to happen to this folk or that folk over their histories, belonged to a sculptress of some skill and very fast eyes. She made a statue of what her eyes saw as just a fleeting glance and set this statue in and among a artfully organized patch of flowers.

And as things so often happen, a visitor saw this statue and asked the owner to make one for him. And so it went. And so it went. Much to the consternation of the Garden Gnomes.

And eventually an entire industry sprang up around these statues and their production. People even wrote fanciful books about the culture of these things. They were all wrong, of course. None of the authors had ever talked with one of these small folk or had ever visited a Garden Gnome village.

The end result of all this was that the Garden Gnomes retreated deeper and deeper into areas where they would not, or could not, be observed.

Young Garden Gnomes, every once in awhile, on a dark, a particularly dark night, would steal one of these statues and hide them away.

Of course, this had no effect on the overall population of these fake garden gnomes. That industry was to well intrenched.

The Divineal of Thantala.

In time before time almost before memory it is told that the Divineal were there, passing through the universe of universes upon business that none dared ask about and few would dare challenge. The few that did, died. This rare occurrence, challenging one of them, and the result of that challenge, was told one to the other, and thus was the tale spread, and The Divineal were left to pursue their own interests. Most of these interests appeared to have something to do with Death. Death as a being, not merely as the end of something.

All the folk of the elseplaces recognized them as none else would dare to wear a deeply hooded robe of dark forest green that was almost black. And none else would presume to carry a short gold staff.

It is said among the many cultures in the universe of universes that few have ever seen the face of the individual hidden in the blackness of the deep hoods. It is also said that to see that face is to die. But, if one had ever done so and survived, none had ever so stated.

It is known and understood by most folk that one does

not approach one of The Divineal and start a conversation. One does not watch one of The Divineal closely. One tries as much as possible to ignore their existence. One hopes to stay alive. It was this understanding that brought into being the label used far and wide for them, "The Sisters of Death." But it never, ever, was used when of them could hear it.

None knew where their elseplace, their home place, was located. None knew which of the many elseplaces, numbers beyond counting, would be the one wherein they resided. And even if one could find out, in some mysterious way, none would dare chose to go to such an elseplace.

The Divineal were polite and very soft spoken, if and when they might chose to speak to someone. And all, but the foolish and soon to be dead, would do all that they were capable of doing, if asked to do something. That is what the folk in the universe of universes believed. And none knew of anyone that had been asked and who had refused and survived.

None knew how many Divineal there were. None knew why or what they were about and most folk felt that the best place to be when one of them was around was to be somewhere else.

The Divineal were like a pebble dropped into a still pond whose action caused ripples to flow out in all directions. And like that pebble, they were totally unconcerned about those ripples.

The Witch Clans.

The Potri witch clan came into existence, as did all the witch clans, during what all the clans call "The Great Migration." From where this migration came is a great matter of debate and argumentation, but not why.

The ancestral clan, or clans, also a matter of intense debate and argumentation, had, through arcane knowledge, come to understand that a disaster beyond the control of any user of magic was about to happen to their homeland.

So they fled out into the universe of universes and over time the witch clan, or clans, splintered and grew into the myriad of clans that are now present.

The long ago seen disaster happened in a single violent explosion that removed their homeland as their sun erupted and ate everything within reach.

Some thing, some event, during that long ago migration and scatter brought into the witch culture a sense of authority coupled with a powerful magic that each clan cultivated. Each clan developed their own clan interests and evolved their own unique concept of magic. The end result of this was a somewhat provincial sense of proper witch attire and proper witch behavior. The pairing of these beliefs with their sense of authority meant that the folk living in the many elseplaces in the universe of universes knew that any witch tended to be rather short-tempered and had a predilection toward violent behavior when the behavior of other folk, witch, magician, or non-magical user, was felt by the witches to be engaged in improper behavior, undesirable behavior, or were just plain irritating.

Most witch clans dressed in wardrobes of midnight black, the exact style of their clothing varying widely. Some of the clans, in the long before before, had, for reasons they chose not to reveal, settled on wardrobes of other colors.

The Faan witch clan is unique. Among all of the witch clans scattered across the universe of universes, they are the only one that does not maintain a clan house. And, unlike all the other clans, the members are all and only generationally linked. The magic of the Faan flows down the female line from mother to daughter.

The Faan clan, unlike the other clans, are trained almost exclusively by their female relatives, mainly by their mother and their aunts. But if a sister has learned some new and unique twist, it may be shared, sister to sister. It is due to this multi-generational sharing and training that has made the Faan noted throughout the witch clans as being the most powerful clan and to be avoided if at all possible. And some few understand that at some point in the long ago long ago, in their mating with their chosen mates-for-life, from other witch lines, that something unusual happened that twisted and transformed their genetic material.

The result of this event was that, at times, their offspring are born with new and unique abilities. This tends to explain why the Faan do not maintain a clan house. Members of their clan, most often, prefer to wander mostly by themselves and to study and collect magic and magic spells. And other things.

The Mage Guilds.

The mage Guilds apparently came into existence in the long ago long ago in a manner none understand or thought to record as this event was in a time when such occurrences were not seen as being important enough to warrant special note.

Magicians are, in one sense, at the opposite end of the magical spectrum from the witches. That is why the magicians and the witches tend to avoid each other whenever possible, especially physical contact. The magic of each tends to be unstable in contact, often resulting in fatal results. However, there is the fact that, at times, in a manner none truly understand, that magicians and witches may have close association, even mates of the others, without dire affects.

The Vander mage Guild, as written in the Histories of the Arcane, was once a sub-Order of the Fanderlaine mage Guild. Little is known of the Fanderlaine and what they thought to specialize their skills upon. The Vander sub-Order eventually split away from the Fanderlaine and pushed deep into the arcane knowledge that was of particular interest to their members. The Vander became the most radical of the experimenters of the mage Guilds and explored many areas of interest to them. This was considered most strange in the mage communities as the Guilds tend to be extremely conservative in their outlook and mage knowledge. Unlike most Guilds, the Vander are almost exclusively female, each member carefully selected for skills and aptitude.

The Anaza Sorcerers.

The Sorcerers were, and are, a small clan and have forever lived in small isolated elseplaces rarely relocating. Small isolated elseplaces were more common in the universe of universes than most of the folk realized. And that suited the Sorcerer clan quite well.

Why they preferred to live this way is lost in the dim reaches of an ancient history begun in a time almost before time itself. Various of the First Sorcerers at numerous points in time in their long, long history had searched their book of lore and learning, The Book Of Songs, for clues as to why this was the way it was. But each had failed. None of them realized, or knew from the oral traditions of the clan, that the Book Of Songs had come into existence long past the time when the reason why could be remembered.

So, as these things happen, the Sorcerer clan has remained reclusive and unknown to the larger universe of universes, not really hidden so much as just being very remote and private.

There was one piece of information known to the clan, a piece of information never allowed to be transmitted to anyone not a member of the clan. And similar to the reason for their preferring small, isolated elseplaces, the acquisition of this piece of information, the how and the when and the why of it did happen, was lost in the time long before before.

Someone, way back then, had learned to recognize the presence of a folk never seen and poorly understood. This recognition was not visual but rather a matter of odor, the odor of blooming flowers. With such an olfactory clue, this small clan of magic users, the Sorcerer clan, knew when the Wood With were around. They had never seen one but the delicate and pleasant odor told them when these folk were about.

The Wood With knew of this strange thing. So they tended to keep a watch on this small group more from a matter of curiosity than of any fear of what that clan might do.

The Sorcerer clan, of course, knew when these other strange folk came and went so they, the Sorcerers, tended to keep Sorcerer business very carefully hidden from these others. And in some strange and subtle way, the clan felt that the Wood With were not to be trusted. It was a cultural tradition, never to be questioned. The reason for this was also lost in the dim historical past. And, of course, they would never attempt to affect the behavior of the Wood With. Tradition also stated that this was not to be done.

The True History of the Magic Users as Discovered by the Divineal.

Many of the witch groups, whether the Witch Clan, the Sorcerer Phylota, the Nagar sort, or the Divineal, have a tale from a time long before long before, and long before written records, of fleeing their homeland before it was destroyed by an event that no magic could prevent. This tale was passed member to member as an oral tradition and eventually was written down. It appears that this event happened.

But, as the magic users scattered into the universe of universes, their knowledge and identities became unique, group to group, and most felt that they were different than all the others.

However, all the groups so far mentioned are witch, even though some felt that others were not and needed to be hunted down and destroyed.

What none of them knew, or understood, is that the magicians were also from this same single event. Witch and magician fled from the same homeland, although, in some manner not understood, the magicians lost the remembrance of that past happening.

The witch and magician groups on that homeland attempted to cast a great spell of prevention. It failed and they fled. None knew that the failure of that spell caused a great change in their magic, with witch and magician forces becoming polar opposites of each other, hence the great danger, now, of mixing, one with the other, magic or personnel, most of the time.

The Wood With.

The Wood With are a small folk. If anyone saw one of this secretive group from a distance, an event so unlikely as to be in the realm of never, it might be thought that what was seen was a very young human child of ten or twelve years of age. Of course, few human children are accompanied by a beast as tall as they are.

The Wood With, from a time before forever, have remained unobserved and unknown, which is exactly what they wish. As a group they are, for the most part, uninterested in the affairs of other sapient beings in all the universe of universes. But, every so often, there occurs a one that attracts their attention. This event is a rare, but not unusual, happening.

The Wood With prefer to live in and among the big trees, taking comfort one from the other. They and the environment blur together where ever they might be. This skill, this cultural attribute, is the main reason, but not the only reason, why they remain unseen and unnoticed.

Their beasts are as unique a species as the Wood With. From an early age one finds the other and from that instant the pair are inseparable. The beasts blend into their surroundings with the same ease as their constant companions.

It is a peculiarity of the Wood With that their presence leaves a faint odor of blooming flowers in the air. In all the time of their existence only one small group have ever realized this fact. But that group's mythology and cultural values are such that the fact that they know this is all that they know. Every thing else they believe, everything else are tales from antiquity with all the error that derives from that.

The Kingdom and Kingdoms of Bahn Duhr Tohr.

The Kingdom of Bahn Duhr Tohr had been, until its most recent merging into a whole, a series of large and small kingdoms, each with a unique name and a unique color scheme. These color schemes were relegated to their Royalty and to their armies. It was very useful to combatants to be able to recognize friend from foe in the chaos of massed combat.

Many of the kingdoms, but not all, could trace their existence back into the dimly remembered past. Some even argued that they existed long before written records came into use. The kingdoms large and small, frequently merged, or broke apart, as the normal political intrigues and royal wheeling and dealing created large kingdoms out of smaller ones, or as so often happened, smaller kingdoms out of larger.

But, in spite of the usual turmoil over boundaries and royal household alignments, all the kingdoms were dependent upon each other as no single one had all the resources necessary for true self-sufficiency.

The bonds between the rulers and the ruled are tight and mutually advantageous. Rulers who did not keep the needs of their folk foremost did not last long. Of course, the occasional battle with a neighbor was accepted as just part of life. Battles were, for the most part, short. This was due to the usual approach to warfare that assumed that most of the fighting would happen between the royalty of the houses in contention. The knights and lessor troops often suffered nothing worse than broken bones. Most of the time this occurred during the first melee and charge.

Grandeville.

Grandeville is a small, rather isolated, rural community of 8,000 population (more or less) tucked away in the mountainous corner of northeastern Oregon. It survives in a provincial unawareness of many things, being overly conscious of the ancestors who settled the place long after the westward migration brought California, Washington, Oregon, and Idaho into statehood.

The town sprawls down from "The Bench," a shallow bench along the edge of the next door mountain slope, to The Blue River, named after the color it has after the first snow melt surges from the canyon and out across the valley proper, always threatening to jump its banks and flood the surrounding farm land.

There are two newspapers published in town, a weekly and a daily (except for Sunday). The Daily, The Grandeville News, tends to ignore anything happening outside the edge of town. The weekly, The Mountain View, tends to ignore anything happening in Grandeville and prints whatever the publisher happens to feel like publishing.

There are a number of local establishments of note:
- The Two Bags Full - a grocery store.
- The Railroad Bar and Grill - "The Rail."
- Big Darlene's Bar
- Johnson's Everything Shop.
- Chen's Chinese Restaurant.
- Leonard's Outdoor Supply Shop.
- The Always Open Gas Pump.
- The Romp and Stomp Motel
- Randy's Truck Corral.

- Dave's Soup and Salad Bar.
- Nan's Clothe Worke.
- Rachel's Thing Shop.
- Dough To Go (doughnut shop)
- The bowling alley with the ever-changing name.

About the Author

George R. Mead began to study anthropology in 1962 after being discharged (honorably) from the U. S. Army, Combat Engineers. He eventually received a B.A., M. A., and Ph. D. in his chosen field. And many years later an M. S. W. in Clinical Social Work. He was worked in aerospace, taught at the college and university levels, worked in a community action agency, ran a restaurant, been unemployed, and worked for the U. S. Forest Service. He is now retired from the work-a-day world but does a certain amount of consulting, writing, and research. He lives seven miles outside of the small town of La Grande, Oregon, with his wife, two cats, and one dog from the animal shelter, Kona.

www.ingramcontent.com/pod-product-compliance
Lightning Source LLC
Chambersburg PA
CBHW060807030726
47503CB00002B/367